MURDER IN A MAYFAIR FLAT

PIPPA DARLING MYSTERIES
BOOK 3

JENNA BENNETT

On the last Friday of every month, Christopher Astley, in the guise of his alter ego Kitty Dupree, has attended a covert drag ball somewhere in London. In April, the ball was interrupted by a police raid that Christopher escaped by the skin of his teeth, only because he was yanked out of the nightclub before the raid started by someone who knew that it was going to happen.

This month, the gathering has moved from the last Friday of the month to the first Saturday of the next, and the arranger has found a new venue. On the first weekend in June, everyone gathers in the old Rectors Club on Tottenham Court Road for a grand old time.

All this is why Christopher's cousin Philippa Darling is alone in the flat she shares with Christopher when Christopher's other cousin, Crispin, Viscount St George, sails through the door three sheets to the wind from celebrating his twenty-third birthday with his usual crowd of extremely fast Bright Young People.

And when a sozzled St George, along with an always-inquisitive Pippa, decide to get dressed up and crash Christopher's drag ball, the night ends with the dead body of a tabloid reporter on the floor of a Mayfair flat, and enough motives for murder to populate an entire wing of Wormwood Scrubs Penal Institution.

Now Pippa and Christopher must determine who wanted the gossip hound dead badly enough to do something about it, all while trying to keep Crispin's name out of the press and their own heads above water.

"Every murderer is probably somebody's old friend. You cannot mix up sentiment and reason."

HERCULE POIROT

CHAPTER ONE

IT WAS JUST after ten o'clock when Evans rang up from the lobby and ruined what was left of my evening.

"Miss Darling? Lord St George to see Mr. Astley."

"Christopher's out," I said, since my flat-mate and cousin had dressed up as his alter ego Kitty Dupree and gone off to his monthly engagement—a drag ball—an hour ago.

After the police raid the last weekend of April—a raid Christopher had escaped by the skin of his teeth, and only because someone who knew it was going to happen had yanked him out of there just in time—the arranger had taken new precautions, and the event had moved from the last Friday of the month to the first Saturday of the next, and so here we were, on Saturday the 5th of June.

As soon as the date registered, I rolled my eyes. "Let me guess, Evans. He's sozzled?"

"Absolutely potted," Evans confirmed. "I don't know if it's safe to allow him to go off on his own, Miss Darling."

No, it definitely wasn't. The Honorable Crispin Astley, Viscount St George, Christopher's other cousin (on the spear side) and heir to the Sutherland dukedom, had recently—as in within the past year—managed to wrap his previous automobile, a Ballot 2 LTS racing car, around a light pole in the West End. He had walked away from that mishap with no worse injury than a bump on the head, but the Ballot had been a complete loss. Now he was driving a Hispano-Suiza H6, with the same engine that Barnato had used for the speeding record at Brooklands in 1924, and I dreaded to think what trouble he could get up to with it in his current condition.

"Better send him up," I told Evans. Against my better judgment, I might add. I'm slightly more fond of Crispin than I used to be—he had rescued me from a rather handsy gentleman at a weekend party last month, so now I had to be grateful—but he was still not my favorite person in the world (that honor would go to Christopher). In his current state, he would undoubtedly prove to be even more of a nuisance than usual.

However, needs must and all that. If I let him leave and he actually died, I'd be sorry. "I'll meet the lift," I added.

"Very well, Miss Darling."

Evans disconnected. I unlocked the front door to the flat—Christopher and I share a service flat in the Essex House Mansions in London—and proceeded down the hallway towards the lift. I could hear the gears engage, but not until I was standing in front of it. It must have taken Evans all that time to maneuver St George into the box and push the button for our floor, I assumed.

I had expected to see St George's pretty face smirking at me through the grille in his usual impudent fashion when the door slid back, but there was no sign of him. From my vantage point, the lift appeared empty. I wrinkled my brows before pulling the grille open and sticking my head inside. "St George...? Are you—? Oh, for God's sake!"

There was a titter, and then Florence Schlomsky, our resident American manhunter, turned away from Crispin, whom she had backed into the corner of the lift next to the button panel. "Hullo, Pippa!"

"Florence," I said severely. "Would you mind unhanding St George so I might have him?"

She had a palm against his chest, keeping him in place, and there was quite a lot of her lipstick—carmine red—on and around his mouth.

He must not realize it, because he smirked. "Evening, Darling. You want me? I thought you'd never ask."

"I'm not asking now," I told him. "You look ridiculous, St George. Wipe your face and come along."

I had to physically enter the lift and push Florence out of my way to appropriate him, which I did by grasping him by the lapel and tugging him after me. He came along as docilely as a lamb, although Florence pouted. "Not fair, Pippa. I saw him first."

"I saw him when he was eleven," I said, "so no joy, I'm afraid. Besides, he was on his way up to see me. Hands off, Florence. Not yours to play with."

"He didn't seem to mind." She glanced at him from under her lashes as she followed us into the hallway.

Florence is not unattractive—she has a wholesome, American face with pink apple cheeks and more than the usual number of teeth, exceptionally straight and white—but she's not the shy and retiring type. Her father has money, and she's in England specifically to barter those dollars for a British title. She would love to snag St George, who is already a viscount at twenty-three, and who will eventually become a duke. It doesn't hurt that he is, in addition to that, both young and handsome, unlike a few of the other specimens of unmarried British nobles, who are neither.

"He never minds," I told her. "He's an incorrigible flirt. I'm doing you a favor, really, by keeping him away from you. He can't be trusted around women."

She gave him another playful glance. "I don't mind."

"You would if you married him and he kept trifling with other women. He just can't help himself, it seems."

The look I gave him was less commiserating than critical, since I absolutely think he can help himself; he just doesn't want to.

"Not getting married," Crispin announced. "Not 'till you say you'll marry me, Darling."

He grinned at me, loose and uninhibited. "We'd have to go off and live in squalor on the Continent, though, 'cause I'd have to renounce the title and estates."

'Renounce' gave him a bit of trouble, I was happy to note. It took him a few tries to get it out.

"That's all right," I told him, since tying myself to St George for the rest of my life was close to the bottom of the list of things I wanted to do. I might accept a proposal if he were dying and it was the only way to save his life, but not otherwise, and I can't guarantee I would do it then. "Keep the title and fortune. I don't want them, or you."

I'd marry Christopher before I married Crispin, and that's saying something, when Christopher has no interest in girls and is the closest thing I have to a brother.

Crispin pouted. "Aww, Darling...!"

I shook my head. "You're terrible, St George. Save your dubious charm for someone who appreciates it."

"Like me," Florence said brightly. "I'd be happy to marry you, Lord St George."

I arched my brows. It seemed Florence hadn't taken herself off down the hallway towards her own flat, the way any decent person would do after being dismissed. She still stood beside the lift, beaming at Crispin.

It would take stronger measures, I supposed.

"That's right," I told Crispin, meanly, "she'd be happy to marry you. So be careful what you say. Someone else might think you meant it, and then you'd end up wed to some woman you don't care about just because you got drunk and careless. If you had said to Miss Schlomsky what you said to me, you'd be on your way to the registrar's office right now."

Florence nodded. Crispin looked horrified.

"Come along," I added, still with that death grip on his lapel. "Goodnight, Florence. Next time, don't be so quick to attach your mouth to him, please. This is the second time in a month I'll have to clean lipstick off his face, and I'm getting annoyed with it. If I can't get it out of his collar, I'll be sending you the bill."

I tugged him after me down the hallway in the direction of our—Christopher's and mine—flat. Crispin, of course, couldn't resist the last word. "Good night, Miss Schlomsky. You'll have to forgive Darling, I'm afraid. She can be so possessive sometimes—"

The sentence was cut off when the flat door shut behind us. That was assuming he'd planned to say anything more, of course. He might not have.

"You're horrible," I told him, as I pulled him, stumbling, across the foyer and into the sitting room. "Over there, on the chair. Sit."

I let go, and watched him make his way across the floor, a bit unsteadily, towards the chair I had indicated. When he reached it, he fell upon it and sprawled, legs akimbo. The grin he gave me was lazy and no doubt intended to be charming. "Evening, Darling."

"Good evening, St George. Do you prefer to use your own handkerchief on your face, or should I bring you something less expensive than a monogrammed silk square?"

From which Flossie's crimson lipstick wasn't likely to ever come out.

"You do it." He put his head back against the chair and closed his eyes. Like Christopher, he has excessively long, curly eyelashes, and the shadows fanned against his cheeks. I shook my head and walked into my room to dig a less ostentatious handkerchief, one in plain cotton, out of my tallboy.

"Here you are." I stopped next to him and held it out.

He didn't open his eyes, just reiterated, "You do it," and patted the arm of the chair to indicate that I should sit down next to him.

I arched my brows at the presumption. "I'm not wiping your mouth for you, St George. You're not two years old."

"You've done it before."

"That was different," I said.

He shook his head against the back of the chair. "No, it wasn't. You may have felt differently about it, but it was the same situation."

It absolutely was not. The last and only time I had wiped lipstick off his mouth had been in public, during a weekend party a month ago, after one of his other conquests had descended on him with glad cries of recognition and the almost palpable need to mark him as her own in front of us all.

On that occasion, yes, I had taken the handkerchief out of his breast pocket and dragged it across his mouth before handing it to him with a rather pointed directive to finish the job himself. We had been surrounded by other people at the time, not been alone in the privacy of Christopher's and my flat, and he had not been sprawled in an armchair, already three sheets to the wind and determined to continue celebrating his twenty-third birthday in style. This was not a situation in which it would be appropriate for me to come anywhere near St George's mouth, with a handkerchief or anything else.

"Do it yourself," I told him again, and dropped the hand-kerchief on his stomach.

He couldn't possibly have felt it, as it fell with the lightest of flutters, but he opened his eyes halfway to peer at me. "You're a hard woman, Darling."

"And don't you forget it," I said. "I'm not wiping Flossie Schlomsky's lipstick off your mouth, St George. I'll sacrifice a handkerchief to the cause, but that's all I'm willing to do. You're on your own with the rest of it."

"Oh, very well." He grabbed the handkerchief, which he passed over his mouth several times. "There. Is that better?"

I narrowed my eyes to see what, if anything, remained of the lipstick, and didn't think about what I was doing until the lips I examined so intently curled up at the corners, amused.

"Damn you, St George," I told him, flushing pink.

"Now, now, Darling." He grinned. "It can't have been that much of a chore. Last time, you told me the pink was becoming. Let me return the compliment."

He managed a credible bow without ever taking his head off the back of the chair.

"Oh, for..." I shook my head. "What are you even doing here, St George? Why aren't you out there with your friends and admirers, celebrating your birthday?"

"I wanted you and Kit there," Crispin said with a pout, as if that made any sense at all. He'd been quite happy drinking and carousing with the Society of Bright Young Persons for the past several years, since he graduated from university and since they started their treasure hunts in the summer of 1924. In all that time, I hadn't gotten the impression that he'd given Christopher and me a thought. It made no sense that he would abandon them before ten o'clock on a Saturday night—and on his birth-day, no less—to show up here.

"Well, I'm sorry to have to tell you," I said, "that Christopher isn't home. He put on Kitty and went out to his monthly engagement."

Crispin brightened. "Did he get dressed up and go to a ball? Is that where he went?"

That was exactly where he'd gone, in an exquisite black gown that had been inspired by the woman with the bright pink lipstick. Lady Laetitia Marsden had worn nothing but black the entire time we'd been at the Dower House in Dorset last month, and when one considered her sleek, black bob—very like the wig Christopher wears when he's dressed up as Kitty—I supposed it had made sense that he would have emulated her style for the next drag ball he went to.

He had looked stunning when he left the flat an hour or so ago—perhaps even more so than Lady Laetitia herself, although I'm not sure she would have been pleased to hear me say so. Nor was I sure Crispin would be pleased, so I kept it to myself.

"That's right," I told him instead. "After the raid in April—did you know that there was a raid on the ball on the night you showed up here to tell Christopher that his grandfather wanted to see him? After that, they moved from the last Friday of the month to the first Saturday of the next to throw the police off. They found another venue, too, of course, but I never knew where they were meeting in the first place, and I don't know now."

"I do," Crispin said blithely.

I stared at him, offended. "You know? How is it that you do and I don't? Did Christopher tell you? Why would he tell you and not me?"

Had he wanted Crispin to accompany him? He had told me, repeatedly, that it wasn't a proper place for someone like me. And admittedly, Crispin runs with a much faster crowd than I do. But still, I'm Christopher's best friend. Crispin is his cousin whom we sometimes tolerate. Surely he wouldn't have done that to me.

Would he?

"Relax, Darling," Crispin smirked. "It wasn't Kit. I imagine you simply don't spend enough time with the right people."

"That doesn't make any sense," I said. "I live with Christopher. He attends the balls. Nobody knows better than Christopher where they are. If Christopher didn't tell you, who did?"

"As I said, Darling—"

"Yes, yes. But surely your set doesn't attend the same events that Christopher's set does?"

"You'd be surprised," Crispin said.

I arched my brows. "Oh, would I? Don't tell me that you have a closet full of dresses and wigs at Sutherland House, St George, that you put on so you can go out to meet men?"

"No, Darling." He smirked. "I like women."

I rolled my eyes. As if there was a female person anywhere in London who didn't already know that.

"But some of my acquaintances don't—Tennant, you know, and Beaton—and the rest will do anything for a lark."

"So you and your friends dress in drag and crash the balls?"

"*I* don't," Crispin said. "Some of the others have been known to. On a dare or for a laugh; you know how it is."

I didn't, actually, but I had heard the rumors. "So why haven't you been known to? Too afraid to risk your reputation as a womanizer to put on a frock? Too much time stuck in the wilds of Wiltshire?"

Where his father was fighting a losing battle of trying to keep Crispin out of trouble and the tabloids?

"That," he said, "plus I stay away because of Kit."

I blinked, and he added, "We look so much alike that I don't want to get him into trouble by showing up in places where there might be confusion about who's who."

That was surprisingly generous of him, and he must have guessed that I was taken aback, because he smiled maliciously. "Didn't think I had it in me, did you, Darling?"

"I'll admit I'm pleasantly surprised," I told him. "I thought you were completely without finer feelings, so I'm pleased to hear that you're not. At any rate, I'm sorry Christopher isn't here to go drinking with you. I'm sure he would have done it if he could."

Crispin smirked. "That's all right, Darling. I'll settle for you."

"Oh, no." I shook my head. "I'm not mingling with your set again. Lady Laetitia will probably be there, and if I have to rescue you from one more woman using her feminine wiles to entrap you into marriage, I swear to God..."

"How about a man?"

I stared at him. My mouth was open, but no words came out, so I shut it. And opened it again. "What do you mean?"

He smiled. Smugly, irritatingly. "I know where Kit is. I'll take you there, if you want."

CHAPTER TWO

THE TEMPTATION WAS TOO much for me, of course. I'd
been curious about the drag balls ever since Christopher started
attending them shortly after we'd moved to London in the
spring. But he'd always kept that part of his life separate from
the part that included the flat and me.

And I'll readily admit that crashing the ball with Crispin,
of all people, gave me pause. I was feeling more kindly towards
him than I used to, but I still wasn't sure I ought to go with him
to an event that was so important to Christopher. What if
everything Crispin had said tonight had been a lie, and he had
some sort of evil plan that would embarrass or damage Christopher, and I could have prevented it, simply by refusing to
accompany him?

Did I believe so? No, of course not. Crispin might not like
me much, but he *was* fond of Christopher, at least as far as I
could tell.

I did what I could to mitigate the risks, however. "You know
that you have to wear a gown, don't you?"

He looked at me down the length of his nose. "Pardon?"

"It's a drag ball. You know, men in women's dresses? Like Shakespeare before women could be actresses?"

"I know what a drag ball is," Crispin said irritably. "And I'm aware of theatrical tradition, Darling. I did theatricals at Cambridge, you know."

And then he arched a brow. "Am I to understand that you want me to wear one of your frocks? The apple green you threatened me with last month, I suppose? I don't think it will fit, Darling. I know that short hems are in fashion, but surely mid-thigh is a step too far."

"Not mine. Christopher's." I grinned evilly. "He has two, in addition to the one he wore tonight. One pink and one blue. And they'll both fit like they were made for you. No thigh-baring necessary."

Crispin's hair is a shade lighter than Christopher's, a silvery platinum rather than sunny barley, and his eyes were his mother's cool gray instead of the Astley blue, but other than that, they are practically identical. Same height, same build, same heart-shaped face with pointed chin and cupid bow's mouth. Christopher's nose was a shade longer, and Crispin has a small scar above his left eyebrow that I had mistakenly thought was from running into a tree, but which had apparently come about as a result of that incident with the Ballot and the light pole.

Other than that, they look much the same. Christopher's gowns would fit Crispin like a glove. One that was made for him.

"You can't be serious, Darling," Crispin said. "You want to go in drag?"

"It's a drag ball!"

"Not everyone dresses up," Crispin said. "As I told you, the Society of Bright Young Persons have crashed the events before, and..."

"You're a coward, St George!"

"If you think calling me names is going to sway me," Crispin said coolly, "you're quite mistaken. I know very well that you don't like me. What makes you think I would care what you think?"

I scowled at him. "We both know you care, St George. You just pretend that you don't, and everyone can see right through it."

He lowered his brows. "You're awful, Darling. If you can see right through it, why do you—?"

"Never mind that right now." I certainly didn't want to argue with him about it. I was still getting used to the idea that he had feelings at all, let alone the fact that I had hurt them when I took Christopher away from him as a child. I didn't want to contemplate Crispin's feelings any further than that.

Instead, I turned my efforts to persuading instead of simply badgering him into it. "It's a drag ball, St George. And Christopher will be there. Do you really want us to walk in there looking like ourselves?"

"Kit will recognize us even if we go in drag," Crispin said. "He'll certainly recognize his own gown."

"Please." I folded my hands and made my eyes big. "For me, St George?"

He looked at me. And sighed. "Fine. But if you tell anyone that this happened—"

"Yes, yes, St George. If I tell anyone that I talked you into wearing a gown and heels—"

His face dropped. "Heels? I have to wear heels, too?"

I managed to refrain from laughing, but just barely, "—you'll do something unspeakably horrible to me—"

He moaned. "How is it that you're not dead yet? How is it that in the last twenty-odd years, no one has murdered you in your sleep and put the world out of its misery?"

I smiled impishly. "Just lucky, I guess."

That, and the only person with that kind of access to me is Christopher, and he doesn't find me as insufferable as Crispin does.

"Why don't you start by removing your jacket and waistcoat," I suggested, "and I'll bring you your choice of gowns. Then you can take them into Christopher's room and finish dressing."

He moaned again, but he did it. Or started to. For all that he had conversed fairly normally with me, his movements were clumsy, and weren't helped by the fact that he was literally sitting on the tails of his formal dinner jacket. It took him the best part of a minute to work out how to wrestle his way out of it. By the time I walked back into the sitting room with a dress over each arm, he was trying to unbutton the white waistcoat underneath, and was having a hard time of it.

"Dear me." I looked him up and down. "I take back what I said about you not being two years old. Do you need assistance, St George?"

He stared at me for a long moment before he shook his head. "No, Darling. I'd rather not have the picture of you working my buttons in my head for the rest of my life. No offense."

None taken, now that he mentioned it. I didn't want the picture of me working his buttons in my head for the rest of my life, either. Or in his, for that matter. "Here you are, then. Light blue and pale pink. Which do you think will go better with your complexion?"

He squinted at the two dresses, one a sky blue with beadwork and one a blush pink with tassels. "Pink," he said eventually. "The blue is a bit too close to the dress Johanna died in last month."

It was, now that he had reminded me. I laid it over the back of the sofa with a wince. "You would have to bring that up. Pink it is, then. Should look well with your eyes."

"Bloodshot?"

"Gray," I said. "Christopher wore the black wig when he left, so I shall have to see if I can wind you a turban or find you a hat of some sort, since your hair isn't long enough..."

I wandered back towards the bedroom, snagging the blue gown off the back of the sofa on the way past, while Crispin continued to divest himself of his clothes. By the time I had hung the blue gown back into the wardrobe and had dug a silk scarf in shades of gray, black, and pink from the tallboy, he was unfastening his cufflinks and shirt studs.

"Gah!" I clapped my hands over my eyes. "What are you doing?"

"What you told me to do," Crispin said with a snigger. "Putting on the pink frock."

I kept my hands where they were. "Can't you do it in Christopher's room?"

"Are you telling me you haven't seen Kit without his shirt on?"

Of course I had. "You're not Christopher."

"We look practically the same, or so you said yourself."

"Well, you're not the same. Go and be private, St George. Don't make me watch you undress."

There was a moment's pause, then— "What if I need help?"

"Undressing?" I said. "You've come to the wrong place, I'm afraid. If you wanted help taking your clothes off, you should have stuck with Flossie Schlomsky. She wouldn't have objected."

"And whose fault is it that I didn't?" Crispin wanted to know. Without waiting for an answer, he added, "So maybe I should go outside and knock on Flossie's door and ask for help, is that what you'd suggest?"

"No," I said. "What I suggest is that you go into Christopher's room—or my room, for that matter, or the bathroom; somewhere that isn't the sitting room—and take care of it yourself. You're an adult, St George, and not so privileged that you can't unbutton your own shirt. You got yourself dressed and undressed during the time we were in Dorset last month. You didn't bring a valet then. You don't need help now."

He heaved a put-upon sigh. "Very well. Where is your room?"

"Into the hall, first door on the left." And whyever he couldn't use Christopher's room was beyond me, but at least he was moving along, so I decided not to quibble. "You've been here before, St George. You weren't even drunk last time."

"I'm not drunk now," Crispin said and brushed past me in his shirtsleeves with the pink gown tossed negligently over one shoulder. "The coldness of your demeanor has sobered me, Darling. I'm as unebriated as a judge and likely to stay that way."

He vanished into the hallway before I could tell him that 'unebriated' wasn't a word. He'd managed to get it out without any trouble, so perhaps he was right, and he had sobered up since he arrived.

I spent the time until he reappeared picking up and folding the jacket and waistcoat he had left crumpled on the chair, and the white bowtie that had ended up on the table along with the cufflinks and studs from his shirtfront. It wasn't my task to do, I supposed—I wasn't his wife, mother, or maid—but I'm tidy enough that the garments offended me, discarded and rumpled on my furniture.

Then Crispin stepped into the doorway from the hall, and I looked up. And blinked. "You... you have hair on your chest."

Crispin glanced down, to where whorls of fair hair peeped out of the deep V of the pink gown. After a second he looked back up at me, nonplussed. "Of course I have hair on my chest."

I gaped at him. "Christopher doesn't."

He smirked. "I'm sure he must, Darling. Most men do. Or perhaps you don't know that?"

"Of course I know that," I said. "But I'm telling you that Christopher doesn't. Since you're supposed to look like him, I suppose you're just going to have to shave. There's a safety razor in—"

"I am not shaving the hair off my chest!" Crispin said, outraged.

I put my hands on my hips. "Well, you can't go out like that."

"Then perhaps we shouldn't go at all."

When I must have looked mutinous, he added, "Or perhaps I can just go as myself. If anyone recognizes me, it'll just look like one more stupid stunt of the usual sort."

Well, yes. But— "I thought you and your Bright Young Set was all about the challenge," I said. "Not afraid, are you?"

He snorted. "Of course I'm not afraid. I shave my face twice a day, Darling. I know it doesn't hurt."

"Then what's the problem? What would it take for you to agree to this?"

"To shave my chest? Quite a lot more than you're willing to bargain, Darling. I have a reputation to uphold, you know."

"A reputation?" I repeated. "For what?"

"Virility," Crispin said with an eyeroll, "what else? What do you think would happen if, the next time I take a woman to bed, there's nothing but stubble on my chest? What would she think of me?"

"Certainly not that the neckline of your borrowed gown was too low to allow you to keep your chest hair." My lips twitched. "I was right, you know. Pink is very becoming on you."

"I'm sure the apple green would have looked better," Crispin grumbled.

"I'm not. If you want to keep the hair, feel free to do so. I'm going to find you a pair of Christopher's gloves and shoes, and then we'll see about an evening cloak of some sort, since you certainly can't walk around outside like that..."

We'd both be arrested before we'd crossed the street if he did. Indecent exposure, indeed.

His eyes narrowed. "And you, Darling? You'll be wearing the apple green, I assume? Or perhaps the savage banana yellow?"

"I was thinking I might borrow your evening suit," I said, and had the pleasure of seeing his jaw drop. "It'll be too big on me, of course. You're a few inches taller than I am, and rather wider across the chest and shoulders. But it seems the least I can do after making you put on... that."

Although perhaps I ought to make it Christopher's suit instead. That way I wouldn't have to strip off to give Crispin back his clothes at the end of the evening.

Yes, perhaps just a bit too intimate, that exchange.

"On second thought," I said, "I'll just go find what I need in Christopher's wardrobe. While I do that, feel free to use my makeup table to do your face. You'll need some rouge and rice powder, and lipstick, and some kohl around your eyes. Eyelash enhancer, if you feel brave."

He blinked at me. I left him standing there while I sashayed down to Christopher's room and dug what I needed out of the wardrobe.

Fifteen minutes later we were ready. I looked rather like a young boy trying on his father's dinner suit, I imagined, while Crispin had somehow managed to put on a more than credible face. The kohl around his eyes brought out the silvery gray of his irises, and he'd had the sense to pick a pink lipstick instead of the red or coral. He'd even been brave enough to darken his eyelashes and brows—and had done it without poking himself in the eye—and it was astonishing the difference it made.

The dress helped, of course, and the silk stockings, and Christopher's second-best pair of pumps, and the elbow-length gloves that hid more muscular development than any woman is likely to have. There was nothing to be done about his shoulders or upper arms. I shoved an evening wrap at him and hoped for the best.

Evans's eyebrows rose high enough to give him the look of a surprised rabbit when we arrived in the lobby, but he opened the door without quibbling and pocketed the coin Crispin gave him. "Good evening, Miss Darling. Lord St George."

"Good evening, Evans," Crispin said with all the dignity befitting his elevated status. His voice—still recognizably male —sounded ridiculous coming from a man in a pink dress with rouged cheeks and a colorful scarf tied around his head.

There was a little confusion as to who should hand who into the car. I tried to push Crispin in first, since I was technically the one in the top hat and he was the one in the gown. But he was adamant that he was driving—I would get behind the wheel of his beloved Hispano-Suiza over his cold, dead body; as if I could have done a worse job than he did of the Ballot—and since he hardly seemed inebriated at all any more, I acquiesced. In return, he allowed me to bow him into the car first and then go around and open my own door.

"So where are we headed?" I asked when he had started the motorcar with a roar of the engine and we were rolling away from Evans and the Essex House Mansions.

He smirked. "Tottenham Court Road. Rectors."

"The nightclub?" I wrinkled my brows and felt the top hat slip down my forehead. "That isn't open anymore, is it?"

He shook his head, focused on slotting the motorcar into traffic. "It was shut down for twelve months two years ago, for violating the liquor laws. But Mitchell is bankrupt and can't get it open again. I guess he's trying to salvage what he can."

"By opening it up to Lady Austin's crowd?" Wasn't that adding insult to injury, in the form of a violation of the buggery laws on top of everything else?

Crispin merely shrugged, and I added, "Have you been there before?"

He slanted me a look. "To Rectors? Once or twice. I was still at Cambridge for most of the time that they were open."

"You had better hope we don't run into any of your regular set this evening," I told him. "You make for a passably pretty girl, St George, but I'd hate to think what Lady Laetitia and her ilk would think to see you now."

He smirked. "She already knows I have hair on my chest, Darling."

"Ugh," I said. "Really, St George? Must you remind me?"

"I didn't realize my chest was so abhorrent to you, Darling."

"Not your chest," I said, irritated, "although I can do without that, too. But must you keep reminding me what a deplorable excuse for a human being you are? I've managed to spend almost an hour with you, and neither of us has tried to murder the other. We're practically getting along. Must you ruin it by reminding me of all the things I don't like about you?"

"My apologies, Darling." He managed a semi-acceptable bow, not easy to do while navigating a fast car along a busy road. "I forget how much my person offends you."

"It's not your person, St George!" I banged my fists against my knees for emphasis. He looked down and then up again, quickly, his cheeks pink.

I added, "It's your behavior. It's the string of women you've apparently taken to bed with no more care than you'd have had in taking them to tea at Selfridges. It's the girl with the baby, and it's Johanna in the garden maze and Lady Laetitia in the parlor and Flossie Schlomsky in the lift this evening."

He winced. "Darling—"

"I understand that you're in love, St George, and I'm sorry that your father won't let you marry her." Whoever she was. I didn't know who he fancied himself in love with, and I didn't— I told myself firmly—care.

"Darling—"

"But your behavior is deplorable. You cannot keep doing this to your family, not to mention to all those women, just because you can't have the one woman you want. It's unjust, and unkind, and... and..."

"Unseemly?" Crispin suggested dryly. "Unsavory? Untoward?"

"Yes! Not to mention indecent, inappropriate, and improper!"

He nodded. "As you say, Darling. We've arrived."

I blinked. "Pardon me?"

"We're here." He gestured around us, to the now-stationary motorcar and the parking attendant who was attempting to take it from us. "This car park is a block away from Rectors. We'll have to walk the rest of the way."

"Oh," I said, flushing. "I'm sorry."

"As you should be." He removed himself from behind the wheel and handed a coin to the attendant. "Keep her in a handy spot, Giles, if you please. I don't know how long we'll be staying or how quickly we'll need to make our getaway."

Giles touched a finger to the brim of his cap. "Right you are, your lordship. I'll keep 'er by the door."

"Thank you, Giles." He nodded to me. "Ready, Darling?"

I was, although I had honestly expected him to come around to my side of the motorcar to open the door for me. Now I did it myself instead. "Ready."

"Then let's go." He gave Giles a nod and offered me his arm.

"Shouldn't I be doing that to you?" I wanted to know.

"You're a bit short, Darling." In Christopher's pumps, he was close to six feet tall. I wasn't wearing heels, so I was my usual five feet six. Looking up at him, I felt much smaller than I usually do. The high-heel difference works in my favor the other way.

"You look nothing like yourself," I told him honestly. "I can't believe the car park attendant recognized you."

"Not so much me as the H6, I fancy. It's rather well known around here."

Of course it was. As was he. I sank my teeth into my bottom lip. "We'll be all right, won't we? Going there, like this?"

He glanced down at me. "Of course we will, Darling. Or if not, at least we'll be together when we end up in jail."

Ugh. "Just don't do anything Christopher wouldn't do," I said.

He smirked. "Under normal circumstances, that warning would work. Tonight, I rather think it should be the other way around. I'm much more likely to behave myself here than Kit would be."

"Just don't get into any trouble," I told him.

"Likewise, Darling. Now, are you ready?" He gestured along the pavement towards the arched doorway up ahead. "That's it, right there. Through and down."

"As ready as I'll ever be," I said, and took a deep breath.

CHAPTER THREE

WHAT LAY behind the front door was a foyer with several other doors leading off of it, and a nun in a black and white habit.

I blinked, taken aback. Of all the things I had expected to see, a nun was not one of them. Crispin didn't look surprised, however, although one corner of his mouth turned up in what was either amusement or satisfaction.

She—he—the nun looked at him, and then looked at me, before inclining her—his—head politely. "Good evening, my lady. Sir."

The voice was most definitely male, a deep baritone. I opened my mouth and then closed it again, unsure whether I was supposed to respond, or Crispin was.

He did it. "Good evening, Sister."

The nun smirked. "Going down?"

Crispin nodded. "If you don't mind." He slipped her—him —a coin, which disappeared into a pocket of the habit. The nun opened one of the doors. A wave of sound burst out of the opening.

Crispin nudged me towards it. "Go on, Darling. Thank you, Sister."

"Always a pleasure," the nun told him. Crispin shoved me through the opening and down the stairs towards the lower level. The door shut behind us with a thud.

The stairwell was only faintly lit, although the walls practically vibrated with the amount of sound that was coming up from below. Music—*le jazz hot*—and voices and the sound of feet.

"A nun?" I said over my shoulder.

"Password," Crispin told me, following me down. "Some of these places operate in secret—"

"I'm aware."

"I'm sure you are, Darling. You need the right password to get in. When the commissionaire is dressed like a nun, the password is always 'sister.' When he's dressed like Sherlock Holmes, the password is 'Watson.' There's a place in Marylebone where you have to use the words 'hair of the dog' to be let in, and one in Spitalfields where you have to tell them that you're there to get lucky."

"Charming," I said. "And you know all this because—?"

He smirked. "I get around, Darling."

Of course. "Well, it's very clever of you."

"I'm a clever boy," Crispin said as we stepped off the staircase and into what used to be—and for tonight, at least, still was—Rectors Club.

Unlike Crispin, I had not been to Rectors before, so I looked around curiously.

We were standing in a foyer. Directly in front of us was an enormous room with a heavy coffered ceiling held up by a row of ornate columns marching down the middle of a gleaming inlaid parquet floor. Off to either side were rows of white-topped tables, and beyond those were walls lined with cozy booths. A small stage at the far end of the room held a jazz band, but the players were visible only occasionally through the mass of bodies on the dance floor. Above the dancers' heads, four large fans kept the air circulating.

At first glance it looked like any of the nightclubs in London. Figures in black tie dancing with figures in slinky gowns. The light shone on brilliantined hair and sparkling beads and jewels, and the fans dispersed clouds of smoke from cigarettes held in corners of mouths and in long, enameled cigarette holders.

It required a closer look to see that at least half the 'women' had shoulders to rival Crispin's. Some had shadowed jaws, and there were quite a few prominent Adam's apples to be seen. Some of the 'women' had hairier chests than he did, too, and had made no efforts to hide it.

On the other hand, some of them were so exquisitely beautiful that I had to look both twice and three times before I could tell that they weren't women at all.

Of course, I ought to be used to that. Christopher in a wig, makeup, and gown is much prettier than I could ever hope to be. I am, at best, cute. In full makeup, Christopher is stunning. And Crispin, even without the wig and with rather a lot more hair on his chest, looked better than most of the 'women' here.

More than one person eyed him with interest, and I took his arm. "Let's sit."

He smirked. "Don't you want to dance, Darling?"

I looked at him from under the brim of the top hat. It was too big, and sat on top of my eyebrows, so I had to tilt my head all the way back to see his face. The only reason it hadn't fallen into my eyes already was because I had more hair than Christopher. "Will you let me lead?"

"What do you think?"

"I'm wearing the trousers," I pointed out.

"Do you think trousers are what makes a man, Darling?"

Perhaps not. "Fine," I said. "You can lead."

I don't know how, anyway. When I learned to dance, it was some ten or eleven years ago, with him and Christopher and a private tutor that Aunt Roz and Aunt Charlotte brought in. I'd had to partner both boys alternately, and they had both gotten practice leading. I had not. My task had been to float, feather-like, in their arms while they'd turned me this way and that.

"You won't step on my toes," I added, "will you?"

He'd certainly done plenty of it back in the ballroom at Sutherland House. Most of it on purpose, as far as I'd been able to tell.

He shook his head. "Of course not, Darling. I've grown out of tormenting you that way."

"But not any other way?"

"You said it," Crispin said, "not me. Now, go find us an empty table and leave your hat on it along with this." He let the evening wrap drop from his shoulders and handed it over.

"Why do *I* have to—?" I began, and then I realized: because I was wearing the pants. Had I been the one in the dress, he would have taken my wrap and put it somewhere along with his topper before escorting me onto the dance floor. With me in the dinner suit, it was my job to take care of him. I rolled my eyes at his smirk. "Fine, St George. I get it."

"Better not call me that," Crispin said. "We should have code names, don't you think?"

"Do you really think that's necessary?"

"I'm certain of it." He looked delighted by the idea. Perhaps he hadn't been joking about the Cambridge theatricals. "You'll be Philip, I suppose?"

"I suppose I'd better."

"Unless you'd like to be Lancelot or Percival? Perhaps Romeo? Something dashing and romantic?"

"Only if you'll agree to be Juliet," I said, certain that that would shut him up. When it didn't—when, indeed, he got an unholy light in his eyes—I added, quickly, "Never mind. I do not want to be Romeo. Or Lancelot."

He quirked a brow. "Petruchio? Perhaps Benedick?"

That would suit our usual back-and-forth bickering, at any rate.

"No," I said repressively. "Phillip is fine. I suppose you'll be Crispina?"

"God forbid. I thought perhaps I might be Georgina."

"Certainly. I'd be happy to call you Georgina." From now until the end of time, whenever he did something to annoy me. "Or Henrietta, if you prefer."

He eyed me, having perhaps realized that he had opened a can of worms. "Never mind. You know, Darling, I think perhaps you should just call me St George. And I'll call you Darling."

"Fine by me," I said, "Georgina."

He closed his eyes. "You're horrid, Darling."

"You asked for it," I told him. "Really, Georgina, you ought to have known better."

He sighed. "I suppose I ought to have. You're not going to forget this, are you?"

Not at all likely. "I'm sure I will," I said, "eventually."

"In a few years?"

"Doubtful. It'll take at least a decade."

"Marvelous." He held out a hand. "Since I no longer have to pretend, give me the hat and the wrap, please, and I'll see if one of the booths is empty."

"I'd say that's highly unlikely," I told him, but I followed behind when he headed up towards the back looking for an out-of-the-way booth that might not have been discovered yet.

The first two we passed were occupied: the first by a party

of four, two men and two 'women,' bonding over glasses of champagne. They all eyed Crispin as he went by, and ignored me completely.

The second booth had a couple in it, attached at the lips, and it was impossible to determine which persuasion they were, although the one who had his—or her—back to us was dressed in a shimmery taupe gown, while the other had the usual black worsted dinner jacket on. I could see the sleeves, if nothing else.

Given the venue, I assumed that we were looking at another pair of men, however. And since staring seemed intrusive, I quickly averted my eyes and scurried off after Crispin.

"This'll do." The next booth was empty, and he dropped the top hat and wrap on the tabletop. "Let's see if that will be enough to claim ownership. If we come back and someone else has taken up residence, we'll just have to figure out a way to share."

"Or take our things and leave," I said, since I was rethinking the whole outing by this point. I felt terribly awkward and out of place, and I had no idea how Crispin could move around so unselfconsciously in what had to be thoroughly unfamiliar circumstances.

But perhaps it was simply that he was Crispin St George, scion of the Sutherlands, and he couldn't conceive of a setting where he wouldn't be welcome, if not with open arms, then at least with the respect accorded his title and family history.

"All right, Darling." He turned to me and held out a hand. "Shall we dance?"

Part of me wanted to crawl into the booth and hide, but the quirk of his eyebrow when I didn't jump quickly enough to agree steeled my spine. "Certainly. Lead on, St George."

"At least you didn't call me Georgina that time," Crispin said, and led me toward the dance floor.

. . .

AFTER THAT, and for as long as we stayed on the parquet, it was pretty much like any other nightclub. The smoke, the music, the shuffling steps of the other couples around us, the occasional unavoidable collision. After a few minutes, I forgot that I was wearing a man's evening suit, and that my companion was wearing a gown and lipstick. At least until I inadvertently looked up and got an eyeful of pink lips and darkened lashes.

"What?" Crispin asked when my lips twitched again.

I stopped pretending I wasn't amused and gave him a broad grin. "I keep forgetting what you look like. Until I look up and see your face. Pink lipstick, eyelash enhancer, and all."

"I have fabulous eyelashes, I'll have you know." He fluttered them. "Everyone says so."

"Far be it from me to oppose all your other women, St George. They're nice eyelashes, I agree." Christopher has them, too, so it wasn't as if they were unfamiliar.

A corner of his mouth turned up, but he didn't let me in on what he found amusing. Instead, he shifted his hand against my back and turned me in the other direction. "At least I have that to recommend me."

"There are worse things you could have," I agreed, and abandoned the subject of his eyelashes to look around. "Have you seen Christopher yet?"

Crispin shook his head. "I imagine he's in a booth somewhere. If he were on the dancefloor, I think we would have seen him by now."

I thought so, too. The room was large and the crowd bigger than I had expected, but there were still only about a hundred or perhaps a hundred and twenty people present. Admittedly, the lights were low and the smoke heavy, but I knew exactly what I was looking for—a shiny black cap of hair and a black dress of crepe de chiffon embroidered with beads, over an underdress of black crepe de satin.

If it was on the floor, I was certain I would have seen it. Christopher—at least in drag—is the sort of thing you notice.

"Look out," Crispin said, and I instantly braced myself for a collision with another dancing couple. It didn't come. Instead, a hand landed on my shoulder.

"Excuse me," a voice behind me said—unfamiliar, but distinctly male, "would you mind if I cut in?"

"As a matter of fact," Crispin began, with an icy glance over my head.

I moved my hand from his upper arm to put it against his chest. "Down, Georgina. He means me, I imagine."

He looked down at me, shock in his eyes.

"He wants to dance with you," I clarified.

"I got it, Darling." He looked up at the gentleman behind me. "I'm sorry, sir. But we're monogamous."

"We're no such thing..." I began, because how dare he, honestly? He's the least monogamous person in England, and ought rightly to have been struck by lightning for telling a tarra-diddle like that.

"Hush, Darling." He had already taken steps to twirl us both to the edge of the dancefloor, away from the gentleman in the dinner suit, and now he wrapped a hand around my wrist and tugged me along behind him, between the round tables and up to the booth we had claimed for our own earlier. "Good Lord, if I had known that that was likely to happen, I never would have agreed to this."

I sniggered. "Nothing happened, St George. A handsome, young man asked you to dance. You said no. Nothing at all happened."

"He was neither handsome nor particularly young. Thirty, if he was a day."

"And you all of twenty-three," I jeered. "Today."

He shot me a scowl over his shoulder. The four people in the first booth still assessed him openly as he stalked by. The couple in the second booth had come up for air now, and did the same. No one spared me a single look. "That was a *man*, Darling. A *man* wanted to dance with me."

"You're dressed like a woman," I pointed out. "What did you expect? Don't you cut in and take other women away from other men on the dancefloor?"

"I am *not* a woman!"

He stopped in front of the booth as if he'd run into a wall. I ran into him, and knocked him forward a step. "Ooof!" he grunted when the edge of the table hit him somewhere sensitive. "Bloody hell, Darling...!"

"Sorry," I said. "Why did you—? Oh."

Our booth—'our' booth—had indeed been invaded and occupied by someone else in the time we'd been gone from it. A young man in horn-rimmed spectacles, this one quite close to our own age, was sitting at the back of it, nursing a glass of what looked like champagne. He was dressed like a woman, in a bobbed, brown wig and a burnt orange gown with beadwork around the neckline, but he was quite clearly a man in spite of it, and of the smear of lipstick he had added to his face.

Two more stemmed glasses were sitting on the table, empty, while a bottle of the bubbly waited in a bucket of ice in the middle of the tablecloth.

The young man—round-faced and impish-looking— smirked up at us, or more accurately at Crispin. "There you are, Astley. I thought that was you."

There was a moment's pause, one that stretched out for long enough that I wondered if the young man had mistaken

Crispin for Christopher and now Crispin had no idea who he was.

But then— "Montrose," Crispin said. "I didn't recognize you for a second. It's St George now, you know."

"Of course it is." The young gentleman nodded. "Congratulations are in order on that, I understand, although I'm sorry for your loss."

He meant the death of His Grace, Duke Henry, of course, and not Crispin's mother, but a shadow passed across his— Crispin's—features nonetheless, at the reminder. "Thank you."

Montrose gave him a brightly inquisitive look from behind the glasses. "I didn't expect to see you in a place like this."

"I'm not usually to be found in places like this," Crispin told him dryly, "and certainly not dressed in my cousin's clothes, but it's my birthday today, and Darling and I decided to do something thrilling to celebrate."

He pulled me forward.

"Thrilling?" The young man's eyes, a clear hazel behind the lenses, fastened on me. "Darling?"

"Miss Philippa Darling," Crispin said formally. "The Honorable Frederick Montrose. Technically, she's my cousin Christopher's cousin, my aunt Roslyn's niece, but the cousin of my cousin is my cousin. Isn't that right?"

"Sounds good to me," Frederick Montrose agreed and turned his attention and his bright eyes back to me. "Sorry, Miss Darling, that I can't get up and greet you properly, but I'm somewhat wedged in here."

"That's all right." I smiled graciously. "It's a pleasure nonetheless."

"Don't say that before you know who he is," Crispin advised me. "Monty writes for The Daily Yell."

Oh, did he really?

"I'm surprised they let you in here," I told him. "I would have expected journalists to be as *de trop* as constables."

He smirked. "Hence the getup, you know?" He waved a hand over his dress, wig, and lipstick. "Protective camouflage. I'm on the trail of a story."

He gestured to the bench beside himself. "Have a seat. I got us a bottle of bubbly. We'll toast your birthday, St George. How old are you today? Twenty-four, is it?"

"Twenty-three," Crispin said, but he nudged me into the booth ahead of him and then scooted in behind me.

Montrose nodded. "That's right. You were always younger than everyone else, weren't you?"

"I'm not that much younger," Crispin grumbled. "Christopher's only two months older than I am."

Two and a half, if you wanted to be particular, but I saw no need to point it out. Instead I watched as Montrose lifted the bottle of champagne and filled the two empty glasses. "Have I met Christopher?" he asked as he poured. "He wasn't at Cambridge with us, was he?"

Crispin shook his head and reached for the glass. I did the same, but instead of taking a sip—I've become somewhat leery of drinks I haven't poured myself—I put it down in front of me. "If you've seen Crispin, you've seen Christopher. They look very much the same."

Crispin slanted a look my way. I was pleased to see that he, too, put his glass down without sampling the contents. We'd both learned something from our trip to Dorset in May, it seemed. "I thought you claimed we're nothing alike and you have no problem telling us apart, Darling."

"*I* don't," I said. "Christopher is a lovely, kind, sensitive soul, and you're a womanizing cad with vile habits and a string of broken hearts in your wake. I have no problem telling you apart. Other people do, however."

Montrose sniggered. "Sounds like she has your number, St George. So is Christopher here, too? I'd like to meet him."

"Somewhere," Crispin said vaguely. "We've lost him for the moment. He looks like me, but in a black gown and wig."

Montrose nodded, scanning the dance floor.

"So what are you really doing here?" Crispin added. "Trying to cause trouble for someone, I suppose? Do you have a photographer hidden somewhere? Can I expect to see myself on the cover of the Yell tomorrow, looking like this?"

Montrose sniggered. "Would I do that to you?"

"You've done worse than that already," Crispin told him, but without sounding very troubled about it.

"It would sell rather a lot of papers," I said thoughtfully. "The scion of the Sutherlands in a dress and makeup at a drag ball. Imagine the scandal."

Imagine Uncle Harold's expression. He'd go apoplectic with rage. Crispin shot me a look, one that made it seem like he was thinking the same thing.

"It would sell a lot of papers if there were any truth to it," Montrose corrected. "But everyone knows there isn't. There's that string of broken hearts you mentioned, for one thing."

"Maybe the reason for the broken hearts is the dress and makeup," I said lightly, and Crispin winced.

"Don't put ideas in his head, Darling, please. It's not the dress and makeup, and you know it."

"Of course." It was my turn to snigger. "My apologies, Georgina."

Montrose brayed. "Oh, Lord. That's too good. Georgina, really?"

"For the occasion," I told him, "I'm Phillip and he's Georgina. What about you? You came here in disguise. Do you have a *nom de guerre*, as well?"

Or a *nom de plume*, perhaps, given his profession.

He chuckled. "I'll have to be Frederica, I suppose. Or Freda. I'm not sure whether that's better or worse than Georgina."

I stuck out a hand. "Pleased to meet you, Freda."

"Likewise, Phillip."

We shook.

CHAPTER FOUR

WE HADN'T NOTICED CHRISTOPHER, but as it turned out, he had seen us, and he showed up at Montrose's—our—table just a few minutes after Crispin and I did, with a look of mingled consternation and worry on his (very pretty) face.

"Pippa? Crispin? What are you—?"

I interrupted him before he could say any more. "There you are! We thought we'd lost you."

Christopher shut his mouth on the rest of the sentence and looked at me. And looked closer. And winced. "Is that my dinner jacket?"

"It's your entire evening suit," I said brightly. "Top hat and all. I considered wearing St George's, but I thought the process of switching off at the end of the night might prove awkward."

Christopher cut his eyes to Crispin for a moment, and something, some thought, passed between them. It was Christopher's turn to look amused while Crispin looked sour.

"So it might," Christopher agreed blandly. "Hello, Crispin. Pretty frock. Although you should have shaved your chest first."

"So Darling tells me," Crispin said, "Why is everyone suddenly so concerned about the hair on my chest?"

"Because you're flaunting it," I told him, at the same time as Christopher asked, "Everyone? Who's everyone?"

"Darling threatened to make me shave it off back in the flat," Crispin said. "Next would be my legs, no doubt, and after that—"

"Stop!" I slapped a hand across his mouth. "For God's sake, Georgina, have you no sense of decorum? Next, you're going to ruin the illusion by telling us all about your hairy back—!"

Montrose sniggered and Christopher choked on a laugh. Crispin's fingers wrapped around my wrist and tugged my hand down so he could speak to me over it. His eyes were deeply annoyed. "I do not have a hairy back, you horrible—!"

"Georgina?" Christopher managed. "Really, Crispin? You couldn't have found something better than Georgina?"

"We don't all have names that lend themselves to abbreviation," Crispin said sourly and let go of my arm. "It's easy when you're Philippa, or for that matter Kit. Harder when you're Crispin Henry Jonathan. Darling suggested Crispina and Henrietta, but—"

Christopher winced. "Yes, I can see why you'd prefer Georgina. We'll just call you Georgie, old chap."

"I'd rather you didn't," Crispin began, but by then someone else had joined us, and he closed his eyes. "Oh, Lord."

The newcomer, at least, was in black tie and not a dress. "St George? Is that you, old bean?"

He didn't wait for an answer, just turned and yelled over his shoulder, "Over here, chaps! Look who I found! It's St George, and he's wearing a frock!"

Crispin sighed. "Yes, Hutchison. It's me."

Soon Hutchison was joined by two other young gentlemen of the Young and Bright variety. They were all in evening kit, and all in much the same state that St George had been in when he'd first arrived at the flat two hours ago. Sauced to the gills, and feeling no pain.

"You remember Montrose, don't you?" Crispin said, and at least Hutchison seemed to, so they must have gone to Cambridge together, as well. "This is my cousin Christopher, and Miss Philippa Darling."

There was a lot of giggling at that, and both Christopher and I had our hands kissed while the others debated which one of us ought rightly have our hands kissed the way we were dressed, while Crispin rolled his eyes. By now he was, as he had told me earlier, as sober as a judge, and he didn't seem to appreciate his friends' inebriation any more than I did. That kind of thing is much easier to deal with when one is properly lubricated oneself.

The three young men had a girl with them, also from the Society of Bright Young Persons, and also deeply inebriated, and she greeted Crispin's appearance with shrieks of merriment. "Mercy, St George, don't you look a picture!"

"Yes, yes," Crispin said, with another eyeroll. "Sit down, Gladys, before you fall down."

He tugged her down on the other side of him, while two of the other three crowded in next to Christopher on the other side of the booth. The final young gentleman—I thought his name was Blanton—squeezed in next to Gladys.

They made short process of Montrose's bottle of champagne, and then they ordered two more. There were toasts to Crispin's old age, as well as to the rest of us.

As they got more and more sozzled, I met Christopher's eyes across the table and tried to communicate how sorry I was. This wasn't at all how I had wanted the evening to go. We— Crispin and I—had just wanted to crash the ball and have some fun. It was supposed to be a lark, nothing more. We'd thought—

or I had—that we'd find Christopher and he'd be annoyed with us, but mostly forgiving and, eventually, happy to see us and touched that St George had wanted him to help celebrate his birthday.

But instead, we had taken Christopher away from the dance floor and his own friends, and had stuck him here, at the back of a booth surrounded by a contingent of St George's set, who all thought we were here to make sport of the occasion.

Which is what we wanted them to believe, of course—especially Frederick Montrose, because if he realized that Christopher was actually a regular here, at this event and with these people, there was no question at all that Christopher Astley—that Kitty Dupree—would show up on the front page of The Daily Yell tomorrow.

Crispin being here, and in drag, was, as Montrose had pointed out, a non-starter. Everyone in London knew his reputation with women, and no one would believe that he had suddenly turned queer. But Christopher was a different story. If that news got out, all sorts of bad things might follow. Ostracization, jail, the disappointment of Uncle Herbert and the worry of Aunt Roz. The tightening of the purse strings to the point where he and I would have to leave London and go back to Beckwith Place—or God forbid, Sutherland Hall—to live.

Crispin wasn't happy about the outcome of the evening, either, I could tell. He joked with his friends and exerted his charm on Gladys, and was successful at both, even in a dress and makeup, but he kept glancing across at Christopher and at Frederick Montrose, and occasionally sideways at me, with concern in his eyes.

Christopher didn't seem terribly fussed about it, honestly. He conversed politely with Montrose, who didn't seem to be asking invasive questions at all, but instead kept his eye on the newcomers more so than Christopher. After a few minutes, the young man whose name I hadn't caught, engaged Christopher in conversation, and after that, Montrose's bright hazel eyes flicked back and forth between the two of them, between Crispin and Gladys, and between Blanton and Hutchison at either end of the table.

Hutchison seemed laid back and at his ease. Blanton, on the other hand, got more and more jumpy as time went on. He perched on the edge of the seat next to Gladys, chewing his fingernails and darting glances, not at Christopher or Crispin or even at Frederick Montrose, but out at the dance floor and the entrance to the club.

And a few minutes later his concern was rewarded, as another young man—this one with heavily brilliantined black hair and flawless black tie—stopped by the table. "Evening, chaps."

He showed all his teeth in a dazzling smile, one that could have given Flossie Schlomsky a run for her money.

Blanton jumped to his feet and snagged his friend by the arm, perhaps to make sure he wouldn't disappear again. "Dom! There you are. I was afraid you weren't going to show up."

He turned to the table before Dom had a chance to respond. "Everyone, this is Dominic Rivers. Dom, do you know everyone?"

Mr. Rivers took in the assembly with large, dark eyes surrounded by lashes that looked—but probably weren't— painted. His hair was dark, his eyes were dark, and his skin was a darker shade of olive than the one most of us sported. He probably came by the thick, dark lashes honestly.

To the best of my knowledge I had never seen him before in my life, and he didn't seem to recognize me, either. He nodded to Hutchinson and the third friend, and winked at Gladys, who tittered. He looked at Crispin for several seconds before he said, tentatively, "Astley?"

"Rivers," Crispin responded. It wasn't precisely friendly, although it wasn't precisely the opposite, either. "It's St George now, you know."

Rivers nodded. "Of course it is. What are you doing here?"

"Celebrating my birthday with a different crowd than usual," Crispin told him lazily. He was leaning back in the booth like he hadn't a care in the world, and like he wasn't dressed in a gown and high heels and couldn't care less what Rivers, whoever he was, might think about it. "My cousin Kit. Miss Philippa Darling."

He gestured to Christopher, on the other side of the booth, and then to me. It ought rightly to have been the other way around, I suppose, but then there were the clothes, again.

"And you remember Montrose, surely?"

Rivers gave a short laugh. "Is that who it is? Evening, Montrose. Not sure I'd have recognized you without St George's say-so."

"I'll take it as a compliment," Montrose said, although it hadn't sounded like one, and his tone indicated that he knew it. "How are things with you, Rivers?"

"Can't complain," Rivers said with a bright smile. "Busy, busy, you know. A pleasure, as always."

He nodded politely—and managed to make it include all of us—before focusing his attention solely on Blanton. "Are you ready to blouse, old man?"

Blanton nodded. "Yes, please, Dom."

Gladys, too, nodded eagerly and started scooting away from Crispin towards the edge of the bench. Whatever Rivers had to offer seemed to conquer even Crispin's charms, and I must admit that my brows arched. Most women prioritize the Sutherland title and fortune over pretty much anything else.

"Where ho?" Montrose asked lightly.

"We're off to Ronnie's place," Gladys said with a giggle.

And then she seemed to remember, suddenly, who she was leaving behind, because she turned to Crispin. "You should come with us, St George."

Crispin blinked, and I have to say, it was quite rude of her to invite him so particularly without including the rest of us. I got the pretty distinct idea that he didn't want to go with her, however, and furthermore, I also got the idea that Blanton and Rivers, and perhaps Hutchison too, didn't want him to come, either.

Or perhaps it was the rest of us they had a problem with. If so, they could just take Crispin and go. I'd stay with Christopher and make my way home with him at the end of the night. It was certainly no inconvenience to me if they took Crispin away.

I had my mouth open to say so when—

"Capital idea," Montrose said brightly, looking from one to the other of them "We'll all go and make one big party of it. Celebrate St George's birthday in style!"

Crispin glanced across the table at Christopher. The fourth young man, the one whose name I didn't know, was also looking at Christopher, and it didn't seem as if Christopher would mind terribly spending more time with him.

Crispin must have seen it, too, because he turned his attention from Christopher to me, via Montrose. The look he and Freddie Montrose exchanged lasted barely a second, but it was noticeably there.

Crispin looked at me. "Darling?"

His reluctance was obvious, at least to someone who knows him well, and I've watched his expressions on and off for twelve years now. I can't read him as well as I can Christopher, but well enough to know that at that moment, he wanted me to say no, to come up with some reason why we couldn't go.

And I'm sorry to say that I did what I usually do in that

situation, which was the opposite of what Crispin wanted me to do, because a large part of my life is about doing what I can to annoy him.

I smiled brightly. "That sounds marvelous. We've got Crispin's Hispano-Suiza; we can take Christopher and someone else. Perhaps you, Mr. Montrose?"

Montrose nodded pleasantly. "That would be delightful. Thank you."

I turned to the only other real woman in the party. "You're welcome to ride with us too, Gladys. If you'd prefer to go with us over going with the young men."

Four of them, in whatever vehicle they had gotten here in. In the Hispano-Suiza, at least I would be there to make sure everyone behaved.

Not that anyone was likely to misbehave, actually. Certainly not Christopher, and I didn't get the impression that Crispin was particularly drawn to Gladys, either, for all that he had flirted outrageously with her. For him, that was practically instinct. And as for Frederick Montrose... well, the idea of him trying to get something going with a young woman in his current getup was too ridiculous for words.

"Darling?" Gladys repeated, as she looked between me and Crispin.

"Just St George's idea of a little joke," I told her, after which Crispin put a hand to his chest and a wounded look in his eyes.

"You cut me to the quick, Darling."

"On a regular basis, I'm sure," I told him, and gave him a nudge with my hip. "Go on, St George. Out of the booth."

He sighed but moved. "On your own head be it, Darling."

"Be what?" I asked, but he just shook his head and looked around.

"Where's my wrap?"

"Here you are." I fished it out of my—of Christopher's—top hat and handed it to him.

He eyed it, and me, and it. "You're not going to help me into it?"

I gave him a look. "It's a wrap, St George. There's no 'into.' You just wrap it around you."

"Wrap it around me then, Darling. You're my escort for the evening, aren't you? Isn't it your duty to make sure I'm wrapped up against the evening chill?"

Now that he mentioned it, I guess it was. I flung the wrap around his shoulders while Christopher somehow managed to get into his own with no problem, as did Montrose. Hutchison did the honors for Gladys. And then we headed out of Rectors and away from the drag ball and down the street to the car park and Giles and Crispin's Hispano-Suiza.

RONALD BLANTON'S place turned out to be an exceedingly lovely flat in a very exclusive mansion block in Mayfair. It quite blew Christopher's and my flat in the Essex House Mansions out of the water. It was twice as big, for one thing, with a proper library, and one more bedroom, and staff quarters. Ronnie had a live-in manservant, an older man with sparse hair who greeted us in the foyer when we walked in, and who displayed no signs of surprise or anything else, not even at the sight of Christopher, Crispin, and Frederick Montrose in their dresses and wigs, nor for that matter of me in my—or in Christopher's—top hat and tails. He merely divested the men of their evening wraps and me of my hat, stowed them in the appropriate closet, and withdrew, at Ronnie Blanton's request, to his quarters for the evening. "Off to bed, Dobbins," Ronnie said gaily, "there's a good chap. We'll take care of ourselves for the rest of the night."

"Yes, Master Ronald." Dobbins inclined his head and withdrew. Rivers and Hutchison shared a snigger, Christopher and I a look.

"Come in, come in!" Ronald waved us all into the sitting room. "Make yourselves comfortable. Hutch, will you do the honors? Dom…"

Dominic Rivers and Hutchison nodded, upon which sign Blanton drew Rivers out through the door into the hall, practically vibrating with eagerness, while Hutchison headed for the bar cart. "What'll it be, chaps?" he asked over his shoulder. "Shall we have more champagne in honor of St George's birthday, or something else?"

"Champagne cocktails!" Gladys giggled, and Hutchison shrugged.

"Someone better check the larder for oranges, then."

Gladys turned toward the kitchen, but the third young man, the quiet one, whom Christopher had told me in the car was named Graham Ogilvie, shook his head. "Better not interrupt, pet. Hutchie'll make you a nice French 75 instead. Won't you, Nigel?"

"Certainly," Hutchison said, and got busy with the bottles. "What about the rest of you? Miss Darling? Or should I say Mister Darling?" He smirked.

"I'll take whatever is convenient," I told him. "A French 75 is fine. So is straight bubbly."

Hutchison nodded. "St George? Mr. Astley? Montrose?"

Crispin said he'd take champagne, as well, and so did Christopher, and Graham Ogilvie did the same. The four of us toasted Crispin with glasses of Ayala, while Gladys giggled over her French 75 and Hutchison poured himself and Freddie Montrose straight brandies.

"What's going on in the kitchen that we don't want to interrupt?" Montrose wanted to know, with a glance at the doorway.

Hutchison shook his head. "Nothing you need to worry about, old chap. That's between Ronnie and Dom."

"Oh, really?" Montrose waggled his eyebrows suggestively. Hutchison rolled his eyes—Gladys giggled—but Ogilvie took offense.

"Listen here, Montrose!" he said heatedly. "It's not like that, but if it were, it would be none of—"

"Easy, Gram," Hutchison told him lazily, from where he had sprawled on the sofa with the glass on his stomach. "Everyone knows it isn't like that. And Ronnie doesn't need you to defend him, old man."

It was fairly obvious to me, even if perhaps it wasn't to Hutchison, that this had nothing to do with defending Ronnie Blanton from whatever Frederick Montrose might publish about him. Graham Ogilvie shot a quick look at Christopher— who wasn't looking at him but was talking softly to Crispin about something or other; I caught the words, "—doesn't really, and you ought to know that, Crispin,"—and then looked away again. I thought perhaps Ogilvie had some inclinations of his own that he didn't want Montrose to make light of, even if it was Ronald Blanton and Dominic Rivers on the chopping block, and not himself and his own feelings.

At any rate, whatever Blanton and Rivers had been doing in the kitchen, it didn't seem at all romantic. Ronnie came back after a few minutes, looking like a new man. Gone were the nervous mannerisms and shaky hands. In their place were bright, shiny eyes with dilated pupils—all that was left of Ronnie Blanton's irises was a thin rim of blue around a large expanse of black—broad gestures, and a sense of palpable excitement.

Oh yes, and a smear of white at the edge of one nostril.

"Cocaine," Frederick Montrose said softly while we watched Ronnie cross the floor toward us while Gladys jumped up from her chair and practically ran over to Dominic Rivers, who was waiting in the doorway. "And now it's her turn."

I lowered my voice to make sure I wouldn't be overheard. "Do they all use it?"

Montrose glanced at me. His own eyes were bright behind the lenses of his hornrims, too, but the pupils were a normal size, neither overly large nor the pinpricks I had once seen on my Cousin Francis. "Not to the degree Blanton and Gladys do. They wouldn't survive without the dope anymore. The others aren't at that point, although I'm sure they indulge, too."

"St George?" I ventured.

We both looked at Crispin, who was still talking softly to Christopher. He noticed us staring and, out of character, flushed pink under the makeup. Christopher looked over too, and smirked, and for a second, he looked so much like his cousin—and Crispin, in his dress and pink lips, so much like Christopher—that it was almost as if they had switched places.

Then Crispin's lip turned up in its usual sneer and things went back to normal. And—

"I know very little about what St George gets up to," Montrose said. And changed it to, "Not aside from what everyone knows, I mean. The tabloids are full of the exploits of the scion of the Sutherlands."

They certainly had been lately. "Women," I said, with a displeased look at Crispin. "Women and more women."

Montrose sniggered. "He does seem popular with the fairer sex."

After a second, he added, "If he does indulge in dope, it's purely recreational. He has none of the signs of being addicted. And while he certainly drinks a lot, and does some truly stupid things—"

Like wrapping the Ballot around the West End light pole, I assumed, unless Freddie Montrose had somehow gotten wind of that young woman with the baby who had shown up at Sutherland House sometime in the last few months.

"—he's not stupid in general."

"And they are?" I indicated Blanton, now sprawled in a chair with a blissful smile on his face while he listened to Hutchison expound on something or other, and Ogilvie, who was watching them from the other side of the table with an unreadable look on his face.

"They're certainly not as smart as they think they are." Montrose leaned forward to put his glass on the table. "The Bright Young People aren't all that bright, when it comes down to it."

He shot me a look before he pushed to his feet. "Excuse me. I'm going to look for the facilities."

I nodded, while he addressed himself to Blanton. "Your toilet, old man?"

"Out the door to the right, third door on the left," Blanton told him.

Montrose ambled toward the door. Hutchison waited until he was into the hallway and out of sight before he said, "Don't you think you ought to go with him, old man?"

"To the toilet?" Blanton giggled.

"He's a reporter," Hutchison said. "He writes for The Daily Yell."

In his current state—or perhaps it was a regular thing—Blanton didn't seem able to add two and two together to make four. Hutchison had to spell it out for him. "Are you sure you want a reporter wandering your flat with Gladys and Dom in the other room, Ronnie?"

It took another second, but then— "Oh!"

Blanton jumped up and ran for the door. Hutchison got to his feet, too. "Excuse me," he said formally, with a small bow. Whatever else was wrong with him, he had lovely manners. "I should go with him. He'll do himself no favors in his current condition."

He headed towards the door, too, leaving Graham Ogilvie in charge of the sitting room. A look passed between the two of them just before Hutchison ducked out of sight around the door jamb, and it was very clearly a passing of responsibility from one to the other. It was beyond obvious that they didn't want any of us—with the possible exception of Crispin—wandering the flat while Dominic Rivers and Gladys got up to whatever they were getting up to in one of the other rooms, and now Graham Ogilvie was responsible for keeping us here.

"What does he think he's going to do?" I inquired of the others. "Burst into the water closet after Montrose and plug his ears?"

"I don't imagine Monty was actually headed for the WC," Crispin asked, "do you?"

"With as much as you've all had to drink," I told him, "I wouldn't be surprised."

He rolled his eyes and turned his attention to Ogilvie, who was perched on the edge of his chair, alternately eyeing us and looking nervously at the door to the hallway. "Don't you think you ought to go with them, old man? Who knows what Blanton might do in his current state? And Rivers isn't quite sane at the best of times, is he?"

Ogilvie hesitated. Glanced at Crispin. Glanced at the doorway. Looked back at Crispin. Who told him, gently, "Hutch might need help keeping Blanton from Montrose's throat. It won't help anyone if Ronnie tries to strangle him."

Ogilvie cast another agonized glance at the door.

"You don't have to worry about us," Crispin added, persuasively. "We're not going to get involved. We don't care what Ronnie and Gladys get up to on their own time and with their own money. Do we?"

He looked at Christopher, and then me. We both shook our heads. Ogilvie looked at us too, and chewed his bottom lip worriedly.

"Go on," Crispin told him. "You know you want to. We'll just sit here quietly and wait for you to come back."

I nodded. So did Christopher. Ogilvie gave us all a final dubious look, before he got up and ran for the door. As soon as he was out of sight, Crispin turned to us both, his demeanor quite different from the laidback ease he had put on for Graham Ogilvie. "Listen. Dominic Rivers is a dope dealer. Ronnie and Gladys are both dope addicts—"

"We're not stupid, St George," I told him.

He gave me a look, but kept talking, "—and Frederick Montrose works for The Daily Yell. He's probably looking for a scoop for his odious newspaper. Now he's managed to put all three of us in what basically amounts to a dope den—"

"Aren't dope dens in places like Limehouse? And not in nice flats in Mayfair?"

"You'd be surprised," Crispin said darkly, and perhaps I would. However—

"We understand all that, St George. But I didn't get the impression that he's particularly interested in the three of us, you know, other than as a way to get to Blanton and Rivers. He even told me that if *you* use dope, you do it only recreationally..."

Both his eyebrows rose. "You asked Monty about me? Do you worry about me, Darling?"

"As a matter of fact," I said, with a grimace, "I do."

He blinked, and for a moment his lips parted in surprise before he firmed them again. "Dear me. I never thought I'd see the day."

"Oh, come off it," I said, irritated. "I may not like you much, St George, but I don't wish you ill—or at least not that amount of ill. Besides, I've already got one cousin who's a dope addict. I don't need another."

"If Francis uses cocaine," Crispin said clinically, "he only does it recreationally, as well. And I'm not your cousin, you know. Contrary to what I said earlier, the cousin of your cousin isn't actually your cousin."

Yes, I was aware of that. But at the moment, it wasn't of much concern.

"I'm actually more concerned about Freddie Montrose's safety than our own right now," I said. "I didn't get the impression that he's out to get either of us. Maybe at first, when he originally showed up at Rectors, he was looking for something salacious he could print about the drag ball. He said he had heard about last month's raid and was hoping for something exciting to happen."

I glanced at Christopher, who made a face.

"But once Dominic Rivers showed up, I think Montrose became more interested in the dope angle than the drag ball. That might even have been why he was there in the first place. It didn't seem as if Rivers showed up by accident, after all, but more like he and Blanton—and probably Gladys—had a meeting arranged."

"Rivers sells dope," Crispin said. "There must have been someone at Rectors he was dealing with. And with all the secrecy, it probably seemed like a safe place to meet with Ronnie and Gladys, as well."

No doubt. "So about Montrose..."

"Monty isn't our problem," Crispin said. "In my opinion we ought to get out of here before something goes wrong and we get caught up in it."

"And leave Montrose to his own devices?"

He looked at me, very intently. "Listen to me, Darling. Freddie Montrose is not our responsibility. He's an adult who came here on his own to—I assume—get dirt for an exposé for his tabloid. We're not responsible for what happens to him."

"So you do think something is likely to happen to him. And you're sitting here instead of getting involved?"

"What am I going to do?" Crispin wanted to know, gesturing to his tasseled gown and strap shoes. "I'm not exactly dressed for a scrap, am I?

Well, no. Nor was Christopher. Nor was either of them, to my knowledge, particularly scrappy by nature. If Crispin got into fist fights, Grimsby's dossier of a month ago hadn't dug it up.

"We can't just—" I began, planning to end with a statement to the effect that we couldn't just leave Freddie Montrose to fend for himself if the others all fell on him. He'd be beaten to a pulp before being tossed out on his ear, and if we could spare him the beating and instead just remove him before any damage was done, didn't we owe it to him—and to our own consciences—to do so?

But that was as far as I got before a shrill scream cut through the interior of the flat, and we all jumped to our feet and ran for the door to the hallway to deal with whatever it was.

CHAPTER FIVE

THE SCREAMER WAS GLADYS, which I had expected based on the shrillness and pitch of the sound. She was standing in the middle of the hallway with both hands pressed to her mouth and her eyes wide as saucers above them. Her pupils were as wildly dilated as Ronald Blanton's had been just a few minutes ago, her irises just the same thin rims around a large expanse of black, and her screams kept leaking out around her fingers.

The other four men were crowded around the open door to a room, all of them peering around the jamb at what lay inside.

And by four, I mean Ronnie himself, Hutchison, Ogilvie, and of course Dominic Rivers. Freddie Montrose was nowhere to be seen.

As we approached—but while we were still too far away to do anything to stop it—Rivers pivoted from the door jamb and swung out with one hand. It landed across Gladys's cheek with enough force to whip her head around, and the crack of it echoed up and down the hallway. I let out an enraged screech of my own.

He glanced in my direction, but didn't pay me any attention whatsoever. Instead, he grabbed Gladys by the shoulders and shook her. "Shut up, you stupid cow, or you'll wake Dobbins, and then hell really will break loose!"

"You bastard—!" I shrieked, surging forward, but Christopher and Crispin grabbed me by the arms, one on each side, and kept me from charging up to Rivers and giving him a piece of my... no, not my mind, but the flat of my hand. If he was of a mind to hit women, I had no objection to returning the favor.

However, they clearly weren't about to let me, and besides, I will say for Rivers that the treatment was effective. Gladys still sniffled wetly, cradling her no doubt stinging cheek, but she had stopped wailing. Rivers let her go and turned back to the open doorway, and to Blanton, who was clinging to the jamb with both hands, all his earlier excitement gone. He was pale and trembling. "Go and make sure she didn't wake Dobbins, and if she did, find some way to put him off. The last thing we need is Dobbins seeing this."

Blanton scurried off without a word. That left an opening in the doorway, but before I could take advantage of it, Crispin let go of my arm. "Hold on to her," he told Christopher, "and don't let go."

Christopher nodded, and shifted his grasp to my elbow instead. "Stay here, Pippa."

"I want to see what's happened," I protested, but Crispin was already on his way towards the door, the heels of his—Christopher's—strap shoes clicking against the parquet floors.

Christopher shook his head. "You already know what happened. There's no need for you to look at it."

"I don't—" I began, but of course, once I thought about it, I knew exactly what had happened. I had been afraid of it as soon as Frederick Montrose left the sitting room. It didn't come as a surprise to see all the color drain out of Crispin's cheeks when he peered through the open door. When he glanced over his shoulder at us, there was a horrified look on his face.

"Let me go," I told Christopher and twitched my arm to get it out of his grip. "They're all just standing around gaping instead of doing something. Nobody's trying to help him."

"If there was anything that could be done, I'm sure someone would do it," Christopher said, and held on. "Look. Crispin's going in."

He was. As we watched, the back of the pink frock disappeared through the doorway.

"If there's anything that can be done," Christopher told me, "Crispin will do it."

"Somebody should do something about Gladys. Get her a glass of brandy or water, at least."

You'll notice that I didn't suggest that *I* should do it. Not only do I not have a lot of patience with the vapors, but I didn't think any ministrations on my behalf would be well received. She was slumped against the wall of the hallway, pale as a ghost except for the one pink cheek that still bore the imprint of Dominic Rivers's fingers. She wasn't having hysterics anymore, so I guess we ought to be grateful for that, but she had tears running down her face, and she kept swiping one hand under her nose, as if that, too, was dripping.

Inside the room everyone was crowded around, there was the sound of a faucet turning on and off. Then a second passed, and Crispin came back out into the hallway shaking water from his hands. Christopher winced, but didn't say anything about the way the droplets were likely to stain the shantung silk of the dress.

"What happened?" I asked. I mean, I knew, but I wanted to hear someone say it, and none of the others seemed likely to put it into words.

"He's dead," Crispin answered, and while I could hear a

very faint tremor in his voice, he sounded mostly calm. "Someone should ring the police."

"No!" Rivers yelped. Gladys made a startled hiccough.

"We can't leave him there," Crispin pointed out. "Dobbins won't want to step over him every time he has to use the butler's pantry for the next week."

"A week?" I repeated. "Surely you know—"

He flicked me a glance. "Yes, Darling. But after a week, the odor will be unpleasant enough that there wouldn't be a question about whether or not to phone the police."

Yes, of course. "I'll do it," I said, and looked around, "if someone can point me in the direction of the telephone."

But— "No!" Rivers barked again. He went so far as to reach out and grab me by the shoulder, which caused Christopher to growl and Crispin's eyes to narrow. They both took a step forward, but before either of them could say anything, Rivers dropped his hand. "Dear me," he said, "I didn't realize I wasn't to touch your precious, St George."

If he had somehow imagined that that pseudo-apology was going to make Crispin calm down, he clearly didn't know him at all. "Shut it, Rivers, or I'll do it for you."

"Oooh." Rivers grinned unpleasantly. "Touchy."

"Stop it," I said severely, "both of you. Now is not the time to see which of you has the bigger—"

"Pippa!" Christopher exclaimed, shocked, and, "Darling!" Crispin said, wincing.

I sighed. "If Montrose is dead, we have to phone the police. We can't leave him there."

"Of course not," Rivers agreed. "We'll take him downstairs and put him in the alley."

He said it as if it were a perfectly reasonable solution to the problem, instead of a suggestion that we interfere with a crime scene and destroy evidence, not to mention the appalling notion of carting around a dead body.

My jaw dropped, and Christopher's tightened. Clearly neither of us had seen this suggestion coming. Crispin's face didn't change, so perhaps he wasn't as surprised as I was.

Gladys nodded fervently, and Ogilvie uncoiled himself from the wall where he had been languidly observing the proceedings. "It had better be the service lift, then."

Rivers agreed with a nod. "We'll need to clean up the blood, too. Blanton will have to send Dobbins out for more towels, I suppose."

"Have you lost your minds?" I asked, and they both looked at me for a moment before they went back to talking to each other, just as if I hadn't opened my mouth.

"She's right, you know," Ogilvie said. "Dobbins would wonder where the towels went. Ronnie shall have to purchase his own whitewares, I'm afraid."

"That's not at all what I meant!" I exclaimed. However, at this point Christopher started to pull me backwards down the hallway towards the sitting room, away from the group in front of the pantry door.

"We can't let them—" I began, resisting the steady pull, but by now Crispin had caught up too, and between them, he and Christopher manhandled me through the door into the sitting room.

Christopher let go, but Crispin didn't. He pushed me a couple further steps into the room and turned to me.

"Listen, Darling—" He's only a couple of inches taller than I am, but he did his very best to loom.

"No, St George," I retorted furiously, hands on my hips, "*you* listen...!"

"Stop it, Crispin," Christopher said. He took his cousin by

the arm and pulled him back a step so he wasn't hissing directly into my face. "You're scaring her."

"No, he's not!"

What he was doing, was making me angrier than I already was. We had to call the police so they could figure out who had killed Montrose, and the last thing I needed was Crispin telling me otherwise.

Crispin, meanwhile, told Christopher, "She should be scared! And so should you. So should all of us!"

"I just think..." I began, and he turned back to me, eyes glinting with temper.

"Listen to me. For once in your life, Philippa, *shut up* and listen to me!"

My jaw dropped. He only calls me by my first name on exceedingly rare occasions, when things are either extremely tense or else extremely important, and if this was one of them, perhaps he was right and I ought to listen.

He waited, and when I—for once in my life—didn't attempt to interject, he went on, his voice low and vibrating with something that might have been anger, but might equally well have been fear. "Someone in this flat is a murderer."

I snorted—that was rather obvious, wasn't it?—and he continued, "At this point, it doesn't even matter who. They all agree on what to do next. They want to get that body as far away from themselves as they can. And if we get in their way, I don't think they would think twice about killing us, too."

"You wouldn't let that happen," I told him. "You and Christopher wouldn't let anything happen to each other, or to me."

"There are more of them than there are of us, Pippa," Christopher said, alternating between watching us and keeping an eye on the hallway. "I'm with Crispin on this. We go along with whatever they say—even if that is taking Montrose's body downstairs and leaving it in the alley—and then we get ourselves out of here. And deal with the rest later."

He exchanged a tense glance with Crispin, who nodded and turned back to me. "Montrose is already dead, Darling. It doesn't matter what happens to his body."

I opened my mouth, but closed it again without speaking.

He continued, persuasively, "What matters is what they do to *us*. And they have very little to lose right now. Let's not make it easier for them."

Christopher nodded. They both looked at me, waiting for me to do the same.

As usual, my first instinct was to argue. I argue with whatever Crispin wants as a matter of course. And I disagreed vehemently that it didn't matter what happened to Montrose's body. It absolutely mattered, albeit perhaps not to Montrose. But I wasn't going to debate the point. They had made their case, and it made sense, and I did want to get out of Blanton's flat with my life. If their way was the way to do it, then I'd go along. Even if it was Crispin's idea.

"All right, Pippa?" Christopher prompted.

I nodded.

"Good." They both turned to the doorway, just in time for Ronnie Blanton to appear.

He glanced around, at Crispin and me still face to face in the middle of the floor, and Christopher a couple of steps away. "Everything all right in here?"

"Delightful," Crispin said, stepping back. If he had been wearing a suit, he would have shot his cuffs. I could see the movement start, and then stop when he realized he was in a gown and elbow length gloves. The frustration on his face would have been funny under other circumstances.

"Darling needed a little convincing," he flicked me a glance, "but we're all on board with doing what's necessary."

Ronnie nodded. His eyes were still bright, but a bit less dilated than earlier. He must have come down off the initial euphoric transport. I wondered whether it always happened that quickly, or whether the current events had had something to do with it. "Dom said to get you."

Crispin looked apologetic. "Are you sure you want to do that, old man? We were in here when whatever happened out there. The less we know about it, the better it might be for everyone."

Ronnie chewed on that for a moment. It looked like it took effort, but at least he was thinking. I allowed myself a moment to hope that he might be reasonable, but then he simply said it again. "Dom said to get you."

The impression he gave was that whatever Dominic Rivers said, Ronald Blanton did. And if Dominic Rivers said it, it was to be done, whether it made sense or not.

"Yes," Crispin said, "but right now we're not actually involved. Don't you think you might want to keep it that way?"

Ronnie eyed him. "You're the ones who brought Montrose here," he pointed out. "That makes you part of this."

I winced. Surely that wasn't true. We were the ones who had motored Freddie Montrose to Mayfair, yes, but he had wanted to go. He was the one who had invited himself to Blanton's flat. Surely it wasn't our fault that he was dead?

Crispin, however, nodded resignedly. And when Blanton said, "Let's go," Christopher headed through the door first, and then Crispin nudged me along ahead of him. In the hallway, they flanked me, one on each side.

Outside the door to the butler's pantry, nothing much had changed. Gladys was still crying, but very quietly now. It was as if she wasn't even aware of the streaks of black makeup trickling down her cheeks. Ogilvie leaned against the wall next to the open door picking at his nails, while Rivers and Hutchison were discussing next steps.

"—wrap his head with something," Rivers said, "since we don't want a trail of blood all the way downstairs..."

Hutchison nodded. "A towel ought to take care of it. And another to mop the blood off the floor. One of the girls can do that while we move the body down to the motorcar."

He flicked a glance at me and Gladys, or perhaps it was at Crispin and Christopher. I opened my mouth—I certainly wasn't going to wipe Montrose's blood off the tiles; that would amount to destroying evidence—and Crispin dug his elbow into my ribs. In its current condition, bare of jacket, shirt, or anything else, it was sharp and pointy, and I closed my mouth again.

"Motorcar?" he repeated. "Would that be *my* motorcar, by chance? I brought Montrose here in the H6, so now I'm responsible for taking him away again?"

"As you say," Hutchison said courteously, "you do have a motorcar."

"And no one else does?" Crispin arched a brow. "The rest of you walked, I suppose?"

Nobody answered. It was quite clear that we had been nominated *in absentia* to transport the body, and nothing we could say would change that.

"Where are we supposed to take him?" I wanted to know. "I thought you were going to put him in the alley. You don't need a motorcar for that."

Had they, by chance, reconsidered, and were going to let us transport him to the police? Or at least to a hospital?

But no, surely not. Nor was I sure I wanted to, actually. Nothing good would come from driving up to Scotland Yard with a dead body in the back of the automobile. That was true whether we'd had anything to do with killing him or not.

"We thought," Rivers said, "that taking him further afield might be a good idea. With the way he's currently dressed—"

He leveled a look through the open door into the butler's pantry, "we thought you might take him back to Rectors."

Where everyone had seen him sit with us, drink with us, and leave with us.

Then again, that was true for everyone else in Ronald Blanton's party, as well. We'd all sat at Freddie Montrose's table, and shared a bottle or two of champagne with him, in full view of everyone in the club, just an hour or two ago.

"Fine," Crispin said, since there was nothing else to say. "Get him downstairs. I'll fetch the motorcar."

He swung on his heel so the pink tassels danced around his calves. "Come along, Kit. Darling."

"They can help us down with the body..." Hutchison began, but a look from Crispin shut him up.

"If we're to be responsible for taking him away, we're already doing more than our share of the work. And I don't want any of us having to explain away bloodstains. It'll be hard enough to make excuses without that, if we're stopped along the way."

"Why would you be stopped?" Blanton wanted to know, and Crispin gave him a crushing look.

"You don't think every one of the London constables know the H6? Most of them probably know it's my birthday, too. You think they won't stop me, to see how much I've had to drink?"

"He has a point," Ogilvie told Rivers. "Perhaps—"

But Crispin had already swept past him to the door, dragging me behind him. "We're off. The rest of you bring the body."

"Might it not be better—" Blanton began, but Crispin kept going.

"If we've been nominated to do this, then let us do it. We'll meet you at the service entrance."

He opened the front door and held it for me. "After you, Darling. You too, Kit. Let's go."

He shut the door gently behind us and breathed out. I felt the same way. Just leaving Blanton's apartment behind was like a breath of fresh air.

"Let's not dilly-dally," Christopher said, making a beeline for the staircase and waving us down ahead of him. "Let's not give them any opportunity to change their minds. We're out of there. Let's keep going."

"Are we going to take Frederick Montrose to Scotland Yard?" I asked, as we clattered down.

Crispin didn't bother to glance at me over his shoulder, just kept going down the stairs, his heels clicking in counterpoint to Christopher's against the marble steps. "Of course not, Darling. Don't be absurd."

"What do you mean? What are we going to do with him?"

"What we said we would do," Crispin said. "Take him back to Rectors."

I stopped, or I would have, if Christopher hadn't been behind me. As it was, I had to keep going whether I wanted to or not. "Have you lost your mind? You're going to drive a dead body from Mayfair to Tottenham Court Road and leave it there? And go home and sleep as if nothing happened?"

"Of course not, Pippa," Christopher said from behind me, and Crispin added, before he could go on, "None of us will be able to sleep after this. Not for days and days."

I stared at him, or more accurately, at the back of his head. He didn't seem to notice, just kept moving down the stairs. "Have you—?"

Lost your mind, was what I was going to ask. I didn't get the chance.

"If you don't mind, Darling," Crispin said, "I am running for my life here. And it's not easy to do in these shoes, in case you were unaware."

"Of course I'm aware, you imbecile. I spend most of my life in shoes like those."

"But do you usually run for your life in them?"

He clattered to a stop at the bottom of the staircase, but didn't wait for me to answer. Instead, he took a calming breath before he told us both, "Now let's all just walk out as if nothing's wrong. If anyone asks, the commissionaire will be able to tell them, quite honestly, that we arrived with Montrose and left without him."

"And that's a good thing, is it?"

"It is, Darling. I'm not going down for this murder if I can at all avoid it. Now come along."

He pushed the door open, took me by the arm, and steered me across the checkerboard floor of the foyer, with Christopher clattering behind. When the commissionaire pulled the front door open with a flourish, Crispin gave him a cheerful, "Good night, Webley."

"Good night, Lord St George," the doorman said. While he eyed me and Christopher, he clearly couldn't place us, because he didn't use our names. His gaze lingered on Christopher, though, and I figured he had probably noticed the resemblance between the two of them. If anyone asked, it wouldn't be difficult to identify both Christopher and me.

But then we were outside in the cool London night air, and on our way along the pavement away from Blanton's mansion block towards the car park where Crispin had left the Hispano-Suiza.

CHAPTER SIX

THE STREETS WERE MOSTLY DESERTED. There were no nightclubs on Blanton's street, and not much else going on, either. Mayfair is more the domain of the old guard, quite settled and conservative, than the Bright Young Set. Sutherland House, for your information—Crispin's bachelor pad when he's in Town—is located here, a few streets west from where we were. Christopher's and my mansion flat, needless to say, is not nearby.

At any rate, it gave us a chance to talk. Not that we got much closer to a solution to our problem.

"We could get in the H6 and go home," I suggested, since it would absolutely be my preference to have no more to do with the situation. "Just leave them there with Montrose's body. Let them deal with it."

They both looked at me, and I added, defensively, "At least we wouldn't be accessories to murder that way. This is an attempt to cover up a crime. Interfering with a crime scene. Defiling a dead body. Tortious interference with a deceased human. Something like that."

"I don't like it any better than you do, Pippa," Christopher said, as he clack-clacked along beside me. He had an easier time walking in the heels than Crispin did. More practice, probably. "But I don't see how we can get around it. If we don't go back with the motorcar, they'll know we've abandoned them, and I'm not sure I want to get on Dominic Rivers's bad side. The others', either, but particularly his. If he makes his living peddling dope, I imagine he won't blink at a few murders."

"He seemed rather upset earlier, didn't he? He's certainly not in the habit of dispatching people."

"This might have been his first actual murder," Crispin said, "if he's the one who did it, but he'll do it again before he lets himself get arrested for it. Or I'm sure he knows someone unsavory he can talk into, or pay, to do it for him. I vote with Kit. We shan't do anything to upset Dominic Rivers."

Fine. I had no particular wish to upset Rivers, either. Although truthfully, the other two seemed more worried about it than I was.

"So what you're saying," I said, "is that we have to go back with the motorcar. And we have to accept Montrose's body. What do we do with it once we have it?"

"We take it to Rectors," Crispin said.

Christopher and I exchanged a glance. "I don't feel as if we should leave him in the alley and walk away, somehow."

"I'm not suggesting we do that," Crispin said, as the entrance to the car park came into view in front of us "I'm not a monster, you know. I'm usually quite happy to save my own skin, but not at the expense of everyone and everything around me."

Before I could say something sarcastic about his concern, or lack thereof, for the rest of us, he added, "Montrose was a friend, at least once upon a time."

I closed my mouth again, and let him talk without interrupting.

"What I suggest," he said, "is that we take him to Rectors, leave him there, and then we go find Tom Gardiner and tell him what we know."

Thomas Gardiner was an acquaintance of both boys' from their days at Eton. He was younger than my cousin Francis by a year or two, and older than Crispin and Christopher by roughly four, which made him a contemporary of my late cousin Robert's. It was that connection that had made him remove Christopher from April's drag ball—kicking and screaming—before the infamous police raid a month and a week ago.

And then he had showed up at Sutherland Hall two days later, as part of the contingent from Scotland Yard that was investigating Grimsby the valet's murder. Tom was a detective sergeant as well as a photography expert on Chief Inspector Pendennis's homicide team.

Last month, when Christopher and I had discovered Johanna de Vos—she of the pale blue dress—dead in Lady Peckham's bedchamber in Dorset, he had told me that he didn't know how to get in touch with Thomas Gardiner. But that was a month ago. Things might have changed.

"Well?" Crispin said after the car park attendant had scurried off to fetch the Hispano-Suiza. "What do you think of my idea?"

"I suppose I've heard worse ones," Christopher admitted.

"Do you know where to find him?"

Christopher nodded. "He has a flat in Chelsea."

That was certainly more information than he'd had last time we'd spoken of it. Back then, he hadn't even had a telephone number with which to contact Tom. And now he knew where the man lived?

I looked at him, but he avoided my eyes. His cheeks were a

delicate shade of pink.

"Do you have his direction?" I asked. "Can we phone him at home? Knock him up and get him to meet us there?"

But Christopher shook his head. "No telephone in his flat."

He must have actually been to the flat in order to know that, it seemed. I arched my brows at him, but he didn't say anything.

"Shall we go and take delivery of the parcel, then?" Crispin asked, as the Hispano-Suiza made its slow way towards us, with the attendant behind the wheel. The headlamps were lit, and for a moment, our shadows were grotesque against the brick wall of the next building. Then the H6 came to a stop next to us and the attendant held the door for Crispin. Christopher handed me into the backseat while Crispin slid behind the wheel. "Ready to blouse?"

"Please," I said, "and for God's sake, St George, can't you just say 'go,' like a normal person? A blouse is something you wear. Or at least I do; you shouldn't."

Christopher sniggered. "She's got you there, old chap."

"Still younger than you," Crispin said. "But fine, Darling. Are you ready to go?"

"Yes," I said. "Let's get this over with as soon as possible. I'm feeling quite nauseated by the whole thing." And quite worried about getting away with it, what's more. "What are we going to do if we're stopped along the way?"

"Pray," Crispin said, and took his foot off the clutch. The Hispano-Suiza rolled off down the street towards Ronald Blanton's lodgings.

THE OTHERS WERE WAITING by the service entrance when we arrived, skulking in the shadows and propping up Montrose's body. He was still in his frock and lady's shoes, of course, but one of Blanton's fluffy towels was wrapped around his head so I couldn't see his face.

"Put him in the back with Philippa," Crispin ordered, without ever getting out from behind the wheel.

I opened my mouth to object, and then thought better of it. He—what was left of Frederick Montrose—had to go into the backseat with me. He couldn't sit next to Crispin in the front seat. Not only was Christopher there, but Montrose would not be able to keep himself upright, and would sway from side to side and probably end up with his head either out the window or on Crispin's shoulder. Which he might deserve—St George, I mean; not Montrose—for getting us into this predicament, but it would be an unpleasant experience for him, and also might put the rest of us in danger of discovery.

And then there was the fluffy white towel, which was like a beacon of light that would catch everyone's attention. And I certainly didn't want to contemplate what Montrose would look like without it. So I swallowed back my revulsion and prepared myself to accept delivery of the body.

Rivers, Hutchison, and Ogilvie spent the next minute wrestling it into the back of the motorcar, where they draped Montrose across the seat with his head—and the towel—in my lap. I choked back the need to gag. Gladys, who was watching from the shadows along with Blanton, stared at me with huge eyes in a white face, and I'm certain I looked very much the same as she did. We shared an uncomfortable moment of kinship as our eyes locked, before Hutchison shut the door behind Montrose and took a step back.

"There we are." His voice was falsely bright, and brittle underneath the brightness. So far, he had kept a stiff upper lip throughout this whole ordeal, but perhaps the task of moving the body had been too much for him. He cleared his throat. "Take him to Rectors and find somewhere to place him, where it'll look like he was killed by someone there. And whatever you do, don't get caught!"

"You don't have to tell me that," Crispin said irritably. "You know, the next time I'm invited for an after-party at one of your flats, I'm declining."

"Should have said no this time," I muttered, and he nodded.

"I can't believe you got me into this, Darling. All I wanted to do was celebrate my birthday with you and Kit, and instead I'm wearing a frock and transporting a dead body across London in the early hours of the morning..."

"It's hardly my fault that you have the sort of friends who kill each other," I retorted. "If I had known this was going to happen, I wouldn't have agreed to it, either. Now stop complaining and drive. The sooner we leave, the sooner we'll be done."

Christopher nodded. "Yes, please, Crispin. Stop talking and go."

"Very well." Crispin put the Hispano-Suiza in gear. "But this isn't the last you'll hear of it."

He took his foot off the brake and we rolled off down the street in the direction of Rectors.

It wasn't a long drive, and traffic was practically non-existent. It was a good thing, because if the trip had been longer and had taken more time, I might have lost my mind. I already couldn't believe we were doing this. How had this evening gone so wrong that simply wanting to have some fun for Crispin's birthday had landed us all in this mess, where we were transporting a dead body across London, with both boys in makeup and frocks and me in Christopher's dinner suit?

And there hadn't been any way around it, either, that I could see. Yes, of course, if we could go back a few hours, to the beginning of the evening, and take a different path, things might have turned out rather differently. Montrose might still be alive, since without Crispin at the table at Rectors, the others might not have noticed him there, and everything might have had a different outcome.

Then again, if I had turned Crispin away when he showed up at the flat, he might have got back into the Hispano-Suiza and wrapped it around another light pole, and he might not have walked away from that. We could be dealing with Crispin's dead body now, and not Montrose's, and despite my own usual feelings of irritation—particularly now, when I blamed him for having got us into this situation—I didn't wish him dead. Christopher would be devastated, and for another thing, I might miss him, too. At least a bit. So while I still felt terrible about Montrose, I probably wouldn't sacrifice Crispin for him.

Probably.

With such pleasant thoughts to keep me company, we crept along Piccadilly at what felt like a snail's pace, keeping a keen eye out for constables or anyone else who might recognize Crispin and/or the Hispano-Suiza. The drive took what felt like hours, although I don't think it can have been more than fifteen minutes before we pulled into sight of Rectors nightclub.

Crispin yanked the steering wheel to the side and we landed at the curb up the street from the nightclub. And there we sat, all three of us gaping, open-mouthed, at the scene in front of us.

"Dear me," Christopher said faintly.

The street outside Rectors was blocked to traffic, but alive with activity. Several police vehicles were parked at angles all over the roadway. Their headlamps cut through the darkness and lit up a scene of almost Biblical destruction. Bobbies in uniform swarmed the building where Rectors was located, running inside and then coming back out, dragging men in evening kit and men in gowns and high heels behind them. The air rang with screams and curses, and there were fisticuffs and attempts to break away from the strong hand of the law. One man, dressed in an elegant champagne gown with strings of beads flapping around his knees, legged it up the street with a constable in pursuit. We ducked down as they ran past, which put me in much-too-close proximity to Freddie Montrose's head.

The constable came huffing back down the street at a jog a few seconds later, so the man in champagne beads must have escaped. We waited until the constable was safely past before we reared our heads again.

"This isn't going to be easy," Crispin said grimly. "There are people everywhere. We can't just haul him out of the backseat in full view of everyone and leave him on the pavement."

No, we absolutely couldn't. "What do we do? Take him back to Mayfair and dump him in Blanton's alley after all?"

"Better to dump him in an alley around here," Christopher said, and then grimaced. "I can't believe we're sitting here talking so calmly about getting rid of a dead body."

No, I couldn't either. "We'd better get out of here as quickly as possible, anyway. This place is swarming with constables. We don't want to give them time to notice us, and then come to investigate what we're up to."

That was surely the very last thing we needed. Not only for all three of us to be caught in drag, at the scene of an illegal drag ball, but to be caught in drag at the site of a raid with a freshly dead body draped across the backseat of our car.

I could only imagine what would happen if that news hit the tabloids.

"Yes, Crispin," Christopher nodded, "get us out of here, please. We can decide what to do with the body once we're away from here."

Crispin nodded. But no sooner had he taken his size 42 T-strap pump off the brake, than a figure materialized beside the car, practically out of thin air.

"For the love of God, Kit—"

It was Tom Gardiner, of course, in his tweed suit and with his Homburg pulled low over his face, but not quite low enough to mask an expression made up of equal parts irritation and fear. It was the kind of expression my Aunt Roslyn—Christopher's and Francis's mother—would get when one of us had climbed up a tree and fallen, and she couldn't quite decide whether to yell at us for being stupid or embrace us for having survived. In the end, she usually did both, and I had the feeling that Tom Gardiner would like to do the same. But of course he couldn't, because not only were we on a public street, with constables running back and forth and a raid going on in front of us, but Christopher was inside the motorcar while Tom was outside on the pavement, and that made the logistics difficult.

And to be honest, I had no idea whether they were in the habit of embracing anyway. I had never seen them do it, so maybe they were not. I had the impression that Christopher rather liked Tom, and Tom had gone out of his way to keep Christopher from being rounded up in last month's raid, so it was possible the feelings were reciprocated. On the other hand, Tom might just be taking care of Christopher because Robbie wasn't around to do it.

None of that mattered at the moment, anyway. Tom wasn't in the embracing part of the process. He was still stuck on the angry yelling. Except he was doing it *sotto voce*, since he didn't want to draw attention to us.

"—have you lost your mind? What are you doing here? You should not be here, especially not now. I thought you'd be inside, so I went in and looked for you—looked for you everywhere!—but I couldn't find you, and now I've been standing here for an hour waiting for them to haul you out in handcuffs...!"

As the diatribe continued, my eyes widened, and so, when I glanced over, did Crispin's. I could only see the back of Christopher's head—or rather, his black wig—so I had no idea how he reacted, but I would guess that his cheeks and the tips of his ears were probably bright red.

And then Tom seemed to recall himself, possibly when he realized that he and Christopher weren't alone. He glanced at Crispin, and did a double-take. And then looked at me and did the same. "Miss... um... Pippa? And Lord St George? What are you doing here?"

He gave us another up-and-down look. But before he had a chance to comment, his eyes fell on Montrose, and his expression changed. "Who's that?"

"His name is..." Crispin cleared his throat. "His name was Frederick Montrose."

Tom's eyebrows disappeared behind the hat. "Was? Are you telling me—?"

He looked from Crispin to Christopher to me and back. "You're surely not telling me that you're driving around London at three in the morning with a corpse in the backseat?"

I winced. Crispin did, too, and I'm sure Christopher must have, as well. We glanced at each other and avoided Tom's eyes and surely looked as guilty as it is possible for three people to look. Neither of us attempted to lie and tell him that no, we definitely were not driving around London at 3 AM with a corpse in the backseat, though.

"What have you done?" Tom asked. He asked very quietly, and I don't think it was only so that no one around us would hear. I think he was also so upset that his response was to turn more quiet so he wouldn't lose his temper and yell. "Who is— who *was* Frederick Montrose and why is he dead in your car?"

He took another look at what he could see of Montrose—the frock, the shoes—and added, "And why is he dressed like that?"

"It wasn't us," I said. And added, winningly, "You know *we* wouldn't kill anyone."

He eyed me. For a second too long for it to be comfortable. "I don't know you very well at all, Miss Darling. I wouldn't have thought so, certainly, but here you are."

He waited a moment for that to sink in before he added, "And he's clearly not a stranger you picked up along the way, if you know his name."

And then he did a double-take. "Wait. Did you say Frederick Montrose? The same Frederick Montrose who—?"

"The Frederick Montrose who wrote for The Daily Yell," Crispin said. "If you were going to say something other than that, I don't know which Montrose you thought he might be."

He gave Tom an arrogant sort of look. Tom looked back at him in silence. It's probably some sort of inferiority complex, honestly, not that I would dare to say that to his face.

Crispin's, I mean. I don't think Tom has any inferiority complexes. But St George becomes extra snotty around certain people, and they always look at him as if he were a small worm they'd like to crush under their heel.

"That's the Montrose I thought he was," he said eventually, after dismissing Crispin and his tone as not being worthy of his time and attention. "Why is he dead, and why is he in a frock? And more than that, why is he in your car?"

He gave Crispin a look. "You know, St George, I never considered seriously that you might have killed either your grandfather or Miss de Vos, but I'm starting to wonder why. It's fascinating how corpses follow you about. How did you come to be in possession of this one, if I might ask?"

"It's Darling's fault," Crispin said, with a glance into the backseat at me.

I scowled at him. "It most certainly is not."

"If you hadn't suggested dressing up and crashing Kit's drag ball—"

"If *you* hadn't shown up in the first place, wanting to celebrate your birthday—!"

"Shhh!" Christopher hissed as our voices got louder. "Keep it down, or the police will notice us!"

"The police already noticed you," Tom said dryly, which was certainly true.

"Not you," Christopher said. "*You* aren't going to arrest us. Are you?"

He gazed up at Tom from under his lashes. He might even have fluttered them, although if he did, it had no visible effect.

"I don't know," Tom told him. "It depends on how persuasive you can be."

His gaze made it clear that Crispin and I were included in the plural 'you,' as well. The reference to being persuasive was not some flirtatious remark that only applied to Christopher, but was aimed at all of us.

"Right now," he added severely, "you're not doing a good job of explaining why I shouldn't."

I took a breath, but then everyone froze as two of the constables down the street very obviously caught sight of us—of the Hispano-Suiza—and started coming towards us.

"Budge up," Tom ordered, and yanked on the door handle. When the door opened, he slid into the front seat next to Christopher, who was smooshed against Crispin's side. The latter growled, but didn't complain. There wasn't anything to complain about. Anything was better than being caught by the London constabulary right now.

"Reverse," Tom said, his voice tight, as the constables drew closer. "Let's go, St George. Stop dawdling."

"I'm not dawdling," Crispin told him through gritted teeth. "We're going. I just need a little room..."

He shoved Christopher back towards Tom for long enough to do what he needed to do. Christopher fetched up against Tom's shoulder with an, "Ooof!" and Crispin got the car going. Backwards, and at speed. The constables dwindled to pinpricks in a matter of seconds. Or if they didn't quite do that, we zoomed backwards down Tottenham Court Road a lot faster than was comfortable or, I assumed, safe.

I was screaming, Christopher was cursing, and Tom was telling Crispin what he was going to do to him—arrest and dismemberment featured large—if Crispin didn't immediately cease to do what he was doing. Crispin was laughing, but then he had been laughing when he wrapped the Ballot around the light pole, too.

"I'm going to kill you, St George," I told him breathlessly. "Let me guess: this was what you were doing last year, when the Ballot bit the dust."

"When the Ballot bit the dust, I was drunk," Crispin told me over his shoulder. His voice was perfectly calm and even, as if this was something he did all the time. As if going backwards down a London street in the middle of the night, dodging around cars and a few pedestrians, didn't faze him at all. "And you won't kill me, Darling. You like me too much for that."

We were coming up on a cross-street, and he zipped around the corner, still going backwards, and then shifted and shot across Tottenham Court Road in the opposite direction. The constables on foot hadn't a hope of keeping up. I hadn't thought it was possible to get up that kind of speed within the city limits, but I had clearly underestimated the Honorable Viscount St George.

"In your dreams," I told him breathlessly. "I will absolutely kill you, St George. And then I'll wake you from the dead and kill you again. I'm sitting in the back of your motorcar with a dead body, you madman. Slow down, unless you want him to fall on the floor!"

Crispin didn't say anything to that, but he did slow down. Just a bit.

"Where to?" he asked Tom, as if we were out for a leisurely Sunday drive instead of a desperate dash through the dark streets of London, running away from the police.

Tom shook his head. "How should I know? What were you planning to do with this body?"

"The plan was to dump it outside Rectors," I told him, "although we had to kibosh that plan when we saw what was going on there."

He shot me a look in the mirror. "Tell me you're joking."

"She isn't," Christopher said. "But it's not what it sounds like, I swear."

"It had better not be," Tom muttered, and turned to Crispin. "Take a left up here. Find somewhere where we can stop and discuss what's going on."

"What does that mean?" Crispin wanted to know. "We can go to Sutherland House or Kit's flat, if you'd like. Or a car park?"

"Not a car park. Nowhere where anyone can get a look into the backseat. And not a place where anyone is likely to recognize us."

"There aren't a lot of those in London," Crispin said dryly. "I'm fairly well known, and so is the car. How about Limehouse?"

"Not Limehouse," Tom said. "We'd stand out like the foreigners we are in Limehouse. Hyde Park will do."

Crispin nodded and turned in the direction of Hyde Park.

CHAPTER SEVEN

WE WERE MOSTLY silent on the drive. Crispin slowed down enough that we weren't in danger of being stopped for reckless driving, and he kept his mouth shut, too. Christopher and Tom exchanged a couple of murmurs, but they were too soft for me to make out. And Freddie Montrose was, by necessity, quiet.

When I first had him dropped in my lap, his body had still been warm, and I had been able to tell myself that he was just asleep, the way Christopher had been back in May, after an overdose of sleeping medication someone had intended for me. He had slept through the entire trip from Dorset back to Sutherland Hall in Wiltshire, and had stayed asleep for another twenty-four hours past that. And that was in addition to the more than twenty-four hours he had already slept by then.

I'm not sure who had been more worried about him, Crispin or myself. We had both been assured, by Francis and by the doctor Tom had called in, that Christopher would wake on his own once the sleeping draught was out of his system, and that he would be none the worse for the experience. And I think we had both mostly believed it. But there had also been, in both of us, the fear that Francis and the doctor were wrong, that Christopher wouldn't wake up, or that when he did, he wouldn't be the same. There was no reason to think so, but I know I hadn't been able to shake the fear, and I didn't think Crispin had breathed easily, either, until Christopher opened his eyes and spoke, and he could tell for himself that all was well.

It had made me regard him—St George, I mean—more kindly than I had been up to that point.

At any rate, at first, I had been able to tell myself that Montrose's situation was like that. He was asleep, not dead, and eventually all would be well.

By now, however, he was cool to the touch, and the comforting lie I had been telling myself no longer held up. I was holding a dead man in my lap, the head someone had crushed in with... well, I still didn't know what weapon had killed Montrose, but his crushed head was cradled in my lap, and a Scotland Yard detective was sitting in the front seat conversing softly with Christopher while Crispin drove us along the winding roads of Hyde Park during the darkest part of the night.

"Pull up ahead," Tom instructed, and Crispin brought the H6 to a stop under a tree whose low-hanging branches partly shielded us from view. When the motor was off, he added, "Tell me everything from the beginning."

We told him everything. Or rather, Christopher did. He did a thorough job, so there was no need for Crispin or me to contribute anything. We lit a cigarette each—or he lit mine and handed it to me—and then we listened along with Tom.

"So these are friends of yours," Tom said to Crispin after Christopher had finished his recitation and was lighting a cigarette of his own.

Crispin shrugged. "I wouldn't go that far. My real friends wouldn't force me to drive a dead man all over London because they couldn't call the police."

"But they're part of the set you spend your time with," Tom said. "The Society of Bright Young Persons."

His tone was deeply ironic. For once, Crispin didn't seem to mind.

"Peripherally," he allowed. "Although I think you overestimate the amount of time I spend with anyone except my father. Three weekends out of four, I'm locked away in Wiltshire, like Rapunzel in her tower."

I snorted. Tom didn't say anything, and Crispin continued, "Montrose was not part of that crowd. He was doing his own thing. Hunting for a story for his paper, most likely. And he wasn't at Rectors because he usually spends time with Kit's crowd, either. But Nigel Hutchison, Ronald Blanton, Graham Ogilvie, and Gladys Long are part of, as you say, the Society of Bright Young People."

"But not Dominic Rivers?"

Crispin shook his head. "Rivers is a dope dealer. Blanton and Gladys use dope..."

"And you don't?"

Crispin looked at him for a moment before he said, "I'm not going to claim I've never indulged. But as a general rule, no. Alcohol is legal, and isn't likely to kill me."

I muttered something, and he tilted his head my way. "I'm sorry, Darling. I didn't catch that?"

"I was making a comment about the Ballot," I said. "I'm sure I don't need to repeat it."

"No, Darling, you don't. You've nagged me quite enough about that incident as it is. With the way you bring it up at every opportunity, one might almost think you care."

He turned back to Tom and continued before I had the

chance to say anything, which was probably for the best. Yes, I cared, but if he tried to force me to admit it, he probably wouldn't like the result.

"Kit's brother Francis uses dope. Not cocaine, not as far as I know, but we all know he's dependent on Veronal, and you saw him that night at Sutherland Hall, Gardiner. The only thing that'll do that to someone's eyes is opium."

Tom nodded. "I daresay you've tried that, as well?"

"Since this isn't an official interview," Crispin said coolly, "I'll admit that I have tried a lot of things. Once. But I don't use dope as a general rule. And I largely don't do business with Dominic Rivers."

"Who does? Other than Ronald Blanton and Gladys Long?"

"A long list of people," Crispin said. "I'll write it down for you, if you'd like. Some of them would be guesses, the others I know about for a fact."

Tom nodded. "I'll take it. But that's for another day. First, we have to deal with this one. Who killed Montrose?"

"We don't know," I said. "Rivers and Blanton had gone off into another room, and when Blanton came back, he was flying high. Rivers then took Gladys off to a different part of the flat. Montrose asked for the loo, and after he left, the others figured out that he was most likely spying on them, and went after him. The three of us were left alone in the sitting room. I thought we ought to make sure that everything was all right—" I slanted Crispin a disgruntled glance, "because I was afraid they would hurt Montrose..."

"You were afraid they were going to kill him, and you sat in the sitting room and waited?"

"No," I said, "Good God, Tom, of course not. We wouldn't have done that. I was afraid they were going to get into a fight. That someone would catch him eavesdropping, and would hit him and toss him out on his ear. I didn't think he would die. That didn't even cross my mind."

Clearly it should have, but even now, after the fact, I had a hard time believing it had happened.

"Did you know these people, Kit?" Tom wanted to know, and Christopher shook his head.

"I met them for the first time tonight."

"It's up to you, then," Tom told Crispin. "You had met them all before?"

"Met them?" He nodded. "Yes. Know them, not necessarily. Montrose and I went to Cambridge together. So did Hutchison, so I'm reasonably familiar with him. He's friendly with Blanton, who's friendly with Gladys. I'm not sure where Graham Ogilvie came from, but he's part of the same clique. I see them off and on on the weekends I come up to Town."

"And Rivers?"

"Rivers comes and goes," Crispin said. "He has a business to run, and better things to do with his time than waste it in idle carousing."

"Undoubtedly," Tom nodded. He had pulled his little notebook and a stub of a pencil out of his pocket and was taking notes. I had no idea how he could possibly see what to write, or how he'd be able to decipher the scratches tomorrow, but the pencil moved steadily across the page. "Any idea where I'd be able to find him?"

"Where he lives, do you mean?" Crispin shook his head, causing his—Christopher's—earrings to dance. It says something that by this part of the evening, I no longer did a double-take whenever I looked at him and realized that he was wearing makeup and a gown. "I don't know. I don't think anyone does. When someone wants Rivers or what he's offering, they'll ring up and leave a message, and Rivers comes and finds them."

"And you know this because—?"

Tom was still writing, not looking up at Crispin, but the latter squirmed guiltily.

"I may have taken advantage of it once or twice."

Christopher caught his breath, and I narrowed my eyes. "That was stupid of you, St George."

"Yes, Darling," Crispin said, "I know."

"People can die from sniffing cocaine, you know. Not to mention that I wouldn't trust Dominic Rivers any farther than I could throw him. I wouldn't be surprised if he laced his powder with arsenic."

"That would be very bad for business," Tom said mildly, and turned back to Crispin. "You know, of course, that cocaine is on the Dangerous Drugs list."

Crispin nodded.

"Using it is illegal."

"I told you that in confidence," Crispin said. "And we're sitting here in my car with a dead body in the backseat. If you wanted me to hang over something, it's more likely to be that."

Tom didn't bother to tell him he was right. "Just out of curiosity, can the three of you prove you didn't kill him yourselves?"

There was a pause. "Not if you won't take our word for it," I said eventually. "We were together when he died, in a different room than where it happened. I couldn't even tell you what he was hit with. I haven't seen his head. They'd wrapped the towel around him by the time they brought him downstairs."

"How do you know it's Montrose?"

"Dress and shoes," I said. "And I think St George looked at him. Didn't you?"

He nodded. His face was pale in the darkness under the tree, but I think he might have turned a shade paler. "He was on the floor in the butler's pantry—"

"So he didn't go to the lavatory?"

He shook his head. "That was just something he said so he could leave the sitting room, Darling. Rivers and Gladys must have been in the kitchen, and he was on the floor of the butler's pantry. I don't know what was used to hit him. There were several things sitting around that may have been heavy enough. Cast iron pans, a marble rolling pin..." He trailed off.

"Nothing with blood on it?"

"Not that I noticed." I could see his throat move when he swallowed.

"He was wearing a wig," I said. "Thick and brown. It might have absorbed the blow and some of the blood."

"You're sure he's dead?" Tom glanced over the back of the seat onto the towel in my lap.

"He's turning cold," I said. "And he isn't breathing. I made sure of it when they loaded him into the car. He's dead, and was dead before we left with him. If he'd still been breathing when we got him in the car, we would have taken him to hospital, and to hell with what they wanted."

But I cast a guilty glance out the back of the Hispano-Suiza, just in case they—Rivers, or perhaps the combination of Blanton, Hutchison, and Ogilvie—were somewhere back there watching.

"Is he still wearing the wig?" Tom wanted to know.

"I'll let you determine that," I told him. "I have no need to look."

"He's not," Crispin said. "Or he wasn't when I saw him on the floor in Blanton's flat."

"We'll have to go through the trash for it, I suppose." Tom looked back down at his notes. "So you three were in the sitting room. Rivers and Miss Long were in the kitchen, or so we assume. Blanton, Hutchison, and Ogilvie followed Montrose. Which of them killed him?"

"I have no idea," Crispin said. "If Rivers and Gladys were in the kitchen, it can't have been one of them—"

"But we don't know if they were in the kitchen," I said. "Maybe they were actually in the butler's pantry, and when Montrose walked in, because he thought they were in the kitchen, one of them picked up the weapon and hit him with it."

"He was hit on the back of the head," Crispin said, "so whoever did it, came at him from behind. Not in front."

"Fine. Rivers left Gladys in the kitchen and walked out into the hallway and from there into the butler's pantry and hit Montrose. Or one of the others did it while Rivers and Gladys were both in the kitchen."

I turned to Tom. "We have no idea. Because nobody told us anything. But one of them did it. Probably not Dobbins. So—"

"Dobbins? Who's Dobbins? You didn't mention anyone called Dobbins."

"Blanton's man-servant," Christopher said. "Blanton sent him to bed when we arrived. I assume he was still there when we left. Rivers told Blanton to go make sure that Dobbins wasn't going to suddenly turn up and discover the body. So I think we can write off Dobbins."

Tom nodded. "That leaves us with the three of you, the innocent bystanders; Rivers, the dope dealer; Blanton and Miss Long, the addicts; and Hutchison and Ogilvie, the concerned friends. Any bad blood between Montrose and any of them?"

"He writes about some of us from time to time," Crispin said, "although it's usually more me than anyone else. He and Hutchison didn't seem terribly pleased to see one another at first, or at least Hutchison didn't seem pleased to see Montrose, but surely it's more likely that Montrose was killed because someone didn't want to appear in print in The Daily Yell tomorrow. Or later today, I suppose I should say."

"That may be what we're supposed to think," Tom said. "What was the nature of the disagreement between Hutchison and Montrose?"

"Lord, I don't know!" Crispin shook his head. "I haven't seen Montrose in months. He writes about me, but I don't see him. And I don't spend all that much time with Hutchison and his set, either. If they'd had a disagreement, I don't know what's behind it."

"We'll figure that out later, then." Tom shut his notebook and tucked it away. "For now, I guess we should decide what to do with your body."

"It's hardly ours—" I began, and then abandoned the futility of that particular argument in favor of one more pertinent. "What do you mean, do with it? Leaving him in the alley beside Rectors is right out, with the raid going on. And I don't feel good about tossing him in the Thames..."

"He'll have to go to the morgue," Tom said, "and without going in the water first. We don't want to destroy any more evidence than you have already."

No, we didn't. And while he probably didn't mean to sound like he was criticizing us, I felt rather bad about it, even so.

"We'll have to invent some sort of story," Tom continued. "One that absolves you from failing to carry out the task they gave you, if St George's friends should ask, and I'm sure they will."

I was sure they would, too. "We obviously couldn't carry out the task the way they wanted. Tottenham Court Road was crawling with constables by the time we got there. And that'll be in the papers tomorrow, no doubt."

Tom nodded. "If you hadn't met me, what would you have done with him?"

"We were going to leave him there and then come find you," Christopher said, "but you found us first."

Tom gave him a look, but didn't say anything.

"Let's just leave him on the grass," I said, with a glance outside the motorcar. "Hyde Park is as good a place as any to get rid of a body. We've been sitting here for ten or fifteen minutes without seeing a soul. We'll just put him under this tree and drive away. Then you, Tom, can pretend to find him and flag down a patrolman. And tomorrow we'll tell Hutchison and his friends that we left Montrose in Hyde Park because Rectors was under attack by bobbies."

There was a moment's pause.

"That seems to cover all the contingencies," Tom allowed grudgingly, "but don't think I didn't notice that you're proposing to leave me holding the body, so to speak."

"Well, it can't very well be one of us," I pointed out, "with the way we're dressed. Although if you want company, I suppose Christopher and I could trade clothes—it's his suit I'm wearing—and then one of us could stay with you. Who would you rather have with you at three AM in Hyde Park, Detective Sergeant Gardiner? Me or Christopher? Both? Or perhaps St George? Christopher's dinner suit would fit him, too."

Crispin held up both hands. "Keep me out of it, Darling, if you please."

"You're just afraid to let me drive your precious car," I told him.

"Yes, Darling, that's what I'm afraid of. Having to strip down to my skivvies in Hyde Park in the middle of the night so I can put on Christopher's dinner suit, that you first have to strip out of... that has nothing whatsoever to do with it. Are you really that sanguine about taking your clothes off in public? Because if so—"

"I'm not," I said. "Hush, St George. What'll it be, Tom? Me, Christopher, or Crispin?"

"Neither of you," Tom said. "Take the car and go home. And stay there until I come and find you."

"When you say home..."

"Your flat. Go to your flat." He pointed a finger at Crispin. "You go with them."

Crispin opened his mouth and then, obviously thinking better of his retort, closed it again.

"Stay with Pippa and Kit until tomorrow. Somewhere where your friends aren't likely to find you. I don't want Rivers and Hutchison and their friends to corner you until we've had a chance to examine the body and decide how to proceed."

I couldn't imagine what Scotland Yard's plans for Montrose's body would have to do with Crispin, Christopher, and me, but it was three o'clock in the morning, and it had been a long night, and it wasn't over yet, so I decided not to argue or inquire. "Let's get this over with, if you please. I suppose I'm going to have to help, so if Hutchison asks, I'll be able to say with honesty that I helped dispose of the body."

"I think it'll be sufficient if you stand and watch, Pippa," Christopher said. "Crispin and I will take care of it."

Crispin grimaced, but didn't object. "Come on then, Kit. Let's get it done."

He opened the rear door of the H6 and began pulling Montrose out of the motorcar.

"Careful!" I told him, as Montrose's head dropped from my lap and landed on the seat next to me.

"He can't feel it, Darling."

"I know that," I said, irritated. "But the towel is slipping, and—euurgh!"

"Don't look," Christopher advised, as he came around the motorcar to help Crispin balance the burden that was Montrose. "We'd have to take the towel off anyway. It doesn't make any sense to leave it."

"It might give Tom something to investigate if we do," I suggested, with a glance at Tom. He was watching the boys' progress from the other side of the Hispano-Suiza. He had his arms folded across his chest, and occasionally he would wince.

I turned back to look at them, and had to admit that they made quite the comical picture—or would have, if the situation had been less dire. All three of them were wearing evening gowns and high heels. Christopher and Crispin were like two bookends holding the shorter, squatter form of Montrose upright. If you didn't look too closely at his head, they may look like two women, or at least two men dressed like women, helping their none-too-sober counterpart home after a night on the town. But the pointed toes of Montrose's strap shoes were digging a furrow in the dirt as they dragged him towards the trunk of the tree, and the back of his head was a bloody mess—I mean that in its most literal sense—and the towel in my hands was soaked with blood, and so, I noticed, were Christopher's trousers...

My stomach lurched, and I turned back to Tom. "Do you want the towel? You're going to have to investigate this case somehow, aren't you?"

"If we'd simply found him here," Tom said, his eyes on Crispin and Christopher as they arranged Montrose's body against the tree trunk, "dressed the way he is, we would assume he had something to do with the raid at Rectors nightclub. We'd talk to the men we arrested and see whether any of them had seen him at Rectors tonight, and who he might have been talking to or sitting with. Through that, we'd likely get a few names we could pursue. Like Kit's and possibly St George's. Kit's known there—"

I opened my mouth, and then closed it again when he added, pensively, "—albeit perhaps not under his own name. But Lord St George is known all over London."

"So you're going to make this difficult for Crispin," I said, pleased.

Tom looked at me for a moment, but didn't comment. "In a normal investigation, we'd likely find a few people who recognized Montrose and who recognized Kit and St George. Someone might have heard one of them introduce the other as his cousin. I assume that happened at some point?"

I nodded. It certainly had. Crispin had introduced both Christopher and myself as his cousins, both to Montrose and to the group of Bright Young Things. The people in the surrounding booths may very well have heard him do so.

"So we'd come knocking on your door, and the door at Sutherland House," Tom said, "and tomorrow morning, that's exactly what shall happen. Take Lord St George with you and keep him there. After what has happened, he might like the company anyway. And tomorrow morning, I'll come talk to you about it, and you'll tell me everything you've already told me tonight, on the record."

I nodded. That was clear enough.

"And at that point," Tom said, "we'll decide where to go from here. But for now—"

He flapped his hands at the motorcar, "—shoo, all three of you. I'll stop by the flat tomorrow morning. I know where it is."

Of course he did. The first time I had seen him had been in the Essex House mansion flat, whisper-yelling at Christopher after yanking him out of April's nightclub raid before he could be arrested, before bringing him home and reading him the riot act.

"We'll be there," I said as I climbed back into the Hispano-Suiza. "You'd better come with us, St George. You can have my bed for the night."

"Dear me," Crispin drawled as he fitted himself behind the wheel, "will you be in it, Darling?"

"I will not," I told him, as Christopher got into the passenger side seat with a snigger. "I thought you'd be more comfortable there than on the Chesterfield, but if you're going to give me trouble about it, I'll leave you to curl up in the sitting room for what's left of the night."

"No, no, Darling." He started the car. "I'd be delighted to kip in your bed, with or without you. You keep the Chesterfield."

I had thought I might creep in with Christopher, actually, but I wasn't going to say so in front of Tom. And besides, it might be better if I didn't. Creep in, I mean. Neither one of us was likely to get a good night's sleep tonight, and trying to do it together would surely only aggravate the problem.

So I nodded and said to Tom, "We'll see you later, then?"

"As soon as I get this business with the body sorted," Tom said. "Don't go anywhere. With luck, it'll take St George's friends some time to track you down, but if they turn up before we've had a chance to talk again, don't say anything other than what we've agreed to."

"Rectors was under siege," I recited, "so we left him under a tree in Hyde Park. And left the towel with him. So sorry. That's all we know."

I tapped Crispin on the shoulder. "Go, St George."

"See you later, Tom," Christopher said, and then we rolled away from the curb and out of the shadow of the tree, and along the tree-lined roads of Hyde Park towards home.

CHAPTER EIGHT

BY THE TIME we got to bed, the sun was rising over the Tower of London and Tower Bridge.

Admittedly, it was June, so very close to midsummer—otherwise it might not have been. In the middle of winter, we would have had several hours to go before sunrise, most likely.

Nevertheless, when there was a knock on the door at around eleven the next morning, it startled me out of deep sleep and I had to scramble off the Chesterfield in the sitting room in my pyjamas, and stagger out into the foyer and over to the door.

It didn't occur to me not to open it. Evans wouldn't let just anyone upstairs without advanced notice—I had cured him of that when he let Crispin up unannounced the first time—so there would either be Flossie Schlomsky outside the door, I figured, or else Tom Gardiner.

As a result, when I found myself face to face with an elegant gentleman in tweed and a houndstooth cap—a gentleman who wasn't Tom—I fell back a step.

"Oh." Good Lord. "Uncle Harold."

My courtesy-uncle by marriage looked down his nose at me.

He's the tallest of the Astleys, at least an inch or two taller than his son, and like his brother and nephews, he has the fair Sutherland hair and the blue Astley eyes. Crispin inherited his platinum hair and gray eyes from Aunt Charlotte, but all the other men in the family tend more toward the warmer end of the spectrum.

There was nothing warm about His Grace's eyes at the moment, however. Nor about his voice. "Where is my son?"

"St George?" It was a stupid question. Uncle Harold had no other sons, at least none he acknowledged. I suppose I was trying to gain time before the inevitable row, since Uncle Harold's demeanor suggested that one was in the offing. "He's still in bed."

If possible, Uncle Harold's eyes got even more frosty. "I don't know what he promised you—" he began, which made no sense whatsoever.

"He didn't promise me anything. He showed up last night, thoroughly pickled. and I put him to bed rather than let him go off in the Hispano-Suiza and get in a motorcar accident again."

Best not to say anything at all about the interlude, I decided. The less Uncle Harold knew about the events of the previous night, the less irate he was likely to be.

"I would have thought you'd be happy that I kept him here instead of letting him go off and perhaps kill himself," I added.

If Uncle Harold was happy, he showed no sign of it.

"Where is he?" He peered over my shoulder into the foyer. St George wasn't there, of course, so I did the only thing I could do, and stepped back.

"Would you like to come in? He's still asleep. My bedroom is—"

Uncle Harold had brushed past me by now, but at the

sound of this, he did an abrupt stop and then a turn. "Your bedroom?"

"The Chesterfield in the sitting room is rather narrow," I said, irritated, "and I thought he'd be more comfortable in a proper bed. If you'll have a seat, I'll go fetch him."

I scooped my own pillow and blanket off the sofa so Uncle Harold could sit down—he watched me down the length of his nose the entire time—and then I wandered into the hallway, where I applied my toes to the door to my bedroom. "St George! Wake up. You have company."

There was a grumble and the sound of bedsprings from inside the room, and I shifted the burden of blankets and pillows to one arm so I could reach for the knob with the other. "I'm coming in."

"No!"

I paid no attention, of course—it was my room, after all—and opened the door to the sight of the future Duke of Sutherland scrambling upright in bed—my bed—with the blankets—my blankets—clutched to his naked chest and his hair sticking up every which way. His cheeks were pink—so was the chest, if it came to that—and his eyes managed to be both sleepy and annoyed. "Damn you, Darling, what part of 'no' didn't you understand?"

"You have company," I told him, as I walked over and dumped the extra pillow and blankets on the bottom of the bed next to him. "Your father's here."

"My...?" He shook his head, apparently to clear it. "I'm sorry, Darling, I must have misheard. Who is here?"

"Your father," I said. "His Grace, Harold, Duke of Sutherland. He's in the sitting room waiting to see you."

"My..." He sounded as if he might have lost his breath for a moment. "My father's here, and I'm... you're... my father?"

I nodded. "I would put some clothes on, if I were you. Who

knows how long he'll be willing to kick his heels in the sitting room before he decides it's been long enough?"

"All I have is yesterday's dinner suit," Crispin said.

"I'm sure that'll be fine. Or I can go into Christopher's room and find something else, if you'd prefer."

"Not a frock," Crispin said.

I gave him a crushing look over my shoulder. "In front of your father? Don't be absurd."

Besides, it wasn't as if Christopher owned anything of that nature that was suitable for day wear. The only time he dresses up is for balls, and sparkling gowns are *de rigueur* for those occasions. But he didn't walk around the flat in skirts and stockings the rest of the time.

"Then yes, Darling. Please. I'd be grateful for something else to wear."

"I'll be right back," I told him. "You might want to run next door to the lavatory while you can. I assume you'd like to face your father with fresh breath."

He grimaced. "I wouldn't mind if I could do that."

"Then come along. And don't bother covering up." He was eyeing the blankets as if he thought about wrapping one around himself. "I promise I won't turn around and look at you as you skulk along behind me. Besides, if I've seen Christopher in his pants—and I have—I've practically seen you in yours, too."

"It's not the same," Crispin grumbled, but he didn't argue. "Very well, Darling. Gather me up some of Kit's clothes and knock on the door with them. I'll dress in there; that way you can come in here and make your own *toilette*. I'm sure those pyjamas didn't do you any favors at all with my father."

Most likely not. "I'll see you in a moment, then."

Or not, as the case may be, since I certainly wasn't keen on getting an eyeful of St George in his underthings, no matter how modern and flippant I tried to sound. Yes, I had in fact seen Christopher in his unmentionables, but that was very different from seeing Crispin in his. They might look the same, but they were two different people. I knew what he'd look like *sans* clothes, because I knew what Christopher looked like without most of his—chest hair notwithstanding—and that was good enough for me.

So I scurried down the hallway past the door to the washroom and knocked on Christopher's door. "Kit? It's me. I need to come inside."

I didn't wait for him to answer, just turned the knob and pushed the door open. Farther up the corridor I could hear St George move from my bedroom to the lavatory, and before I could fall into temptation and sneak a peek over my shoulder, I ducked into Christopher's room and pulled the door shut behind me.

"What's going on?" my cousin asked sleepily from the bed. "Is it Tom?"

"Worse. I need to borrow some of your clothes for St George."

"Take whatever you want," Christopher said and waved a hand towards the wardrobe. "What can be worse? Rivers and Hutchison?"

"Worse than that, too. It's the Duke."

"The what?"

"Your Uncle Harold," I said, while I flipped through the shirts in the wardrobe. "Crispin's father."

"Uncle Harold's here?" Christopher sat up with a jerk. "Why?"

"I have no idea." I pulled out a white shirt and draped it across the bottom of the bed before I went back for more. "Somehow, he must have figured out that Crispin's here, because the first words out of his mouth were, 'where's my son.'"

I grabbed a pair of flannel bags and tossed them after the shirt, before I turned to Christopher with both hands on my hips. "More accurately, it was 'where *is* my son.' He pronounced every word. Very distinctly. And in a very cold sort of voice, as if he thought I was hiding him."

I turned back to the wardrobe. A pair of socks and a waistcoat followed the trousers. And then a tie. "He can use his own cufflinks, I assume? And his own suspenders."

"I'm sure he can," Christopher said. "So Uncle Harold is upset."

"He's..." I hunted for the appropriate words. He wasn't upset, exactly. He'd been quite cool and collected. "—displeased. With Crispin and with us. Or at least with me. I have no idea what I've done to get on the wrong side of your aunt and uncle, but Aunt Charlotte would look at me like I had crawled out from under a flat rock while she was alive, and now Uncle Harold is doing the same thing."

"I don't imagine it's anything you did," Christopher said. "Other than simply being here, and breathing. I think it's more likely to be something—"

A knock on the door derailed the sentence, and when I crossed the floor and opened it, I was presented with that eyeful of St George I hadn't wanted.

"Gah!" I clapped my hands to my eyes. "Good grief, St George. Have you no sense of modesty whatsoever?"

"You're not so brave when it's *you* faced with something you don't want to see," Crispin said maliciously, "are you?"

He stepped through the door and to the side before flapping his hands at me. I could see them through the gaps in my fingers. "Shoo, Darling. I'll dress in here. Go to your own room and get out of your jimjams, there's a good girl."

"I hate you, St George," I told him, as I made my way through the door with my hands still covering my eyes. "Your clothes are on Christopher's bed. Or pick something else out of the wardrobe if you'd rather. And don't make your father wait any longer than necessary."

"No, Darling. Off you go." He shut the door on my heels. I stuck my tongue out at it before I ran back up the hallway and into my own room to—as he put it—get out of my jimjams.

WE FACED Uncle Harold as a united front. Christopher had gotten up along with Crispin, and we were all dressed and mostly presentable when we bearded the Duke in his—or our—sitting room. Crispin had slicked his hair back into its usual smooth helmet—it was rather a shame to see those flyaway wisps disappear—and so, of course, had Christopher. In their flannel bags and sleeveless jumpers, standing side by side in front of the Duke, they looked as much like twins as they had back in the Eton days, when I'd first landed in the family.

We all looked a bit the worse for wear, I'm afraid. We could brush our teeth and I my hair, the boys could slick their flyaway strands back against their skulls, and I could put on makeup to brighten my face, but there was nothing we could do about the bloodshot eyes from too much champagne and not enough sleep the night before.

Uncle Harold looked at us all, up and down, from where he sat ensconced on the Chesterfield, while we stood in a row in front of him like three misbehaving school-children.

"Well," he said. And stopped. Expectantly.

I didn't say anything. He wasn't *my* father, nor was he properly my uncle. The title was only a courtesy, and I already knew that he didn't like me much, even if I didn't know why. I could perhaps guess that it was my German heritage—my late father had been German, and that wasn't a positive association, even so many years after the Great War—but that was a guess, nothing more.

When no one else spoke up either, His Grace, the Duke, continued. "What do you have to say for yourself?"

There was a beat of silence. "Are you speaking to me?" Crispin wanted to know. "Or to Kit or Pippa?"

Uncle Harold's eyes narrowed. "Much as I would enjoy the opportunity to air my concerns regarding Christopher and Miss Darling, I'll leave that to my brother. You, however, St George—"

"I haven't done anything!" Crispin protested.

His father drew in a breath and swelled up.

"Why are you here, Uncle Harold?" Christopher interjected. As his uncle let his breath out again, Christopher continued, "I mean, what made you think Crispin would be here? He doesn't usually visit us when he's in Town. Normally, he spends the night in Sutherland House."

He used to, certainly. But perhaps the realization that the staff at Sutherland House had gossiped uninhibitedly to Grimsby the blackmailing valet about all his moral crimes and misdemeanors, had disenchanted St George of the idea of taking refuge there. Why go somewhere you know people will take note of everything you do and report every little transgression back to your father and, in the past, your grandfather?

"Did Rogers phone you when I didn't come in last night?" Crispin wanted to know. He sounded both outraged and hurt. "Have you instructed the servants to spy on me, Father?"

"They always did," Uncle Harold said coolly. "It wasn't until your grandfather's manservant came home with an itemized list of your indiscretions that we realized how bad things had gotten, however."

He let that sink in for a moment before he added, "When you left the Hall yesterday, I notified Rogers to expect you, that you were driving up to London. When you hadn't shown your-self at Sutherland House by six this morning, Rogers phoned the Hall to let me know."

"And you roused Wilkins and drove up to find me." Crispin sounded bitter.

"I waited until a decent hour," his father informed him, "before I woke the chauffeur, but yes, essentially that is what happened.

"And here I find you," Uncle Harold continued, "in Miss Darling's bed."

His tone was bland to the point of offense, and Crispin flushed. Christopher's jaw tightened. Before either of them could speak, I said, "I resent that," since I did, in fact, resent it.

Uncle Harold turned his attention from his son and nephew to me. His eyebrows were elevated, and he looked vaguely surprised, as if I were a piece of *objet d'art* or furniture that had spoken up. In his world, perhaps women were a lower form of life that didn't talk back unless expressly spoken to. Aunt Charlotte had been quite ladylike and quiet, now that I thought about it.

I, however, was raised by my mother, adventurous enough to leave her own country and settle down in another, and then by my mother's sister, and Aunt Roz isn't quiet at all, even if she is in every respect a lady.

Besides, this was 1926, and we no longer held to the mores of a bygone era. Young women are thoroughly modern and forward these days.

So for good measure I added, "It's not as if I were in there with him, you know. If you're worried about who your son and heir shares his bed with, I'm not the one you should be looking at. Unlike certain other women I could mention, I'll lend St George my bed, but I won't share it with him."

I sneered at Crispin. He sneered back.

Uncle Harold's lip curled in a smirk. "She's got your number, doesn't she, boy?"

"Yes, sir," Crispin said. And then he directed a resentful look my way, as if it were my fault that his father talked to him like he were still in short trousers.

Uncle Harold chuckled. "Serves you right, boy. Sowing your wild oats all over the place—"

"Yes," Crispin interrupted loudly, "thank you, Father. So you thought I might be here. Has something happened, that you came running to find me? Or did you plan to rescue me from Darling's non-existent wiles?"

"I resent that, St George," I said, stung at this dig to my charms. "I'll have you know that—"

He sighed. "Yes, yes, Darling. I misspoke. I didn't mean to suggest that you don't have wiles. Just that you're not wasting them on me."

"Ah." I waved my hand. "In that case, carry on."

"Thank you, Darling." He gave me a truncated bow before turning back to his father. "Is something wrong?"

Uncle Harold flapped his hand dismissively. "Nothing at all, boy."

"So I don't have to drive home to Wiltshire this exact moment?"

"I think it would be a very good idea if you went home to Wiltshire," Uncle Harold said, "but it doesn't have to be this moment. If you would like some time to say goodbye to your cousin and his..."

There was a pause.

"Cousin?" I suggested.

Uncle Harold hesitated, and when he couldn't lay his thoughts on the word he wanted, he went on as if it had been there, "—you may drive down this afternoon."

"But I'm expected home for supper?"

"Naturally," Uncle Harold said.

Naturally. "Take care, St George," I told him. "We'll miss you."

"Yes, I can hear the sincerity dripping off your words, Darling." He rolled his eyes. "We both know that you aren't going to miss me, so why say it? Why not just leave well enough alone and say nothing?"

"I might miss you," I said, "the same way I'd miss a toothache."

"No doubt." His voice was dry. "And I'd miss you the way I would miss—"

"St George!" his father barked, and Crispin flushed and bit back whatever awful thing he had been about to say.

I sniggered, but before I could speak again, there was another knock on the front door.

"We might as well not have a doorman," I told Christopher as I headed for the foyer to let whoever was knocking into the flat. "Evans just keeps sending people up with no warning. I thought it was bad when St George showed up a month ago, but at least then Evans thought he was you. This time—"

Uncle Harold bristled, but by then I had left the sitting room and was in the foyer, and mercifully out of range of anything he might have had to say about me to his son and nephew.

I'll admit to some trepidation when I turned the lock and pulled the door open. I thought it was most likely to be Tom Gardiner, and I wasn't terribly keen to discuss yesterday's murder in front of Uncle Harold. But I thought I could at least trust Tom to keep his head until we could get rid of Crispin's father. The latter might evince some surprise that a Scotland Yard detective came to visit his nephew and his nephew's cousin at what was practically the crack of dawn on a Sunday morning, but if Tom just played his part right and made the whole thing seem friendly and non-professional, I thought we could probably push Uncle Harold off without him being any the wiser.

On the other hand, it might be Florence Schlomsky, and I wasn't nearly ready for another encounter with her. Her behavior *vis-à-vis* Crispin yesterday evening had been brazen to the point of embarrassing—for me, I mean. Not for Flossie, certainly, and probably not for Crispin, either, since he doesn't embarrass easily. But I could only imagine how Uncle Harold would react to such behavior.

Unless I was wrong about Uncle Harold, of course. He might think a liaison between his son and the American heiress would be a good thing. The Sutherlands are hardly paupers, and St George certainly doesn't have to go fortune-hunting to maintain his standard of living, but there's nothing wrong with accumulating more money than one has already, either, and Florence was in possession of a tidy fortune.

Having thus prepared myself, I pulled open the door and came face to face... not with Flossie Schlomsky, but with—

"Miss Long?"

CHAPTER NINE

"MISS DARLING," Gladys Long sniffed. "Is Lord St George here?"

She peered past my shoulder into the foyer.

The sniff wasn't condescending. She was crying, actually, choking back tears. Her eyes were red and swollen—bloodshot, too—and her cheeks were wet. She kept dabbing at them with a handkerchief that looked positively sodden. I peered at her, as closely as I could without actually leaning in, but I could see none of the signs of yesterday's excesses. Her pupils were a normal size, neither too large nor too small, and while she was wound up, it wasn't the manic, chemically induced excitement of last night.

"He's inside," I said. And since I hadn't really a choice, I added, "Would you like to come in?"

She nodded eagerly. "Please."

I still wanted to know how she had gotten up here without being announced—perhaps Evans was susceptible to bribery, or perhaps she'd given him a sob story so he had felt sorry for her; I felt bad for her too, right now, so I couldn't exactly blame him—

but it didn't seem like the time to inquire. So I merely stepped aside and gestured her into the foyer so I could close the door behind her.

"Through the door on the other end." I waved her to go ahead of me, and raised my voice. "Visitor for you, St George."

He lifted his head to look at the doorway, but so, of course, did Christopher. So, for that matter, did Uncle Harold, who twisted to peer over the back of the Chesterfield. Faced with all three of them staring at her, Gladys gulped. "St George?"

Her voice shook as she looked from Crispin to Christopher and back. Or perhaps from Christopher to Crispin and back. It was fairly obvious that she had no idea—or not much of one—which of them was which.

I will admit that to someone who didn't know them well, they did look very much alike at the moment. Crispin was wearing Christopher's cream-colored flannel bags and a light gray jumper, while Christopher was wearing his own gray bags and a blue jumper. Up close, you would be able to tell that the jumpers matched their eyes, Crispin's gray and Christopher's blue, but Gladys wasn't close enough to them for that. She had stopped just inside the door, and now she eyed them both with the expression of a rabbit facing a pair of snakes.

Then—

"Gladys," Crispin said, his tone somewhere between surprised and apprehensive, and Gladys focused on him, looking relieved.

"St George!" She rushed across the floor and threw herself in his arms, clutching handfuls of his, or Christopher's, jumper. He looked like he wanted to object—Christopher, I mean, about the jumper—but he refrained.

Crispin caught her, but not without a grimace. One she, thankfully, didn't see.

"There, there." He patted her awkwardly on the back.

Perhaps it was his father's presence that inhibited him, because he'd certainly made a much better fist of it last night. "What's wrong, Gladys?"

"Everything," Gladys wailed, clinging like a vine. "That wretched journalist is dead, and Dom is gone, and Ronnie's a mess, and Hutchie said that I should come and ask you about last night—"

I caught Crispin's gaze over Gladys's head, and drew a finger across my throat. He arched a brow. "Really, Darling?"

I rolled my eyes. "Of course not, St George."

I didn't want him to kill her. I simply wanted him to shut her up before she said something we'd all regret. She'd already come quite close to the line with that remark about the dead journalist, and the last thing we wanted was for Uncle Harold to get any inkling of what we'd been up to last night.

Christopher, who has more experience interpreting my body language, came to the rescue. "Come and have a seat, Miss Long," he said, "and Crispin will mix you a drink."

He detached her quite deftly from his jumper, while Crispin, looking relieved, headed for the bar cart.

"Father?" he asked over his shoulder. "Would you like something to drink?"

Gladys gulped, as if she had just now realized who Uncle Harold was, or perhaps realized that he was there at all. The buckle in her knees could have been an attempt at a curtsey, or simply a reaction to the news. At any rate, she dropped into the chair with a horrified whisper of, "Your Grace?"

Uncle Harold inclined his head regally. "And you are, my dear—?"

"I'm sorry, Father," Crispin said from over by the wall. "This is the Honorable Gladys Long. You know her people, I'm sure. Gladys, my father, the Duke of Sutherland."

Gladys gulped again.

"Darling?" Crispin added. "Kit? Something to drink?"

It was a little early for me, honestly, but under the circumstances... "I'll have whatever Christopher's having," I said, as Christopher made his way over to Crispin and the bar cart. "Miss Long? What would you like?"

Gladys requested a Gin Rickey, and since that was simple enough to fix, we all had them. All except Uncle Harold, who sipped on straight bourbon.

"So, Miss Long..." he began, with what I assume he thought was an avuncular twinkle in his eye, but which really looked much more like beady inquisitiveness, "you and my son are close."

Gladys giggled nervously. "Yes, sir. Your Grace."

"Did you help him celebrate his birthday last night?"

She shot a glance at Crispin. "I... um... yes, Your Grace."

"Where did you go?"

"A group of us went to Rectors," Gladys said, which of course was true as far as it went, "We met St George and his party there. And then we finished up in Ronnie Blanton's flat in Mayfair."

Uncle Harold looked politely puzzled. "Rectors night-club?" he echoed. "I thought that shut down." He glanced at Crispin. "Didn't Mitchell run afoul the licensing laws?"

Crispin nodded. "Yes, Father. The club isn't open to the general public anymore, but last night, it was used for a special event."

"Your birthday?"

I smirked, and so did Christopher. "No," Crispin said, straight-faced. "Just a celebration of some kind. A ball, if you will. A hundred or so people. Most of them had no idea who I was."

"So I won't be getting a bill for the hiring of Rectors for an evening's debauchery?"

Crispin shook his head. "No, sir. It was nothing to do with me. We just went there. Kit, Philippa and I, Gladys and her friends. Freddie Montrose, an old schoolmate from Cambridge."

A shadow crossed his face when he mentioned Montrose's name. I waited for Uncle Harold to comment on it, but if he noticed, he chose not to remark.

"And then you came back here," he said instead. His Grace's tone, or rather, his lack thereof, made it abundantly clear how he felt about that fact.

"Kit, Pippa, and I did," Crispin nodded. "Gladys stayed on in Blanton's flat. Or at least she was still there when the three of us left."

Uncle Harold nodded, but before he could ask any more questions, there was yet one more knock on the door. I exchanged a glance with Christopher—our flat was beginning to look like Victoria Station—and turned to Gladys. "Did you come alone, Miss Long, or is one or more of your friends outside?"

"I came alone," Gladys said, with a slightly fearful glance at the door. Hopefully, that meant that at least we didn't have to worry about it being Dominic Rivers.

I started to push to my feet again, but Christopher put a hand on my shoulder to keep me down. "I'll go."

He uncoiled himself from the arm of the chair. Like me, he probably expected our most recent visitor to be Tom Gardiner, and he wanted a moment alone with him before ushering him into the sitting room.

It was perfectly understandable, so I nodded and sat back. Crispin had been hovering behind us, perhaps keeping the chair, and Christopher and me, as a buffer between himself and Gladys, but now he came around to take Christopher's spot. His father watched him do it, eyes flicking from Crispin to me and back, but he didn't comment, although it looked as if he thought about doing so.

Instead, he turned back to Gladys with a benign smile. "And how are your parents, Miss Long?"

Gladys said that her parents were fine—"Thank you very much, Your Grace,"—and continued on to her father's bulldogs and her mother's embroidery. I let it fade into the background while I strained my ears for noises from the foyer.

There were Christopher's footsteps across the parquet, and there was the key turning in the lock. The slight squeak of the hinges as the door opened—we'd have to oil those—and then...

"Now, don't you give me that look, Mr. Astley," said Flossie Schlomsky's voice. "You know you're happy to see me!"

Crispin choked on his Gin Rickey. The only reason I didn't, was because I hadn't taken a sip.

"St George!" Uncle Harold exclaimed, shocked, and Gladys squeaked nervously.

"Would you like me to thump you on the back, St George?" I inquired solicitously, while out in the foyer, Flossie Schlomsky continued, "Say, Mr. Astley, is your cousin around?"

Crispin shook his head violently and warded me off with a raised hand.

"Pippa?" Christopher's voice said faintly. "Yes, she's inside—"

"No, silly boy!" From the archness of Flossie's voice, she had smacked him on the arm with her gloves in some revolting parody of the ever-popular Jane Austen. Flossie probably thought it was how we all behaved here in Merry Olde England.

"Your cousin St George," she continued merrily. "I had a little petting party with him in the elevator last night, until Pippa came along and interrupted, and I was hoping..."

For more, no doubt.

Next to me, Crispin was wiping gin and tonic off his face with a serviette, while out in the foyer, it was Christopher's turn for a coughing fit. It must have concerned Flossie, who inquired, "Gosh, Mr. Astley, are you okay?"

"Fine," Christopher managed. "Yes, Crispin's still here. So is his father."

If he had thought that that piece of news might deter Flossie—I'm sure he hoped it would—he couldn't have been more wrong. She clapped her hands together. "The Duke is here? Oh, I have to meet him! Please, Mr. Astley, won't you introduce us?"

There was nothing Christopher could say to that except, "Yes, of course, Miss Schlomsky," so he said it.

Next to me, Crispin quivered, like a racehorse at the gate.

"No," I told him, and even went so far as to put a hand on his knee to keep him in place. He froze. "This is your own fault. You should have told her no yesterday. If you insist on spreading your favors around indiscriminately, you'll have to learn to deal with the consequences. Now you have to stay here and take your medicine like a good little gent."

"Have I told you lately that you're vile, Darling?" He didn't wait for me to answer, just got to his feet as Christopher escorted Flossie through the door to the sitting room. "Miss Schlomsky. What a delight to see you again."

Gladys, in the other chair, eyed Flossie up and down and sniffed. This time the sniff was definitely condescending.

"Oh, let's not stand on ceremony," Flossie said merrily. "I told you yesterday to call me Flossie."

"Of course you did." Crispin managed a polite bow. "May I present my father, the Duke of Sutherland? You know Darling and Kit, of course, and this is the Honorable Miss Gladys Long."

Flossie noticed Gladys for the first time, and the two of them stared, narrow-eyed, at one another. Until Uncle Harold cleared his throat, and then they both jumped.

"Florence," I said sweetly, since I couldn't bring myself to use the sickeningly sweet diminutive. "Uncle Harold just stopped by to order—I mean, to request that Lord St George return home to Wiltshire. You're just in time to say goodbye."

Crispin looked relieved. Flossie looked disappointed. Uncle Harold looked surprised. He opened his mouth, and then seemed to think better of what he was about to say, and closed it again.

"Miss Florence Schlomsky is one of our neighbors here at the Essex House Mansions," I told him. "It seems she and St George had an encounter in the lift yesterday evening."

Flossie giggled. Crispin winced.

"Miss Schlomsky is American," I added, as if Uncle Harold couldn't figure that out for himself from the accent. "Her father owns a series of dime-stores in Toledo."

"Where?"

"Somewhere in America," I said, before Florence could offer directions. When she'd tried to offer them to me, I had been completely lost, and I had every reason to think the same would be true of Uncle Harold. An eighteen hour drive west of New York, and then north... really?

Uncle Harold nodded, as if the explanation was sufficient. "How long have you known my son?" he asked Flossie. "I hope I'm right in assuming that last night's encounter wasn't the first time you met?"

Flossie giggled. "Not at all, Your Highness. Lord St George and I met a couple of months ago. He gave me a lift to a party at Lady Montfort's."

She bent an adoring eye on Crispin. His father did the

same, less adoringly. "You went to a party at Lady Montfort's, Crispin?"

I hid a smile. Of course he hadn't. Flossie had attached herself to him, in the belief that he was Christopher, and he had dropped her off at the staid Lady Montfort's soiree—after a heavy flirtation, no doubt, since he just didn't seem able to help himself—before he had gone on to a much less staid get-together at the Jungman Sisters', one that had featured plenty of alcohol and Bright Young Things.

And the next day he had complained to me about being 'saddled' with Flossie, when truly, he could just have kept the charm to a minimum and gone on his way without a lot of pretty words.

"You're such a charming lad, St George," I told him, and he looked down at me, startled, "the way you just can't seem to keep from turning your wiles on every woman you meet."

The startled look turned into a sneer. "Oh, lovely, Darling. A compliment and a dig in the same sentence. How very typical of you."

"There was no compliment in that sentence," I informed him, "although I can see where you might have been confused."

The sneer intensified, and reached its apex when I added, "I can't see this dubious charm of yours myself, but there's no denying its effectiveness. Can't you just keep it to yourself, St George?"

"I'm afraid I can't, Darling. Besides, as you so often tell me, it's not me, it's—"

"Your title and fortune. Yes, I know I've said that." *Ad nauseam*, in fact. Over and over, until I've made him believe it. "I've changed my mind, St George."

His eyebrow arched in inquiry, and I added, "Clearly there's more to it. Your title and fortune doesn't explain... them."

I nodded to Gladys and Flossie, who were sizing each other up, rather like two cats in an alley, while His Grace, the Duke, watched in consternation. "They've both got fortunes of their own, so they don't need yours, and yet they look ready to scratch each other's eyes out. And I heard what Laetitia Marsden said last month, you know."

"Heard what, Darling?"

"In Christopher's room," I said, "the morning after all the excitement. She did her best to persuade you to marry her. She'd take you even knowing that you don't love her, it seems. And she's got both a title and a fortune, so all she wanted—"

Had been him.

His lips curved, in a smirk this time. "Perhaps there's something you're missing, Darling."

"Perhaps there is." I gave him a dubious up-and-down. "You must have something to recommend you, I suppose, if all these women keep coming back for more."

"I suppose I must. Any time you'd like me to demonstrate, Darling, you just let me know."

"Demonstrate what?"

"My dubious charms, as you like to call them... Darling."

His voice softened on the last word, as if he were using it as an endearment and not simply my name. It was entirely without the sarcastic undertone it usually has, while the smirk turned from self-satisfied to something far more dangerous. Even his eyes changed, from clear, cool gray to something darker and moodier. From one moment to the next, he went from looking like my rather annoying personal nemesis to a handsome young man bent on seduction.

And then he blinked, and it all went away.

My breath seemed to have gotten stuck in my throat during the second-long interlude. I had to clear it away before I could tell him, "Impressive, St George. I didn't think you had it in you."

"You don't know me very well," Crispin said depreciatingly.

I didn't know that side of him, certainly. Although if that was how he looked at all the young women who fell for him, it was hard to blame them for their reactions. In my case, of course, the effect was mitigated somewhat by the fact that it was so clearly put on. He'd never look at me like that under normal circumstances, and we both knew it. But if not for that, and for the fact that for twelve years, he had been my least favorite person in the world, I might have felt a little quiver in my own diaphragm, too.

And because that idea was abhorrent, I shuddered. "Please don't do that to me again. That was horrible."

He sniggered. "I'll spare you my attentions from now on, Darling. It's not as if you appreciate the effort, so I might as well refrain from throwing my pearls before swine."

Swine, was it?

"Go away, St George, and take your pearls with you. And if you call me a sow one more time, I'll slap you."

"I didn't—!" he began, offended, but the look on my face must have convinced him that he was better off putting some distance between us, because he got to his feet. "Very well. I'll go keep Gladys and Florence from coming to blows, shall I?"

"Do," I told him. "And if they start taking potshots at you, don't expect me to come to your aid."

"Of course not, Darling. I never do."

He walked away. I watched, eyes narrowed, as he shared a smile between the two girls, both of whom promptly ignored the other to dimple back at him.

They're both of the healthy, blooming variety. Florence has bouncing, brown curls, pink cheeks, and those perfectly straight, American teeth, while Gladys is a sunny blond, with blue eyes and that typical English Rose complexion. At the moment, they were both gazing up at him with shining eyes and parted lips as if he'd hung the moon—or as if they each hoped for a kiss.

"Pshaw!" I said. Not an expression I'd ever expected to use, I might add, but there's a first time for everything, and the situation seemed to call for it.

"St George?" Christopher's voice asked from next to me, as he dropped down on the arm of the chair where Crispin had been. It was as if they were playing musical chairs with the arm of mine. "What did he do this time?"

I glanced up at him. "Called me a pig."

His eyes widened. "Not really?"

"Of course, really. It was all about how he wasn't going to throw his pearls before swine—me being the swine, naturally, because I didn't show proper appreciation for the way he decided to demonstrate his skill in seduction..."

"Is that what that was?" Christopher said, looking enlightened. "I wondered why you were looking at him like that."

"Like what? The same way I looked at Geoffrey Marsden last month?"

Geoffrey Marsden, Lady Laetitia's brother, had put his hand on my knee against my will and refused to budge when I tried to move away from him.

"Oh, no," Christopher said, shaking his head. "Not like that at all. You looked at Marsden like you wanted to punch him in the nose. You looked at Crispin like you wanted to grab him by the ears and pull him down for a kiss."

"Eeurgh!" My face twisted—I had looked at him the way Gladys and Florence did?—and Christopher smothered a chuckle.

"Don't worry. It didn't last long. By the time he walked

away, you looked at him exactly the same way that you looked at Marsden."

Good to know. "He's a pig, speaking of them."

"Marsden? Definitely."

"Crispin," I said. "How dare he turn his wiles on me like that?"

All right, so perhaps I might have asked for it. I won't say that I didn't. But still, how dare he? I certainly hadn't asked for *that* kind of demonstration.

"Well," Christopher said apologetically, "it must be galling for the poor bloke, to have practically every girl he meets fall at his feet, while you make it clear just how much you despise him—"

I snorted. "Yes, poor little rich boy, with his title and his fortune and his good looks. If you ask me, it's good for him to realize that there are women who won't come running just because he crooks his finger."

"Well said, Miss Darling," Uncle Harold's voice said. I think it might have been the first time in my life—or at least in the part of my life I've lived since I came to stay with the Astleys—that Uncle Harold has looked upon me with approbation.

And not only that, but he put an avuncular hand on my shoulder and smiled—actually smiled—down at me. "That's absolutely right, isn't it? It's a lesson every young man has to learn, that not every woman finds him irresistible."

"That's true," I told Uncle Harold, while in the back of my mind, I wondered what on earth he was on about. Crispin was his only son; shouldn't he want him to have whatever he wanted? I was fairly certain that Uncle Herbert would never have said such a thing had I been talking about Christopher.

Of course, there was no reason at all why Christopher would worry about women finding him attractive, but for purposes of this conversation, that was beside the point. Uncle Herbert would have wanted every woman on the face of the earth to find Christopher irresistible if that was what Christopher wanted. It was strange that Uncle Harold didn't feel the same way.

On the other hand, I was certainly violently opposed to Crispin getting whatever he wanted, especially today, so I could hardly quibble.

"I hope he wasn't impertinent?" Uncle Harold asked.

I gave him a tight smile. "No more than usual." Crispin was usually impertinent, or rude, or smug or sarcastic or snide, but I wasn't about to tell his father that.

"My apologies," Uncle Harold said, with the semblance of a bow.

A bow! And to me, of all people.

"There's absolutely no need for you to apologize," I told His Grace graciously, while next to me, Christopher looked as astonished by this sudden affability as I was. "And if I want Crispin to say he's sorry, I'll make sure he does, never fear."

Uncle Harold chuckled. "I don't doubt that at all."

He patted my shoulder approvingly before turning to Christopher. "I'm going to take my leave. If you would tell my son to make his way home when he has extricated himself from Miss Long and Miss Schlomsky?"

"You don't want to tell him yourself?"

He flicked a glance at me. "I'm sure he wouldn't want to be interrupted, Miss Darling. I'll see him at Sutherland Hall tonight."

He gave me a nod, and gave Christopher another, and then he vanished into the foyer without sparing another glance for his son and heir.

CHAPTER TEN

ONE OF US should have shown him out, of course. It was our flat, and it would have been proper etiquette to show a visitor to the door. But I was frankly so astonished by the whole conversation that all I could do was stand there and gape, while Christopher seemed to be in much the same state.

"Is it me," I asked when we'd heard the front door shut, "or did something very strange just happen?"

"I'd say so. Did Uncle Harold just pat you like you did something right?"

He had. "I'm floored," I said. "I thought Uncle Harold and Aunt Charlotte disliked me."

"I don't think it's that," Christopher said fairly, "so much as it's the fact that Crispin..."

He trailed off when the latter turned around at the sound of his name and arched a brow. "Telling tales, Kit?"

And then he seemed to register the absence of Uncle Harold, because he looked around the sitting room. "Where did my father go?"

"Back to Wiltshire," I said. "He said to tell you that he'll see you at home."

Crispin nodded. "I suppose that's my prompt to leave. Sorry, ladies."

He shared a charming smile between Flossie and Gladys, who both looked disappointed.

"When will you be back in London, St George?" Gladys wanted to know. "We're having a treasure hunt next weekend. Will you come?"

She peered up at him with limpid, blue eyes.

"If Father doesn't keep me chained to the old grindstone," Crispin told her, "I'd be delighted."

Gladys looked triumphant as she shot a sideways look at Florence. Not to be outdone, Flossie asked, "Will you be coming back to the Essex House Mansions then, Lord St George?"

"I would be delighted to come back to the Essex House Mansions," Crispin said with a flicker of a glance at me and Christopher; Gladys looked angry, Flossie triumphant, "although if my father is going to come haring up to London to look for me if I don't show up at Sutherland House, I suppose I had best go there instead."

"Your clothes, St George," I said, and handed him the bundle of evening kit from last night. "You'll just have to put one of the maids on to getting the lipstick out of the collar, I'm afraid. I didn't have time to try to do anything about it."

"That's all right, Darling." He tucked the bundle under his arm. "It won't be the first time, or I imagine the last. Besides, I have other shirts. And plenty of maids."

Of course he did. "Just bring Christopher's clothes back the next time you're in Town," I said. "Next weekend, you thought?"

"Perhaps." He turned to Gladys, who was tugging on his sleeve. "Yes, Gladys?"

"Hutchie dropped me off," Gladys said. "Can I beg a lift home, St George?"

She fluttered her lashes at him. Flossie looked like a thundercloud, which sat strangely on her pink-cheeked countenance.

"Of course," Crispin said, which in all honesty was the only thing he could say.

"Don't dally," I told him.

"No, Darling." His lips twitched, and I realized, a second too late, that with my use of that particular word, not only had I told him not to waste time—which was what I had intended to convey—but also not to engage in any kind of time-consuming flirtation.

"You know what I meant," I said severely. "Don't dawdle, St George. Your father is expecting you, and it's a long drive to Wiltshire."

"Of course, Darling." But his face was still amused when he turned to Christopher. "See you around, old chap. Thanks for the hospitality and the clothes."

Christopher nodded, and Crispin turned to Flossie and snatched her hand. "Miss Schlomsky."

He looked deeply into her eyes, and then lingered for a second with his lips against her knuckles. Flossie tittered and Gladys's eyes narrowed.

"Enough, St George," I said, and Crispin desisted.

"Of course, Darling. I assume you don't want me to kiss your hand?"

"No." I tucked it behind my back for good measure. "Keep your cooties to yourself."

He nodded. "Come along then, Gladys. Let's blouse."

He swept her ahead of him out of the flat. Flossie followed

them into the hallway, forlornly. I assumed she had planned to stand in front of the lift door with them, gazing hopelessly at St George, until the lift arrived and took them away, but I had no desire to see it. I shut the door after them and breathed a sigh of relief. "Thank God. We're finally alone."

"YOU DID WHAT?" Tom said.

He had finally turned up, still in the same tweed suit and Homburg as last night, looking like he hadn't been to bed yet.

"Tom." Christopher looked relieved to finally see him. I was, too, if it came to that.

"Do you have news for us?"

"Let's sit down." Tom gave a comprehensive glance around the sitting room. I had cleared away the used glasses and had fluffed the pillows and straightened everything up, so there was no sign that we'd had visitors just an hour ago. "Is Lord St George not here?"

"He headed back to Wiltshire," Christopher said. "Uncle Harold showed up here this morning with blood in his eye, and basically ordered him home. He took Gladys with him."

"Your uncle showed up? And took Gladys Long with him to Wiltshire?"

Christopher shook his head. "Uncle Harold showed up looking for Crispin, and so did Gladys. To talk about yesterday, she said."

"At Nigel Hutchison's request," I added, "or so she told us."

"And you didn't think to hold on to her?" Tom looked from one to the other of us.

I hadn't thought of it, to be honest. I had been more than pleased to see the backs of both Gladys and Florence Schlomsky, and for that matter of Crispin himself. Although now that he'd brought it up, I suppose I should have realized that Tom would want to speak to Gladys if the opportunity presented itself.

"We didn't know when you were going to get here," Christopher said. "We couldn't keep her indefinitely, and she seemed eager to get back to her friends. She asked Crispin to take her, and—"

He trailed off at the look on Tom's face.

"And you did what?" the detective asked.

"We didn't do anything," I told him. "Gladys wanted to go home. She said Hutchison had dropped her off here, and she asked St George for a lift. He left to take her home and then drive back to Wiltshire."

At whatever point he could bear to drag himself away from her charms, I assumed.

Tom's eyes widened during this recitation. "You sent your cousin, by himself, back to a group of people who you know killed someone yesterday? Why would you do such a thing?"

I blinked. So did Christopher. I don't think either of us had thought of it that way.

"They're not going to hurt Crispin," Christopher protested, although I could hear the concern in his voice. "He's one of them, isn't he?"

"Is he?" Tom let the question hang in the air for a moment before he added, "Montrose was also one of them, or close enough. Cambridge educated, and an Honorable. And where is he now?"

At the morgue, I assumed, but I didn't think now was the time to ask. Tom had clearly meant the question rhetorically.

"We didn't think—" I began, and Tom nodded grimly.

"That, if you'll forgive me, is obvious. Where does Miss Long live?"

I didn't know, and said so. Tom turned to Christopher, who also shook his head. "No idea, I'm afraid."

"So you sent your cousin off somewhere you don't know, with a woman who might have committed murder last night..."

"We get it," I interrupted, "all right? We get it. And we already feel bad about it, so stop rubbing it in, please. What can we do to find them? Or at least to make sure that St George is all right?"

And if he wasn't, to catch whoever had made him not so.

Although I honestly didn't think Gladys would have hurt Crispin. She had seemed genuinely taken with him—the way most women seemed to be when he turned on the charm—and I didn't think she was enough of an actress to fake her reaction to Flossie Schlomsky, either. I also doubted that she was the one who had killed Montrose. She was a small girl, for one thing, who might have had a problem both hitting hard enough and reaching high enough to bash a man over the head, even a medium-sized one like Frederick Montrose. If she had been in the kitchen with Dominic Rivers when Montrose entered the butler's pantry, she couldn't have gotten to him anyway. And if either of them had left the kitchen to give Montrose a crack on the head, it was more likely to have been Rivers. Not only was he a man, with the usual masculine proclivities for needing to protect the weaker sex, but he had more to lose than Gladys. Being a dope addict is one thing, being a dope dealer quite another.

Or it might have been Blanton, Hutchison, or Ogilvie, of course, who hadn't been in the kitchen to begin with.

And if Gladys had taken Crispin there this afternoon—to Blanton's flat, or Rivers's ditto—then I wouldn't necessarily put it past one of them to hurt him, even over Gladys's objections.

"We know where Blanton lives," Christopher said, "so why don't we start there? If no one's home, maybe Dobbins will be able to tell us where to find Gladys Long. Or if not her, then one of the others."

It was a reasonable suggestion, so that's what we did. Gathered our outerwear and, in my case, my reticule, and headed downstairs to the lobby, where Evans was ready to whisk the door open as we left. "Lots of visitors this morning," he remarked as we filed through.

I nodded. "And you didn't announce any of them, Evans. What happened?"

"His Lordship said he wanted to surprise his son," Evans said. His Lordship being Uncle Harold, the Duke of Sutherland, I assumed. Evans ought rightly to have called him His Grace, but at least His Lordship was better than Flossie's Your Highness. "The young lady was crying—" of course she had been, "—and Detective Sergeant Gardiner showed me his credentials and told me he was expected."

He slanted a look in Tom's direction before he focused his attention back on me. "Was he wrong?"

I shook my head. No, Tom had been expected. The others hadn't.

Although there was nothing to be done about it now. "I don't suppose you happened to catch where Lord St George and Miss Long were off to, did you? Did either of them say anything in your hearing?"

"I'm afraid not, Miss Darling. But I heard her tell him to take a left at the next corner, if it helps."

It certainly didn't hurt, anyway. "Thank you, Evans," I said, and scurried after Christopher and Tom through the door.

TOM HAD ARRIVED at our place in one of the Crossley Tenders that the Metropolitan Police had invested in since the War.

Not one of the wireless-equipped vehicles that the criminal classes—and Crispin's Bright Young Set—had nicknamed 'flying bedsteads,' but a perfectly normal Crossley Tender without the immensely large antennae on the roof.

I crawled into the back seat, leaving the front next to Tom empty for Christopher, and we bumped along at a good clip and arrived outside Ronald Blanton's mansion block after some twenty minutes or so of city streets and city noises.

Christopher and Tom murmured to one another in the front seat for the duration of the drive, but I spent the time in silence. It would have taken effort to keep up with their conversation, both for me to actually hear what they said over the sound of the motor, and then the mental effort required to keep track of their words and perhaps respond to them in a focused, mindful way, and I didn't have it in me. I was sitting in the back seat worrying about—of all people—Crispin.

If anyone had told me two months ago that I would be concerned about Crispin St George's wellbeing, I would have laughed.

Unpleasantly.

I would have assured whoever it was that Crispin could drop dead for all I cared. And I would have meant it (with, of course, the requisite nod to the fact that Christopher was likely to be devastated, and I didn't want anything to devastate Christopher). But as for me and the bane of my existence, my own personal nemesis... why would I care whether he lived or died?

That was before the events at Sutherland Hall in April, of course, and before the events at the Dower House in May. Before the death of his mother, and before I realized that his relationship with his father was less than stellar. Before I knew that he was in love with a girl he couldn't have, and that the fast living and all the other women and the excesses and the death-defying stunts were intended to keep his mind off what he couldn't have.

Before all of that, I would have been happy—or at least not sad—to see the back of him. Now it was two months later, and it turned out that I cared. At least enough that the idea that we might have sent him off with Gladys only so something terrible could happen to him, gnawed at my insides.

Tom was right: someone in Ronnie Blanton's flat last night had killed Montrose. The rest of the group might know who, or they might not. Gladys, specifically, might know who, or she might not. But whoever it was, might have decided that he or they would be safer with Crispin out of the way. And once they had disposed of him, they might decide to come after Christopher and me.

So I sat in the back seat of the Tender and chewed on my cuticles and tried not to think about the trip through London in the back of the H6 in the wee hours of last night, with Montrose's dead body on the seat next to me, and his head in my lap... and I tried not to imagine that it was Crispin's head that was cracked like a nut, and his blood that soaked into my— into Christopher's—trousers as we traversed the streets—

"Here we are," Tom said, his voice cutting through my imaginings like a knife through butter. "Better if I stay with the motorcar, I think. We don't want them to realize that you're talking to Scotland Yard until it's absolutely necessary. Are you all right, Miss... Pippa?"

I opened my eyes, to see that Tom had pulled to the curb down the street from Blanton's mansion block, far enough away that nobody was likely to notice him, or to notice whose car Christopher and I had arrived in. Christopher had already exited the Crossley, and was waiting for me to do the same. They were both eyeing me with concern.

I nodded. "Fine, thank you."

"You're a little pale," Christopher said, looking anxious. "Did it make you feel unwell, to ride in the back? You can have the front seat on the way back, if you'd like. I didn't think you suffered from travel sickness."

"I don't usually. And it isn't that. I feel fine. I'm just worried."

"About Crispin?"

I nodded. "What if we get up there, and he's on the floor with his head bashed in, and—"

"Pippa." He took me by the shoulders and peered down at me, blue eyes intent. "Listen to me. Nothing has happened to Crispin. They wouldn't hurt Crispin, all right? He's their friend. They just wanted to know what happened last night. That's all."

"You don't know that," I said, even as I recognized that what he said made sense. "What if we get up there, and—"

"Miss Darling." Tom nudged Christopher out of the way and put his own hands on my shoulders. "Pippa. Kit's right. I shouldn't have worried you the way I did. It's not at all likely that anyone has done anything to St George."

"Then what are we doing here?" I exclaimed, my voice shrill, and a passerby, a man in a top hat and frock coat, shot me a look.

Christopher waved him on, and after a look at Tom, and at the car, with its official MP logo, the gentleman hurried past.

"Pippa," Tom said again, looking deeply into my eyes. His were hazel, clear and kind. "I'll be very surprised if anything has happened to Lord St George. Kit's right. It's much more likely that they simply wanted to know what happened last night. As long as he sticks to the story we concocted, he has nothing to fear. He's as involved as they are, after all. He was the one who disposed of the body."

I had no answer to that, and he added, "We don't even know that Miss Long brought him here."

"They might be in her flat," Christopher shot in, "doing unmentionable things to one another."

My face twisted, and Tom let go of my shoulders, but not without a quickly suppressed chuckle. "There you are. You and Kit go knock on Blanton's door and ask for Gladys's direction, and when we get there, we shall find St George doing up his buttons."

"If we do," I said viciously, "I'll kill him myself, for scaring us this way."

Christopher took my arm and pulled me into motion down the pavement, away from Tom and the official Crossley. "He's probably halfway to Wiltshire by now, Pippa," he told me as we walked. "Taking out his frustrations on driving too fast and scaring the sheep."

"Frustrations?" I echoed. "What does *he* have to be frustrated about?"

It was a rhetorical question, so I wasn't surprised when Christopher didn't answer it except with a cryptic, "Let me count the ways."

"Yes?"

But he didn't, because by then we had reached the steps up to Blanton's mansion block, and the commissionaire, a different one than last night, opened the door for us. His gaze moved over me without recognition or interest, but he did a double-take when he got to Christopher. "Lord St George. Here to see Mr. Blanton, sir?"

Christopher opened his mouth, and then closed it again.

"Yes, please," I said, "Carlton."

He was wearing a nametag, and it was an easy thing to read it while Carlton's attention was fixed on Christopher.

Who nodded. And cleared his throat. "Yes, please, Carlton. If you'd clear us up?"

"Of course, my lord." Carlton pocketed the coin Christopher slipped him. "You and the lady go on up in the lift, and I'll let Mr. Blanton's man know you're here."

"Thank you," Christopher said politely, and nudged me ahead of him toward the lift. "Go on, Pippa."

"Is anyone else up there, Carlton?" I wanted to know over my shoulder. "Mr. Hutchison? Miss Long? Mr. Rivers?"

"Just Mr. Blanton and his man," Carlton said. "You go on up, my lord and miss. I'll let Dobbins know you're coming."

Christopher shoved me into the lift ahead of him. "He doesn't want to talk, Pippa," he murmured. "Wait until we get upstairs. If Blanton's home, he'll tell us where to find Gladys."

I leaned against the wall of the lift and folded my arms over my chest.

Half a minute later we were on our way down the corridor to Blanton's flat, where Dobbins had already unlocked the door and was peering out.

Or no... it wasn't Dobbins at all, it was Ronald Blanton himself, something which became clear when he pulled the door open with a cry of, "St George!"

"Mr. Blanton," I said politely as I stepped across the threshold. "How are you holding up?"

He looked dreadful, I have to say. His eyes were bloodshot, his skin was pasty, his hands shook, and he looked worse than he had in Rectors yesterday, before Rivers came along and doctored him up. It had been a while since he'd had a hit of dope, I surmised, and he was in withdrawal. Hopefully he hadn't expected Crispin to be able to fix it for him, because if St George was distributing cocaine, I would have something to say about it.

Christopher followed me across the threshold and turned to face Blanton, who greeted him feverishly. "St George! I've been so worried. What...?"

And then he stopped, and peered suspiciously into Christopher's face before recoiling a step. "You're not St George."

Christopher shook his head. "I'm his cousin, Christopher Astley. We met last night."

"Of course we did." Ronnie began giggling. Once he'd started, it seemed to take him effort to stop. "Of course we did," he said again once he'd gotten himself under control. "You looked rather different then."

Christopher nodded. "You remember my cousin Pippa, I'm sure."

Ronald looked me up and down. "You looked rather different, too," he said, "but yes, I do."

"We were hoping to find Lord St George." I cut to the chase, since nothing seemed to be gained by beating around the bush. "Miss Long stopped by the flat and took him off somewhere. Since he's not here, could you perhaps tell us where to find Miss Long's residence?"

Blanton blinked at me. "Gladys did that?"

"At Mr. Hutchison's suggestion, apparently. You don't know anything about it?"

He shook his head, and kept shaking it for a bit too long. As if he couldn't work out how to stop. "I haven't seen anybody today."

I eyed him narrowly. He didn't appear to be lying. At least St George wasn't tucked away in a closet somewhere in the flat, or in the butler's pantry, breathing his last, then.

"Can you tell us where to find Gladys Long?" Christopher asked. "I'd like to catch my cousin before he goes back to Wiltshire."

Blanton turned to him. And eyed him in a silence that went on for long enough that I was going to prompt him by the time he said, "She has a one-bed flat in a mews in Belgravia. The long one, near Eaton Square Garden. Starts with an E."

"Eaton Row? Or Eaton Mews? Maybe Ebury Mews?"

"One of those," Blanton agreed with an owlish nod, which was no help whatsoever. Eaton Row and Eaton Mews are as distinct from one another as Ebury Mews is from both of them. Nor are they the only three mews in that area. Not even the only three that start with an E. "It has a green door, and a green stable door next to it. She's on the first floor, above the old stable. Lucky thirteen."

He giggled.

"The street number is 13?" That would be a help, anyway. Number 13 with a green door; we ought to be able to find that, even if we had to look in a few different mews before we did.

"What about Hutchison and Ogilvie?" Christopher asked. "Where can we find them? And Rivers?"

Blanton peered at him. "Are you trying to find them before they go to Wiltshire, too?"

"Don't be stupid," Christopher said irritably. "If I can't find my cousin at Gladys's, I'll have to search for him elsewhere. And it's possible she took him to see Hutchison or Rivers." Since there weren't here.

Blanton shook his head. "Nobody goes to see Dom. Dom's on the telephone. If you want to see Dom, you ring him up, and he comes and finds you."

Just as Crispin had said, as a matter of fact.

"His direction, then. I'll try to phone him."

Blanton blinked for a second before raising his voice. "Dobbins? Where are you, Dobbins?"

There was no answer, and after a moment Blanton giggled. "I forgot. I sent Dobbins out for cigarettes."

"Can you find it yourself?" I wanted to know, and Blanton rattled it off. From memory. I assume he must have rung it up enough that it had imprinted itself on his brain, and so he could recall it, even in his current condition. He was twitching and jumpy and clearly unable to hold a single thought in his head for more than a second or two, but he had Dominic Rivers's direction at the top of his mind.

"Where do Hutchison and Ogilvie live?" Christopher asked.

"They share a bachelor pad in Kensington," Blanton answered. "At the top of one of the mansion blocks. The big ones across from the Royal Albert Hall."

"Albert Hall Mansions?" The blocks around the Royal Albert Hall make the Essex House Mansions look positively anemic. They're enormous, with six or seven floors, taking up large sections of each city block. "Do you know which building? The number of the flat? The floor they're on?"

"The attic," Blanton said. "The bachelors are at the top of the world."

He giggled again.

"But you haven't seen them today?" Christopher prodded.

Blanton shook his head. "I haven't been out, have I, and no one's come to see me. I'm not feeling so good, you know."

"No," I agreed, "I imagine you're not. We're not, either. Murder has a way of doing that."

Blanton blinked at me. "Murder?"

"Frederick Montrose," I said. "He died last night, don't you remember? Right there?"

I pointed to the door to the butler's pantry. Ronald turned to stare at it with an expression that was caught somewhere between disbelief and shock.

"That was real?"

Christopher and I exchanged a glance. "Yes," Christopher said, "it was."

"Did you think it wasn't?" I added.

Ronnie attacked one of his fingernails, his eyes wide and

unblinking above his hand. "I thought it couldn't be, you know? People don't die here."

He was lucky he wasn't dead himself, in my opinion, if he was so far gone that he couldn't tell a dead body in his own flat from a hallucination.

"Freddie Montrose did," I said. "Someone hit him over the head and left him on your pantry floor. Was it you?"

Ronnie shook his head. And kept shaking it long after he should have stopped.

"Do you know who?" Christopher asked.

Ronnie kept shaking his head, but said, "No," as if he didn't realize he was doing it.

"You left the parlor first. After Montrose asked for directions to the lav, you know."

Ronnie nodded. And kept nodding. But— "I don't remember that," he said.

"You don't remember looking for Montrose? After Nigel Hutchison reminded you that he was a reporter and maybe you should go with him rather than let him roam the flat?"

Ronnie shook his head.

"So you have no idea who hit him?"

"No," Ronnie said.

It might have been the truth or it might not. There was no way to know. He was adamant about it, anyway. We tried in a couple of different ways to approach the subject and get a different answer, but Ronnie kept reiterating, with words and gestures, that he didn't know what had happened to Montrose. He might even have believed it. In the end, we thanked him for the information he had given us—locations for Gladys Long, Hutchison and Ogilvie, and a way to contact Dominic Rivers— and took our leave. Dobbins was still not back when we left.

CHAPTER ELEVEN

"NO LUCK?" Tom wanted to know when we were back beside the Crossley.

"Not in as far as finding St George or Gladys Long." I made my way into the back of the vehicle as I spoke. "Blanton was the only one upstairs. He said he's been alone all morning. And incidentally, he doesn't remember the murder. Or says he doesn't."

Tom's eyebrows arched. "Is that so?"

"That's what he claimed," I said, as Christopher fitted himself into the front seat next to Tom. "He was in awful shape. Twitching and sweating the way he did last night, while he was waiting for Dominic Rivers to turn up."

"Withdrawal symptoms," Tom nodded, not without sympathy. "He's addicted to dope, and if he doesn't get it regularly, that's what happens."

That was a load off my mind, actually. Nothing to do with Blanton, but I had never seen my Cousin Francis behave that way, which surely meant that his addiction was far less severe than Blanton's.

And Crispin had all his faculties, with no shaking or sweating or twitching whatsoever, so I probably didn't have to worry about him, either. Not as far as that was concerned, at any rate.

Although I was frankly shocked that Ronald Blanton claimed not to remember anything that had happened last night. A murder had taken place in his Mayfair flat, and he didn't remember it? He had helped carry Frederick Montrose's lifeless body down several flights of stairs and had loaded it into the back of a car under cover of darkness, with its head wrapped in a towel so blood and brain matter wouldn't get everywhere, and he said he couldn't remember it?

"Dope can do strange things to people," Tom said, when I opined as much. "You said he had just taken a hit when this happened? He might have been in a world of his own, and everything that happened around him took on a dream-like quality. Cocaine is a strong stimulant. It makes the user feel euphoric. All of real life, especially the bad parts, might have taken a back seat to that."

He turned to Christopher. "Did he know where Miss Long or any of the others can be found?"

"Hutchison and Ogilvie share a place in Kensington," Christopher said, "next to the Royal Albert Hall. It might be in the Albert Hall Mansions, or it might not. Gladys Long has a mews flat in Belgravia. It's either Eaton Row or Eaton Mews or perhaps Ebury Mews. Or something else. He thought it started with an E, although I'm not sure how far I trust Ronald Blanton's recollection. But I assume we start there?"

"If your cousin departed with Miss Long," Tom agreed, "let's do. We can always go to Kensington if they aren't there. But it's not on the way, so let's not waste time on a detour there at the moment."

He turned south toward the river and Belgravia.

I sat in silence a moment, until I couldn't stand the silence any more. (It didn't take long.) "Is there a reason you're worried about wasting time?"

Or to put it more bluntly, when he had told me not to worry about Crispin, that nothing was likely to have happened to him, had Tom been lying and I really ought to worry? Did he think that time was of the essence, and that was why we were haring off toward Eaton Square without stopping in Kensington first? Was Tom afraid of what we might find there?

Tom met my eyes in the mirror. "It's not because I've had second thoughts and believe we'll find St George dead in a pool of blood, if that's your concern. If we find him at all, I'm sure he'll be, as Kit said, doing up his buttons."

"Dallying with Gladys?"

He nodded. "But the sooner we can put this to bed—no pun intended—the sooner the both of you can stop worrying about him. So we should go there and see if we catch them *in flagrante*."

I grimaced. So did Christopher. I deduced he wasn't any more eager to see his cousin in the act of seducing Miss Gladys Long than I was.

"And if they're not there," Tom added, "we'll try Kensington next. Did Ronald Blanton say anything about where Mr. Rivers might live?"

"Dominic Rivers's whereabouts are not known to the rabble," Christopher said dryly. "If Blanton wants him, he rings him up, and Rivers comes to him. The same thing Crispin said. It seems Rivers doesn't want house guests."

"No," Tom agreed, "I wouldn't either, if I were Dominic Rivers. That way he can control as much of every encounter as possible. If anything spooks him about any of it, he can leave with no one being the wiser. He probably had you under observations at Rectors last night, for a while before he made his presence known."

He might very well have done. The place had been full of moving bodies, music and noise, and it would have been quite easy for someone to stay out of the way and keep observation before he decided it was safe to approach.

"But we got his direction," Christopher added, "so we can ring him up and try to arrange a meeting. And then nab him when he turns up. And put the thumbscrews to him." He grinned.

"Bloodthirsty," I muttered and he slanted me a look.

So did Tom. "It would be well deserved," he said. "People die from cocaine use, you know. There was Billie Carleton at the end of the war—the actress; you might remember her, or were you too young?—and you heard of Billy Chang and the situation with Freda Kempton a few years back, didn't you?"

I had, indeed, heard of that situation. So had all of London, and all of England for that matter, as it had been front page news everywhere.

Freda Kempton, a dance instructress at a London club, had died from an overdose of cocaine in—if memory served—1922. Billy—Brilliant—Chang was a Chinese dope merchant from Limehouse who was suspected of having supplied her with the drugs. He had something of a harem of young women he both gave dope to and dallied with, it seemed.

He hadn't been found guilty of her death—she had taken the overdose herself, perhaps by accident or perhaps on purpose—but a couple of years later, the police had arrested Chang for dope dealing. He had served his sentence in Wormwood Scrubs, and then been deported. There were rumors that he had set up shop on the French Riviera, although he might equally well be in Hong Kong, or even back in Limehouse by now. It was said that when the boat carrying Billy sailed away from the Royal Albert Docks, a young woman left behind called after it, "Come back soon, Chang!"

"You shouldn't feel sorry for Rivers, Pippa," Christopher told me now. "Even if he didn't have anything to do with killing Montrose last night—and we don't know that he didn't—you saw how Blanton was today. That's Rivers's doing, too."

Of course it was. "It doesn't matter," I said. "And it's not that I'm feeling sorry for him. If he killed Montrose, he deserves prison. If he's dealing dope—"

Christopher opened his mouth, and I went on, "—and there doesn't seem to be any question about it, then he deserves prison for that, too. I just object to the thumbscrews."

"We don't torture suspects anymore," Tom said blandly. "Nor would we have to. There's plenty of evidence against Rivers for dope dealing, even if most of it is circumstantial."

He glanced at Christopher. "Do you have any reason to think he's the one who coshed Frederick Montrose?"

"Not except for the fact that he was there when it happened and had a motive," Christopher said. "If Montrose planned to write about him in The Daily Yell, he would have had every reason to want to silence him."

Tom nodded. Christopher continued, "But Montrose died in the butler's pantry, and if Rivers and Gladys were meeting in the kitchen, that makes it more likely that it was one of the others. Someone who saw him spying on them and decided he shouldn't be allowed to."

"So Blanton, Hutchison, or Ogilvie."

Christopher nodded. "Although if Rivers and Gladys met in the butler's pantry and not the kitchen, and Montrose walked in on them, it could have been either of them, too. Do you have any idea what he was hit with?"

"Do you?" Tom retorted. "You were the one who was there."

"I didn't see the body before it was moved," Christopher said. "Or his head while he was in the car with us."

"Doctor Curtis looked at him this morning and said it was something heavy and smooth with a round edge."

"So a champagne bottle," I said. "Or a rolling pin."

Tom shot a quick look into the back seat where I was sitting. "Is there a reason you're mentioning those two things?"

"Only because we were drinking champagne last night, and a rolling pin is something one might easily find in a butler's pantry. But it was something like that?"

"Something very like that. A bottle of champagne might have shattered on impact, and there were no glass shards in the wound or liquid on the clothes, so the rolling pin is perhaps more likely. But from what we know, I think it might be either."

"It's a shame you can't just go up there with a search warrant and look around," Christopher said, and Tom nodded.

"But that would give away that we know one of them did it. And it would also give away that the three of you told us. So we'll hold off on that for a little while longer."

He turned the corner from Grosvenor Place onto Ebury Street, and continued, "Right now, we're interviewing everyone we pulled in from the raid last night. The minute a single one of them puts Montrose together with Blanton, Hutchison, and Ogilvie, or Rivers and Gladys Long, or even the three of you, I shall be all over Blanton's flat with a search warrant. But for now, I'm waiting for an excuse."

"And if you don't get one?" I asked.

He shot me a look in the mirror. "Then, tomorrow morning, we lie. We can't afford to let it rest any longer than that. One of them might get restless and decide to leave."

"If anyone leaves," Christopher said, "won't it be whoever did it? And then you can just nab him?"

After a second he added, "Or her?"

"We can't rule out Gladys Long," Tom agreed, turning yet another corner. "Montrose wasn't a particularly tall man, but Curtis said he was most likely bending down when he was hit. The blow came from above. None of you are tall enough to manage that without standing on something, I assume? And I assume he's likely to have noticed someone climbing up on a crate behind him and waving a champagne bottle around?"

Of course he was likely to have. "So he was bending over to put his ear to the keyhole," I said, "or the crack in the door, and someone approached from behind and hit him. Any one of us could have done that."

Tom arched a brow, and I added, "Well, not Christopher or Crispin. We were in the other room together. But any of the others. Hutchison was a touch taller than Montrose, I'd say. Blanton and Ogilvie were approximately the same height as him, and Rivers was perhaps an inch shorter. Gladys is rather small. Which wouldn't matter if he was leaning over. But I'm not sure she'd be strong enough to hit him hard enough to crack his skull. He was wearing a bobbed wig on top of his own hair, and whoever hit him, hit hard enough to break his skull through both."

"What happened to the wig?" Tom wanted to know, and I shook my head helplessly. I didn't know what had happened to anything other than the body, and only because we'd been responsible for it. But what the others had done to the butler's pantry after we had left with Montrose's body, I couldn't say.

"We have no idea," Christopher said. "The others were going to clean up. We could have asked Gladys, except Crispin's father was there this morning, and it didn't seem like a good idea. I suppose Crispin might have asked while they were alone in the car. That was likely why she wanted him alone in the first place. So she could ask him about what we did last night. Hopefully he had the sense to ask questions back."

"If he found out," Tom said, "he didn't come back to your flat to report it."

"He might not have had time to return before we left for Mayfair," I pointed out. "Or he might still be with her, and he's planning to stop in again before he sets out for Wiltshire."

Or he'd send us a note, although by the time he posted it, it might take a day or two to reach us.

A part of me would be relieved to find him still with Gladys. At least I could stop worrying about him then. Even if there admittedly was another part of me that was busy thinking up snide remarks about men who spent inordinate amounts of time wooing the opposite sex.

"There was no point asking Blanton," Christopher added, "since he said he doesn't remember anything that happened last night. If the wig had been in his flat, surely he would have made mention of it, at least."

"One of the others likely disposed of it elsewhere," Tom said, "on their way home." He pulled the Crossley up to the side of the street. "This looks like a good place to park. Eaton Row and Eaton Mews are that way, Ebury Mews over there."

He pointed to the left and right.

"Blanton said she's in a first-floor flat with a green door and a green stable door and the number 13," I said. "Although between you and me, I don't know how reliable he is."

Or whether he'd even told the truth. He might have lied, just to ensure that we wouldn't find Gladys.

"Let's start looking, then." Tom led the way across the street and into the maw of the mews.

Christopher and I followed. And then we trudged along, looking left and right, with me hanging on Christopher's arm so the uneven cobblestones wouldn't turn my ankle if I stepped wrong.

"There's number 1 3," Tom said after a minute or two. "The door's black."

It was. The rest of the building was whitewashed, and there were cheerful gingham curtains in the upstairs windows. I had a hard time reconciling the Gladys Long I had met last night and this morning with gingham fabric, but I suppose she might have had a more domestic side that she didn't let out often.

"So do we think Ronnie made a mistake," Christopher asked, eyeing it, "or do we think Ronnie lied, or is this a different mews than the one Gladys lives in?"

"I vote for a different mews," I said. "I don't think he was in any condition to lie, although it's quite possible he misremembered. But he also wasn't certain about the mews, so I think it's a different one."

"We could knock?" We both looked at Tom, who had the official credentials to do that sort of thing.

He shook his head. "I'm not on an official visit here. I think it's better if we draw the least possible attention to ourselves. If we fall short in the other mews, as well, we can always come back."

He headed for the mouth of the mews with us behind.

"I haven't seen the H6 anywhere," Christopher commented a few minutes later, as we entered the second mews on our list. "If Crispin's still here, it ought to be parked somewhere in sight. The mews itself is too narrow to park a motorcar in."

It was. And no, I hadn't seen the blue Hispano-Suiza either. It's a fairly distinctive car, not easy to overlook, so if it had been anywhere around, we'd have noticed it.

"Perhaps he simply dropped her off and went on his way," Tom said as we trudged forward, keeping our eyes peeled for number 1 3. This surface was a bit easier to navigate than the previous, the cobblestones flatter and less uneven, so I was managing under my own steam.

"Or he might have put the motorcar elsewhere while he went inside her flat," Christopher added. "There must be car parks nearby, where he could leave it. Out of sight."

There must be. And the suggestion was logical. I wanted to believe it, but...

"Or if something's wrong," I said, "he's lying in the backseat with his head in Gladys's lap right now, while Hutchison or Ogilvie or even Rivers drives the car and the body somewhere where they can leave what's left of him."

There was a pause. Christopher and Tom exchanged a glance.

"You know," Christopher said, "Crispin's right. You do have a vile imagination."

I shot him a look. "I don't think this kind of thing was what he was referring to when he said that, Christopher."

"No," Christopher agreed, "I know very well that it wasn't. But that's quite an ugly picture you painted. You don't really believe...?"

"Let me put it this way," I said. "I would be delighted to walk into Gladys's flat and find her and St George in bed together. Delighted by it. I'd be happy enough that I wouldn't even give him a difficult time."

"That's quite delighted," Christopher said dryly.

I nodded. Yes, it was. Quite a lot more delighted than he—Crispin, I mean—would deserve under those circumstances. But if that's what happened, I'd bite my tongue on any unkind words, nonetheless.

"Until Tom mentioned it earlier," I said, "I didn't really think that any of us were in danger. It hadn't crossed my mind that we could be. But someone in that flat perpetrated violence last night, Christopher. Someone who wasn't you or me or St George. And if they know that he can identify them..."

"Number 13," Tom's voice cut into the conversation. "And it's green."

We came to a stop beside him, all three of us looking at the small brick house with the green door and a green stable door side by side on the lower level, and two windows up above. The curtains weren't gingham this time, but looked soft and elegant, with an expensive sheen. Lavender silk, or perhaps satin.

"That looks promising," Tom said.

I nodded. "The curtains look like they might belong to Gladys Long. She was wearing lavender last night. And the number 13 and the green door are right."

He shot me a look. "Would you like to do the honors?"

I shot one back. "Knock, you mean? Of course, if you'd like me to."

I walked up to the door and applied my knuckles to it. And stepped back and listened for any sound from inside.

None came. They were probably upstairs in her bedroom and couldn't hear. I knocked again, harder.

"Nothing?" Tom asked. He and Christopher had gathered in behind me now.

I shook my head.

"Probably wore himself out," Christopher muttered, "and is asleep."

My face twitched into a grimace. "Did he wear her out, too?"

He shot me a bland look. "If he were here, I'm sure he'd tell you that it has been known to happen."

No doubt. "I would hope he wouldn't be so uncouth as to tell me anything of the sort," I said, applying my knuckles to the wood one more time. "Although being intimately familiar with him—if not quite so intimately as Gladys—I wouldn't put it past him, honestly."

Christopher shook his head. "Nor would I. Try the knob."

"We can't just walk in—" I began, but Tom reached past me and twisted the handle.

The door opened and we peered into a dimly lit hallway with a staircase to the first floor.

"Five will get you ten they're in bed together," Christopher whispered.

"As long as he's not on the floor with his head bashed in, I don't care," I whispered back.

Tom, meanwhile, had taken a step into the narrow space and raised his voice. "Metropolitan Police. Is anyone home?"

There was no answer, and my heart started beating faster as he headed for the stairs.

Logically, I knew that there was no real reason to suppose Crispin would be dead on the floor of the flat upstairs. If he wasn't in bed with Gladys, he was more likely to be elsewhere. On his way home in the Hispano-Suiza, probably approaching Frimley or Basingstoke by now, or else off somewhere with Gladys herself, and Hutchison and Ogilvie. They may not even be threatening him, but might simply want to know what he had done with Montrose's body last night.

So logically, there was no reason why I should be watching Tom's ascent up the stairs with dread. Even so, emotionally, I was waiting for disaster to strike.

Halfway up, he turned to us. "Aren't you coming?"

"Are you sure you want us?" Christopher answered. "It's not exactly regulation, is it?"

"None of this is regulation," Tom said. "You're here. You may as well be ready to help, should I need it."

The suggestion that Tom might need help was all it took to get Christopher racing up the stairs. I dragged myself up behind him, reluctantly. If Crispin was up there, he certainly wasn't likely to attack Tom for walking in on him, and I didn't see who else might want to do harm to any of us.

At the top of the stairs was another door, this one white. Tom stopped and knocked, with Christopher right behind him. I climbed the last couple of steps and listened, too. Our breaths were louder than usual in the narrow confines of the enclosed staircase, but other than that, there were no sounds from inside.

"Knob?" Christopher suggested, and his voice sounded funny, as if he, too, was expecting something bad to be lurking behind the door.

Tom pulled a handkerchief out of his pocket and draped it over his hand before he reached out and twisted the knob. The door opened. He raised his voice. "Hello?"

There was no answer.

"This is Detective Sergeant Thomas Gardiner with Scotland Yard. I'm coming in."

"Crispin would certainly answer that if he could," I muttered, and Christopher nodded.

"Sounds empty."

It did. "Better let Tom go alone. It might be illegal for him, too, to walk in without a warrant or due cause, but I'm certain it's more illegal for us."

"We're concerned about your cousin's wellbeing," Tom told me with a glance over his shoulder. "Or at least I know you are, so I'm indulging you by making sure he's not here and bleeding out on the floor."

"Thank you," I said. "I think."

Christopher fumbled for my hand. "Just wait, Pippa. I'm sure there's nothing to worry about. Nothing at all."

Certainly.

"We didn't see the motorcar outside," he added, as if rambling on and reiterating things we already knew made him feel better, and perhaps it did, "and nobody's answering up here, so chances are they didn't come back here at all when they left us. She told him to take a left, didn't she?"

"That's what Evans said she said. This would have been a right, wouldn't it? If they were going directly here. But they hadn't been at Ronnie Blanton's flat. Unless he'd forgotten that, too."

"Or was lying," Christopher said.

Yes, of course. "You're not actually helping, you know."

He squeezed my hand. "I'm sorry. I think perhaps I am a bit more worried than I'd like you to believe."

"I'm going to kill him," I said. "If he isn't already dead, I'm going to murder him for scaring us this way."

Christopher nodded. "I'll help you. Although I'm sure he's not doing it on purpose, you know. He's probably going home, headed down the Salisbury Road at forty-five miles per hour, scaring the sheep and everyone else on the road, and not sparing us a thought."

Perhaps. It was a nice picture. I focused on it until I could breathe again. I was just starting to feel better where there were footsteps inside the flat, and then the door opened and Tom's face appeared in the crack. "Come inside."

The voice was grim, and so was the face.

"What's wrong?" I asked, while my heart started to beat hard enough to knock a hole in my ribcage.

He eyed me. "I need an official identification."

"Of?"

"The dead body on the bedroom floor. Grab her, Kit."

My knees buckled, and I would have dropped to the floor had Christopher not caught me around the waist and kept me upright.

CHAPTER TWELVE

"THAT'S HER," Christopher said half a minute later, and I swallowed and nodded.

"Yes. That's Gladys Long. Or at least it's the girl who was introduced to us as Gladys Long at Rectors nightclub last night."

The same girl whom Crispin had introduced to his father as Gladys Long this morning. The same girl he had walked out of our flat with, and gotten into the Hispano-Suiza with, and driven away with.

"I think we can take it as established, then," Tom said, "that this is Gladys Long."

We probably could. Or at least that it had been Gladys Long. Now, the girl was just an empty husk on the bedroom floor.

Approximately a month ago, at the Dower House in Dorset, Christopher and I had walked into a different bedroom and found a different young woman dead.

Johanna de Vos, she of the pale blue dress.

She had been strangled, and had put up a fight before she

succumbed. Her face had been bruised and dark, and her tongue had been sticking out, while her pretty blue dress had been tangled around her limbs from her struggle to overcome her assailant.

When Tom had brought us into the bedroom here, I had been worried that we'd be faced with the same sort of situation.

But this scene was nothing like that one. Gladys was still fully dressed, in the smart summer frock from earlier, with her silk stockings in place and her dainty shoes buckled. If there had been any kind of hanky-panky going on between her and Crispin, she had dressed and reapplied her lipstick afterwards. It was red and shiny, a bright gash across her pale face.

She was lying on her stomach on the floor next to the bed, with her head turned towards the single window. It looked out onto the back of the mews, where a few straggly weeds were clinging to life. Her eyes were wide open and vaguely startled under plucked, arched brows. If it hadn't been for the pallor of her skin and the messy wound on the back of her head, she might simply have surprised herself by stumbling.

"She's been dead less than an hour," Tom said.

"An hour ago we were on our way to Blanton's flat. Do you suppose, if we'd been quicker...?"

I swallowed back the wave of guilt that the question posed, and tried to be reasonable about the whole thing. "If he would have told us exactly where to go, maybe. It wasn't our fault that we had to hunt for the place."

I glanced at Gladys again. "Whoever did it must have been waiting for her to come home. It's a good thing St George resisted the urge to come upstairs."

"How do you know he did?" Tom wanted to know, and I turned to him.

"Resist, do you mean? He must have. Otherwise he'd be lying here himself, with his head bashed in, don't you think?"

His expression didn't change, and I added, "Surely you don't believe—?"

"Don't be silly, Pippa," Christopher said. "Crispin would never..."

He trailed off when he noticed the look on Tom's face. "You can't seriously think that my cousin had anything to do with this?"

"Of course not, Kit." Tom sounded impatient. "For one thing, you both claim that he was with you last night when Montrose got it."

"He was absolutely with us when Montrose got it," I said firmly. "And I'm not sure I appreciate the implication."

He didn't say anything, and I added, "But yes. All three of us were together in Blanton's sitting room. Crispin could not possibly have hit Montrose, nor would he have had any reason to do so. Even if Montrose planned to do an exposé on Lady Austin and the drag balls, Crispin wouldn't have been implicated in that. Everyone knows his reputation with women."

"He might have done it for someone else," Tom said, and he rather ostentatiously avoided looking at Christopher as he did it.

The latter took offense anyway. "If you think I would rather someone die than have it exposed that I go to drag balls..."

"Of course you wouldn't, Kit. But St George may not have known that."

"Of course he knows that," I said crossly. "He's not stupid. And if you knew how much it annoys me to have to admit that, you wouldn't make me do it. Besides, he would never cosh an old schoolmate over the head simply to spare Christopher embarrassment."

"Although that's all completely beside the point," Christopher added, "because he was in the sitting room with us when

Montrose was killed. Nor would he do…" he pointed at Gladys, "this. He may have his faults, I'm not saying he doesn't, but he's not the kind of man who hits women."

"And for your information," I said, hands on my hips and a scowl on my face, "the reason I said that he hadn't come upstairs with her, is that her clothes are on and her lipstick intact. He must have dropped her off outside the door, or outside the mews altogether, if he couldn't get the Hispano-Suiza to the door, and she walked the rest of the way on her own."

"If her job was to get him here for Hutchison or Ogilvie or Rivers to talk to," Tom said, "would she agree to that?"

"She may not have had a choice," Christopher answered. "Crispin is nothing if not stubborn. And he has good reasons for not wanting to toy with loads of women at the moment."

I snorted, because it seemed to me that he toyed with plenty of them. However— "The girl he wants to marry? I suppose so. Although it didn't stop him from flirting with Gladys last night."

"There's a big step from flirtation to what you're suggesting," Tom said. "Fine. I shall take your word for it that he had no opportunity to attack Montrose last night, and therefore no motive to attack Gladys Long today. But I will have to track him down to talk to him."

I couldn't imagine Christopher having a problem with that. I certainly didn't. In fact, if I could have snapped my fingers and had Crispin materialize in front of me right now, I would have done it. While I believed what I had told Tom—if St George had come upstairs with Gladys with the idea that they would share her bed, chances are she would have been more disheveled than she appeared—it was not impossible that he had come upstairs with her for another reason, and the other reason was the person who had killed her. If she had told him that Dominic Rivers was waiting, for example, Crispin might have decided to take the opportunity to talk to Rivers to find out what the other man knew about Montrose's death.

And then there was the possibility that not just Rivers, but Hutchison and/or Ogilvie had been here, and between them, they had killed Gladys and overpowered Crispin, and then taken him with them when they left.

Did I think that that had happened? Perhaps not. It was much more likely that he had simply dropped Gladys off at the door and gone on his way. But it wasn't impossible that something had gone wrong. So if I could have waved my magic wand and conjured him in front of us at that moment, I would have done it, if only so we could all be assured that he was in one piece.

"I shall have to make inquiries," Tom said thoughtfully, "after I call in the Yard. I'll have to go up and down the mews and knock on doors, I suppose. See what, if anything, anyone might have seen."

He turned to me and Christopher with sudden purpose. "You two had better make yourselves scarce. I'll walk you to the entrance to the mews and see if I can flag down a constable, while you go on home. There's no need for you to stick around, and much better if you don't."

Christopher opened his mouth, presumably to argue, and I took his arm. "Of course."

Tom gestured to the door, and I headed that way, towing Christopher behind me. Downstairs, Tom secured the front door as best he could without the key, before he led the way up the mews in the direction we had come.

We hadn't gone more than a few steps before a door opened on the other side of the narrow roadway, and a young woman a few years older than the two of us—around Tom's age, give or take a year—appeared.

She was dressed in the current fashion, a drop-waist dress and strap shoes, with a cloche hat pulled down over black curls. A pair of dark eyes surveyed us from under the brim.

"Good afternoon," Tom said, nudging the brim of his hat. "Have you seen the young woman who lives across the mews today? Miss Long?"

The neighbor peered past him to the house, and then looked at Christopher and me. "*He* ought to be able to tell you that," she said, nodding at him. "Dropped her off about an hour ago, didn't he?"

"Did he?" Tom shot a glance over his shoulder, a warning to us—or to Christopher, specifically, I suppose—not to speak. "An hour ago, you said?"

"About that." She put her hands on her hips and eyed him. "What's this about, then? Who are you?"

Tom told her who he was, complete with a flashing of credentials. "We're actually trying to find the young man you saw. He didn't come back after taking her home."

The young lady gave Christopher another look. "Twins, are they?" She didn't wait long enough for any of us to give her an answer, which was just as well, since they're not. "He didn't stay long. Walked her to the door, had to be convinced to come upstairs, it looked like, and then came back out a few minutes later, looking like he couldn't get away fast enough."

I wanted to look at Christopher, but decided it would probably be best if I didn't.

Of course, just because he'd been in a hurry didn't mean he'd killed her and was running away from the crime scene. She might have thrown herself at him, and he had wanted to get away from her before she gave pursuit.

That would not be quite in character, admittedly—I had yet to see St George run away from any woman, dead or alive— but if he was serious about this girl he claimed to be in love with, maybe it had taken effort to resist Gladys's attempts at seduction.

Or he might have watched someone else bash Gladys over the head when she walked through the door, and he'd run away before he could get bashed, too.

Tom must have followed that same train of thought, because by the time I came back to the conversation, he had inquired whether the young woman had seen anyone else go into Gladys's place today, with her or alone.

"She was brought to her door by a young man early this morning," the neighbor said, and went on to describe a man in evening dress who might have been Dominic Rivers, Nigel Hutchison, or Graham Ogilvie. Blanton's hair was too light to be called dark, even in the twilight before dawn, and of course both Crispin and Christopher are fair-haired. Not that either of them had brought Gladys home this morning. "He waited for the light to go on upstairs, and then he went back up the mews. Parked his car at the entrance, no doubt."

Tom nodded. "And you haven't seen anyone else come or go?"

"I saw her leave," the young woman said. "Just before eleven, that was. She walked out by herself. When she came back, she was with the young man." She shot a look at Christopher. "The twin."

"And nobody came by while she was out?"

"Nobody I saw," the neighbor told him. "But I wasn't keeping an eye on the door. I hear it bang sometimes, and if I'm near the window, I'll look out. But if I'm at the back of the house, then I won't hear it and won't look out." She stuck her hands on her hips. "Are you going to tell me what's happened?"

Tom hesitated, but considering that there would soon be other detectives, not to mention a mortuary car, showing up across the way, I assume he figured there was no reason to keep mum. "She's dead. We're trying to figure out how many people had access to her flat this morning."

"I only saw the one." She glanced at Christopher, and then at me. And she must have seen something in one or both of our faces, because she added, "But I was in the kitchen most of the morning. Any number of people could have come and gone through the front door if they were quiet about it. I only heard the young lady and gentleman—your brother," she nodded at Christopher, "because they were laughing."

"Getting along well," I said sourly, "were they?"

"They certainly looked like they did." She eyed me for a second before she turned her attention back to Tom. "If he did something to her, he went from happy and laughing to murderous in very few minutes."

"It happens," Tom said, although he must have felt both Christopher and me staring daggers at him, because he added, "yes, yes. I know. He wouldn't have."

"No," Christopher said tightly, "he wouldn't."

"And you didn't see anyone else approach the place?"

The young woman shook her head. "But as I said, I wasn't keeping watch, and most of the morning, I was on the other side. Someone could easily have come and gone, and I wouldn't have noticed."

Tom nodded. "Thank you for your time."

He turned to walk away, but halted when she said, "Is this... Was she... Do I have to worry about...?"

Someone attacking her, she meant. If someone had attacked Gladys, were the other young women in the area likely to get attacked, too?

I shook my head. "Not at all," Tom confirmed. "It was personal, and related to something that happened last night. Nothing to do with you or anyone else. You don't have to worry."

She looked relieved.

"If you remember anything else, or you happen to notice someone coming around after we're finished here today, I would appreciate if you'd let me know." He pulled a card out of his pocket and handed it to her.

She looked at it. "Detective Sergeant Gardiner?"

Tom nodded.

"A pleasure to meet you." She dimpled at him under the cloche, and next to me, Christopher's eyes narrowed. "Are you headed out? I'll walk with you, if you don't mind." She turned towards the entrance to the mews, and Tom did the same. As we fell in behind them, I reached down and took Christopher's hand. It was stiff in mine for the first second, and then he relaxed.

"It's going to be all right," I told him.

He glanced down at me, a flash of blue. "I feel like I should be the one telling you that, Pippa. You seem to be more worried about Crispin than I am."

That hadn't been what I was referring to—I was talking about Tom, currently striding along ahead of us, in pleasant conversation with a woman he'd just met—but now that he mentioned it...

"Aren't you worried?"

He shrugged. "I suppose I am. A little. Although unlike you, I know that he wouldn't do something like this."

"I know that, too, Christopher!"

"Do you?" He eyed me. "Because it's just over a month since you were convinced, and tried to convince me, that he had murdered not just Grimsby, but Grandfather."

"That was different," I said crossly. "It made sense. I made a very good case for why he might have done that. There were motives and means and opportunities and everything. There's no reason at all why he would have done this."

"If she came on to him and wouldn't let go...?"

"Don't be ridiculous, Christopher," I said. "She wasn't a succubus. It's not as if he doesn't know how to extricate himself from women when he's done with them, you know. I heard him let Laetitia Marsden down at the Dower House last month. She kept pushing him to marry her, and he made it very clear that he wouldn't."

"I didn't hear that," Christopher said, his tone interested.

"You were asleep," I answered. "Or unconscious. Whichever that overlarge dose of Veronal did to you. I was upstairs on the landing, and he was talking to Lady Laetitia in your room. Besides, you know what happened with Johanna before she died. He turned her down flat, too. If Gladys did anything he didn't like, he would have dealt with it, and her, and not by killing her."

Christopher nodded, and I added, "And unlike Tom, who wasn't there, you and I know perfectly well that he had nothing to do with what happened to Freddie Montrose. He was with us, and neither of us killed Montrose. It makes sense that whoever did that, did this."

"Because Gladys knew what happened," Christopher said.

I nodded. "I'm not concerned that Tom is going to lose his mind and arrest St George. I am—or at least I was, before we ran into Tom's new best friend—"

Christopher snorted.

"—concerned that Rivers and company got hold of him. But if he left here under his own power, and only a few minutes after he walked in, he must be all right. He's probably on his way home, like you said."

"I'm sure he is. Hopefully he'll be all right when he hears that Gladys is dead."

Lord, yes. Johanna had been killed after St George turned down her advances. If Gladys had been snuffed out after the same sort of scene, I could only imagine the effect it would have. Crispin is highly strung and prone to drama anyway. He would probably imagine himself as some sort of jinx who got women murdered when he said no to them. And God only knew what he would start doing then.

"I shall have to set him straight," I said, more to myself than Christopher.

"If anyone can do it," Christopher answered dryly, "it's you, Pippa."

WE PARTED from Tom and his new admirer outside the entrance to the mews. And we did it without a word. Or at least without much of one.

"You know where to find us," I told Tom, and he nodded, distracted both by the young lady, who was still hanging prettily on his every word, and by the need to flag down a constable for backup.

Christopher said nothing, and I noticed Tom glancing at him once or twice. But of course he was busy, and we had an audience, and were in public, and anything beyond what I had already said would be too much. So I smiled politely, and Christopher nodded, and then Christopher and I set off up the pavement towards the nearest tube station, while Tom focused on getting the attention of the constable who was making his slow and ponderous way towards the mews.

"Home?" Christopher wanted to know as we approached the underground.

I glanced at him. "I'd rather go to Royal Albert Hall and see if we can find Hutchison and Ogilvie. If we show up out of the blue, it's possible that one of them gives something away, about Gladys or about who might have hit Montrose."

And if they didn't, we might at least be able to assume that neither of them had had anything to do with it. Or perhaps not. But Tom was clearly going to be busy with Gladys's body for a few hours yet. And he had nothing to tie Gladys to Nigel Hutchison or Graham Ogilvie, nothing beyond the confidential information we had passed him last night, so we might as well do what we could as amateur sleuths, at least until we were taken off the case.

"It's a nice afternoon for a stroll," Christopher said agreeably, which I took to mean that he had made the same calculations I had made, and come to the same conclusions.

We came up into the sunlight again at Knightsbridge, and from there we strolled the kilometer along Carriage Way, with the city on one side of us and the green grass and trees of Hyde Park on the other. The bright sun and blue sky of the Sunday afternoon were almost impossible to reconcile with the four people—or three people and a detective—who had disposed of a dead body under the trees across the street in the darkness of last night.

The red brick and white trim of the Albert Hall Mansions was visible from several blocks away, but it wasn't until we had rounded the corner of Kensington Gore that we saw the dome of Royal Albert Hall itself, with the elegant façade of the Albert Court Mansions beyond.

"No H6," I commented, looking around at the various parked motorcars.

Christopher shook his head. "He's on his way home, Pippa. Safe and sound."

He put his head back and peered up at the nearest building. "It's enormous."

It was. And there were several other buildings, too, all equally large. "It's a pity Blanton couldn't give us better directions than he did. A green door isn't going to be much help this time."

Christopher shook his head. "If he's right about them sharing a suite on the attic level, that's somewhere to start, though. And each building must have a commissionaire, don't you think?"

I would expect so. These were expensive flats, more expensive than mine and Christopher's, and both Hutchison and Ogilvie must be well off, if they were part of Crispin's set. The Society of Bright Young Persons isn't open to the working classes, only to the upper echelon who can afford not to work for a living.

And yes, I do know that I can count myself among that number, as Christopher is basically keeping me—or perhaps it's a little more appropriate, and not so pejorative, to say that his parents are keeping both of us. We would probably be welcome in the Society, or at least Christopher would. My heritage tends to preclude me from that sort of thing. One-half German is still too German for post-War England.

At any rate, the mansion flats were such that they should certainly have a commissionaire on duty.

"Shall we inquire?" Christopher suggested, and led the way into the nearest block.

CHAPTER THIRTEEN

WE GOT LUCKY, as it happened. Misters Hutchison and Ogilvie were residents of the first mansion block we walked into. The porter confirmed that the pair lived on the "bachelor level," or in other words, the attics.

"Would Mr. Hutchison or Mr. Ogilvie be at home to visitors?" Christopher asked.

The porter suggested that he might inquire.

"So they're at home?" I asked. "You haven't seen them leave?"

The porter looked at me down the length of his nose. "Shall I just inquire, madam?"

Not a gossip, then. I sighed and nodded. "Yes, please."

The porter rang upstairs. And someone was at home, because the porter said politely, "Lady and gentleman to see you, Mr. Hutchison."

"Mr. Christopher Astley and Miss Philippa Darling," Christopher told him.

The porter repeated it, and gave Hutchison a second to respond. Which he must have done with vigor, because the porter went into a litany of yeses and nos, culminating in, "I haven't seen him this afternoon, sir."

I opened my mouth to tell him that if Hutchison was inquiring about Crispin, we were looking for him, too. Christopher put his foot on my toe and applied pressure, and I closed my mouth again.

"Yes, sir," the porter said. "Right away, sir."

He nodded to us. "Take the lift up to the seventh floor. Mr. Hutchison will meet you."

Lovely.

When we exited the lift on the top floor, Hutchison was waiting.

He was perfectly put together, in the same type of casual flannel bags that Christopher was sporting, and the same kind of knit jumper.

You may wonder about the jumpers, seeing as we were past St George's birthday and almost a week into June.

England is cold and gray a lot of the time, and this year, June was no exception. We had started the month with eleven degrees on the first, and although things were warming up a bit by now, overcoats and pullovers were still *de rigueur*. If we were lucky, we might get something that resembled summer in July or August, but for right now, it still felt a long way off.

At any rate, Hutchison was dressed in weekend casual, and his expression when he eyed us was part suspicion, part worry. "Miss Darling. Mr. Astley."

"Hutchison," Christopher said smoothly. "We were hoping to find my cousin."

Hutchison blinked. "St George? Why? Was he coming to see us?"

The blink looked genuine, as if he'd been sincerely surprised by the suggestion, but of course that kind of thing is easy to counterfeit.

"We thought he might," I said. "He left our flat with Miss Gladys Long. When he didn't come back, we went to Mr. Blanton's flat first, since we knew where it was. When St George wasn't there, Blanton gave us your direction, and we came here next."

"St George went off with Gladys? He'd be at her place, then, wouldn't he?"

"We don't know where to find it," I said plainly. "Blanton talked about a mews in Belgravia, and a green door, but he didn't know which one. He knew where you lived, so we came here first."

"I see." Hutchison's lips twitched. "Well, Gladys lives in the Ellery Mews, number 13, and I haven't seen St George so far today."

"Thank you." Christopher turned toward the lift, and Hutchison added, "Not so fast."

Christopher turned back, brows elevated. So were mine. I could have sworn that Hutchison had been chivvying us along as quickly as possible, but perhaps his tone and his desires were at odds.

"Yes?"

Hutchison looked around, furtively. There was no one visible on the landing, but he gestured to the door to his flat. "Come inside."

Christopher glanced at me. I shrugged. I did take a bit better of a grip on my reticule, however, as we followed Hutchison toward the door to the flat.

"After you." He bowed me inside.

I could tell that Christopher was on the verge of offering to go first, and that would rather give away the fact that we were worried about being attacked, so I shot him a look of warning and raised my head high as I passed through the door into the flat.

Nothing hit me on the back of the head, and I relaxed my grip on the bag.

"Is Mr. Ogilvie not home?" Christopher asked as he entered behind me, with a quick glance around.

We were standing in a foyer, not dissimilar to the one in the Essex House Mansions. Parquet floor, tall ceilings, ornate cornices. The room was bigger and the ceilings taller than the ones at home, but the parquet floors were the same.

Hutchison shook his head. "Gram went out. May I take your coat, Miss Darling?"

He hovered expectantly.

"That's all right," I told him. "I doubt we'll be staying long."

"We just wanted to know if you'd seen Crispin," Christopher added. "Or Miss Long."

"I haven't seen either of them today," Hutchison said promptly.

"You didn't drop Miss Long off outside our place and send her upstairs to talk to my cousin?"

Hutchison shook his head. "Is that what she said I did? If she went there, she went on her own. Or with someone else."

"Why would she lie about it?"

"No idea," Hutchison said. "I assume she might have wanted to know what happened last night, but I didn't speak to her."

He gestured to the door at the end of the foyer. "I want to know that, too, now that you're here. Come in and have a seat. Drink?"

I declined. Someone had almost killed me with a poisoned drink a month ago—and had put Christopher out for several days when he drank it instead. In this situation, and with this group of people, it was far safer not to take any chances.

Not that Hutchison seemed particularly homicidal at the moment. He came across as a rather pleasant young man without a care in the world. If he had killed Gladys—and he might have; Ogilvie wasn't here to give him an alibi—it hadn't had much of an effect on him. He'd been far more distraught last night, or this morning, over Montrose.

"It's not much of a story," Christopher said, and perched on the arm of the chair I dropped into. "We loaded the body into Crispin's motorcar and drove back to Rectors. By the time we got there, the street was covered with constables and police cars. I even saw the Flying Bedstead."

"Did you?" I said, looking up at him. "I didn't notice it."

He nodded. "It was there. Parked on the other side of the street. At any rate, we couldn't unload Montrose's body. And after a minute of watching, someone noticed the H6 and started coming toward us. So we bloused out of there and over to Hyde Park. We left him under a tree."

Hutchison looked taken aback, perhaps at the abrupt end to the story. "And no one saw you?"

"If anyone had been there," I said, "we wouldn't have done it."

He nodded. "And the police didn't recognize St George's motorcar? They're fairly familiar with it."

"If anyone did, they didn't come looking for him at ours," Christopher said evenly. "If someone went to Sutherland House to look for him, we wouldn't know about it."

"But they also wouldn't have found him," I added. "And now, I assume, he's on his way home. You really haven't seen him this morning?"

Hutchison shook his head. "I haven't seen anyone. Gram was here when I woke up, but that's all."

"Where did he go? And when?"

Could he have been the one to drop Gladys off? Or the one to kill her? Or was Hutchison simply lying, and he himself had dealt with Gladys?

He eyed me for a moment before he said, "He didn't say."

"How many ways out of this building?"

Hutchison's lips twitched. "Two. Front door and back stairs."

So Ogilvie—or for that matter Hutchison himself—might have left and come back without being seen by anyone.

"What happened last night?" Christopher cut in. Hutchison looked at him, sort of blankly, and he added, "We were in Blanton's sitting room. Montrose left, and then the rest of you followed. The next time we saw you, he was dead and you were all standing around the body."

"Someone killed him," Hutchison said.

Christopher nodded. "That much we know. We thought perhaps you'd give us a little more information."

Hutchison eyed us both for a moment in silence. "Wouldn't you rather not know?"

"I would rather it hadn't happened at all," I said honestly. "I feel terrible about it."

He sighed. "Believe me, so do I. I had nothing against Freddie Montrose. We went to school together. We were friends, of a sort."

After a moment, he added, "Of course, the fact that he—an Honorable, of all things—chose to go to work for that awful tabloid and dig up dirt on all his friends... well, it was difficult to reconcile that with friendship. But I certainly didn't want him dead."

"Who did?"

He glanced at me. "I don't know."

It was impossible to say whether he was telling the truth or not. He looked and sounded like he was telling the truth, but if he had killed Montrose, he had every incentive for not admitting it.

"How can you not know?" Christopher asked. "You were there."

"So were you. And you don't know."

"We got there after it happened," I said. "We were still in the sitting room when Montrose was hit."

He eyed me. "Well, so was I. By the time I got to the butler's pantry, he was on the floor, bleeding."

Again, it was impossible to tell whether it was true or not. It might have been. Or he might have been shielding whoever had killed Montrose. There was just no way to know.

"What happened after we left last night? Or this morning?"

"We cleaned up," Hutchison said. "Wiped the blood off the floor, cleaned the rolling pin in the sink—couldn't get rid of that; Dobbins would notice—but we took the dirty towels with us when we left."

"And did what with them?"

"Left them in a rubbish bin halfway between here and Mayfair," Hutchison said. "We put Ronnie to bed—he had crashed by then—while Rivers took Gladys home. And Gram and I came back here."

And went to bed, I assumed. I hoped they'd spent a restless night, although to look at Nigel Hutchison now, with his rosy cheeks and bright eyes, that didn't seem likely.

"And you really don't know where Ogilvie went this morning?" Christopher asked, and Hutchison turned to him.

"You would have to ask him."

"He didn't tell you where he was going?" Or did Hutchison just not want to tell us?

"We don't live in each other's pockets," Hutchison said. "He said, 'I'm going out for a while, Hutch,' and he left. I was still in bed."

"So he left early?"

"Early enough, considering how late we got in. Why so many questions?"

Wasn't it obvious? I was attempting to determine who had had the opportunity to kill Gladys Long.

But because we hadn't mentioned Gladys's death, or the fact that we knew about it, I was severely limited in what I could do.

"Just curious," I said, and Hutchison nodded. "So you've been home alone."

"Most of the day, yes. I was thinking I might go by Ronnie's place and see how he's holding up. You said you saw him earlier. How was he?"

"Rough," Christopher said. "It's been a while since he's had a fix, and it shows."

Hutchison rolled his eyes. "What happened yesterday probably scared Dom off, and now he won't come back. I guess I'll have to go and deal with it."

"Is there a reason Blanton can't deal with it himself?" fell out of my mouth, and Hutchison glanced at me.

"He doesn't always think straight, you know?"

Clearly. Especially not under the current circumstances. "Could he have killed Montrose, if he thought Montrose was going to expose Rivers and perhaps get him arrested?"

Hutchison's face closed up. "You'd have to ask him," he said again.

I waited, and after a moment, he added, seemingly reluctantly, "He's not much of a fighter. That's why he likes to escape."

I nodded encouragingly, showing him that I could certainly relate to that.

Not personally, of course. I have no problem being combative. Some people—whose names might be Crispin Astley—would say I'm too combative for my own good.

Or rather, it's probably Christopher who would say it. Crispin doesn't seem to mind my antagonistic attitude, or at least he gives as good as he gets. And Christopher, for all that he's much less aggressive than I am, has no escapist streak, either. It's Crispin who likes to drown his sorrows in women, alcohol, and fast motorcars.

"Difficult home life?" I suggested.

That's Crispin's problem, after all. If his family—or his father—would just let him do as he wants, and would let him marry the woman he thinks would make him happy, even if she isn't a suitable wife for the future Duke of Sutherland, he'd have no need to escape.

Perhaps the same was true for Ronald Blanton.

Hutchison eyed me narrowly. "What do you know about it?"

"Not much," I admitted readily. "My parents are dead. But I have a few people in my life who have a habit of escaping into things that aren't necessarily good for them, and in at least one case, it's a parental problem."

While in Francis's situation, of course, it went back to the war.

Which put Blanton's and Crispin's indulgences in perspective, when I thought about it. What, after all, did they have to escape from, compared to the memories of death and destruction that keeps Francis up at night?

"Ronnie's father is an arse," Hutchison said. "If he wasn't such a tosser, Ronnie wouldn't be the way he is."

That might very well be true. If Uncle Harold wasn't the way he is, chances are that Crispin would be different, as well.

Then again, Crispin is responsible for his own actions, and the choices that lead to them. And so was Ronald Blanton. His father surely wouldn't actually want Ronnie to be sniffing cocaine at every opportunity. Ronnie himself had made that choice. In exactly the same way that Uncle Harold didn't want Crispin to carry on the way he did. Crispin chose to do it. Quite possibly in order to punish or otherwise simply annoy his father, but it was nonetheless his own doing, and not Uncle Harold's.

"We'll just carry on," Christopher said into the silence, "and let you do the same. Miss Long lives in Ellery Mews, you said?"

Hutchison nodded. "Number 13. With a green door."

We thanked him for the help, even though it was information we already had, and took our leave, while Hutchison went off to prepare himself to rescue Ronnie Blanton.

"WHAT DO YOU THINK?" I asked Christopher when we were back on the ground level and on our way back towards the Knightsbridge tube station. "Would Hutchison's need to take care of Blanton extend to committing murder for him?"

Christopher glanced over at me. "I shouldn't wonder. He seemed quite protective of Blanton. And quite upset about his father."

I nodded. "He showed no sign of knowing that anything had happened to Gladys, though."

Christopher shook his head. "But he could just be a good liar. He was alone in the flat. That means he could have left and gone to Belgravia and come back without anyone knowing. Ogilvie was gone, and he said there was a back entrance he could have used so the doorman wouldn't have seen him."

"It was interesting that he denied dropping Gladys off at our flat this morning. She said he had."

"One of them was lying," Christopher agreed. "But it might have been Gladys. If she wanted Crispin to give her a lift back."

"There was no need to mention Hutchison if it wasn't true,

though. She might have simply said, 'I came here on my own.' It would have accomplished the same thing."

"That's true."

"So why would Hutchison lie about it? And if he didn't want to admit to having done it, why not make sure to tell her not to mention it?"

"No idea," Christopher said. "I'm not sure why it would even matter. Although, if he did kill Gladys, he might not want to admit to having left the Albert Hall Mansions. If he didn't leave, he couldn't have done it, after all."

"Should we go back and ask the doorman what he noticed about Hutchison's and Ogilvie's comings and goings?"

"He wouldn't tell us even if we did," Christopher said, looking left and right to cross the street. "Better to tell Tom what Hutchison said and have him ask. The porter would have to tell Tom the truth, I assume."

I would assume the same, although, as we all know, it can be dangerous to rely on assumptions.

"You spent a bit of time talking to Graham Ogilvie before the whole thing fell apart last night," I said. "At Rectors and in Blanton's flat later. What was your impression of him?"

Christopher didn't answer immediately, and I added, "Did he strike you as someone who could commit murder? Or as someone who uses dope? Just because Blanton and Gladys were the only two people Rivers fixed up last night, doesn't mean that some of the others might not be indulging, as well. Once Montrose was discovered to be dead, everything else fell by the wayside."

Christopher nodded. "It was loud in Rectors, so it wasn't as if we could have much of a heart to heart. He mostly asked whether I went to the balls a lot, and whether I always got dressed up, and things like that. I avoided being specific, since you never know who you might be talking to..."

He trailed off with a grimace. "He didn't strike me as a constable in mufti—not that intoxicated and with the group of friends he had—but it never hurts to be careful."

No, it didn't. The buggery laws are still on the books, and arrest and conviction can result in anything from fines to hard labor. Admitting to anything at all would have been quite stupid of Christopher, and he's not.

"Did you form an impression as to why he was asking?" I wanted to know.

He shot me a look. "I got the impression that it was more of a personal interest."

"Oh, really?" I smirked.

"Not like that, Pippa. He wasn't trying to flirt with me. It was more that he was interested in the balls and the lifestyle than in me personally."

"For his own sake?"

"Or someone else's," Christopher said. "And to answer your question, he didn't strike me as particularly homicidal. Or even particularly upset with Frederick Montrose. He didn't sit there and scowl at him or anything of that nature. As far as I can recall, he didn't say a single word about him. No, wait..."

"Yes?" I said.

"He asked me whether I knew him. I said no, that Crispin was the one who had gone to Cambridge with Montrose, not me."

I tucked my hand through his arm. "We went to Oxford."

Christopher nodded and patted it. "We did."

"And I got a degree." I smiled, self-satisfied.

"You did," Christopher agreed. "You wouldn't have done if you'd gone to Cambridge."

No, I wouldn't. A year after Oxford matriculated the first woman in 1920, Cambridge University had held a vote on doing the same thing, and instead of awarding women degrees, the day—October 20th, 1921—had ended with fourteen hundred male students rioting at Newnham College, breaking down the gates and threatening the two-hundred-odd female students.

In fact, here we were, in the summer of 1926, almost five years later, and female Cambridge students still weren't full members of the university.

"I wonder if St George was there," I said thoughtfully. "He was at Cambridge in the fall of 1921, wasn't he?"

"We were at Oxford in the fall of 1921," Christopher answered, "so I assume so. What—?"

I told him, and he shook his head. "Oh, no. I hardly think he would have taken part in terrorizing women students, Pippa."

"He's quite fond of terrorizing me," I pointed out, even if, perhaps, calling it terrorizing was a step too far.

Christopher slanted me a look. "He's not really, you know. He respects you. Perhaps not to your face—"

There was no 'perhaps' about that.

"—but he's not a chauvinist. He may play fast and loose with a lot of girls' affections..."

"May?" I inquired.

"But they're not girls who are likely to be hurt by it. He doesn't seduce the servants, or anyone who isn't perfectly well aware of what he's doing. No one who isn't willing to play along."

Perhaps not.

"I hope he's all right," I said.

Christopher nodded. "I do, too."

CHAPTER FOURTEEN

WE DECIDED to take afternoon tea at the Ritz, since we were in the neighborhood anyway. And if you wonder how the Royal Albert Hall and Knightsbridge come to be in the neighborhood of the Ritz Hotel, it was because we also decided to go by Sutherland House in Mayfair on our way home, just to ascertain that Crispin wasn't there.

There was absolutely no reason to think he'd be there, of course. He ought to be somewhere in Hampshire by now, if not actually into Wiltshire itself. At the very least, he should be moving through Surrey at quite a slow pace. But because there was no way to know for certain where he was, and because Sutherland House had a telephone we could use to ring up the Hall and inquire of Tidwell the butler whether Crispin had made it home, we decided we might as well take advantage of it. The weather was pleasant, if a touch on the cool side—all the better for walking around London—and afternoon tea at the Ritz is always a pleasant experience.

Thus fortified, we set out towards Sutherland House, and arrived some twenty minutes later, to ring the bell.

"Rogers," Christopher said when the door opened, and slipped past the butler into the marble foyer of the elegant old townhouse. "We're looking for my cousin."

There was a beat as Rogers shut the door behind us and turned to eye him. "I'm sorry, Master Christopher. I'm afraid his lordship isn't here."

He glanced at me, and for a second something flickered across his face before it turned impassive again. He inclined his head in something halfway between a nod and bow. "Miss Darling."

"Rogers," I said. "It's been a while."

Christopher and I had come up to Sutherland House occasionally when we were younger and had been living with Christopher's parents at Beckwith Place. But the Town house had been in use more by Duke Henry himself while he'd been alive, and by Uncle Harold and Aunt Charlotte, and over the past couple of years by Crispin. Christopher and I didn't come here a lot. It was perhaps not surprising that Rogers should be taken aback to see us now.

"He hasn't been by?"

Rogers shook his head. "No, Master Christopher. His Grace was here this morning looking for him."

"He found him," I said, and when Rogers turned a politely inquiring eyebrow my way, I added, "He spent the night with us. St George did, I mean. His Grace—Uncle Harold—showed up at the flat this morning looking for him."

Rogers nodded. "It might have been suggested that he should try there."

Oh, might it, really?

"Who suggested it?" I wanted to know, since the passive tense made it appear as if Rogers was trying to avoid responsibility for siccing Uncle Harold on us.

But before I could get an answer, Christopher entered back

into the conversation. "Never mind that right now. We last saw him—saw them both—around midday. Did either of them come back here?"

"No, Master Christopher," Rogers said. "No one has been here since His Grace left with Wilkins this morning."

"Would you mind if we made use of the telephone?"

Rogers twitched a brow. "Of course not, Master Christopher. Who will you be ringing up?"

"Sutherland Hall," Christopher said. "I want to know if Crispin made it home."

"Of course." Rogers gave another of those not-quite-bows. "Allow me."

"If you please, Rogers." It was abundantly clear that Rogers didn't want either of us to do it, after all.

"This way." Rogers led the way out of the foyer and down the hall, into the nearest parlor. There was a telephone on a table by the wall. "Just a moment, Master Christopher."

He headed that way, picked up the ear piece, and issued an order into the mouth piece. Seconds passed. Then—

"Good afternoon, Sutherland Hall. This is Rogers at Sutherland House in Town. I have Mr. Christopher Astley here for Lord St George. Is he available?"

A faint buzzing or quacking noise issued from the ear piece. Rogers grimaced. "I see. And His Grace?"

There was more buzzing.

"One moment, Tidwell," Rogers said, and dropped his hand from his ear to address Christopher. "Tidwell says that his lordship has not yet made it home. His Grace got there several hours ago."

As he should have, if he had left London when he said he was going to. Crispin had taken Gladys home after that. Although he ought still, in my estimation, have made it home by now. Or at least he ought to be close to it.

"Let me talk to him," Christopher said and reached for the ear piece. After a moment he added, "Please."

Rogers relinquished it, although in my opinion he did it reluctantly. Christopher put the receiver to his ear. "Is that you, Tidwell? This is Christopher Astley. Is my cousin not home yet?"

The receiver quacked.

"M-hm," Christopher said. "M-hm. Well, I tell you what, Tidwell—"

But Tidwell must not have wanted to be told what, because he spoke again.

"I see," Christopher said. "Yes, I quite understand, Tidwell. But listen here—"

Tidwell didn't want to do that either, obviously, because he continued to speak.

"Give him to me," I said impatiently and snatched the receiver away from Christopher's ear. Really, if you want something done right, you're better off doing it yourself. "Tidwell, this is Pippa Darling. Is St George not home yet?"

"No, Miss Darling," Tidwell said.

"Well, something's happened here in Town that he needs to know about. When he comes in, will you tell him that Christopher or I shall find a telephone box later this evening, and ring back? And for him to make sure he's available when we do?"

Tidwell said he'd pass on the message whenever Crispin (at long last) showed up, and I thanked him and was about to disconnect when something crossed my mind. "Tidwell?"

"Yes, Miss Darling?"

"At what time did Uncle Harold come back this afternoon?"

"His Grace arrived at four-fifteen," Tidwell said. "In the Crossley with Wilkins."

Not enough time for Uncle Harold—or I suppose Wilkins the chauffeur—to have murdered Gladys Long, then. Not that I thought either of them would have wanted to. But it was just as well to have it established that they couldn't have.

"Thank you, Tidwell," I said. Tidwell assured me that he was happy to be of service, and we hung up on mutual goodbyes.

"What on earth, Pippa—" Christopher said, appalled, and I shrugged.

"It's just as well to be certain."

"Why on earth would Uncle Harold want to murder Gladys Long?"

Rogers choked on what must have been an inhalation, and Christopher glanced at him before he turned his attention back to me. "It wasn't as if Crispin was serious about her, you know. And even if he were, Uncle Harold might actually approve. She's an Honorable, after all, and one hundred percent British."

Yes, she was. Unlike yours truly, not to mention whoever the girl was that Crispin fancied. That was part of what Uncle Harold had against her, apparently. She was both foreign and common, according to what we—Christopher and I—had heard Uncle Harold hiss at his son through Crispin's sitting room door back in April. Gladys was—had been—neither foreign nor common, so truly, the whole thing had probably been a bit of obsessive madness on my part.

And speaking of obsessive madness...

"Rogers," I said. "Tell me about the girl with the baby."

Rogers looked partly appalled, probably at the suggestion that Uncle Harold had killed anyone, and partly nonplussed. The conversation must be moving too fast for him. "Pardon me, Miss Darling?"

"The girl," I said. "With the baby. The one who showed up

here a few months ago and suggested that St George was the baby's father."

The one I had learned about back in April, and whom I had been curious about ever since.

Rogers's face cleared, although he said, "That's not precisely what happened, Miss Darling. The young woman showed up looking for His Grace's grandson."

And how was that any different from what I had articulated?

"You mean, she didn't ask for him by name? Lord St George?"

Or Crispin Astley, I suppose. This had happened before Duke Henry died, so Crispin had been a mere Honorable back then.

Rogers shook his head. "No, Miss Darling. 'The old Duke's grandson,' was what she said. She didn't use any name at all."

But Crispin was the one who occasionally used Sutherland House as his love nest while in Town, so he was the obvious culprit. His Grace, the late Duke, had had more than one grandson, however.

I turned to Christopher. "Anything you'd like to say?"

He stared at me, appalled. "Good grief, Pippa. You're accusing me now?"

"You're a grandson of the old Duke's too, aren't you? If it wasn't Crispin who got her with child..."

I trailed off, blinking, as we both realized the corollary. If it hadn't been Crispin's doing, and it certainly hadn't been Christopher's, then the only other option was Francis.

"No," Christopher said, shaking his head. "That's not possible."

Of course it was possible. And it was certainly more likely than that Christopher was the guilty party. Although it was still possible that Crispin was lying, or that he simply didn't remember. The way he carried on, I wouldn't be surprised. If Ronald Blanton could forget a murder in his own flat, Crispin could certainly have forgotten one of the several dozen women he must have bedded in the last year or two.

"Thank you, Rogers," I said, although he had given me precious little to be grateful for. I was sorry I had asked, to be honest. "I don't suppose she left a name or a direction?"

Rogers shook his head, but volunteered the following information. "She wasn't someone we had seen before, Miss Darling. When the young master brings a woman by, they're usually loud enough that we get a look at her."

Yes, the staff at Sutherland House had gotten a look at an even dozen or so women over the past year, all of whose names they had shared with Grimsby, who had shared them with His Grace, the late Duke Henry, and with Crispin's father. He had also noted them down in his book. And then, somehow, the pages had ended up in my possession—an event which had never been satisfactorily explained, by the way; at least not as far as I was concerned—so now I knew the names of all the women St George had dallied with recently, too.

"If Lord St George should happen to phone," I told Rogers, "or turn up in person, will you tell him that we're looking for him?"

"Yes, Rogers," Christopher added, "please do."

Rogers inclined his head. "Certainly, Master Christopher. I'll let him know."

Wonderful. I had gotten the distinct impression that until Christopher added his exhortations to mine, Rogers hadn't planned to do a thing, which was galling, but at least now he had promised.

"Whatever possessed you to check Uncle Harold's alibi, Pippa?" Christopher wanted to know when we were back outside Sutherland House and standing on the pavement with the door shut behind us. This close to midsummer, the evenings were long, but dusk had started to creep in along the bottom edges of the buildings.

I opened my mouth, but before I managed to get anything out, a motorcar bounced up to the curb in front of us.

"There you are," a voice said, and Tom's face appeared in the opening between the door and the roof. "I should have guessed I'd find you here."

"If you're looking for St George," I said, "they haven't seen him."

"Nor have they seen my Uncle Harold since he left this morning," Christopher added, coming up to stand next to me. "He's back home. We rang up Sutherland Hall. But Crispin hasn't made it back to Wiltshire yet."

Tom's brows furrowed, what we could see of them beneath the Homburg. "He should have made it back by now, shouldn't he?"

"One would think," I agreed. "Especially with the way he drives."

Fast, and without much care for comfort or whoever else might share the car or the road with him.

"Although the way he normally drives," Christopher added, "makes it more likely that he might have gotten into an accident between here and there, too, I suppose."

Wonderful. Something else to worry about.

"We told Tidwell to tell him that we want to speak to him," I said. "We planned to find a call box later on this evening, and try again."

Tom cogitated for a moment. He looked from me to Christopher, to the polished stone façade of Sutherland House behind us, and back to me and then finally to Christopher. And seemed to make a decision. "Hop in."

"Pardon me?"

"Get in the car," Tom reiterated.

"Why? Where are you taking us?"

"To Wiltshire," Tom said. "You're both standing here worrying, and I must speak to St George anyway. He was the last person seen leaving Gladys Long's home this afternoon, and as such—"

As such, he was a suspect. He had to be.

"Surely you don't think—" I began, dismayed, but desisted when Christopher nudged me.

"Just climb into the back of the motorcar, Pippa. If he's willing to take us with him, don't you think we ought to go?"

Perhaps we ought. Or rather, we certainly ought to go. If I had had a motorcar of my own, I would have been halfway to Wiltshire in it myself by now.

"It'll be quite late by the time we arrive..." I demurred.

"So we'll prevail on Mrs. Mason to put us up for the night," Christopher said. "It's not as if Sutherland Hall doesn't have plenty of empty bedrooms. Although if she refuses—or if Uncle Harold does—we'll drive to Beckwith Place and have Mother do it. She won't mind."

If we turned up at the doors to Beckwith Place past midnight, begging for shelter because Uncle Harold had turned us away, I didn't imagine Aunt Roz would be exactly pleased— neither with the late hour of our arrival or with Uncle Harold— but yes, Christopher was most likely right: she would take us in and prepare rooms for us. And Beckwith Place wasn't *that* far from Sutherland Hall.

"Fine," I said, and crawled into the backseat of the Crossley after which Christopher climbed into the front seat next to Tom. "But only because I really am worried."

"We both are," Christopher told me and shut the door before nodding to Tom.

.   .   .

THREE QUARTERS OF AN HOUR LATER, we had put London behind us for the upper parts of Surrey, and Tom had updated us on the investigation as it stood.

"There was nothing in Miss Long's flat to point to any culprit other than St George. The—"

"What do you mean," Christopher interrupted, "*other than Crispin?* Surely you don't think that Crispin—"

"He was there," Tom said. "He was seen leaving the premises at around the time that Miss Long died. And he seems to have vanished. That's a sign of guilt, if ever there was one."

"Don't be ridiculous," I told him. "You know as well as I do that he'd never do something like that. If he was going to kill someone, it would be me, not Gladys Long."

Christopher opened his mouth, presumably to protest, and I carried on as if I hadn't noticed. "And he wouldn't bash her over the head. It would be so very easy for someone who knew her to make Gladys Long's death look like an accident. All anyone would have to do, would be to give her an overdose of something."

I waited politely, but when neither of them spoke up, I added, "All her friends surely knew that she took dope. Everyone in Blanton's flat last night knew it. Crispin certainly knew, probably before last night. He spoke of it as if it was commonly known. If he had wanted her dead, he could have joined her in a spot of cocaine, made sure she got more than was good for her, and left her there, with the dope. And voila, accidental overdose. Or even suicide, if someone wanted to pin Montrose's murder on her."

Tom still didn't protest, so I went on, "As we saw yesterday, she was certainly amenable to taking dope from Dominic Rivers. She might have been equally amenable to taking it from someone else. Certainly from St George; she was cuddling up to him all last night, and she did her best to cut Flossie

Schlomsky dead this morning. If he offered her cocaine, she would have trusted him and taken it. And he's not stupid, so he'd know all this. If for some reason he wanted Gladys dead, he would have done it in a way where he didn't look guilty. He would certainly have made sure that no one saw him coming or going from her place."

"That's if it was premeditated," Tom said. "If it wasn't..."

"If it wasn't, things must have gone from laughing and joking to murderous in a hurry. You heard what your new friend said. They looked happy when they went into the flat."

"So what's your explanation, then?" Tom wanted to know.

"I think it's pretty obvious, don't you? One of the four men in the flat last night—the four who were there in addition to Christopher and Crispin, and of course Montrose—took her home this morning. Both Blanton and Hutchison gave us her address, or at least directions for how to find her, and if Hutchison knew where she lived, Ogilvie would have done, as well. And if Rivers doesn't allow people to come to him, but he comes to them, then he probably knew, too."

"I'll accept that Ronald Blanton, Nigel Hutchison, Graham Ogilvie, and Dominic Rivers all knew where Miss Long lived," Tom said.

"One of them killed Montrose, and Gladys Long might have known who."

Tom nodded. "Seeing as she's now dead, and not by her own hand, it isn't likely that she was the one who killed Montrose, I suppose."

No, it really wasn't. Christopher was shaking his head, too.

"She was a dope addict," I said, "which made her perhaps less than stable. She might have gotten jittery and wanted to confess. She went to see St George this morning, perhaps of her own volition. She told him that Hutchison had dropped her off, but Hutchison denied it. If he, or one of the others, thought that she was waffling and might give them away, that would be a reason to get rid of her."

"But going to see St George wouldn't suggest that," Tom said. "He was already involved. So were you and Kit."

That was true, of course. I glanced at Christopher. "They made sure—very much so—that we shouldn't find out who killed Montrose. No one admitted to doing it. Not last night, and not today either. Ronnie Blanton said that he didn't remember anything that happened last night, and Nigel Hutchison said Montrose was already dead when he came on the scene in the butler's pantry."

"But they could have been lying," Christopher shot in.

"Yes." Blanton could have lied about what, if anything, he remembered, and Hutchison could have lied about Montrose already being dead when he saw him. "At any rate, if they didn't want us to know who did it, and if they were afraid Gladys would spill the beans to St George, that would be a reason to get rid of her."

"But if so," Tom asked, "why drop her off at all? Why not kill her then, before she had a chance to talk to anyone? And then take the body somewhere and dump it?"

That was a good point, and gave me pause for a moment while I thought it through.

"Perhaps they all agreed that Gladys should talk to St George? They must have wanted an update on what we did with Montrose's body last night. The discovery wasn't in the morning papers, right?"

Tom shook his head. "We let it into the afternoon papers, though. Male body found in Hyde Park, with possible ties to the raid on Rectors that was front page news in the morning edition."

"Did the article give his name?"

"None of the papers had that. Although I'm sure people are

starting to talk. What a way to go, for someone who wasn't involved in the lifestyle at all. Dead, in a dress, in Hyde Park." He shook his head. "He'd never live it down, were he alive."

"Did you know Freddie Montrose?" I wanted to know, and he met my eyes for a moment in the mirror.

"Remotely. He was a tabloid journalist, I'm a copper. And we went to university together for a couple of years, although I'm not sure I knew him then."

"Cambridge?"

He nodded.

"I didn't realize you went to uni with St George."

They'd been at Eton together for a year—so had Tom and Christopher—but no one had mentioned Cambridge.

"For a short while," Tom said, "and only because of the war. I would have finished and gone by the time he came along if not for the time I spent in France."

Of course. Tom was four years older than Christopher and Crispin, the same age that Cousin Robbie would have been, had he survived his own detour to France. Crispin, like Christopher, went from Eton to Cambridge—or Oxford, in Christopher's case—at eighteen. Tom spent his eighteenth year, and possibly his nineteenth, fighting in the Great War.

"I started at Cambridge in 1919," Tom said. He must have noticed the calculations going on in my head. Or perhaps he was simply used to having to explain. "Almost a year after the Armistice. I was twenty."

"So you were there for the Storming of the Gates."

"Newnham College in 1921?" Tom made a face. "I should hope you would know me well enough to realize that I wouldn't take part in intimidating coeds."

"Of course." I did, in fact, realize that. Anyone who had gone through the fighting in France the way Tom had, and who had seen the worst of war, wasn't likely to participate in riots here at home. Especially over something like women's right to proper degrees.

"And no," Tom said, clearly reading my mind; it was becoming a bit uncanny by now how everyone could tell what I was thinking, "I don't know whether Lord St George did, but I would warn you away from jumping to conclusions, Pippa. For someone who refuses to believe him guilty of harming Gladys Long, you're awfully quick to think that he would do other terrible things."

I huffed and leaned back, folding my arms over my chest. Although I couldn't refrain from saying, "He would have been eighteen. A fairly new-minted eighteen. It wouldn't have been surprising if he did some stupid things."

"He wasn't sent down, anyway," Christopher said. "And if he'd ended up in the papers, Uncle Harold would have had something to say about it, not to mention Grandfather, so I can't imagine that he did anything too awful. Why are you so interested in who took part in the riots anyway? It was ages ago."

"I'm not sure," I admitted. "It's just all the talk about Cambridge, I suppose, and all the people who attended. Crispin. Montrose. Hutchison. Tom—"

"Do you suppose Cambridge and the riots might have had something to do with what happened?" Tom asked, eagle-eyed. "Kit's right, you know. It was a long time ago. And no one died."

It had been five years, give or take. And yes, that was quite a long time to wait for revenge, if there had even been something to revenge. "In the riots, you mean?"

Tom nodded. "Proctors kept the male students from breaking down the gates to Newnham. It must have been traumatic for the women who were inside, but I've never heard that anyone was hurt. The papers took a dim view of the proceedings, of course..."

I nodded. I remembered that. We'd sat in Oxford, a few miles away, patting ourselves on the back because of how much better we had handled the whole affair a year previously—when neither Christopher nor I had been students, incidentally. There had been no riots in Oxford. But I did remember the headlines, and the male Cambridge students' outrage that they were being vilified in the press while the women students, whom they considered to be the interlopers, were made out to be the victims.

"It's probably just a coincidence," I said. "I don't know why my mind connected the two."

"It's a point of fact," Tom answered. "The victim as well as two of the suspects—"

Christopher and I both grimaced.

"—were at university together when something traumatic happened there. There might be a connection. When I get back to Town, I shall have to look into everyone's background and determine whether anyone else in this case has a connection to Cambridge. And when we get to Sutherland Hall—"

He eyed me in the mirror. "—St George can tell us what he was doing during the storming of the gates, and perhaps that will set your mind at ease."

I made a face. Knowing that Crispin hadn't taken part in terrorizing female students in 1921 would certainly make me feel better about that particular aspect of the situation. But my mind wouldn't be at ease until I knew who had killed Montrose, and now Gladys, and that no one I knew or cared about was likely to hang for it.

CHAPTER FIFTEEN

WE DROVE into the courtyard at Sutherland Hall well past supper. It was closer to eleven, actually, and I was surprised to see lights above the ground floor of the house. I would have expected Uncle Harold, at least, to have gone to bed by now.

"Crispin's lights are out," Christopher said, glancing up at the dark windows on the first floor of the east wing where his cousin lives.

"I suppose we could check and see whether the H6 is in the garage." I peered out into the darkness beyond the courtyard, into the area where I knew the old carriage house to be.

"Someone's coming," Christopher said, and after a moment, my eyes made out what he had already seen: a dark figure moving towards us across the grass. For a second, the moon glimmered on a head of fair hair, and then the figure came close enough that I recognized Wilkins, the chauffeur.

He did a sort of double-take when he saw Christopher. "Mr. Astley?" His attention moved from Christopher to me and then Tom, whom he must have recognized from the last time Scotland Yard was here. Wilkins looked even more concerned.

"Wilkins," Christopher said. "Is my cousin home?"

Wilkins's eyes flickered towards the windows on the upper story. "He ought to be, Mr. Astley. He brought the H6 back a couple of hours ago."

I let out a breath I hadn't realized I was holding, and Tom slanted a look my way.

"Shall I put the car away?" Wilkins added, with a glance at the police Crossley.

Christopher deferred to Tom, who shook his head. "Just leave it. We may not be here long."

"Go on off to bed, Wilkins," Christopher added. "If we want the motorcar moved into the carriage house, we'll do it ourselves."

Wilkins didn't look too pleased about that—I guess perhaps he felt that the carriage house and the vehicles inside it were his domain, and he didn't want anyone else to deal with them—but he nodded.

"Let's go," Christopher added and took my elbow. "Come along, Pippa. Tom."

He headed for the front door to the Hall, which, by now, Tidwell the butler had pulled open.

"Mr. Astley?"

"Good evening, Tidwell." Christopher pulled me across the threshold into the Hall, while behind us, Wilkins left the courtyard in the other direction, to make his way back to his rooms above the garage. "You remember Detective Sergeant Gardiner, of course."

"Detective Sergeant." Tidwell gave Tom something between a bow and a nod. "And Miss Darling."

"Hello, Tidwell," I said. "We're looking for St George."

"His lordship is in the parlor." Tidwell glanced down the east wing hallway.

I scowled. "Let me guess. Is he drinking his supper?"

"His lordship ate first," Tidwell said, which meant that yes, he was drinking. But at least he wasn't doing it on an empty stomach.

"What about Uncle Harold?"

Tidwell turned his attention to Christopher. "His Grace went up to bed, Mr. Astley."

"There's no need to disturb the Duke," Tom told Tidwell. "We'll just head on down the hallway and have a talk with Lord St George."

Tidwell looked torn, as if the police showing up to talk to Crispin was something Crispin's father really ought to be informed about—and it probably was—but at the same time, he wasn't any more eager to disturb Uncle Harold's beauty sleep than the rest of us.

"It's all right, Tidwell," Christopher said. "We just want to see that he's all right. Pippa's been worried."

I rolled my eyes, but I couldn't very well deny it, so I didn't try.

Tidwell eyed me for a moment before he turned back to Christopher. "Anything else, Mr. Astley?"

Christopher shook his head. "We'll just find Crispin. Can we stay the night, Tidwell, or should we plan to drive to Beckwith Place after this?"

"I'll inform Mrs. Mason to have the usual rooms made up," Tidwell said.

I made another face—sleeping in my usual room would put me at the far end of the west wing across from Tom, and would put Christopher at the far end of the east wing across from Crispin, an arrangement Aunt Charlotte had come up with before she died, God knows why—but I didn't complain. It was better than getting back into the Crossley to drive to Beckwith Place in the middle of the night.

"Thank you, Tidwell," Christopher said. Tidwell inclined

his head and withdrew. Christopher turned to Tom and me. "Shall we?"

I twitched my elbow out of his grip. "I think we should. And before he gets so soused that he won't be able to speak sense anymore."

I didn't wait for the others, just headed down the hallway towards the parlor at a good clip, my heels clicking against the floors.

"Is that you, Sadie?" Crispin's voice oozed out of the parlor as I approached the door, and my eyes narrowed.

"You utter bastard, St George."

He was sniggering when I appeared in the doorway. "Good evening, Darling. I thought that would get you."

It had, but I wasn't about to admit that to him. Instead, I put both my hands on my hips and scowled. "I suppose you saw us arrive through the window, did you? Do you have any idea how worried we've been? We haven't seen or heard from you for almost twelve hours—"

"You didn't see or hear from me for several weeks prior to that," Crispin pointed out. He was lounging in his chair with a glass of what looked like brandy lazily balanced on his stomach, and he looked quizzically at me. "Why on earth would you—?"

But by then first Christopher and then Tom had appeared in the doorway behind me, and Crispin's face lost the smug expression and he sat up. The brandy sloshed against the edges of the glass and he moved it to a little table at his elbow with the air of someone bracing himself. "Now what?"

"Gladys Long is dead," Tom said, without any attempt to soften the blow at all.

It was probably deliberate—he wanted to get Crispin's honest first reaction—but I could have told him that it was a bad idea. It isn't easy to stagger while sitting in an easy chair, but Crispin managed it. He turned as white as a corpse—not difficult to do when you're naturally pale to begin with—and his lips parted in something that was part inhalation, part the sound you make when you're unexpectedly hit in the stomach.

"For God's sake," I told Tom irritably as I crossed the floor, "was that necessary?"

"I rather think it was." He sounded not remorseful at all.

"Well, I hope that display convinced you that he knew nothing about it." I dropped down on the arm of Crispin's chair and faced Tom.

Even Christopher seemed to think that Tom had gone a step too far this time, because he came to perch on Crispin's other side. "Honestly, Tom..."

"It's just as well to be certain," Tom said. He looked from one to the other of us, and then turned his attention squarely on Crispin. "Have a sip of brandy, St George, and prepare to answer some questions."

"You absolute tosser," Crispin told him, breathlessly. "How dare you spring something like that on me?"

He had to stop to catch his breath, and I put a hand on his shoulder, and accidentally made a shiver run through him.

"Buck up," Tom said unsympathetically. "We don't have time for your dramatics. You were seen leaving her flat just before one o'clock this afternoon. You'd better have a good explanation, or I'm going to have to haul you back to London and book you on suspicion of murder."

There was a pause, and then Crispin blew. "How dare you talk to me like that, you wanker? You show up here, with my cousin and my... my..."

He didn't seem quite able to articulate what I was to him, which was fair considering our relationship, and so he went on without specifying, "—and you dare to accuse me of being a murderer? To my face? In my own home? You absolute, utter—!"

"Shhh." By this point he was practically hyperventilating, and I did something I had never expected to do, and put an arm around his shoulders before I tilted my cheek against his temple. "It's all right, St George. He didn't mean it."

And if he wasn't quiet, he'd wake up Uncle Harold, and then the fat would truly be in the fire. And at that point we could probably forget about spending the night, too.

Tom muttered something—it was probably, "Did, too!"—and Christopher shot him an hostile look before turning back to Crispin, with a calming hand on the latter's arm. "She's right, old bean. None of us think you did it."

"*He* does!" Crispin snarled, pointing at Tom.

"I promise you he doesn't. Not really." I shot Tom a look that told him he had better not disagree with me, or something painful would happen to him. "He just wanted to see your reaction. He knows better than to think you would kill someone."

"I would kill *him*," Crispin said viciously, "with pleasure right now!"

"Not something you want to say to a policeman," Tom told him blandly, while I tried to implement what I thought were calming strokes on Crispin's back. He twitched irritably.

"But fine," Tom added. "Convince me you didn't do it."

"How am I supposed to do that?" Crispin threw his hands up in the air and dislodged my arm while he was at it. "And stop patting me, for heaven's sake, Darling; I'm not five years old with a splinter!"

I huffed. "Fine." To hell with him. "I was only trying to help."

"Next time—" Crispin began, looking at me down the length of his nose, which was quite the feat when he was sitting on the chair and I was on the arm of it. But then he seemed to think better of what he had been planning to say, and added, "Never mind."

Christopher muttered something, and Crispin shot him a sour look.

"Yes," he told Tom, "I was there. Of course I was there. Kit and Darling both saw me leave with her. I suppose I could lie and say I dropped her off at the entrance to the mews—she lives in a mews flat, down in Belgravia..."

Tom nodded. "I wouldn't advise you to lie about it. You were seen going into her place—"

"Had to be convinced to go upstairs, the neighbor said," I added, and Tom shot me a look.

"—and then you were seen coming out ten minutes later. Looking like you couldn't get away fast enough, was the expression, I believe."

He flicked me a look, and I made a face. That had indeed been the way the neighbor had described it. And it painted quite an ugly picture.

"I feel like I'm back in Dorset," Crispin muttered. "Last month I was supposed to have strangled Johanna de Vos in the five minutes between the time I came in from the garden and the time I entered the room I shared with Kit. At least you're giving me twice as much time to get the job done this time."

"She wasn't—" I began, and subsided when Tom glanced at me.

Crispin shot me a look too, but when I didn't say anything else, he went on. "She wanted me to stay and... uh... make her feel better."

Tom's lips twitched. "Petting, dope, or both?"

Crispin flushed a deep pink that was frankly laughable considering his reputation. "For God's sake, Gardiner—" He shot me an agonized look.

"She knows what you get up to," Tom told him, while

Christopher added, "She's under no illusions about you, I'm afraid, Crispin."

"Figures," Crispin muttered with a scowl. "Fine. If I have to talk about it, then… both, I suppose. The dope was a given. The rest was implied, but I didn't stay to find out the details."

"And she was alive and well when you left?"

"Of course she was alive and well! If I went around murdering all the women who make indecent propositions to me, England would be littered with corpses."

"Excuse you," I muttered, and he arched a brow my way.

"I thought you were under no illusions?"

"I'm not. But there's no need for you to flaunt it, is there?"

"The nice policeman asked, Darling." He smirked. The chance to bicker seemed to have restored some of his self-possession.

"Stop flirting," Tom ordered irritably, and I turned a look of outrage on him. Next to me, Crispin did the same. We both had our mouths open to explain, hotly, that we were certainly not doing anything remotely like flirting when Tom went on. "So you left. Did you see anyone you knew on your way out of the mews?"

Crispin shook his head, but then seemed to think better of it. "There was a red Morris Bullnose parked down the street. Ronnie Blanton drives one."

"What do Nigel Hutchison and Graham Ogilvie drive? And Dominic Rivers?"

Crispin thought about it. "I have no idea how Dom gets around. He shows up out of a bottle, like a genie. When I see Hutchison and Gram, they're usually with Ronnie in his motorcar."

"You and Nigel Hutchison were at Cambridge together."

Tom slid smoothly into the next line of questioning, as if it were merely small-talk. To further the impression, he stopped looming and took a seat on the chair on the other side of the table. Now that things had calmed down a little, Christopher took me by the arm and pulled me over to the Chesterfield, where we sat down side by side.

Crispin watched for a moment before he turned back to Tom. "That's correct."

"What about Ronald Blanton and Graham Ogilvie?"

"Gram went to university somewhere in Scotland," Crispin said. "Aberdeen, Glasgow, maybe even Edinburgh."

"And Blanton?"

"He might have been at Cambridge, but if he was, I don't remember him. I wasn't close to Hutch either, if it comes to that, but at least I remember him. But it's a big place, isn't it? I didn't know everyone, not even the ones in my own form. Do you remember Ronnie Blanton?"

"I was a few years ahead of you," Tom said mildly, "but no, I don't. I barely remember you, and it was only because I already knew you. I don't remember Nigel Hutchison at all, and for all I know, both Blanton and Ogilvie could have been there."

"Montrose was," I interjected. "A year or two ahead of Crispin. Do you remember him?"

Tom shot me a look. "Now that you mention it, no. But those of us who were older and had been through the war tended to keep to ourselves."

And small wonder. The idea of Tom getting up to the kinds of immature antics that Crispin had undoubtedly done, was laughable.

"Did Gladys attend university?" Tom wanted to know, and Crispin looked at him for a moment in silence. I could practically see the wheels inside his head turn. One of the more attractive things about Crispin, if I were to admit that such things exist, was the way his mind worked. He's remarkably quick to catch on to things, whether said or merely implied. Or even jealously guarded.

"She didn't attend Cambridge, if that's what you mean. But no, I don't think she did."

"Do you remember the storming of the gates?"

Crispin made a face. "That awful event at Newnham College after the vote in -2 1? Of course I do."

"Were you there?"

He turned to look at me, and it took a second for him to respond. "At Newnham College that evening? No, Darling. I don't terrorize women in their beds."

I rolled my eyes, and a corner of his mouth turned up. After a second, he added, a bit reluctantly, "I was part of the crowd in King's Parade when Reverend Hart said to 'go tell Newnham and Girton.' But I didn't fancy being sent down, so I went up to my rooms instead of to Newnham with the others."

"Did any of the others go?" Tom wanted to know, and Crispin turned back to him.

"Any of the crowd we've been talking about? Not Hutchison, certainly. He had a sister at Newnham, if memory serves. But Freddie Montrose did, although I'm sure it was more for the news value than because he cared about the verdict. He wrote for The Granta. I remember he got in a bit of trouble for an editorial later that month."

"One of the editorials trying to justify the whole thing as a prank?" I asked, outraged, and he shot me a look.

"Yes. One of those."

And here I had rather enjoyed Montrose's company for the few hours that I had known him. I made a face. "I hope he got sent down."

"Now that you mention it," Crispin said, "I think he probably was."

He turned back to Tom. "Why all the questions? I assumed Monty was killed because he was spying on Dominic Rivers."

"Doesn't everyone in your set know that Rivers is a dope dealer?"

"Of course they do," Crispin said. "But that doesn't mean that people like Ronnie Blanton or Gladys want him to be arrested. Or that they want to be featured in the press as addicts themselves. They're—" he made a face, "they *were*, I guess, in Gladys's case—dependent on family money and parental good-will to stay in Town and live in the manner to which they are accustomed."

"Can you think of any reason why anyone would have wanted to get rid of Gladys Long?"

"Only that she was there when Monty was killed," Crispin said. "She certainly wasn't at Newnham in -21. But everyone in that flat—" he glanced at me and Christopher, "everyone other than the three of us, could have known who did it."

"She didn't tell you?"

Crispin shook his head. "I asked. She said she didn't know. That she was in the kitchen with Dom when it happened. That when they came out into the hallway, the other three were clustered around the door to the butler's pantry, and Monty was on the floor."

And that might have been the truth.

On the other hand, if she hadn't known who the killer was, why get rid of her?

"Did she talk about going to the police?" I wanted to know, and Crispin shot me a look.

"She didn't bring it up. I did. I said, if she and Dom could vouch for each other, it had to be either Blanton, Hutchison, or Ogilvie who had killed Monty, and why didn't I drive her to Scotland Yard so she could tell the police what she knew?"

"But she said no."

Crispin nodded. "I didn't get the feeling that she was worried, if it matters. Not about anyone coming after her. She felt bad about Monty, but he wasn't a friend, and she was more concerned that one of the others might be arrested for it. It didn't seem to be about her own safety at all. She said she had to keep quiet so they'd be all right."

"And the car you saw could have belonged to Blanton, or could have been used by Ogilvie or Hutchison?"

Crispin nodded. "I imagine Ronnie would have been happy to lend it to either of them, had they asked."

"Blanton was at home when we stopped by," Christopher said. "Dobbins was out, so Blanton was alone in the flat. He could have left, before or after that, and no one would have known about it."

"And Hutchison was alone at his and Ogilvie's place," I added. "So Ogilvie was out, perhaps in the Morris. Then again, Hutchison could have been out and made it back by the time we got there. Even without a motorcar."

"There's no reason to think it was either of theirs anyway," Crispin said. "London is full of Morris Oxfords."

Yes, it was. They're a lot thicker on the ground than Hispano-Suizas. Especially bright blue ones.

"At any rate," I said, "none of them have an alibi for Gladys's death. Except perhaps Ogilvie, depending on where he spent the day, and with whom. Blanton and Hutchison were both alone. Hutchison said he didn't drop Gladys off at our place, by the way. And if Ogilvie had the motorcar, I suppose he couldn't have. But we don't know that Ogilvie did. Or that Hutchison didn't."

"Or that anyone dropped her off," Christopher added. "Perhaps she took the tube. We did."

I nodded. "We should ask Evans. He might have noticed how she arrived."

"If whoever dropped her off didn't want to be seen, he would have parked out of sight of Evans," Christopher said, which was certainly true. "And with everything that's happened today, we did nothing about contacting Rivers."

"He wouldn't have talked to you anyway," Crispin said. "He requires a personal introduction, and although last night might have served as that under normal circumstances, he'd be extra careful today. If anyone is to contact him, it ought to be me."

"He won't come here to do business, surely?" I looked around the parlor, and by extension, Sutherland Hall, the village of Little Sutherland, and all of Wiltshire, hours away from London.

"If I paid him enough, he would," Crispin said dryly, "but I imagine it would be easier if I were in Town."

"You'll come back up to London tomorrow morning, then?"

It was Tom who asked, and Crispin eyed him warily for a moment. "Are you arresting me?"

Tom rolled his eyes. "Not unless you want to confess to killing either Frederick Montrose or Gladys Long."

"Of course I don't. Although I imagine you could still arrest me—" he glanced at Christopher and me before looking back at Tom, "—arrest all three of us, for driving around with the body in the back of the motorcar. Not to mention for leaving it in Hyde Park instead of taking it to Scotland Yard or to hospital."

"That's true," Tom agreed pleasantly. "I could do that. So you'll come up to London tomorrow morning?"

Crispin's eyebrow arched. "Blackmail, now?"

"Just say you'll do it," I said, irritated with the back and forth. "You know you're going to, so just stop playing games and say you will."

He glanced at me. "Of course I will. I don't have to be threatened into it. I feel bad enough about Monty as it is. If you and I hadn't gone to Rectors last night, and he hadn't recognized me, and Hutchison hadn't recognized me, and Montrose hadn't seen an opportunity to get close to Dominic Rivers..."

"He might have wound up dead in Blanton's flat anyway," I said. "He and Hutchison went to Cambridge together, too, after all. And at any rate, you are not responsible for either of their deaths. If you weren't the one who picked up the rolling pin—Hutchison said it was the rolling pin, Tom—and brought it down on Montrose's head, it wasn't your fault."

"It feels like my fault," Crispin muttered.

"Then come to London tomorrow," Tom said, "and contact Dominic Rivers and help me figure out what happened."

"You know them all better than we do," Christopher added. "They won't talk to us. They might talk to you."

Crispin nodded.

"We should all get some sleep," I said, and pushed to my feet. "Mrs. Mason should be done with the extra linens by now. If not, I'll help her."

I extended a hand to Christopher, who took it and let me haul him to his feet. When I turned to do the same to Crispin, he eyed my hand with all the enthusiasm of a dead spider.

"Suit yourself," I told him. "We'll see you tomorrow, then. Get some rest."

"I think I'll just stay down here and wake Gladys," Crispin said, and reached for the glass of brandy. Christopher and I exchanged a glance, but neither of us said anything. We just took Tom with us and headed out the door and upstairs.

CHAPTER SIXTEEN

WE GOT BACK to London in time for luncheon, and that was in spite of getting up and out of Sutherland Hall early enough that Uncle Harold never realized we'd been there. Let's just say that Tom's police issue Crossley didn't travel the way Crispin's H6 did.

Of course, Tom didn't motor the way Crispin did, either. No death wish, for one thing. No reckless disregard for life or limb, for another.

So naturally Crispin grumbled the whole way about being stuck behind the Crossley and not being able to give the Hispano-Suiza her legs.

"There's nothing we can do until we get there anyway," I reminded him.

I was in the passenger seat of the H6, while Christopher was keeping Tom company in the Crossley. Crispin had insisted on bringing the Hispano-Suiza so he wouldn't have to suffer the indignity of taking the train back to Wiltshire at the end of our adventure, and of course the Crossley had to return to London and the police garage. So there were four of us traveling back, in two vehicles. I could have been difficult and insisted on riding in the Crossley as well, I suppose, but it seemed churlish to make Crispin do the drive by himself, especially after having done it yesterday, and besides, I thought Christopher might appreciate the time alone with Tom.

"You phoned Dominic Rivers from the Hall before we left," I continued, "and set up the appointment, and that is really all you can do until we get back to Town. We're lucky you could do that much. At least we won't have long to wait for him."

"At the rate we're going," Crispin grumbled, drumming his fingers irritably on the steering wheel while eyeing the motorcar ahead of us balefully, "we'll miss him altogether."

"We won't. There's plenty of time. You're just being impatient."

"Am not." He slanted me a look. "I have an infinite amount of patience, I'll have you know. If I didn't, I would have married Laetitia Marsden by now."

"She certainly pushed hard enough for it," I agreed. "All that talk about how ideally suited you are and how much fun you would have together, with indecent glances and strokes of her hand while she said it, no doubt—"

"Good God, Darling." He looked appalled. "Just how much of that conversation did you overhear?"

"I think I heard most of it. She was still complaining that you weren't talking to her when I came upstairs, so I can't imagine that I missed much on the front end, and of course you know I was on the landing when she walked out. So I imagine I heard all the important bits."

"Of course you did."

The car ahead of us wasn't moving, nor were we, so he leaned forward and banged his head against the steering wheel a couple of times, I assumed to show his frustration. With me, I gathered, and not the traffic.

I sniggered. "Honestly, I'm proud of you, St George. I've always thought you were spoiled, but you're sticking to your convictions in spite of nobody letting you have what you want, not to mention all the temptations in your path."

He snorted. "Don't be too impressed, Darling. I'm taking full advantage of the temptations, as I'm sure you know."

"Not the advantage you could take," I said. "You turned down Gladys, and Lady Laetitia, and Flossie Schlomsky..."

"*You* took me away from Flossie Schlomsky."

"If you had given me any kind of indication that you wanted to stay with her, I would have let you," I said.

"Would you, indeed?"

Absolutely not. "She's so managing, she might have managed you right into marriage. That seems to be what she's aiming for. She said as much, didn't she? And I just can't imagine having to face Florence across the Christmas goose for the rest of my life."

He shuddered. "Nor can I. I suppose I owe you a debt of gratitude, Darling."

"Don't mention it," I said. "It was entirely selfish on my part, I assure you."

"But you plan to be around in twenty years, at the Christmas table, it seems."

"If I'm not married to someone else by the time I'm thirty, I'm marrying Christopher," I said, and had the pleasure of seeing his jaw drop. "It'll be a marriage of convenience, of course. Christopher will continue to do what Christopher does, and I'll live a life of leisure off the Sutherland money."

"That's appalling," Crispin said. "Don't you want children? Don't you want a husband who loves you? Don't you want..." He trailed off, his cheeks darkening.

I sniggered. "Of course I do, St George. But Christopher loves me, and we can adopt a child—I think Christopher would rather that than produce his own, especially with me—"

His jaw dropped again. "But... it wouldn't be a Sutherland!"

"It'll be something like tenth in line for the title," I said, "after you and whatever children you engender, and then Uncle Herbert and Francis, and whatever children Francis and his wife—probably Constance—generate. Christopher's and my child would make it nowhere near the Sutherland title. But we can make it a girl, if you'd prefer. That way it won't matter anyway, with the silly inheritance laws. If you're adopting, you can choose what kind of baby you get, and I bet most people want boys. Girls are always second class citizens. So we'll pick a girl and it'll all work out."

I sat back in the seat, well pleased with my plan. Next to me, Crispin opened and closed his mouth like a frog.

"You're joking," he said, after a minute had passed and he had found his voice. "You must be."

"I assure you, I'm not. But it's only if no one else wants to marry me, you know. I have seven years to find a different husband. Or six-and-a-half, at least. Plenty of time. Marrying Christopher is just the backup plan if finding a husband the usual way doesn't work out."

"You're mad," Crispin said.

"I don't know why you would say that. It makes sense to me. We're best friends, we live together already, we could make a happy life together as we get older. Although Christopher isn't madly keen on the idea, of course..."

He had his heart set on being a bachelor, he'd told me, with all that that entailed. Not that he had said that last part; I was inferring it.

"No," Crispin said, "I quite get that. I'm not madly keen, either. Why on earth are you praising me for not marrying Laetitia, if you're planning to do this to yourself?"

"That's entirely different," I told him. "I'm not in love with someone else. You are. And I'm waiting until I'm thirty, and it's only if no one else wants me. You're twenty-three. Barely. You should wait for Uncle Harold to come to his senses and let you marry who you want."

Or wait for him to die, which had been part of the conversation I had overheard, as well.

Uncle Harold, I mean. Not Crispin. People might die of a broken heart in fiction, but not in reality.

"And if he doesn't?" Crispin wanted to know.

"Then I guess, eventually, you'll have to decide whether she's worth giving up the title for. If she is, then you go and live happily with the woman you love in some little hamlet on the Continent. I hear Italy is lovely. If she's not, you do your duty and marry someone like Laetitia or Flossie Schlomsky and carry on the line. At least your children will be Sutherlands. Perhaps it wouldn't be so bad."

"It would be terrible," Crispin said. "Nothing against Laetitia; we've certainly had some good times..." His lips curved in an unpleasantly reminiscent manner, and I fought back the desire to smack him, "but she's just as managing as Flossie, and I'm sick and tired of being managed."

"Aww, poor baby," I told him. "All these women falling at your feet, and you don't like them handling you."

He scowled. "You're awful, Darling. I don't know why I attempt to be myself around you. All you do is make fun of me."

I suppose I did. But what did he expect, when he said things like that? "You could make it a little less easy, you know."

"I'm sure I could," Crispin said, "but that would rather defeat the purpose, wouldn't it? So you think I should marry Laetitia after all? Or perhaps Flossie? Or..."

He trailed off, and I could see his throat move when he swallowed.

"I'm sorry," I said, in complete sincerity this time. "I don't know how close you were, but it must have been a shock. Especially the way Tom sprang the news on you. And after what happened with Johanna, too."

He slanted a look my way, but not far enough to actually connect with my gaze. "I feel like Jonah. Death and destruction everywhere I go. Every woman I touch ends up dead."

"Let's hope not," I said. "As you said, England would be littered with corpses."

He sniggered. It didn't last long, but it was a laugh. I counted it as a win. "I suppose you're right. Although it hasn't been as many as you think. Not quite enough to litter the countryside."

"If they all dropped dead, I'm sure we'd notice," I said. "You're not jinxed, St George. Gladys's death had nothing to do with you. Someone thought she knew too much and decided to get rid of her. I'd stake my life on it. And as for Johanna..."

"That did have something to do with me."

"Only peripherally. And it wasn't as if you led her on, you know. You were honest, at least if what you told us about it was true..."

He shot me another look. This one connected, and was offended. "I wouldn't lie about it, Darling."

"Then you have nothing to feel guilty about," I said. "You have every right to turn women away, just like I have every right to turn men away. I assume we agree that I do? That every woman has the right to say no?"

"Of course, Darling. You're not required to cater to some man's desires just because you're a woman." He muttered something that sounded like, "Blast him," which probably referenced the handsy Geoffrey Marsden. I had been thinking about him when I said it, and it seemed as if Crispin had been, as well.

"And you're not required to cater to every woman's desires just because she wants you to," I said. "You're allowed to say no, as well. And if something bad happens to her later, it won't be your fault."

He nodded, but muttered, "Still feels like my fault. If I had stayed with Gladys, maybe..."

"Whoever it was probably wouldn't have come in if he'd known you were there," I said. "Or if he were that desperate to murder Gladys, he might have decided you were an acceptable loss, too. So it's a good thing you weren't."

"Happy I didn't end up dead, Darling?"

"Of course," I said steadily. "We were worried about you, St George. It took forever for you to get home. We called the Hall from Sutherland House around six-thirty or seven, and you still weren't back. We envisioned you tied up in some basement somewhere, having matches stuck under your fingernails."

He sniggered. "Sorry, Darling. I got caught up with a waitress in a pub along the way. I stopped somewhere in Hampshire, and..."

I raised a hand. "Spare me the details, St George. I can fill them in for myself."

"Of course, Darling." He focused forward on the road again, smirking. I folded my hands in my lap and considered whether attempting to smack that stupid, self-satisfied expression off his face would result in the motorcar going off the road and us both possibly getting hurt, and whether it might be worth it.

IN SUCH SCINTILLATING COMPANY, we arrived at Sutherland House with some twenty minutes to spare before the time when Dominic Rivers was expected.

"Better get the police car out of the way," I advised Tom, who nodded.

"Finch is coming to pick it up. I'll be staying here with St George."

Crispin muttered something. Christopher and I both looked at him, but he didn't repeat it. That was fine by me, since I assumed it was just some variation of how he didn't need a nanny.

"The two of you," Tom added, "should run along now."

What?

"What do you mean," I said, "run along? You're not letting us stay?"

"This is a murder investigation," Tom began.

"A murder investigation you wouldn't even be a part of if we hadn't given you the body!"

"A body you might not have given me at all," Tom said, "if I hadn't found you outside Rectors with it in the back of the motorcar."

"We told you—!"

"I know what you said, Miss Darling." It was always Miss Darling when he was trying to put me in my place. He only called me Pippa—rarely—when we were on friendly terms. "I have only your word for it. You might have made it up on the spot when I caught you red-handed, so to speak."

"We really were going to contact you, Tom," Christopher

said. "We would have brought the body straight to you if we hadn't been worried that one of the others was watching."

I nodded. "We're trying to help you. St George has contacted Rivers so you can talk to him—"

"St George has to stay," Tom said, with a look at him, "obviously. But you and Kit—"

"He already knows we're involved! We were there the other night. He won't be surprised to see us."

"You can't make us leave," Christopher added. "This is Sutherland House. We're—or at least I am—a Sutherland. You're not making the staff leave, are you?"

Tom shook his head. From his expression, he was chewing his tongue so he wouldn't say something he might regret later.

"We'll stay out of the way if you want us to," Christopher said. And added, with a glance at me, "Pippa ought to, at least. I don't like putting her and Rivers in a room together. Bad enough that he knows who she is from the other night..."

Crispin nodded. I sniffed. "I can take care of myself!"

"I'm sure Gladys Long thought the same," Tom said.

Christopher continued, as if neither of us had spoken, "—but I think I ought to be here. Visibly. Just in case he was the one who bludgeoned Gladys—"

"And Montrose," Crispin shot in.

"—and he decides to take the fireplace poker to Crispin next."

None of us had anything to say in response to that. Crispin looked mildly offended, as if he were thinking of claiming, as I had, that he could take care of himself. But at the same time, he seemed gratified that Christopher wanted to go out of his way to ensure his safety, and so he bit his tongue.

"For what it's worth," he said, "I don't think Rivers would quibble about Kit being here. He already knows we're cousins, and it's not something we can deny anyway, as much alike as we look. But I hope you don't imagine that you can sit in on the appointment, Gardiner. No offense, but he'll peg you for a copper the second he walks through the door."

"None taken," Tom said calmly. "I'll wait in the next room until you hand him the money and he hands you the dope. Then I'll arrest him. And don't even think about making use of it while I'm here, because—"

"I wasn't." Crispin rolled his eyes. "I assumed you'd want it for evidence. I'll just pay for it, shall I, and then hand it over to you?"

"That would be most excellent," Tom said, ignoring the sarcasm, as a weedy-looking young man around thirty slipped around one of the pillars from the street and stopped next to the Crossley. "There you are, Finch. Cutting it a little close, aren't you?"

"If *you'd* been here sooner, *I* would have been here sooner," Detective Sergeant Finchley said as he slid behind the wheel of the Crossley. "I'll come back once our man is safely inside the premises, shall I?"

Tom nodded. "Get well away from here. If he sees a police car anywhere in the neighborhood he might balk."

"I'll make sure I'm a distance away." Finchley didn't wait for an answer, just steered the Crossley into the street and away.

"Shall we?" Tom gestured to the front door, which Rogers was holding open.

"My lord. Back so soon?" The butler bowed Crispin inside. "Master Christopher, good to see you again. Miss Darling. Mister..."

"This is Detective Sergeant Gardiner with Scotland Yard," Crispin said, handing off his hat and gloves. "And we're expecting a Mr. Dominic Rivers to turn up in the next fifteen minutes. When he arrives, will you show him into the green parlor, Rogers?"

"Yes, my lord." Rogers took the rest of the hats and gloves, as well. "Is there anything else you require, my lord? Refreshments? Luncheon?"

"I could eat," Christopher said.

Crispin nodded. "Something simple, Rogers. And enough for everyone. We drove up from Sutherland without stopping for anything but petrol."

"Yes, my lord." Rogers bowed himself out, carrying all our hats and gloves.

"In here." Crispin headed for the green parlor, which wasn't really green, per se. Its walls were more of a golden yellow damask; it was the furniture that was sage green. He dropped down on one of the hundred-year-old sofas with no respect for its age and kicked his legs out. "This do you, Gardiner?"

"This ought to work just fine," Tom said, looking around. "You intended for me to go behind the screen, I assume?"

There was a lovely screen painted with scenes of rice paddies over in the corner, hiding the parlor telephone from view—the one we had used to ring up Wiltshire last night. The telephone table was flanked by a chair to make the person making the call comfortable, and which ought now to make Tom equally so.

Crispin nodded. "I thought it might suit."

"It'll suit very well," Tom decreed, after looking at it. "So you two will be in here. I will be behind the screen. Where will Miss Darling be?"

There wasn't enough room for me behind the screen with Tom, or I would have suggested it. "I don't suppose Sutherland House is built the way Sutherland Hall is, is it, with priest holes and secret passages everywhere?"

Crispin shook his head. "I'm afraid not, Darling. Different era altogether. There are the servants' stairs, of course, but they're not accessible from this room."

No, I could see that they weren't. There were a couple of tall windows on one wall, showing an angled view of the courtyard and the back half of the Hispano-Suiza in front of the stairs, and then there were the doors to the foyer and the one to —if memory served—another sitting room next door, but that was all.

I had my mouth open to suggest that I should lurk in the sitting room when Crispin spoke again.

"I suppose we could borrow a cap and apron from the staff room, and you could flit around the parlor pretending to be a housemaid. I'd quite like to see that."

"I imagine you would," I said. "What is it with you and women in uniform, St George? Last month it was WPCs. This month it's housemaids? You even called me Sadie last night. Is there something I should know about?"

He eyed me down the length of his nose. "You know very well there isn't. I only said that because I knew it was you, and I figured it would get a rise out of you. Which it did. So I was right. But as I have told you before, I have never seduced a housemaid, and I do not—"

He bit back the rest of the statement—most likely a declaration that he did not have a particular interest in women in uniform—with a flush when Rogers came back through the door rolling a cart holding trays full of easily-managed comestibles. Deviled eggs, dainty cucumber sandwiches, that sort of thing.

I sniggered, but didn't ask him to finish his sentence. I thought about it, but I didn't. "That looks lovely, Rogers," I said instead.

"Thank you, Miss Darling. Is there anything else I can do

for you, my lord?" He looked at Crispin, who had returned to his usual color.

The scion of the Sutherlands shook his head. "No, thank you, Rogers. Just go wait for Mr. Rivers to arrive. I'll see him in here."

Rogers nodded. "Right away, my lord."

He withdrew, and closed the door to the foyer behind himself.

"Deviled egg, Pippa?" Christopher asked.

Crispin muttered something, in which I thought I caught the word 'fitting,' and I smirked. "Yes, please."

"Better take it to go," Tom said. "He should be here at any moment."

I nodded. "Put a few things on a plate, Christopher, and I'll take it into the sitting room. Yes... I think that's the motorcar now."

There was the sound of an engine in the courtyard outside. We all turned to the windows, in time to see the bullet nose of a Morris Oxford pull up behind the Hispano-Suiza.

"Blanton's car?" Tom muttered, even as he withdrew backwards from the windows and toward the telephone screen.

Crispin shrugged. "Perhaps not. Everyone who's anyone has a red motorcar."

"So why is yours blue?" I wanted to know.

He shot me a look. "Because I'm not like everyone else, Darling. Now take your deviled eggs and scarper before he notices you peering at him through the window."

Outside, Dominic Rivers had turned off the engine of his— or perhaps Blanton's—motorcar and was climbing out. I reversed away from the window the same way Tom had done. "I'll be in the sitting room." At least until Tom made his presence known. At that point I might present myself back in the parlor, as well.

The bell rang, and I ducked through the door into the next room at the same time as Rogers's measured steps crossed the floor of the foyer. I heard the front door open, and then—

"Dominic Rivers to see Lord St George."

"This way, Mr. Rivers. His lordship is expecting you." Rogers shut the door, presumably on Dominic Rivers's heels, and added, "May I take your coat and hat?"

I imagined that Rivers unloaded them, and then Rogers's voice came back. "This way, Mr. Rivers. His lordship is in the green parlor."

Rivers muttered something, and even from this distance I could make it out as a variation of, "Must be nice." Rogers, of course, being the consummate professional, didn't respond in kind.

"Mr. Rivers, my lord," he intoned instead, this time in the door to the parlor. I made sure I was tucked away out of sight from the doorway as Dominic Rivers made his way into the room. "St George."

"Rivers."

Crispin's voice was cool. There was a pause, a slight one, before he added, "You remember my cousin? Christopher Astley."

"Pleasure," Christopher murmured, and I imagined them shaking hands. Or perhaps not. I was standing behind the door into the sitting room, and while there was a gap where the hinges were fastened, I didn't dare put my eye to it, just in case Rivers noticed the movement.

He was clearly looking around, because after a moment he said, "Nice little place you've got here."

There was mockery in his voice, but it covered something deeper. Anger, at a guess. Perhaps envy. And it was honestly difficult to blame him for that. Crispin was definitely one of the haves—title, money, good looks, mansion in Town, country seat in Wiltshire...

Rivers, meanwhile, was probably not of the same exalted stratum, or he wouldn't be dealing dope for a living.

Or perhaps he was, and was simply being rebellious.

"It's certainly better than Southwark," Crispin said, which might have been an insult, or merely a supercilious comment of the type at which he excelled. I wouldn't put the insult past him, although I doubted that Rivers lived in Southwark. Or if he did, it was by choice. His motorcar—if it was his—was an almost new Morris Oxford in gleaming red, and if he could afford that, he could afford better than Southwark.

Rivers snorted, but didn't respond. I dared to do a quick turn of my head into the gap between the door and the jamb and saw that he had his back to me. So I turned the rest of my body, too, and put my eye to the gap.

And thus I got to watch as he put a hand in his pocket and pulled out a small paper bag, which he extended towards Crispin without a word.

The latter arched both brows. "What's this?"

"What you asked for," Rivers said.

"Is that so?" Crispin reached out a hand, and Rivers dropped the bag into it.

"I assume you won't need my help in making use of it?"

"No," Crispin said, although he frowned slightly as he gauged the weight and size of the bag in his hand. "This isn't my first time, after all."

Rivers nodded. "Then maybe you won't mind checking that everything is all right?"

"Of course." Crispin opened the twist and peered into it. After a moment, he dipped two fingers in. When they came out, they were holding a square of something small and white, almost like a sugar cube, but a bit bigger and, perhaps, slightly squishy.

Did cocaine come in chunks? I had always thought it was a powder, not that I have any personal knowledge, but that's what I've been led to believe.

Was this cube, whatever it was, perhaps covered in the stuff?

Crispin eyed the cube for a second, brows raised, before he lifted it to his mouth. And popped it inside.

CHAPTER SEVENTEEN

MY EYES BUGGED out and my mouth opened on what I can best describe as a silent scream. Through the gap in the door, I saw Christopher's jaw drop, too. His hand twitched towards his cousin, but it was far too late for either of us to do anything to stop him. All we could do was watch, wide-eyed, for what felt like an eternity—my heart hammered against my ribs as I waited for him to fall to the floor and go into convulsions—while Crispin chewed. Finally, he swallowed and extended the bag to Christopher. "Delicious. Turkish Delight, Kit?"

Christopher peered into the bag and then up at Rivers. "Is this some sort of joke?"

"Your cousin asked me to bring him sweets," Rivers said coolly.

"You knew what I wanted, though. And it wasn't Turkish Delight."

He closed up the bag and put it on a nearby table before he folded his arms across his chest. "Would you care to explain what's going on?"

"Shouldn't that be my question?" Rivers wanted to know.

"Should it?"

Rivers's handsome face hardened, and his posh accent dropped off for something rather less polished. "Think I'm stupid, do you? I haven't heard from you in ages, and suddenly you ring me up out of nowhere, not two days after Freddie Montrose dropped dead, wanting me to believe you're looking for candy?"

"First of all," Crispin said, his face dark, "Monty did not merely *drop dead*. If anything, he was dropped. And furthermore—"

Rivers held up a hand. "Be that as it may, it's been months since you rang me up wanting anything, St George. So yes, I'd say something's going on. You're trying to trap me into something. And it's not going to work. I'll take payment for a hundred grams of Turkish Delight, if you please, and then I'll get out of your house before you spring something else on me."

"Now, what would I spring on you, Dom?" Crispin smiled in a not-at-all reassuring way. "I just wanted to talk to you about what happened the other night. The only way to get hold of you, is to ring up, so I did. The sweets were an excuse, I admit it. But all I want to do, is talk."

Rivers shook his head. "I don't know what happened the other night. It was nothing to do with me. You think I go around killing people? Not precisely good for business, is it?"

"I imagine not. You've heard about Gladys Long, I suppose?"

Rivers's eyes narrowed. "What about Gladys Long?"

"She's dead," Crispin said, and this time it was Rivers who staggered. Just a quick wobble, though, and then he had his feet under him again.

"You're lying."

Crispin shook his head. "I'm not. Someone killed her. Yesterday afternoon. The same way they killed Monty."

Rivers turned pale. Or rather, as his skin was olive, he turned sallow. "But Gladys didn't know anything. She was in the kitchen with me when... when it happened."

"When someone in that flat killed Monty, you mean."

Rivers winced, but nodded. "The two of us were in the kitchen. It wasn't until we came out that we saw the other three standing by the door to the butler's pantry. You two were still in the sitting room with your other cousin. The girl."

"Here's the problem," Crispin said. "Freddie Montrose and I weren't close. We went to university together, but that's a few years ago now, and he was older than I. Lately, he has spent what feels like half his time putting my face on the front cover of his vile tabloid and getting me in trouble with my family. I'm lucky I haven't been disinherited with some of the stories Monty has put in print."

Rivers nodded.

"But nobody had the right to kill him. If *I* didn't want him dead, I don't see why anyone else would have."

"You weren't the only one he wrote about," Rivers pointed out.

Crispin arched a brow. "Was I not? Had he already done an exposé on you? I rather assumed that was why he attached himself to the party that night."

"Me?" Rivers said, and shook his head. "Oh, no. I usually manage to stay out of the tabloids. Saturday night was an anomaly. I didn't recognize him in the frock and wig, or I would have kept my distance and caught up with Ronnie and Gladys outside. But no, I wasn't talking about myself."

"Who, then?"

Rivers hesitated. When he didn't immediately start naming names, Crispin added, blandly, "I suppose you can prove where you were yesterday afternoon between noon and two, can you? And that you were nowhere near Ellery Mews or Belgravia?"

It was so smoothly done that Rivers might not even have felt the knife slide in. At least not until Crispin twisted it, his voice hardening, "Because I was there at that time, and I saw a red Morris Oxford parked on Eccleston Street. I was the last person to see her alive, you see—save for the person who killed her, of course—and so I have vested interest in finding someone else who was there at that time, so they don't put me away for it."

"Ronnie Blanton," Rivers said. His voice was sour, as if the name had been dragged out of him quite against his will, and perhaps it had been. Albeit not so much against his will that he had kept quiet about it.

Crispin arched a brow. "What about him? He visited Gladys yesterday?"

"I don't know anything about that," Rivers said, "but Frederick Montrose wrote a story about Ronnie a month or two ago. The same type of thing that he does about you. Except Ronnie's father isn't as forgiving as yours seems to be, and Ronnie cares a lot more than you do."

"Cares about what?"

"About anything," Rivers said. "If Montrose had written a story about how, to celebrate your birthday, you dressed up in a gown and high heels and crashed a drag ball at Rectors nightclub where you had champagne with a table full of men in drag, you would have thought it was all good fun. Ronnie would have hidden away at home for a month to cope with the shame."

And would have needed extra doses of dope to deal with the embarrassment, probably.

"It would have been good fun," Crispin said with a snigger.

"Nobody's going to believe that I've suddenly gone over to the dark side, you know."

He smirked at Christopher, who rolled his eyes. "That's easy for you to say, Crispin. Your reputation precedes you. Although I don't think Uncle Harold would have been as sanguine about the whole thing as you seem to think he would be."

"I'm usually more worried about Philippa than Father," Crispin said. "All Father can do is disinherit me. Darling can eviscerate someone with words and leave them bleeding on the floor. Although luckily she was at Rectors with us this time, so I don't imagine there's much she can say."

"I wouldn't be too sure," Christopher said, which was certainly the same thing I was thinking right then. Eviscerate him? Really? How deplorably dramatic.

"At any rate," Crispin said, dragging the conversation back on track, "Monty wrote something about Ronnie, did he? I must have missed that."

"You were stuck in the country, as I recall," Rivers answered. "It was during that period after your grandfather died."

Of course. Uncle Harold had kept his only son chained up in Wiltshire between the murders and the funerals so he wouldn't scandalize society by appearing on the front cover of the Tatler—or, I suppose, The Daily Yell—with a drink in one hand and a wench in the other before his mother and grandfather were in the ground.

"I rather thought I might hear from you at that point," Rivers added, "but alas..." He spread his hands.

Because a Crispin who was mourning the death of his grandfather and his mother might have wanted the oblivion found in some of what Rivers was peddling, I assumed. It didn't make me like Rivers any more.

But at any rate, deprived of his favorite subject, Freddie Montrose must have decided to write about Ronnie Blanton instead. I hadn't seen the article either, or if I had, I hadn't thought to remember any details about it.

"What did Monty write about Ronnie?"

"The usual claptrap," Rivers said. "The drinking, the parties, the dope. There was a treasure hunt that weekend—sorry you missed it, old chap—where everyone got up in fancy dress and tried to climb Cleopatra's Needle..."

"Cleopatra's Needle isn't climbable," Crispin said coolly. "I've tried. So drinking, parties, dope. Women?"

It was Rivers's turn to snigger. "Not for Blanton."

I waited for Crispin to glance at Christopher. He didn't. "Ronnie's queer?"

"Who knows?" Rivers shrugged. "He's working hard to hide something."

"Other than the murder?"

Rivers didn't respond, and Crispin added, "Have you seen him since Saturday night?"

"Saw him yesterday afternoon," Rivers said. "He's in bad shape."

Yes, he had been. We had seen him yesterday as well, and he had absolutely been in bad shape. But at least now we knew that Rivers had been out in his red Morris Oxford yesterday. Whether that meant that he had also gone to see Gladys Long, was of course a different story.

The conversation lagged for a moment, and I waited for Tom to make himself known. When he didn't, and when no one else said anything, Rivers spoke up again. "Is there anything else I can do for you? Otherwise, I'm going to take my leave."

"Feel free," Crispin said, waving a hand at the door. "How much do I owe you for the Turkish Delight?"

Rivers smirked. "Keep your money. It was worth it to see the look on your face when you saw what was in the bag."

Crispin nodded. "Let me walk you out."

"When you can just summon the butler to show the riff-raff out? Don't bother."

"It's hardly like that—" Crispin began, but Rivers was already on his way toward the door to the foyer. Crispin must have decided against running after him.

We all waited—I know I did—for Tom to do something. To stop Rivers, to follow him. But nothing happened. We could hear Rogers materialize in the foyer with Rivers's outer garments, and then the door closed on Rivers's heels with a, "Good day, sir," from Rogers. I stayed where I was while I listened to the Morris's engine engage in the courtyard, and then the sound of it rolling away.

"Are you still awake back there?" Crispin asked, and that was when the legs of Tom's chair scraped as he got to his feet. Crispin added, "It's all right, Darling. You can come out. He's gone."

"I'm aware." I rounded the door jamb into the green parlor. "I heard every word. I thought you wanted to talk to him, Tom?"

"There was nothing I could do," Tom said, with frustration and unwilling amusement mingled on his face. "We all know he deals dope. But we can't prove it. Not from that conversation. Clever bastard."

Crispin nodded. "He didn't say a single word you could use to hold him, did he?"

Tom shook his head. "Not a one. Did you suspect he was going to do this?"

Crispin snorted. "Of course not. I've bought from him before; I thought he'd jump at the opportunity to take my money again."

"The look on your face," Christopher said with a gurgle of laughter, "when you looked into the bag and saw the Turkish Delight...!"

"The look on Christopher's face," I said crossly, "when you popped whatever it was in your mouth. Really, St George, have you no concept of the way we worry?"

"You thought I was going to fall down and froth at the mouth? Darling, it's almost as if you care." He flapped his eyelashes.

"There's no need to be facetious," I told him. "I don't want you dead, you know. And if he did kill Montrose and Gladys, and thought you knew that he had done, he might have tried to kill you, too."

"I suppose he might have done. It really was just Turkish Delight in the bag, though."

He glanced at Tom. "Shouldn't you be going, Gardiner, before he gets too far away for you to catch up?"

"Finch is on him," Tom said.

"Not in the police car, I hope?"

Tom glanced at me. "Of course not. We're not stupid, you know."

Of course not. "Did you plan this?"

"Yes," Tom said. "And no. I thought he would show up with the dope and try to exchange it for money, and I would be able to arrest him. That was what I hoped would happen. Finch has been in place outside so we'd be able to transport him to Scotland Yard once we had him. But just in case something went wrong, I had him fetch one of the unmarked cars. He'll realize, when Rivers leaves on his own, that he needs to follow. If he manages to stay on him, we might at least have an idea where to find Rivers for next time. He probably won't answer a summons from here again."

He slanted a sideways look at Crispin, who shook his head.

"Not bloody likely. I'm on the *persona non grata* list now, I imagine."

"That's all right," I said. "You don't want his dope anyway."

"Of course not, Darling." He rolled his eyes, but didn't wait for me to answer, just went on. "We did learn a few things, I suppose."

"Rivers seemed shocked to hear about Gladys's death," I said, "so he was either surprised or he's a very good actor."

Tom nodded. "I wasn't able to see anything from where I was sitting, but that did sound like a genuine reaction."

"It looked like one, too," Christopher said, and added, "although I suppose you never know. Some people lie superbly."

"You know him best," I asked Crispin. "What do you think?"

"About his reaction? It looked genuine to me. But you never know, do you? And I told him the truth: I did see a red Morris Oxford on Eccleston Street after I'd left."

"But there are lots of those. Ronnie Blanton has one, too."

"They all piled into it outside Rectors that night," I said, "and drove to Mayfair in it. And after it all happened, after we took off with Montrose's body and they cleaned up the flat, Hutchison and Ogilvie might have borrowed it to get home. And they may have kept it until yesterday."

"Hutchison said Gladys drove home with Rivers," Christopher said. "He had his own automobile there that night. I didn't see it, but it might well have been a red Morris Oxford."

"So to recap, Hutchison and Ogilvie could have been in possession of Blanton's red Morris yesterday afternoon. Or Blanton could have been."

"Or I could have seen a completely innocent red Morris that didn't belong to anyone we know," Crispin added, "and whoever killed Gladys got there on the tube."

Yes. That covered it.

"I wish we could eliminate at least one of them. But I don't see how. They were all by themselves when we saw them yesterday. Blanton was in Mayfair, Hutchison in Kensington. Dobbins, if we're considering him, was out somewhere, looking for cigarettes for Blanton. Ogilvie was also out somewhere; Hutchison said he didn't know where. He might have been driving Blanton's motorcar, or he might not. Dobbins could have been driving it, for all we know, or it might have been sitting in Blanton's garage."

"Or that might have been it, outside, just now," Tom said.

"Rivers was wherever Rivers holes up, but he did say he'd gone to see Blanton at his flat. What was that remark about Southwark, by the way, St George?"

Crispin smirked. "That's what is known as a dig, Darling. His accent is common as dirt when he forgets to put on the posh vowels. I thought I'd make a reference to it."

"Of course you did." I rolled my eyes. "It's a miracle no one has murdered you, St George. And speaking of that... eviscerated? Really?"

"Right," Crispin said. "When I said that, I forgot you were listening. I should have kept my mouth shut."

"Yes, you should have. I'm sure your remark about Southwark didn't make Rivers any friendlier."

"Likely not." He sniggered. "So where are we now? Any closer to where we want to be?"

"If Rivers was telling the truth," Tom said, "and he was in the kitchen with Miss Long when Mr. Montrose was killed—and that's the same story she told, wasn't it?"

Crispin nodded.

"Then we're down to the three young men. All of whom had the opportunity to visit Ellery Mews yesterday."

"But if Gladys and Rivers were in the kitchen together

when Montrose was killed," I objected, "she couldn't have known which of the other three did it. So what was the reason for killing her?"

"They might have told her," Christopher suggested. "Or she overheard. After we left Sunday morning. While they were cleaning up. They probably discussed what had happened."

"If that's the case, Rivers would have known, too. Wouldn't he? He was there, if Hutchison was telling the truth when he said that Rivers took Gladys home."

"But Hutchison could have been lying," Christopher said. "Rivers could have run off immediately. Or Rivers could have been lying about not knowing. They could all be lying."

"I'm inclined to take Rivers out of the equation, myself," Crispin said after a moment's silence.

Tom's eyebrows rose. "Are you really? For what reason?"

Crispin glanced at him. "It makes sense that he and Gladys would be in the kitchen together. He had brought her dope and she would want to use it. She wasn't in as bad a shape as Ronnie, but I could tell she wanted a hit. He probably set it up for her. And if they were in the kitchen and he was busy fiddling with the cocaine, he might not have noticed Monty in the butler's pantry."

"*She* might not have noticed," Tom corrected, "but he might have. He wasn't high, was he?"

We all shook our heads. "He knows better than to use the merchandise," Crispin opined. "He's seen all too well what happens when you do."

Tom nodded. "And of everyone there, Rivers is the one with the strongest motive for wanting Mr. Montrose out of the way. Rivers was actively breaking the law. If Montrose did something to expose him, he would go to prison. The others—or Ronnie Blanton and Gladys Long, at any rate—were just users. He's a dealer. If he did notice Montrose listening in, he had a very good reason to kill him. And if he did, Gladys Long would have seen him do it. So out of everyone, Rivers is the one most likely to have needed to kill her."

Yes. That did make sense. But...

"I know I didn't see his face," I said, "but he seemed sincerely shocked when St George told him that she was dead."

"I did see his face," Christopher agreed, "and he was. And not just that, but he seemed frightened by it. As if they really had been together in the kitchen, and they really hadn't seen what happened to Montrose, and he couldn't imagine why anyone would want to kill her."

"But since they had," Crispin added, "he was afraid that he might be next."

"That was the impression I got," Christopher nodded.

"So we're no further along than we were." Tom sounded cross. "Other than that the three of you seem to think that the person with the strongest motive didn't do it, and someone else did."

I glanced at Christopher, who glanced at Crispin. "I suppose so," the latter said. "Although I'd like to point out that, since we don't know what motives the others might have had, we don't actually know that Rivers was the person with the strongest motive."

"But it's a good one," I added quickly, when Tom's face darkened, "we agree."

"Here is what I want you to do," Tom said to Crispin, ignoring my attempt to cajole him into a better humor. "Contact your friends—all three of them: Blanton, Hutchison, and Ogilvie—and invite them over for a discussion. Gladys Long is dead, and someone might connect her to Mr. Montrose's body —after all, they were seen sitting together at Rectors, and sitting with the rest of you, as well, and some of you have recognizable faces—and that might mean you're all in danger of being arrested. You want to talk about how to handle the situation. Get your stories straight, so to speak."

Crispin nodded.

"You be here, too," Tom told Christopher, "since you were at Rectors that night, and of everyone there, you're perhaps the one most likely to be recognized by the regulars."

Christopher nodded. "Out of curiosity…"

"Yes," Tom said. "A couple of the people we arrested that night pointed fingers at you. Not as yourself, of course, but as Kitty Dupree. And a few made comments about your 'sister' being there, as well."

He turned back to Crispin. "Get them to talk about things. Montrose, Gladys Long, Cambridge, articles in The Daily Yell, cocaine… as well as what happened on Saturday night. See if any of them lets anything slip. Accuse Rivers and see if they jump to agree that he must be guilty."

"Leave it to me," Crispin said.

"I'll have to, won't I?" Tom turned to Christopher. "Whenever he loses control of the conversational ball, chuck it back to him."

Christopher nodded. "I don't know them. I probably wouldn't be talking much anyway."

"What about me?" I wanted to know, since my name hadn't come into this at all so far. "I was there, too, you know."

"But you won't be here for this," Tom said. "They're much more likely to talk freely without your presence."

"Oh, wonderful." I stuck my bottom lip out. "I'll just sit at home alone and wait to be murdered, shall I? What if the killer really is Rivers, and he comes for me?"

"Evans will stop him in the lobby," Christopher said.

"He didn't stop anyone who wanted to come upstairs yesterday."

"That's true. Perhaps it's better if you stay with us. Just not in the same room."

"You want me to skulk next door again?"

"I'll be skulking next door," Tom said, "and so, I imagine, will Finchley. You're welcome to join us."

In that case...

"I would be delighted to skulk with you," I said.

CHAPTER EIGHTEEN

ONCE WE HAD HASHED out the verbiage (and Tom had officially approved it), Crispin penned the notes to Blanton and to the combination of Hutchison and Ogilvie and dispatched them with two of Sutherland House's footmen, who were told to request a reply from each recipient. While we waited for them to come back, we polished off the food Rogers had brought into the green parlor earlier, and went over the plan in more detail. By the time each footman returned with the response that the recipients would be here at nine that evening, we were still sitting around the table batting about ideas for how to bring up the various subjects Tom wanted introduced.

But once it became clear that we—or Crispin—would indeed be hosting the murder suspects to Scotch and cigars—or more likely cigarettes—that evening, Tom got to his feet and stretched. "I'd better go. I'll have to talk this plan over with Chief Inspector Pendennis before we can move forward. And he'll need to get the commissioner onboard, I daresay. We'll be tricking the children of some very upstanding citizens into making admissions about all sorts of illegal behavior. Wouldn't want to do that without official approval."

"Is there a chance that your superiors won't allow things to go forward?" I asked, as Tom shrugged into the tweed jacket he had taken off before sitting down at table.

"They can't do anything about St George hosting friends for the evening. Even if they're people Scotland Yard suspects of being complicit in one or more crimes. The worst case scenario is that I'm told I can't be here. If I can't—"

"I'll take notes. And we'll all try to remember everything we can of what they say."

"If anyone confesses to murder," Christopher added, "obviously we won't forget that."

Tom nodded. "I'll most likely be back here by eight, at the latest. I have to check in with the boss, and with Finch on how he did on tailing Dominic Rivers, and on anything new that might have come up in either investigation. There are people going door to door in Ellery Mews and people talking to everyone who was arrested at Rectors. All we need is a single break, just one person who saw something definitive..."

He trailed off, wistfully. The three of us who were left exchanged glances.

"We'll figure it out," Christopher said. He cleared his throat diffidently. "Would you like me to take you to Westminster in St George's motorcar? He won't mind if I borrow it, I'm sure."

The expression on Crispin's face indicated that yes, he did mind, although to his credit he didn't say the words out loud.

"That's not necessary," Tom said. "It's not a long walk, and I daresay the fresh air and exercise will help me prepare my case for the commissioner."

Christopher nodded. "Let me walk you out, then."

They headed out together. Tom fetched his hat from Rogers and then the front door closed behind them.

"I wouldn't be surprised if Kit hangs on all the way to the Embankment," Crispin said.

I wouldn't, either, but it didn't seem very nice to say so. "I'm sure Tom will send him back before they get that far. He'll turn around at the next corner, most likely."

"Would you care to make a wager?" Crispin wanted to know. "I'll give you excellent odds on him not coming back for an hour, at least."

"I have better things to do with my money than risk losing it to you," I said severely, "and you should be more careful with the Sutherland fortune than that."

He lifted a shoulder. "I don't see why, Darling. There's plenty of it. More than I can use up in a lifetime, even in particularly riotous living."

"Then perhaps you should endeavor to do something worthwhile with it," I told him. "There are lots of people less fortunate than you, you know."

"Of course I know it, Darling. Sadly, I'm not in charge of the fortune yet. For now, that sort of thing is in my father's hands, not mine. Perhaps you should appeal to him for a donation to your favorite charity."

"Oh, yes," I said, "I can see that going over well. Although truth be told, he seemed rather happy with me by the time he left Christopher's and my flat yesterday afternoon."

"Did he really?" He was still sprawled in one of the chairs, while I had gotten to my feet to watch Christopher and Tom walk away through the window, and now he watched me from out of narrowed eyes. "Why was that?"

"I have no idea," I said, stopping behind the chair I had been sitting on earlier, on the opposite side of the table, with my hands on its back as I peered back at him. "I believe I said something derogatory about you—something along the lines of 'poor, little, rich boy with every woman he meets falling at his feet'—it was after you decided to turn your wiles on me, you remember, so I was a bit put out with you—but I have no idea why that should have pleased your father."

"Indeed," Crispin said, watching me. "But he seemed happy, did he?"

"He seemed to be." I hesitated. "I can't help but have noticed that the two of you don't get on very well. I don't think I've ever taken note of it before, or at least not in the same way. Is it something new?"

"Since Mother died," Crispin said. "Or slightly before."

He looked away for a moment before he added, "Although I don't suppose we've ever had the kind of relationship that Kit has with Uncle Herbert. It doesn't seem to matter what Kit does; Uncle Herbert and Aunt Roslyn—and you—love him in spite of it. Father's regard has always depended on my behavior, and not whether or not I am—"

He broke off and shook his head, and picked up the conversation again in a different spot. "I never doubted that Mother loved me, even if she was never as warm about it as Aunt Roz. She was always perfectly correct, and so was father, but it was rarely warm. Smothering at times, on Mother's side, but not actually warm. And then came that weekend at Sutherland Hall, when Grimsby regurgitated all of the secrets he had dug up about everyone..." He made a face.

"And Uncle Harold heard yours and was appalled?" I said sympathetically.

He nodded. "Yes, Darling. He heard mine and was appalled."

"I'm so sorry," I said. "Although truthfully, you know, I read your list of peccadillos, and I'm not surprised."

He scowled. "For the last time, Darling, I don't know the girl with the baby. I have never seen her before. She—"

"Yes, yes," I said, batting his protestations away. "So you've said. But it's not just that, anyway. It's all the other women. And the parties and the alcohol and the Ballot. And the fact that you have Dominic Rivers's private direction and have bought dope from him in the past. If I were your parent, I would be appalled, too."

"Eviscerated," Crispin said dryly. "Bleeding."

I snorted. "You look perfectly fine to me."

He smirked. "Why, thank you, Darling."

"I didn't mean it that way," I said, "as you very well know."

The smirk broadened. "Of course, Darling."

I rolled my eyes. "Come off it, St George. You own a mirror. You know what you look like. And even if you didn't, all the women falling at your feet would tell you."

"You don't fall at my feet, Darling. Perhaps it means more, coming from you."

"In that case," I told him, "you're nice to look at, St George. You look just like Christopher, don't you? Sadly, you don't have his personality, and yours rather ruins the effect."

"There's the Darling we all know and love. For a moment there, I was worried you had lost your edge."

He pushed to his feet. "I'm going to go upstairs to my room for a bit. Mop up the blood, you know. You can do what you want. Stay here and wait for Kit, or go home. Make yourself at home in the library. Whatever you want. I have—"

A shadow crossed his face. "I have some things to think about."

I nodded, and watched him head for the door. He was almost there when I raised my voice. "Crispin?"

He spun on his heel, brows elevated, and I flushed. I don't usually use his given name—it sits uncomfortably in my mouth, and I didn't know why I had done it this time. But I pushed through. "Do you know who the killer is?"

He looked at me in silence for a moment before he gave a single shake of his head. "I don't."

"Do you think you may have guessed?" Was there someone he suspected, and a reason to suspect them?

"I have an idea," Crispin said.

"Will you tell me?"

He shook his head.

"Will you tell Tom? When he comes back, and before the others arrive?"

"No." He shook his head again. "I won't. I might be wrong. And even if I'm not wrong, I'd rather pretend I am until I can't pretend anymore."

So a friend, then. Although they were all friends, at least to a degree, I supposed. Even Dominic Rivers.

So I nodded, and let him pass out of the parlor without stopping him again. Without insisting that he tell me, or tell Tom at the first opportunity.

By the time I reached the foyer myself, he was halfway up the stairs, but he stopped politely when I said his name again. Or his title, this time. "St George?"

"Yes, Darling?"

"I'm going to go home for a while," I said. "As Tom said, I think I could use a walk to clear my head and think things through."

He nodded.

"When Christopher comes back, would you tell him where I've gone? And that he can either follow me home or stay here, it doesn't matter."

Crispin nodded. "Yes, Miss Darling," Rogers intoned.

"I'll be back before eight."

"Come at seven," Crispin said. "We'll have supper before things get hairy."

I nodded. So did Rogers, seemingly in approval of the plan.

"Get some rest, St George," I said. "It's going to be a difficult night."

"Yes, Darling." He continued up the stairs. Rogers handed me my hat and gloves and reticule and bowed me out the door. I headed down Park Lane in the direction of home.

I DID NOT RUN into Christopher on the way, nor did I see anyone else I knew. By the time I got to the Essex House Mansions, my cheeks were nicely pink and I couldn't wait to get out of the frock and shoes I was wearing. I had put them on in a hurry yesterday morning, when Uncle Harold startled us awake by knocking on the door, and since then, I had walked all through Belgravia and Knightsbridge in them, had discovered a dead body, and spoken to several potential murderers, and had driven to Wiltshire and back. I wanted a bath and a fresh set of unmentionables, not to mention some time to myself. I had spent the walk turning over all the facts of the crime—the two crimes—and thought I might have figured out what Crispin thought he knew, but I still needed a bit more time to put the pieces together.

Evans saw me coming and swung the front door open. "Afternoon, Miss Darling."

"Afternoon, Evans," I said politely. "Any mail?"

"Not so far this morning, Miss Darling."

"Any visitors?"

"Not since yesterday, Miss Darling."

I glanced around the lobby, quite as if I expected to see him materialize out of thin air, which of course I didn't. "I don't suppose Christopher's home?"

"I haven't seen Mr. Astley since yesterday, Miss Darling."

I nodded. "By the way, Evans. When Miss Long arrived

here yesterday, did you happen to notice if anyone dropped her off? Or whether she walked up to the door?"

"A young gentleman in a red motorcar dropped her off, Miss Darling," Evans said.

So that eliminated precisely no one. "Did you happen to get a look at the young gentleman?"

But Evans shook his head. No, of course he hadn't. "The top of the car was up, Miss Darling. I saw that he was a young gentleman in a tweed jacket and a soft cap, but I didn't get a look at his face. He didn't get out of the car to open the door for the young lady."

I nodded, disappointed. "Thank you, Evans. I don't suppose you'd recognize the gentleman if you saw him again, would you?"

Perhaps we could have Evans lurk outside Sutherland House this evening, and finger—as the professionals say—either Blanton, Hutchison, or Ogilvie when they turned up.

And if he didn't recognize either of them, then it might have been Dominic Rivers in the motorcar.

Although did it really matter who had dropped Gladys off? She had told Crispin it was Hutchison. Hutchison had said it wasn't him. One of them had lied. But did it really matter who? Whoever it was, needn't have been the person who killed her. It was no crime to drive Gladys to our flat and drop her off.

"I don't imagine so, Miss Darling," Evans said apologetically. "As I said, it was only a glimpse. The gentleman stayed inside the motorcar."

I thanked him and headed upstairs, where the first thing I did, after stripping off the clothes I had worn for far too long, was to fill the bathtub with a lot of lovely warm water and bath salts and sink in to my neck. Then I lay there, while the water lapped gently at the bottom of my hair, and thought things through.

From the beginning.

Crispin and I had gone to Rectors to look for Christopher. Montrose had been there, as he had said, in the hopes of experiencing another raid or something similar. Something newsworthy for his tabloid.

Blanton, Hutchison, Ogilvie and Gladys Long had been there for fun, or perhaps to meet Dominic Rivers.

As Blanton had said (and Crispin had confirmed), customers did not seek Rivers out. He came to them. So it was likely that Rivers had told Blanton to meet him at Rectors. He might have been doing business with someone else there, and Blanton was, according to the hints Rivers had dropped, uneasy about his sexuality.

When we all left Rectors to go to Blanton's flat, Montrose had attached himself to the party. Logically, he must have noticed Blanton's symptoms and/or had recognized Rivers, and had decided that the dope angle was a better scoop than another potential raid. He had come with us to Mayfair to dig up more information.

Montrose had been killed in the butler's pantry while Christopher, Crispin and I were sitting in Ronnie Blanton's parlor.

Dominic Rivers and Gladys Long had been in the kitchen, at least if you believed what they said. They had both said the same thing on separate occasions.

Furthermore, there was really no reason to think they hadn't been where they said they were. Whether or not they'd been in the kitchen made no difference to the case against either of them. If Rivers had killed Montrose and Gladys knew it, they might have made an agreement to lie. Rivers had Gladys over a barrel, since he controlled her access to the dope she needed, and so she would have agreed to lie for him, to keep the supply coming. They could have noticed Montrose spying on them through the door between the kitchen and butler's pantry—a door which gave them access to Montrose in a way that the rest of us in the flat didn't have, without having to go out into the hallway—and then Gladys watched Rivers kill Montrose.

As Tom had pointed out, Rivers probably did have the best motive of anyone in the flat for wanting Montrose out of the way, and in this scenario, Gladys's murder made perfect sense. She knew that Rivers had killed Montrose, and even if she had agreed to keep mum about it, he might have felt safer with her dead.

Or perhaps Gladys was the one who had noticed Montrose spying on them while Rivers was getting her dope ready, and she was the one who had picked up the rolling pin and whacked him over the head. Whether she'd been strong enough to do that was questionable, but say for a moment that she had. Rivers might have been induced to lie for her—he'd want to keep her as a client, and he would have been happy to have Montrose out of the way himself, I assumed—although this scenario did not explain who might have killed Gladys or why.

Blanton, Hutchison, and Ogilvie had been in the parlor with Crispin, Christopher, and me when Montrose excused himself to look for the loo. Blanton had been flying high after his own excursion into the kitchen with Rivers. Hutchison had been mixing drinks, and Ogilvie had been chatting with Christopher.

Practically as soon as Montrose left, Hutchison sent Blanton after him, and as soon as Blanton left, Hutchison had excused himself, as well. That might have taken a minute, perhaps two. Ogilvie had looked very uncomfortable for another minute or two, before Crispin managed to talk him into following the others. And then the three of us had had a conversation that must have lasted a few minutes before Gladys started screaming bloody murder—pardon the pun—in the hallway.

She had told Crispin—and so had Rivers, separately—that they had seen the others at the butler's pantry door when they'd left the kitchen, and that was the first they knew that anything had happened to Montrose.

That might be true, or it might not.

Hutchison had told Christopher and me that when he'd arrived in the butler's pantry, Montrose was already dead. If he had been telling the truth, Rivers, Gladys, or Blanton had to be the murderer.

If Gladys and Rivers had told the truth *and* Hutchison had told the truth, it had to be Blanton.

Unless Hutchison had gone somewhere else before the butler's pantry—there might have been a search on for Montrose throughout the flat; nobody had known exactly where he'd be, I assumed—in which case, Ogilvie might have had time to kill him, too.

Or Hutchison might have lied and killed Montrose himself.

This was getting me no closer to a solution. I turned around in the tub, and made the water slosh against the edges before it settled down again.

Crispin thought he knew who the killer was, and seemed sad about it. That meant it was most likely someone he would consider a friend. He might not include Rivers in that designation, and he had said, hadn't he, that he and Ogilvie weren't close?

And so I seemed to be back to Hutchison and Blanton again.

Crispin had seen a red Morris Oxford parked outside the mews when he came out after walking Gladys to her door. Blanton owned a red Morris Oxford. Hutchison could have had access to Blanton's red Morris Oxford.

Of course, Rivers also had a red Morris Oxford, which rather muddied the waters.

Of the four of them, we knew that Rivers and Ogilvie had been out and about yesterday, while Blanton and Hutchison had been at home when Christopher and I stopped by.

But we'd only seen them for a few minutes each, and there was no reason why they couldn't have left their respective flats before or after we'd been there.

Blanton claimed that he didn't remember any details about the murder, even that it had taken place at all.

Hutchison claimed that he didn't know who had killed Montrose.

Rivers claimed the same, only from the vantage point of the kitchen.

Ogilvie, as the last person out of the sitting room, was the least likely to have seen anything, I assumed.

Any one of them could have killed Gladys, or so it appeared to me, but it was really only the killer who had motive, wasn't it, and that equation only worked out for Rivers.

But Crispin wouldn't have been upset at the idea of Rivers as the murderer.

So what was I missing?

I stood up in the tub and reached for the towel.

"Blanton," I said out loud. "You're missing Blanton."

Blanton, whose flat it was. Blanton, whose drug habit it was. Blanton, whose Morris Oxford it was. Blanton, who had had a nasty article written about him by Freddie Montrose just last month.

Blanton, whose father wasn't as forgiving as Uncle Harold; not that Uncle Harold seemed to be particularly forgiving.

Ronald Blanton, who had been the only one out of the sitting room before Nigel Hutchison.

If Rivers had seen Blanton kill Montrose, he would have

wanted to keep it quiet, both because he'd like to keep Blanton's custom and because the man had done him a favor, honestly.

Gladys and Hutchison and Ogilvie would all have wanted to keep it quiet because they cared about Blanton.

And Crispin would feel bad about it, because he did consider Ronnie Blanton a friend, and probably also because of Blanton's fragility and his less-than-stellar relationship with Blanton Senior, which Crispin could probably relate to.

"It's Blanton," I told the empty flat as I left the bathroom and stepped into the hallway. "It has to be."

CHAPTER NINETEEN

THE THREESOME TURNED up together in the red Morris Oxford just before nine o'clock. By then, we had dined on Beef Wellington and mash in Sutherland House's sumptuous dining room—rather too big and too opulent for the three of us, especially since Christopher and Crispin hadn't bothered to dress for the occasion, and my gown really wasn't anything special.

It was, in fact, the yellow crepe with the silver spangles that Crispin had likened to the divine Josephine Baker's famous banana skirt in Dorset last month, and I waited for him to make a comment about it. But while he eyed it sideways and smirked, he said nothing.

Tom and Detective Sergeant Finchley arrived in time for pudding—spotted dick—and after that, we got busy arranging the parlor for guests.

"You go behind the screen this time, Miss Darling," Tom said. "It might be interesting to see whether any of them—and if so, which of them—is nervous enough to check the room for listening ears."

"None of them might," I protested.

He nodded. "But if one of them does, I'd rather have him find you than me."

"He could find none of us, if nobody hides behind the screen."

"But if nobody checks and you're allowed to stay there, you'll be able to hear everything much better than we will, in the other room," Finchley said, and that, of course, was true.

"They won't think anything of it, if it's you," Tom added. "If they find one of us, the jig is up."

Yes, of course it was. I quite saw why neither of them could hide there. I just didn't understand why *I* had to. If they didn't want me involved in the conversation—and Christopher and Crispin clearly didn't; they were both shaking their heads vigorously—shouldn't I simply hide somewhere else to begin with?

"Perhaps this time we could go with the maid's uniform?" Crispin suggested. "You could flit in and out with trays and buckets of ice."

"You don't think the other three would recognize me?"

"I doubt they'd look at you closely enough for that," Crispin said. "They'll either simply see the uniform and dismiss you as unimportant, or they'll notice the figure but not the face. Depends on whether they're snobs or chauvinists."

"I didn't get the impression that either Blanton or Ogilvie were the type to notice women's figures," I said, "so you'd better hope they're both snobs. And Hutchison seems the most observant of all of them—he was the one who first figured out that Montrose wasn't looking for the toilet in Blanton's flat the other night—so I wouldn't be surprised if he looked past both and recognized me. Especially since I spoke to him face to face just yesterday."

"Yes," Tom said as Crispin pouted, "let's not play games of

that sort with Miss Darling. Although now that I think about it…"

He eyed Finchley, who eyed him back.

Crispin sighed. "Who wants to be the butler and who wants to be the footman?"

"I'm older," Finchley said.

"I'm stouter," Tom answered. Which wasn't technically true—he wasn't stout at all, but he was more muscular than Finchley, who was tall and lanky.

They eyed one another in silence for a few moments, and then Tom turned to Crispin. "Take Finchley with you and find him some sort of uniform. Not a housemaid, please. But whether he's a butler or a footman I really don't care about, as long as he has license to loiter in the front hall."

"Leave it to me," Crispin said and waved Finchley to precede him through the door.

Tom looked around, rubbing his hands together.

"If you're putting Finchley in the front hall and Pippa behind the screen, where are you going to be?" Christopher wanted to know.

"I figure I'll just skulk behind the door to the drawing room, you know. It worked for Miss Darling earlier."

"You'd better hope neither of them think to check in there," Christopher said, but Tom merely shrugged.

"I'll have to count on the two of you to prevent that, I suppose, if it comes to it. You're both clever boys, and St George is quite used to throwing his weight around. I'm sure I can rely on you both to keep the others in line."

And so it was. Crispin brought Finchley back, arrayed in one of Rogers's black suits with a red waistcoat (to set him apart from any of the guests who may be wearing white tie—not that Christopher or Crispin were) and then Rogers was given the evening off while Finchley took Rogers's place in the foyer. He was at least twenty years younger than the venerable Rogers, and a lot less dignified, and he kept repeating the words, "May I take your coats and hats, gentlemen?" under his breath while we waited.

It was a few minutes before nine when we heard the second Morris Oxford of the day roll into the courtyard and come to a stop behind the Hispano-Suiza.

"And so it begins," Tom said softly and vanished into the darkness of the sitting room. I headed for the screen in the corner while Christopher and Crispin stayed where they were, seemingly at their ease in a chair each, nursing an after-dinner brandy.

"Wait for the knock, Finchley," Crispin called. "We don't want them to think we're improperly eager."

"No, my lord," Finchley's voice floated back, and Crispin grinned.

Christopher sighed, and I ducked behind the screen and made myself comfortable in the chair beside the telephone table. In the foyer, faintly, there came the knock on the door, and then Finchley's measured steps across the marble floor.

"Good evening, gentlemen."

"Nigel Hutchison, Ronald Blanton, and Graham Ogilvie to see Lord St George," Hutchison's voice said.

"His lordship is expecting you." I could hear the shuffling as Finchley stepped backward and the other three came inside. Finchley shut the door. "May I take your hats and coats, gentlemen?"

There was the swishing of fabric and then Finchley's voice came back. "His lordship is in the green parlor. If you'll follow me."

Multiple footsteps crossed the foyer, and then came Finchley's voice again, more distinctly now. "Your guests have arrived, my lord."

"Show them in, Finchley," Crispin said, and there was the sound of steps and greetings and finally, Finchley's voice.

"Do you require anything else, my lord?"

"We'll pour our own drinks, Finchley," Crispin said. "Go off and polish the silver."

"Very well, my lord." Finchley withdrew. I heard the soft click of the door latch and a moment of silence.

"He's new," Hutchison said, "isn't he?"

"New under-butler. It's Rogers's evening off." If the question had disconcerted Crispin at all, it didn't show in his voice. "You remember my cousin Kit, of course?"

There was a murmur of greeting.

"Can I offer you something to drink?" Crispin asked. And then he added, his voice half amused and half concerned— "Whatever are you doing, Hutchison?"

Hutchison was prowling, clearly. I could hear his footsteps coming closer to the screen behind which I was sitting. His voice was louder, too, than earlier. "Just making sure we're alone."

"My staff knows better than to gossip," Crispin said coolly, with a hint of offense in his voice. "Or perhaps you're worried that I have Scotland Yard stashed up the chimney?"

I couldn't see him, of course, but I know him well enough to recognize the particular tone that went along with an arched eyebrow.

There was a pause, in which I imagined that Hutchison might have exchanged a look with Blanton and/or Ogilvie.

"But if it will make you feel better," Crispin said, with what was surely a negligent wave of his hand, "go ahead, by all means. Look around to your heart's content. I'll pour. What'll it be, gentleman? We have all the usual poisons."

I could hear the sound of his footsteps cross the floor to the bar cart, and then the clinking of glasses and decanters.

"Gin Rickey for me," Blanton's voice said, "if you don't mind."

"I'll have the same," Ogilvie added.

"You know," Crispin's voice said, over the sound of the clinking of glasses and sloshing of liquid; as he went on, I realized he was addressing Hutchison, "you're not the only person to show up here today with suspicions. I asked Dom to stop by this afternoon, and do you know what he brought me? A hundred grams of Turkish Delight."

He waited for the laughter to subside. Blanton was howling like a hyena, so it took a while. "Not at all what I wanted, of course. But that's what he brought, so I had to be satisfied with it. It's in that bag over there, if anyone's interested."

There were footsteps, perhaps Blanton's, and then the rustling of the paper bag. And a snigger.

"I wanted to talk about Dom," Crispin added, as he handed the drinks around. "What'll be, Hutchie? D'you want a Gin Rickey or something else?"

"Whatever you're having is fine," Hutchison said. He had moved away from the screen now, I was happy to hear. Blanton, meanwhile, must be the one chewing on the Turkish Delight, because all Crispin got from him was a grunt. Ogilvie said, "Thank you."

"Brandy?" Crispin must have reached for another decanter, because I heard the clink of a glass and the sloshing of liquid. "Top off, Kit?"

"Not quite yet," Christopher said. "Better to keep all our wits about us for this conversation, I think."

"Hear, hear." Crispin must have toasted him, I imagined. "I couldn't agree more, old bean."

From the other three, there was a rather distinct silence. "What is that intended to mean?" Hutchison wanted to know.

"Make yourselves comfortable." I heard the sound as

Crispin dropped back into his chair. "This could take a while."

"What's going on, St George?" Blanton wanted to know. He giggled, but he also managed to sound concerned at the same time. "What about Dom?"

"Nothing that I know of," Crispin said. "You heard about Gladys, I assume?"

Neither of the other three said anything, which I figured meant that yes, they had all heard about Gladys.

"She turned up yesterday morning," Crispin said, "in Kit and Philippa's flat. Looking for reassurance."

The way he said it made it sound like women regularly took refuge in his arms when things went wrong, and that he regularly 'reassured' them. I made a face at the mental image the words engendered.

"I took her home, and after I left, someone else walked in and hit her over the head. And now I've got police knocking on my door, thinking I did it. And all because Freddie Montrose spent the last six months putting my face all over his odious magazine so everyone in London recognizes me on sight!"

His voice started out bland, but by the time he stopped speaking, it was both injured and full of bitterness. Theatricals at Cambridge, indeed.

Ronnie Blanton sniggered, of course. Everything seemed to strike him as funny. Hutchison said coolly, "What's this got to do with Dom? You said you wanted to talk about him."

There was a beat of silence. I imagined Crispin eyeing Hutchison. "I didn't ask any questions the other night," he said. "I took Monty's body and got rid of it, and I didn't insist on knowing what had happened. But with the police looking at me for Gladys..."

There was another pause.

There was a click of glass against wood, and I imagined Crispin putting the brandy glass on the little table next to his chair. "You heard about the raid on Rectors, didn't you? We had to leave Monty in Hyde Park instead of in the alley off Tottenham Court Road. But he was still in the dress and ladies' shoes, wasn't he? So Scotland Yard have been asking questions of the people they arrested during the raid, and some of them saw us all together at Rectors."

"All?"

I couldn't quite make out who asked the question. Most likely it was Hutchison again, but it could have been either Blanton or Ogilvie, as well.

"I don't know which of us—or which of you—they recognized," Crispin said. "All I know is that they recognized me. And Kit."

I imagine he flicked a glance at Christopher—and so did everyone else—before he continued. "And they described Monty well enough that the police identified his body from it. So now they're thinking that I must have killed Monty, too. And if they take a close look at the H6, they might find some of his blood in there. A single drop would be enough, wouldn't it? And if that happens, my goose is cooked."

Nobody said anything to that. Crispin's voice hardened. "I refuse to end up in Wormwood Scrubs over something I didn't do. They've been careful not to out and out accuse me. But if they do, I'm pointing the finger at someone else."

The pause this time was longer. Nobody broke it.

"And so we talk about Dom," Crispin said.

Up until now, I had been all right behind my screen. I had been able to keep up with the conversation and make educated guesses about everything else based on the sounds people made. Footsteps, the clinking of glasses, the shifting of bodies. But suddenly, it was as if everything stopped. No one said a word. No one moved. I didn't even hear anyone draw breath.

Then—

"Dom?" Blanton repeated, with a shrill undertone in his voice. Hard to say whether it was from fear or something else. "You think Dom did it?"

"It was either him or one of us. I don't suppose anyone wants to confess?"

No one did, it seemed, because that awkward silence descended again.

"I know it wasn't me," Crispin said. "And I know it wasn't Kit. And let's be honest, chaps, Dom had more reason than the rest of us to be afraid of what Monty might write. We would be embarrassed if he wrote another article about us, and it might get us in trouble with our families or with other people whose opinions we care about..."

Here someone made a noise, and Crispin stopped talking for a moment. When whoever it was didn't carry on with a comment, though, he picked up the sentence again, "—but I know my father isn't likely to disinherit me over it. If he does, the title will go to my Uncle Herbert—no offense, Kit—and I can't see Father letting that happen as long as he has an heir of his own. I don't imagine yours is likely to take that step, either, Ronald?"

Here was where being behind the screen was inconvenient. Blanton didn't answer with words, he either nodded or shook his head. I surmised he responded in the negative, because Crispin said, "But Dom would go to prison if word got out that he's peddling dope. Just look at what happened to Chang. Fourteen months in Wormwood Scrubs, and deportation."

"They couldn't deport Dom!" Blanton exclaimed, horrified.

I imagined Crispin's brow creeping up his forehead. "I imagine they could, you know. His mother was something in the foreign way, wasn't she? Italian or Portuguese or something of that nature? I wouldn't be surprised if they put him on the first boat back to Lima."

"Lima is in Peru," Christopher said. "You're thinking of Lisbon."

"Am I?"

"You must be. Lima is nowhere near Portugal." Christopher sniggered. "That's what comes of a Cambridge education, old chap. Should have gone to Oxford with me."

"Then I wouldn't have had the pleasure of beating you in the boat race, *old chap*," Crispin retorted.

"Only in -22 and -24! Oxford beat Cambridge in -23!"

"By a three-quarter length," Crispin sniffed. "We beat you by four-and-a-quarter lengths the other two years."

"A win is a win," Christopher said, and I had to admire how effortlessly they had introduced Cambridge into the conversation.

Blanton was still on the possible deportation of Rivers, however. "They can't do that!"

"If he killed Monty," Crispin said, "frankly, I don't care what they do with him."

Nobody said anything, and he added, "Look, I'm no fonder of The Daily Yell than you are. But I knew Monty. We went to university together, speaking of Cambridge. With you too, Hutchison. You remember Monty from school, don't you? He was a decent chap back then, wasn't he?"

"He was all right," Hutchison said. "I didn't know him well. He only attended for the first two months of my first term, I think. He got sent down after that editorial he wrote excusing what happened at Newnham."

"But it was just a prank, wasn't it?" Crispin didn't wait for a response. "And it's still not right that he was murdered. I mean, he wasn't hurting anybody that night at your flat..."

This must have been aimed at Ronald Blanton, who made a non-committal noise.

"I think he was awful," Graham Ogilvie said. "I, for one, am not sorry he's dead."

There was the sound of shifting as the attention moved from Blanton to Ogilvie. "Oho," Crispin said, and I recognized the slight maliciousness of his voice. "Would you like to confess to the murder, then, Gram?"

"Not me," Ogilvie said evenly. "He was dead by the time I had made my way to the butler's pantry. But he wrote an article about Ronnie a few weeks ago that made his old man practically foam at the mouth. And all because *you* were holed up in the country out of range."

"I could hardly help it that my mother and grandfather died." Crispin's voice was cool. "My father made it absolutely clear that my usual exploits were not to be tolerated until the scandal had blown over. But I'm sorry about the article, old chap."

This last must have been directed at Ronnie, who said something vague.

"What were we talking about...?" Crispin continued cheerfully. "Oh, yes. Dom. If none of us here killed Monty, it had to be Dom, didn't it? And if he did it, and Gladys saw it, then he had reason for wanting to get her out of the way, too, didn't he? And between us four, or five—"

He lowered his voice. "When I came out of the mews onto Eccleston Street yesterday, I saw a red Morris Oxford bullnose parked at the curb. And do you know what Dom drives?"

"A red Morris Oxford," Blanton said coldly. "So do I, you know, St George."

"But were you there?" Crispin shot back.

Blanton must have opened his mouth, because Ogilvie turned on him. "Be quiet, Ronnie. You know very well that you were not in Ellery Mews yesterday afternoon."

"Fine," Blanton said sulkily. "But that doesn't mean it was

Dom."

"It doesn't mean it wasn't," Crispin retorted. "Look, I don't want to accuse anyone. But somebody did it, and I know it wasn't me. It seems to me that Dom had the best motive. And if none of the three of you did it, who's left? It can't be Gladys."

There was a moment's silence, and then Hutchison said, "I agree with St George. It's time we face facts. If the police have connected St George to Montrose and Gladys, it's only a matter of time before they connect the rest of us. We have to get our stories straight."

"But I need Dom..." Blanton moaned.

"We'll find you someone else, Ronnie. St George is right, you know. It's what makes the most sense. Monty was already dead by the time I saw him—"

"Yes," Ogilvie said fervently. "Me, too."

"—and if you can't remember anything that happened that night, it's just as well to agree that Dom did it. It makes sense."

"Yes," Blanton admitted, "but—"

Hutchison's voice turned coaxing. "I'll make sure you get what you need, Ronnie. But you won't get it in prison, right? So let's just agree that it was Dom, and when the police show up—if they do—that's what we tell them. Monty was already dead when we saw him—that's the truth—and it had to be either Dom or Gladys who did it. That's true, too, isn't it?"

There was a pause.

"Yes?" Blanton said, although he still didn't sound certain.

"Good man." There was the sound of a slap on a shoulder.

"We all agree, then," Crispin said. "Other than Gladys, and she couldn't have hit herself on the back of the head, the only person who could have killed Monty was Dom. And that's what we tell the police."

There was a murmur all around.

"To Monty," Crispin said. "May he rest in peace."

CHAPTER TWENTY

YOU MAY HAVE THOUGHT that was the end of it, but they kept things going for several hours beyond that point. Tom must have wanted to kill them all, and so, I'm sure, did Finchley. I, at least, had a chair to sit on, but I had to be more quiet than the other two, since I was actually in the room with the rest of the party. So I sat there behind the screen, still as a statue on the uncomfortable telephone chair, while my posterior slowly turned numb and while my brain did the same. Every once in a while, someone—Crispin or Christopher—brought the conversation back around to the events of two nights ago, or to Gladys, or to Dominic Rivers and his business, but it didn't sound as if anything got accomplished by it. At one point, Crispin inquired after Hutchison's sister—there was the suggestion that something had happened between them at Cambridge, since Crispin didn't seem to have met a girl he hadn't tried to charm—and Hutchison's voice turned prickly when he said that his sister lived in the country with their mother and father.

"Not married yet, then?" Crispin asked.

Hutchison said stiffly that no, she wasn't.

"Remember me to her the next time you go down to visit, old chap," Crispin said, with what sounded like a condescending slap on the shoulder. I was frankly surprised that Hutchison didn't smack the no doubt obnoxious look off his face—I would have been tempted—but the conversation moved on from there without bloodshed.

It was almost midnight by the time Finchley finally got them out the door and I heard the Morris's engine engage in the courtyard. I waited until the sound of it had faded into the distance before I got to my feet (with an unbecoming groan, like a Rock of Ages, or an old person) and staggered out from behind the screen and into the room.

"That lasted forever!"

"We couldn't ask the initial questions and then push them out the door, Pippa," Christopher said. He had also stood up and was stretching, while Finchley and Tom were making their way in from the foyer and the sitting room, respectively. "They would have become suspicious if we hadn't been willing to sit and gab."

Crispin nodded. He was rotating his head and shoulders. "They went through rather a lot of Father's gin and brandy, but it wasn't entirely wasted. We did learn a few things."

"Such as?"

"Not in here." He shot a look towards the windows. "It's possible to see through these windows from the street, and we don't want them to turn around and get a glimpse of us all standing here nattering." He took my arm. "Into the sitting room. Someone close the door behind us."

A minute later we were seated in the next room, away from any possibility of being viewed from the street, and Crispin had pulled the heavy damask curtains across all the windows for extra privacy.

"Isn't this rather obsessive?" I wanted to know, as Christopher handed me my own gin and tonic before dropping down onto the Chesterfield next to me.

He shook his head. "I don't think so, Pippa. Hutchison was definitely suspicious. He almost found you less than a minute after he walked into the room. Crispin had to talk fast to get him to abandon the search."

The latter nodded. "The other two seemed willing to trust that we were all on the same side, but Hutchie was definitely wary. He was suspicious of Finchley, too. You wouldn't have been able to see it, but he kept shooting glances at the door to the foyer for a while after he sat down."

"That's right," Christopher nodded. "He didn't bring it up again, but he kept looking in that direction. At least until he got far enough into the conversation to forget. If he ever did."

"Was it me?" Finchley wanted to know. "Did I do something wrong?"

Crispin sniggered, but shook his head. "No, Finchley. You were the perfect under-butler. You can keep calling me 'my lord' for as long as you'd like."

Tom rolled his eyes. "They were willing to talk in spite of it, it seemed."

"For the most part," Christopher said. "Every once in a while, something would come up that they all three, or one or the other, clammed up about."

"Like Hutchison with his sister," I said. "What was that about, St George?"

Crispin leaned back in his chair, languidly. He had declined another drink, having pickled his liver sufficiently already this evening, so his hands were folded across his stomach but with no glass in sight. "The usual, Darling. Hutchison has an older sister by two years or so. She was at Cambridge when we started there."

"At one of the women's colleges?"

"I'm fairly certain it was Newnham," Crispin said. "Didn't I mention that earlier?"

He had, now that I thought about it. "Did something happen to her?"

"She's twenty-five or -six," Crispin said, "not married, not living in Town, buried somewhere in the dark of Shropshire with her parents, and her brother gets prickly when I ask a question about her? I'd say so."

"I thought the rioters didn't actually get into Newnham? No one was hurt, you said."

"No one that I know about," Crispin said. "But the run on Newnham wasn't all that happened that day, you know. All day long, the crowd in the King's Parade would hassle women students who walked by. It needn't have been an out-and-out assault for someone to be upset by it."

No, I supposed it needn't have been. "Did you know her? Hutchison's sister?"

"Only inasmuch as I knew any of the older students," Crispin said. "She'd come around now and then to see her brother. We were introduced."

"But nothing happened that would make him prickly about you in particular asking questions about her?"

"Did I seduce the girl? Is that what you're asking?" He slanted an amused look my way. "No, Darling, I did not seduce Hutchison's older sister when I was eighteen. You give me far too much credit."

"I would hardly call it credit," I said, while Christopher sniggered. "And after all, we all have to start somewhere, don't we?"

Crispin nodded gravely. "Indeed, Darling, we do. But in this case, no, I barely knew the girl, and only from having been introduced to her by her brother. Nothing happened that would make him object to me inquiring after her. Unless my reputation has preceded me, and my merely asking questions about any woman's health and wellbeing is abhorrent to her relatives."

"There's always that possibility," I agreed.

"I got the impression that this was more of a general thing, though, and not targeted at me in particular. The girl—woman now—is not quite right, and he didn't like to talk about it."

Christopher nodded. "That was the impression I got, too. He didn't like the reminder and didn't want to discuss it."

"Hutchison and Ogilvie both sounded rather protective of Ronald Blanton," Tom said. "Would you say that's correct?"

Christopher and Crispin both nodded. "In their own ways," Christopher added. "Ogilvie is sweet on him, I think."

"Romantically attached? Does Blanton reciprocate?"

"I'm hardly an expert on other people's feelings," Christopher began, and Crispin made an amused noise. Christopher shot him a look but refrained from comment, although what comment he could have made, I have no idea. He continued, "But I would guess, from his general behavior and everything we've learned about him so far, that Blanton inclines that way but is desperately trying to suppress his feelings because his father disapproves. One of those stringent old gentlemen who told his son not to be a nancyboy, I imagine."

Tom nodded. "So Ogilvie is in love with Blanton and is protective of him because he cares."

"That was my impression," Christopher said, and Crispin nodded.

"Nigel Hutchison does not incline that way at all," he said. "He likes women, and overall, they seem to like him. He and

Gladys had a thing going for a while, if that matters. I'm not sure whether it was over or not, by the time this all happened. He and Blanton go way back, though. I'm honestly surprised it's not the two of them living together instead of Hutchison and Ogilvie, although I suppose it might have been old man Blanton putting his foot down again, and refusing to let his son share a flat with another man."

"But he'll have Dobbins live in?"

He flicked a glance my way. "I'm sure Dobbins reports to the old man, Darling. And he's hardly going to engage in sexual escapades with Ronnie, is he?"

"From what you just said, Hutchison isn't, either."

He shrugged, acknowledging my point. "In any case, Hutchie is protective of Blanton because they go back a decade, at least. We knew them at Eton, didn't we, Kit?"

"You may have," Christopher said. "I didn't."

Crispin nodded. "Blanton's the soft type," he told Tom, "you know? Sensitive. Delicate. The sort that either gets picked on or turns malicious to avoid it."

"Like someone else we know," Christopher said dryly.

Crispin twitched irritably, as if a mosquito had stung him. "Hutchison's less exalted socially than Blanton," he added, "but he's more of a scrapper. The two of them gave each other something the other needed at Eton. So while Hutchison's reason is different from Ogilvie's, he also feels responsible for Blanton. They're both protective of him."

"And do you suppose there's a particular reason why they both might feel that Blanton needs protecting?" Tom wanted to know. "In this particular instance, I mean? Beyond the friendship and possible romantic feelings?"

There was a pause while, I assumed, both Christopher and Crispin tried to sort out what Tom meant.

"They think—or know—he's guilty of murder?" Christopher suggested eventually. "Is that what you're saying?"

Tom eyed him for a moment. "You tell me."

Christopher glanced at Crispin, who made a face, and then back at Tom. "He doesn't strike me as someone who turns to violence as his first option in most instances. Like Crispin said, he's soft and sensitive. But he certainly wasn't in his right mind on Saturday night. He had just taken a rather large dose of cocaine and was clearly flying high. Adrenaline pumping off him in waves."

I nodded. Blanton had certainly come across that way, delicate or not.

"And there was a reporter in his flat," Christopher added, "spying on his dope dealer. Unless that rolling pin was laid out in plain view somewhere, Blanton might be the only one of us who would have known where to find it."

"And if Montrose was on the floor when Hutchison came into the butler's pantry," I added, "and Rivers and Gladys didn't kill him, Blanton is the only one who could have."

Tom nodded and turned towards Crispin. "Your thoughts, St George?"

I did the same, turned and looked at Crispin.

Earlier, in the bath, I had arrived at this same conclusion. Blanton had to be the guilty party, and Crispin knew it, and that was why he felt bad this afternoon.

Like Hutchison and Ogilvie, perhaps Crispin too felt a little protective of Ronnie Blanton. Perhaps he saw something of himself in the other man.

Soft and sensitive, with a father who didn't understand him.

It was my turn to twitch at the sting of a mental mosquito. During our formative years, I had usually felt like Crispin was the one with the upper hand, and that I was the one who had to develop a thicker skin to deal with the blows he dealt. (And he did deal them, make no mistake. There was no love lost between us on either side.)

But I had undoubtedly contributed to that hard shell and sarcastic tongue he hid behind, too. I'd given as good as I got. Such as the suggestion that he was only worthwhile in anyone's eyes because of his title and money—something I had told him so often and in so many different ways that I had managed to sink it so deeply into his brain that he now, apparently, believed it himself.

Yes, I had my own share of blame to shoulder for turning Crispin the way he was.

But my self-reflection was neither here nor there at the moment. Tom was waiting for Crispin's response to the question of whether Ronald Blanton might be guilty of Freddie Montrose's murder, and Crispin was eyeing his folded hands, refusing to meet Tom's gaze.

"Crispin," I said gently. For the second time today, too; it was unprecedented. He looked up, startled, and so did Christopher.

I ignored the latter, even when his eyebrows arched with speculation. Instead, I kept my gaze and my attention focused on Crispin. "Ronnie Blanton comes across, as you say, fragile. Or I suppose what you said was sensitive and delicate, but it's the same thing really, isn't it?"

He didn't answer, and I went on, "If he hit Montrose on the head under the influence of his dope, I'm not sure he can really be blamed for it. And it's easy to feel sorry for him. He comes across as pitiful much more than as a cold-blooded murderer."

Crispin nodded.

"But Freddie Montrose didn't deserve to die. He didn't even do anything to anyone. And Gladys certainly didn't deserve to have someone she considered a friend, someone she invited into her home because she trusted him, send her to the mortuary with parts of her skull embedded in her brain."

He winced.

"Whoever did that, needs to pay. It's only fair. Even if it is someone who only did it because he didn't see any other way out."

"I just can't see him do it," Crispin said. "Do for Montrose, yes. Blanton was as high as a kite on Saturday night. He might not even have been aware of what he was doing. He told you on Sunday that he couldn't remember, didn't he?"

He appealed to Christopher, who glanced at me and nodded.

"But I can't see him going to Gladys's flat, lying in wait until the coast is clear, and then going upstairs and hitting her, all the while knowing that I'd be blamed for it. He likes both me and Gladys more than that."

"But if not Blanton, then who?"

"Dom," Crispin said promptly. "I'd rather have it be Dom."

I could believe that. He had certainly made a convincing case for it to the others. "But do you believe it was?"

"I want to believe it was. It makes sense that it could have been."

"I think we would all be more comfortable with that scenario," Tom admitted. "And it might turn out to be true. He did have a motive for both. Or he had a motive for Montrose, and if he killed Montrose, that gave him a motive for Long. So it might be him."

Crispin slanted a look his way. "But you don't think so."

"I think the way the other two were trying to protect Ronald Blanton was interesting," Tom said, and Finchley nodded agreement. "But that doesn't mean he did it, either.

They could be protective for other reasons, such as his mental state and the dope. It isn't proof."

No, it wasn't.

"How do we get proof?"

The words came from me, and before I was aware I was going to say them.

"I don't know," Tom admitted. "All the physical evidence, at least for Montrose's murder, is gone. We know where he was killed and how he was killed and to a degree why he was killed. We know how the body was moved and why it ended up in Hyde Park."

Here, both Christopher and I winced. Crispin, of course, didn't.

"We know one of a small group of people did it. We think we know who. But we have no way to prove it. And with the way things are, we—"

He glanced over at Finchley, "We can't even initiate a thorough investigation, because we're not supposed to know any of those things. If we go to Blanton's mansion block, or Hutchison's and Ogilvie's mansion block, and start asking questions about their comings and goings, word is going to get back to them that Scotland Yard is asking questions, and then they'll start to wonder why."

"But would that be a bad thing?"

"It would make them wonder who had talked," Tom said. "And if they felt threatened enough, they might decide to go after whoever they thought was to blame. The way they—or one of them—went after Miss Long."

"And again I ask, would that be a bad thing?"

"I know what you're doing, Pippa," Christopher shot in. "You're trying to set yourself up as bait. It didn't work out so well the last time you did it, remember."

"I wasn't the one who got hurt then," I pointed out. "It was you."

"That's what I meant. I'd rather not get hurt again because you've decided to play heroine."

Crispin sniggered. "I'll take the brunt this time, Kit. If anyone gives Darling a poisoned drink, I'll take it."

"These people seem more inclined towards crushing skulls," Tom said dryly. "It's harder to come back from that."

"Yes." I nodded fervently. "Let's try to make sure that no one here gets hit over the head with anything. I don't want that to happen to either of you. Or myself."

"Then perhaps what we should do—" Crispin began, and stopped speaking again when there was the sound of a knock on the front door. "Now who on earth could that be?"

We all exchanged a speculative glance before Tom jumped to his feet.

"Get the door, Finch. Hit the light switch on your way out. Kit, St George, back into the parlor. Miss Darling..."

"Behind the screen?" I suggested, as everyone scurried to obey.

Tom shook his head. "This time, just stay in here with me. We have to make it look as much as possible as it did when they left. If it's one of them coming back, they'll expect that."

"And if it isn't?"

It was Crispin who asked, on his way through the door into the green parlor.

"Do your best," Tom said. "And be ready to duck."

Crispin made a face, but followed Christopher into the parlor. The sitting room plunged into darkness as Finchley turned the light off before opening the door to the hallway. We could hear his steps proceeding regally toward the foyer. From the room next door came the sounds of Christopher and

Crispin dropping back into the chairs they'd been sitting in earlier.

"If he prowls," Christopher said, "make sure he doesn't get access to the back of your head. Between everything on the bar and the fireplace poker, there are plenty of things someone could use to brain someone else in here."

"With both of us in here and Finchley in the foyer, I don't think anyone would dare try," Crispin responded, "but we'll both be careful."

Out in the foyer, Finchley's steps came to a stop and we heard the sound of the door being unlocked. "Sir," Finchley said.

"Good evening again. Is Lord St George still up?"

That was Hutchison's voice, wasn't it? I exchanged a look with the dark shadow that was Tom. All I could see of him was the gleam of his eyeballs when he moved his head and the light from next door hit them.

"His lordship is in the green parlor," Finchley said. "May I take your hat, Mr. Hutchison?"

"I'll keep it," Hutchison said. "I don't imagine I'll be staying long."

Well, that could either sound very ominous or like no big thing, couldn't it?

There were footsteps across the foyer floor and then Finchley's voice. "Mr. Hutchison to see you, my lord."

"Thank you, Finchley. You can go back to the silver."

Crispin waited for the door to close between the foyer and parlor before he added, "Back so soon, Hutchie? Did you forget something?"

"I wanted to talk to you without the others present," Hutchison said.

There was a pause, and then Christopher said, "Oh!"

Hutchison must have been eyeing him expectantly, I suppose. "You mean me too. Crispin?"

It was quite clear, at least to me, that he really didn't want to leave Crispin alone with Hutchison. I didn't want to leave Crispin alone with Hutchison, either. I had grave misgivings about Hutchison coming back like this, on his own, without his friends.

But— "It's all right, Kit," Crispin said languidly. "Go on up to bed. Darling's probably waiting for you to tuck her in, anyway."

I fought back a sniff. Hutchison sniggered. There was a moment's silence while Christopher took stock of the situation and decided what to do. He probably tried to communicate mentally with Crispin, to register his displeasure at the suggestion, and I'm sure it ran off Crispin's back like water off the proverbial duck. Eventually he said, reluctantly, "If it's what you want."

"I don't mind you being here, Kit. You know that. But if Hutchison wants privacy, we should give it to him."

"Fine," Christopher said. "I'll see you in the morning?"

"I'll be here. I don't imagine Father will be sending out the search party until noon, at the earliest."

"Goodnight, then," Christopher said, followed by a polite, "Mr. Hutchison."

His steps receded towards the foyer door. Crispin waited until it had opened and closed before he turned his attention back to Hutchison. "Have a seat. Another brandy?"

Hutchison must have shaken his head, because nothing happened. And he also didn't sit, because when Crispin's voice came back, it was amused. "Prowl the room, by all means. There's nobody here but you and me. Check behind the telephone screen, there's a good chap. See? Perfectly empty and safe. So what's this about? And why wasn't my cousin welcome to stay for it?"

Hutchison must have been satisfied with his survey of the room, because I heard the noise of springs as he seated himself in one of the chairs. "No offense," he said, "but I don't know your cousin. I only know you."

"And what is it you feel you can tell me that my cousin can't hear?"

"About Ronnie," Hutchison said. "I need to tell you about Ronnie."

CHAPTER TWENTY-ONE

"WHAT ABOUT RONNIE?"

Crispin's voice was perfectly level, but he added, "I think I might want another brandy for this after all. Are you sure you don't want to join me, old chap?"

"Go on, then," Hutchison acquiesced, and the room was silent for a moment or two, broken only by the faint sounds of Crispin pouring brandy into two glasses. After bringing one to Hutchison, we heard him sit back down in his own chair.

"Sorry, old man. You were saying?"

"It's not that I think you're wrong about Dom, old bean," Hutchison said. "I agree with you. We should get our stories straight, and it makes sense for us to agree that Dom did it."

"Of course it does." The room was so silent that when Crispin took a sip of brandy, I could hear him swallow. "You said it yourself, didn't you? Monty was dead on the floor when you saw him. That's what you said, wasn't it?"

"Yes," Hutchison said calmly, "that was what I said."

"And you were only the second one out of the sitting room after Ronnie, so..."

He trailed off, and it sounded quite convincing. The silence that followed was that of a man contemplating an unpleasant possibility, reluctantly and without the courage to ask outright whether his supposition was correct. I'm sure it wasn't all feigned, either. Crispin really didn't like the idea that Ronnie Blanton was guilty.

"I thought," Hutchison said delicately, "since we're all on the same side now, you should have all the facts."

"Hutchie..." It was part disbelief, part moan of protest.

"You've known Ronnie as long as I have, St George. First term at Eton, right? You know he would never do something like this if he were in his right mind."

"Ronnie?" Crispin bleated.

"When I left the sitting room, and you and your cousins and Gram, and I went into the hallway, the door to the butler's pantry stood open. I stuck my head in, and Montrose was on the floor by the butler door. The door into the kitchen, where Dom and Gladys were. Ronnie had the rolling pin in his hand and he was giggling."

There was an awful silence before— "He was high," Crispin said heavily.

"As a kite. I don't think he knew what he was doing. He wouldn't do something like that in his right mind, St George!"

"No, of course not," Crispin said. "He isn't... Ronnie's not like that."

"He was high, and that's Dom's fault, isn't it? And it was Montrose, and you know Montrose published that awful article about him just last month. And Montrose was spying on Dom and on Gladys, and if word got out about Dom, Ronnie would lose his supplier, and I don't think he could survive that."

I imagined that Crispin nodded, with what was no doubt a very pained expression on his face. I felt pain of my own, too. Everything Hutchison said was true. It made sense. And it made me feel horrible for Ronnie Blanton. But it didn't excuse murder. Not of Montrose, and certainly not of Gladys Long. Whatever the situation had been Saturday night, or in the early hours of Sunday morning, Ronnie hadn't been high yesterday afternoon. Gladys's murder had been committed by someone thinking coldly and clearly, who had made the decision to do it and then gone through with the plan.

"He didn't realize what he was doing," Hutchison said again, persuasively. "He was laughing, St George. And now he doesn't remember doing it. If you ask him, he can't remember hitting Montrose. He thought it was all a nightmare until your cousins showed up yesterday and asked him about it."

"That's awful," Crispin said, sounding awful himself.

"We can't let him go to prison for something he doesn't even remember doing."

Crispin took a breath. And another one. "That's all well and good, Hutchie," he said, "but if Dom didn't do it, is it really fair to—?"

"It's his fault that Ronnie did it, isn't it? It's his fault that Ronnie is the way he is. He started him on the dope, St George. Whether he ends up in prison for being a dope-merchant or for being a murderer, does it really matter? He deserves prison, doesn't he?"

"I suppose he does," Crispin admitted reluctantly. "But Gladys, Hutchie... if Ronnie killed Gladys—"

"He didn't," Hutchison said.

"How could he not? Whoever killed Monty surely killed Gladys. And it made sense when I thought Dom did it. But if Ronnie doesn't even remember killing Monty, why would he attack Gladys? He wouldn't have had any idea that she'd seen him, would he?"

Hutchison didn't answer, and Crispin added, "If Ronnie didn't do it, who did? It couldn't have been Dom. Not if he and

Gladys were together when Ronnie killed Monty. And it wasn't the same kind of murder, Hutch. Ronnie might have whacked Monty in the heat of the moment and under the influence of dope. But whoever attacked Gladys did it deliberately. Whoever it was waited until I had left and then he went into her place and killed her. It wasn't a crime of passion."

"Gram," Hutchison said, and Crispin went silent. I imagined his mouth opening and closing like a fish's, although that might have been just in my mind.

"Ogilvie?" he managed, finally. "Graham Ogilvie killed Gladys?"

"Makes sense," Hutchison said, "doesn't it?"

"But—" I imagined more of the fish-imitation. "Why?"

"He and Ronnie are close," Hutchison said. "Close, you know?"

It was followed by a sort of pregnant pause, expectant and a bit heavy. Then Hutchison added, "Gram's a little... twisted up where Ronnie's concerned."

"Twisted up?" Crispin echoed.

"Gram's queer," Hutchison said bluntly. "And he's in love with Ronnie. And Ronnie..." He trailed off.

"Isn't?" Crispin suggested.

"I don't think anyone knows what Ronnie is or isn't. Not even Ronnie. He goes hot and cold. Drives Gram mad. One day they're happy as turtledoves, and then Ronnie gets a letter from his old man, and he won't talk to Gram for a week. He holes himself up in his flat and dopes himself to the gills, and then he comes out of it and comes back and cries and begs Gram's forgiveness, and the whole thing starts over again. He doesn't have the courage to tell his father to stuff it so he can live his own life the way he wants to, but he can't bring himself to let go of Gram, either."

"It isn't always easy to stand up to your parents," Crispin

said. "If yours are happy to let you live your own life the way you want to, consider yourself lucky."

I imagined Hutchison shrugging. He might not have, but it fit the general tenor of the conversation. "I'm fairly certain Gram went for Gladys," he said, without responding to the bit about parents. "We talked about it in the car last night, how she must have known what had happened. She was rocky that night."

"She was rocky yesterday morning," Crispin said. "She showed up at Kit's and Philippa's looking like she hadn't slept. And when I drove her home, she asked me whether I thought there was ever a good reason to keep quiet about something like murder."

"What did you tell her?"

"That we were all keeping quiet about murder," Crispin said. "And that I planned to continue to keep quiet about it, since I didn't fancy going to prison."

After a second he added, "Although that was before the police started looking at me. I think she'd understand if I didn't keep quiet at this point. Don't you?"

"Just as long as you stick to the plan," Hutchison said coolly. "Dom did it. He had motive and opportunity, and after Gladys saw him kill Montrose, he had to get rid of her. You said that you saw a red Morris Oxford near Ellery Mews. It might have been his."

"I assume it was really Ronnie's? And Ogilvie was driving it?"

"I think it might have been Dom's," Hutchison repeated, with rather heavy emphasis. "It makes sense that it would have been, really. Much more so than anything else."

"Of course." Crispin returned to his usual suave self. "Of course it would be. That makes perfect sense, doesn't it? I'm glad we had this little chat, Hutchie. It's good that we're all on the same page now."

"Isn't it?" Hutchison must have gotten to his feet, because I heard the chair squeak. "I'll see you around, St George. Keep me up to date with anything that happens."

"Of course, old bean." I heard Crispin get to his feet too, and then two sets of footsteps headed for the door. "You do the same."

Hutchison murmured something that sounded like acquiescence, and then there was the sound of the front door opening—Finchley was out of sight, it seemed, because I didn't hear his voice—and then Crispin giving Hutchison his goodbyes. The door closed again, and I heard the sound of the bolt sliding home. Several seconds passed—I counted, and got past thirty—and then came Crispin's voice. "He's gone. Everyone back into the sitting room."

He fetched his own glass on his way through the parlor, and turned off the parlor lights before shutting the door between the parlor and sitting room. Christopher came clattering down from the upstairs in slippers; he had taken the opportunity to change into a pair of pyjamas—one of Crispin's, I assume, since we hadn't brought a change of clothes of our own—and a robe. Tom gave him an arched brow, but no comment. If Finchley noticed, he didn't show any signs of it.

"Make yourself at home, Kit," Crispin sniggered.

"Just returning the favor from last night, old chap. You raided my closet, I raided yours."

Crispin nodded. "No worries. There are plenty of pyjamas. Enough for everyone. You might have to roll up the sleeves and legs, though, Darling."

"I'm not wearing your pyjamas, St George," I said, while Tom told him, "We're not staying."

He glanced at Finchley, and added, "We still have reports to write. But very quickly... what was all that about?"

"What happened?" Christopher wanted to know, indignantly. "I didn't hear it. Everyone else got to stay, and I didn't get to hear what happened."

Crispin opened his mouth, but Tom got in first. I guess he was in a hurry to get to those reports. "He still thinks that they should pin the blame on Dominic Rivers, but he wanted St George to know the truth, now that you're all on the same side."

"And what's the truth?" Christopher glanced back and forth between the two of them.

"According to Hutchie," Crispin said, "Ronnie killed Monty under the influence of cocaine and in a fit of madness that Monty was spying on Dom. Yes, Darling—" because I had opened my mouth, "that's what it amounted to. And then Gram Ogilvie killed Gladys because she had seen Ronnie do it."

"And Ogilvie did this because...?"

"Of his deep and abiding passion for Ronnie," Crispin said.

I eyed him. "You sound like you don't believe it."

He made a face. "It's not that I don't. It makes sense. It accounts for everything. I can see it happening that way."

"You can see Graham Ogilvie killing Gladys Long because she was a threat to Ronald Blanton?"

"Yes," Crispin told Tom, who was the one who had asked. "I never had a problem with the idea of Ronnie killing Monty. It made sense, under the circumstances. I won't say I like it, but it makes sense. But I didn't think he would have killed Gladys. Not the way it happened. He's just not a cold-blooded murderer. And if it happened this way, then he isn't."

"But Ogilvie is. Do you believe Ogilvie is capable of cold-blooded murder?"

"Easier than Ronnie," Crispin said. "Hutchie was telling

the truth about Gram and Ronnie, you know. I've seen them at it."

Christopher nodded. "Ogilvie was talking about some of this on Saturday night. He didn't name names, but it was about how someone could live openly in that kind of relationship, and whether I thought it was possible, and how does my family feel about me being the way I am…"

"We feel just fine about you being any way you want to be," I said, and was pleased to see that Crispin nodded, too. "We just want you to be happy."

"Thank you, Pippa." Christopher smiled. "Anyway, it would not surprise me to hear that Ogilvie was in love with Blanton. It wouldn't surprise me to hear that he was the one who killed Montrose, either, the way he was talking about him, and that article Montrose wrote about Blanton. Although I don't see how he could have made it to the butler's pantry before Blanton and Hutchison did…"

"He couldn't possibly," I said, "when he left the sitting room at least a minute after them. But if he would have been willing to kill Montrose over Blanton, he might have been willing to kill Gladys, too, to keep him out of prison."

Christopher nodded. So did Crispin.

"So you're all in agreement," Tom said, looking from one to the other of them. "Blanton killed Montrose, but has forgotten about it, and Ogilvie killed Long because she knew that Blanton had done it."

"Is there some reason not to believe it happened that way?"

"None I can think of," Tom said calmly. "All right. That's a lot of progress for one evening. Get some sleep, and we'll talk again tomorrow."

He headed for the door, with a wave for Finchley to follow. "It's the Yard for us, Finch."

"Um…" Finchley said. "Shouldn't I change out of his lord-ship's livery?"

Crispin sniggered. Tom rolled his eyes. "Yes, Finch, let's do that, please. I'd hate to think what the chief inspector would say, to see you come in like that."

"Chief Inspector Pendennis is tucked up in bed," Finchley said as he made his way towards the door, "and he'd say I was doing my job."

He headed for the back of the house. "Back in a few minutes."

Tom nodded. He didn't move, nor did Christopher. Crispin eyed them both for a second before he turned to me. "Come along, Darling. Let me find you a place to sleep. Kit's already in his pyjamas—or in mine—so you might as well plan to stay the night, too. No point in trekking back to the Essex House Mansions at this hour, when we have plenty of beds here."

"If it's not a bother," I said, and let him guide me out the door to the hallway, leaving Christopher and Tom alone in the sitting room.

"No bother at all." He gestured me to proceed up the stairs ahead of him at the same time as he called over his shoulder, "Lock up after them, Kit?"

Christopher's voice floated out of the sitting room with the confirmation that he would do so, and Crispin and I headed up the stairs. "The last time you were here," he asked, "did you stay in the yellow bedroom? It's been a long time, but I seem to remember you being in there. If not, there are plenty of other chambers to pick from…"

"The yellow room is fine," I said. "I'm really not difficult, you know, St George."

"Of course not, Darling." He smirked. "You'll let me know if you'd like me to rustle up a pair of my pyjamas for you, won't you?"

"I'm not wearing your pyjamas, St George!" I took a breath and uncrossed my eyes. "I'll sleep in my unmentionables before I wear your pyjamas."

He clapped a hand to his chest, as if I had mortally wounded him. Or as if his heart had done a hop and a skip in his chest. "Better not mention your unmentionables, Darling. You'll give me palpitations."

"Be serious, St George," I said. "And on that note, honestly, how are you feeling about what happened downstairs? Hutchison, and Blanton, and Ogilvie?"

He didn't answer immediately, just opened the door to what I remembered as the yellow bedroom, and gestured me across the threshold. Then he leaned a shoulder on the jamb as I looked around.

The room was fine, and I turned back to him. "I figured out that you suspected Ronnie Blanton, you know. After we talked about it earlier, I went home and thought about it, and I realized that it had to be Blanton you suspected. You wouldn't feel as bad for either of the other two. You don't feel as bad about the idea that Ogilvie, with malice aforethought, killed Gladys, as you do about Ronnie Blanton killing Frederick Montrose while he was out of his mind."

He didn't say anything at first, just watched me from the doorway with both hands sunk in his pockets. I was starting to worry that I was wrong, that it wasn't what he had thought, when he finally answered. "That's right. I feel terrible about Ronnie. I feel terrible about Gladys, too. She didn't deserve to die. Nor did Monty, really. Whatever he did, wasn't worthy of being murdered over. But I don't feel very sorry at all for Graham Ogilvie. He did what he did in his right mind, and with calculation. Hard to feel sorry about something like that."

Yes, it was. "He did it to protect Blanton," I said. "There might be some mitigating circumstances in that."

Crispin shrugged the shoulder that wasn't up against the door jamb. "Not sure I care."

I wasn't sure I did, either. "Maybe they'll end up in prison together. Ogilvie might like that."

"I suppose he might," Crispin said, and glanced around. "Will this suit?"

"It will suit just fine. Thank you for putting us up for the night."

"This is Sutherland House," Crispin said. "Kit's as much a Sutherland as I am."

Perhaps not quite as much, being several steps further away from the title. And I wasn't a Sutherland at all. "Still. It's kind of you."

"Oh, yes," Crispin said. "Kind. That's me."

I mimicked his stance, leaning against one of the bedposts. "You're not so bad, you know."

A corner of his mouth turned up. "Faint praise?"

I rolled my eyes and pushed away from the post. "Go to sleep, St George."

He sniggered. "Yes, Darling. Sleep well."

"You, too," I told him, and shut the door as he headed down the hallway towards what I assumed was his own bedroom whenever he visited Town.

I heard Christopher come up the stairs after a few minutes, and then a short conversation between him and Crispin in the hallway. There was the sound of a door shutting, and then a knock on mine.

"Come in," I called. Crispin had already been in the doorway to my room, and wasn't likely to come back, so this had to be Christopher.

The door opened. "Gah," Christopher's voice said. "I know we're the next thing to siblings, Pippa, but that doesn't mean I want to see you in your unmentionables, you know."

"I've seen you in yours," I pointed out, as I draped the yellow gown I'd been pulling over my head over the counterpane for the night. "Male and female both. If it doesn't bother you, I don't see why it would bother me."

"There's nobody who would care about you seeing me in my unmentionables."

"Tom?"

"No," Christopher said, although his cheeks darkened to pink. "And anyway, Tom—or someone else like that—would know that you don't care about me and my unmentionables."

"Well, there's no one who cares about me and mine, either."

Christopher muttered something. I caught the words 'St George' and shook my head irritably. "Just because your cousin is girl-mad and wants to see everyone's unmentionables doesn't mean I have to indulge him, Christopher. Did the detectives leave?"

He nodded. "What did you think about what happened downstairs?"

"Hutchison, you mean? And Blanton and Ogilvie? Hutchison's explanation makes sense. I can see it all happening that way. Can't you?"

"I suppose I can," Christopher said, "but I just don't want to admit it."

"Whyever not? It doesn't matter to us, surely? I mean, I'm sorry it happened. Of course I am. But it was just a fluke that we were here."

Christopher nodded. "I just don't want Ronald Blanton to be guilty, I guess."

"Why not?" And then something struck me, and I added, "Oh, Christopher. You didn't—?"

"No, of course not," Christopher said, shaking his head. "No, nothing like that. I just... I guess I see a little bit of myself in him, you know, and in some ways I see even more of Crispin, and I definitely see Francis, and I don't like to believe that any of us is capable of murder."

"You're not," I said. "And under normal circumstances, I'm sure Ronald Blanton isn't either. If he did it, it was only because he wasn't in his right mind."

"If?" Christopher tilted his head to the side.

"A figure of speech." I shook my head. "I don't like it any more than you do, Christopher. It's one thing when murderers are cold-blooded and nasty. It's something else when you feel sympathy for them."

Christopher nodded.

"But Freddie Montrose didn't deserve to die that way. And if Ronnie Blanton killed him, then he deserves to pay the price."

"If, again."

"Hutchison said it was him," I said. "You didn't hear him, but he said he came into the butler's pantry and saw Montrose on the floor and Ronnie standing over him with the rolling pin." Laughing. I pushed that particular bit of information aside, and added, "Can you think of any reason why Hutchison would lie?"

Christopher shook his head. After a second he offered, "Not unless he did it himself."

"Do you have any reason to think he would have done?"

"No," Christopher said. "I guess I just don't feel good about convicting a man for murder on someone else's say-so when he doesn't remember doing the crime."

No, I could understand that. But—

"I don't see any way around it, Christopher. If Blanton's memory of that night is gone, and we only have what everyone else says to figure it out, then I don't see that we have much choice. Better to convict the right man, even if he doesn't remember what he did, than the wrong one."

"I suppose."

"And we're not in charge of anyone's conviction anyway, you know. We're not even in charge of arresting anyone. Tom will arrest who he thinks is guilty, and his superiors have to agree with him, so it's not just Tom's whim. And then that person will get a fair trial. And if the jury convicts him, then maybe it's because he was guilty. But either way it won't be up to us."

Christopher nodded. "I know you're right, Pippa. I don't necessarily like it, but I know you're right."

"Then go get some sleep," I told him, "so we can be of some use to Tom tomorrow if he needs us. Or Crispin, if he needs us. Or anyone else who may need us."

He nodded. "Good night, Pippa."

"Good night, Christopher," I said, and then I proceeded to lay awake for half the night myself, thoughts spinning, until the square of the window started to get lighter with the rising of the almost-midsummer sun.

CHAPTER TWENTY-TWO

"I THINK we should go see Ronnie Blanton," I told Crispin over breakfast.

He arched a brow, and so did Christopher. They exchanged a look.

"And tell him what?" Crispin wanted to know. "That Nigel Hutchison says he's guilty of murder even if he can't remember doing it?"

"I suppose something like that. I feel badly for him. I understand that if he did it, Tom has to arrest him. If he's done it once, there's the possibility that he might do it again, to someone else. For as long as he keeps sniffing cocaine, he's going to be a danger to himself and others if indeed he committed this crime, but..."

"There's that 'if' again," Christopher said. "Twice."

I shushed him. "But does he even know that Hutchison says he did it? Does he know he did it? Has anyone explained to him that he did it? Or does he really remember it all, and when we spoke to him Sunday afternoon, he was simply pretending not to remember? If that's the case, I would feel a lot better about the whole thing. Wouldn't you?"

"I wish I had been there for that conversation," Crispin said thoughtfully. "I might have been able to tell whether he was fibbing or not."

"I wish you had been there, too." Instead of driving Gladys home and getting caught up in her murder and giving us all such a scare for the rest of the day. "But we can fix that this morning, by going to see him again. And you can look at him and try to determine whether you think he's lying or telling the truth."

"I'd be delighted," Crispin said. "He should know what's being said about him. Are you in, old man?"

"Whatever you want," Christopher said. "I suppose we'll be going by the flat first, so Pippa can get into something other than a robe or yesterday's gown?"

I hadn't thought that far ahead, to be honest, but yes, I suppose we had better. It wouldn't look good to show up in Ronnie Blanton's flat in yesterday's gown. I wasn't looking forward to doing the walk of shame in front of Evans, either, to be honest. I'm not used to coming home after breakfast the next morning, the way I had been doing for the past few days.

"There might be something around here that would fit you," Crispin began, "if you're not—"

"—averse to spending the rest of the day in one of your girl-friends' castoffs? Good Lord, St George, do you run them off so quickly that they don't even take the time to put on their clothes?"

He sniggered. "I was thinking of something of my mother's, Darling. She left a few things here."

"I don't think your mother's clothes would fit me, St George," I said, and pushed away the instinctive revulsion that the idea caused. "Nor would I look very good in them, I imagine."

Aunt Charlotte had been a silvery blonde with the gray eyes her son had inherited and an hourglass figure that she liked to enhance with tight waists and prominent bosoms. I was half her age, with brown hair and green eyes and what's generally called a boyish figure. My looks lend themselves well to the current tubular fashions. Aunt Charlotte would look ridiculous in my clothing, and I would look ridiculous in hers.

"It's kind of you to suggest it," I told Crispin, "but I'm afraid you're just going to have to make the detour to the Essex House Mansions."

"Of course, Darling. The image of you in mutton sleeves and corsets will stay imaginary for now."

It absolutely would. "I'm starting to worry about you, St George. First it was Christopher's evening suit..."

"That was your own idea, Darling."

"Then it was a maid's uniform. Then your pyjamas. And now it's mutton sleeves and a corset? Do you have a burning need to make me a laughing stock?"

"Yes, Darling," Crispin said, while Christopher shook his head with a sigh. "It's my one goal in life. I will take you to the Essex House Mansions so you can dress in your own clothes. Then we will go see Ronnie. Does that make you happy?"

"Quite," I said.

"Then my life is complete." He reached for the marmalade.

"When do we leave?"

He sighed. "Whenever you want, Darling."

"Marvelous," I said.

WHAT I WANTED WAS to leave as soon as possible. What happened, was that Crispin informed me that nothing good would come from reviving Ronnie at the crack of dawn—by then it was nine o'clock—and that we should take our time over breakfast. As a result, it was after ten by the time we finally rolled up in front of the Essex House Mansions and I jumped out.

"Will you be coming up, or waiting here?"

"It's a nice day," Christopher said, "and I don't have to change. We'll just wait for you outside."

I scurried in, past Evans who held the door for me, and I would have scurried all the way to the lift had I not heard his voice behind me. "Good morning, Miss Darling. Miss Darling...?"

"Yes, Evans?"

I skidded to a stop in the middle of the lobby.

"Gentleman to see you last night," Evans said.

A gentleman? Really?

"Who? Why?" After a moment I added, "When?"

"The gentleman didn't give a name," Evans intoned, "or a reason. It was late. After you had gone out again to meet his lordship and Mr. Astley."

"Well, what did the gentleman look like?"

Young, Evans said, and fair-haired.

So... Ronnie Blanton, perhaps? None of the others were what I would call fair—Dominic Rivers certainly wasn't, although if the other three had been at Sutherland House, he was the obvious suspect. Except he wasn't fair-haired by any stretch of the imagination.

Detective Sergeant Finchley was fair, but he had also been at Sutherland House. And then, of course, there were the young men of my acquaintance who were not involved in this particular murder case. My cousin Francis, for instance.

Although if it had been Francis, surely he would have

announced himself. He might even have talked Evans into letting him into the flat.

"Had you ever seen him before? It wasn't the gentleman who dropped off Miss Long the other morning, was it?"

After some cogitation, Evans said that he couldn't be sure, but that it was possible it had been. Of course, it was also possible that it hadn't, So that got us no further.

"Thank you for letting me know, Evans," I said. "Next time, try to get him to leave a name."

"I tried this time, Miss Darling," Evans said, sounding wounded. "The gentleman wouldn't oblige."

"Then you did everything you could, Evans. I'll be back down in a few minutes. Excuse me." I dashed into the lift, pulled the grille shut behind me, and punched the button for our floor. The lift jerked and started its slow way upwards.

When I pulled the grille away half a minute later, I found myself face to face with an apparition of pink flounces and bright teeth. "Hullo, Pippa!"

"Florence." I blinked. "Don't you look cheerful?"

"Luncheon at the Ritz," Flossie said. "Say, Pippa…"

"Isn't it a bit early for luncheon? We just finished breakfast."

Flossie's eyes wandered up and down over my frame. Her pink flounces belonged to a day dress—and it was a bit early in the day for the way it looked, but I supposed it was warm enough that a case could be made for cap sleeves—while I was still rather obviously dressed in yesterday's dinner gown. Flossie tittered. "Late night, Pippa?"

"I spent the night at Sutherland House," I said, "with Crispin and Christopher."

If I had thought that that rather bald statement would have put her off—and I admit it, I had hoped it would—I was wrong. Her eyes lit up. "Is your cousin here?"

"Christopher's downstairs," I said coldly, "in Crispin's motorcar."

It was a good thing that I had made my way out of the lift and out of the way as we had spoken, because at the sound of this, Flossie lunged forward. "See you, Pippa!" she called as she yanked the grille over the opening to the lift.

The doors slid shut on my response. "Of course, Florence. Have a nice luncheon." I rolled my eyes and hurried down the hall to the flat so I could change.

When I came back downstairs, in what I like to think is a rather becoming summer frock of flowered rayon, with ruched shoulders and a three-tiered, flounced skirt, she was leaning on the Hispano-Suiza, pink-cheeked and healthy-looking, flashing every one of her blindingly white teeth.

Not at Christopher, of course. Not that I wanted her to do that. But the dead set she was making at Crispin was rather annoying to watch, it was so blatantly obvious. And he was clearly enjoying it, too, smirking back at her.

"Excuse me, Florence." I nudged her out of the way with my hip so I could climb into the rear of the motorcar. "I'm here, St George. Dressed and ready to go. Weren't you the one who was so eager to get going earlier?"

"No, Darling," Crispin said, "that was you. I was the one who said it was too early and we should wait. Don't you remember?"

Of course I did. "Well, it's not too early any longer. We're wasting time."

"Of course, Darling." Crispin smiled at Florence, in something that looked like shared amusement—whatever it was, it made me squirm—while Christopher eyed me with a smirk that made him look remarkably like his cousin. I rolled my eyes at him, and he grinned.

"It was lovely to see you again, Florence," Crispin said, in a voice that practically dripped honey. I wanted to kick the back of his seat, but I refrained. "I hope to see you again soon."

"You know where to find me," Florence said cheerfully. "See you, Pippa. Mr. Astley."

She stepped back, and Crispin let out the clutch. I breathed out a sigh of relief as we moved away from Florence. "I can't for the life of me understand why you put up with her."

"She's not so bad," Crispin said, one hand on the wheel and one elbow negligently balanced in the open window as we rolled off in the direction of Mayfair and Ronald Blanton's flat. "And it's nice not to have to work so hard."

I scoffed. "When do you ever have to work hard to get women to notice you? They fall all over themselves to get your attention. Knock each other out of the way, too."

"You'd know, wouldn't you, Darling?" He sounded amused. Christopher chuckled, and I flushed at the reminder that I had indeed hip-checked Florence out of my way so I could get into the motorcar. I'd been referring to the way she had practically bowled me over upstairs to get into the lift, but it seemed I had no room to talk.

"Must be my title and fortune," Crispin added musingly, "I suppose."

"Clearly," I said sourly and settled into the backseat to brood.

THE TRIP to Ronnie Blanton's flat didn't take long, and after being announced, we headed up in the lift.

"So we are telling him... what?" Christopher wanted to know as the doors clanged shut behind us and the lift started rising with a jerk. "What are we here to do, exactly? Warn him? Discover how much, if anything, he remembers of Saturday night?"

"I'm not certain," I admitted. "I just feel very bad for him. And this seems like the right thing to do. Even if I'm not entirely sure what we're doing here."

"Let's just talk to him," Crispin said, watching the numbers as the lift rose. He had his hands in his trouser pockets and his hat pushed to the back of his head, and his posture looked relaxed, but there was tension in the set of his jaw and around his eyes.

And of course there would be. He considered Ronnie Blanton a friend, while Christopher and I barely knew him. This had to be more difficult for him than for us.

"I'm sorry this is happening," I told him. "If I hadn't wanted to surprise Christopher on Saturday night..."

He flicked a quick glance down at me. "It was my own fault, Darling. I was the one who showed up in your flat and told you that I knew where to find him."

"I shouldn't have gone along with it," I said.

"Neither one of you could have known what would happen," Christopher said sharply, "so just stop wishing you'd done something different and deal with what is."

After a second he added, "But for what it's worth, I'm sorry, too, Crispin."

Crispin nodded.

Ronnie Blanton was waiting in the doorway to his flat, and although he was mostly dressed, his feet were bare and his shirt-collar open. His hair was ruffled, not yet slicked back for the day, but his eyes were clear. For once, he appeared to be neither intoxicated from his dope nor in desperate need of a fix. We had come at an opportune time, it seemed.

"Back already, St George?" He sniggered. "To what do I owe the pleasure so early in the morning?"

By now it was almost eleven, but Ronnie seemed to have rolled out of bed and thrown his clothes on when the summons came from downstairs that we were here, so I suppose for him it was early.

"Something came up last night," Crispin said. "We wanted another chat."

Ronnie glanced over his shoulder into the flat. "Come on in. Should I call Nigel?"

"That's up to you," Crispin said, as he crossed the threshold, "but not for our sake. You're the one we wanted to talk to."

Ronnie looked puzzled. "Why? Nigel's the one who's been handling everything." He shut the door behind us when we were all inside the foyer.

"No Dobbins?" Crispin ignored the question to look around.

"It's his day off. He left after dinner yesterday."

No wonder Ronnie had slept late. No Dobbins to drag him out of bed.

"Perhaps we could sit down?" Crispin suggested.

"Of course." Ronnie waved us into the same sitting room in which we had sat three nights earlier. He seemed oblivious to the connotations, but I glanced at the chair where Frederick Montrose had spent the last few minutes of his life and swallowed.

"Something to drink?" Ronnie asked, blithely.

"It's a bit early, old bean," Crispin told him kindly. "Besides, I'm still half-soused from last night."

He wasn't, really. Not that I had noticed. Like Ronnie, he was bright-eyed and looked fresh. But it made for a handy excuse, I suppose. And it *was* a bit early to start imbibing.

Ronnie nodded. "What can I do for you, old chap?"

"We wanted to ask..." Crispin said, and stopped.

Ronnie blinked politely. "Ask what, St George?"

I looked from Crispin, who seemed as if he had lost his ability to form words, to Ronnie, who was waiting patiently for him to recover it, to Christopher, who eyed one and then the other of them with concern.

"About Saturday night," I said, and my voice sounded too loud and too brash, even in my own ears. I winced and moderated it. "Or Sunday morning, I suppose. We wanted to ask you what you remember about Saturday night and Sunday morning."

A cloud crossed Ronnie's countenance. "Weren't you here yesterday and asked me that?"

"It was Sunday, actually. But yes. We were here, and we asked you that."

He nodded. "I don't remember Saturday night. Or not much about it. We went to Rectors, because we heard it was going to be open for a special event, and Dom said he'd meet me there. And we brought Gladys, because she needed to see Dom, too. And then, when Dom showed up, we came back here. And Dom and I went into the kitchen..."

He trailed off, eyes fixed on something far away.

"We're interested in what happened after that," Christopher said gently. "Can you remember anything that happened after you went into the kitchen with Dominic Rivers?"

"Dom fixed me up." Ronnie giggled. "That's what he does, you know? Fixes you up so you can deal with your life."

There really wasn't anything any of us could say to that, so none of us tried.

"And then you came back to the sitting room," Christopher said. "In here." He looked around. "Do you remember that?"

His voice was soft and coaxing, and I guess the fact that he looked so much like Crispin probably worked in his favor. Ronnie seemed to respond well to him.

He didn't remember coming back into the sitting room, however.

"Dom took Gladys off," Crispin said, and Ronnie turned to him and blinked. "No?"

Ronnie shook his head. "I don't remember that. I was probably pretty high by then, wasn't I?"

"You were feeling no pain," Crispin agreed. "And then Freddie Montrose asked for the lav. Do you remember Monty being here? And us? We brought him with us from Rectors?"

Ronnie blinked. "Ye-e-ees?"

"He asked for the lav. And Hutch suggested that you should go after him—"

"To the lav?" Ronnie started to laugh, but he subsided after a few seconds, and began to gnaw on one of his fingernails instead. His eyes were huge and worried above his hand.

"He didn't go to the lav," Crispin said gently. "He went to the butler's pantry so he could listen to what Dom and Gladys were doing in the kitchen. Probably so he could write about it for his rag."

"I don't remember that," Ronnie said.

"You don't remember going into the butler's pantry and seeing Freddie Montrose hunched over by the butler door with his ear to the crack?"

Ronnie shook his head. " I went to the lav."

"You... what?"

"I went to the lav," Ronnie repeated with a nod. "I remember now. Nigel said to go after Freddie Montrose, and Freddie went to the lav. So I went to the lav."

"Freddie did not go to the lav," Crispin said. "Freddie went to the butler's pantry."

"Well, I didn't know that," Ronnie retorted, "did I? He asked for directions to the lav. So I went to the lav."

"That makes perfect sense," I said soothingly, and he shot me a look. "But he wasn't there, was he?"

Ronnie shook his head. "The lav was empty. So I used the

toilet." He giggled. "We'd had a lot of champagne, hadn't we? It was your birthday, wasn't it, St George?"

Crispin nodded. "It was, old man. I was drinking champagne in your sitting room with my cousins, and you were looking for Freddie Montrose in the lavatory. Do you remember what happened after that?"

"The door to the butler's pantry was open," Ronnie said. "And I remembered that Nigel wanted me to find Montrose, so I went across to it, and..."

His face clouded over.

"And what did you see?" Crispin prompted, when Ronnie said no more.

But before Ronnie could answer, the door to the sitting room flew open, and Nigel Hutchison burst through, followed by an out-of-breath Graham Ogilvie.

They were both in the same state that Ronnie had been when he'd opened the door: hair disheveled, shirts unbuttoned, no ties or socks. Ogilvie wasn't even wearing a shirt, just an undershirt. I eyed it, brows arched, and he flushed.

"Don't," Hutchison panted. "Don't say it, Ronnie."

"Don't say what?" Ogilvie wanted to know. "What's going on?"

"We're trying to ascertain how much Ronnie remembers from Saturday night," Crispin told him, and Ogilvie immediately walked to Blanton's chair and stood beside it, ranging himself aside his... paramour?—with a hand on his arm.

"You don't have to tell them anything, Ronnie. Just because we're all supposed to be on the same side now, doesn't mean you owe them anything."

He shot us all an unfriendly look.

"I don't mind, Gram," Ronnie said, looking puzzled. "I don't know anything the rest of you don't, do I?"

Nobody had anything to say to that, it seemed, or at least no one attempted to interject anything.

"I didn't realize the two of you were here," Crispin said, looking from Ogilvie to Hutchison and back. "Ronnie didn't mention it."

"Certainly I did, St George," Ronnie said, and giggled. "I asked if you wanted me to call Nigel, don't you remember? Did you think I meant to ring him up?"

"I suppose I did," Crispin admitted. "But no matter. We discussed it this morning, the three of us—"

He included Christopher and me with a look, "—and decided we needed to talk some more about Saturday night."

"What's to talk about?" Hutchison moved, subtly but clearly, to put himself between Crispin and the duo of Ronnie Blanton and Graham Ogilvie.

Crispin opened his mouth, and then closed it again. And shot a look at Christopher and me.

We knew, of course, but the others didn't, that detectives from Scotland Yard had heard every word that was said in Sutherland House last night. They had no idea that even now, Detective Sergeants Gardiner and Finchley, and presumably Chief Inspector Pendennis, were planning to move, with all the force of the law, against Ronald Blanton, to arrest him for the murder of Frederick Montrose.

And we couldn't tell them, not without admitting our own involvement with Scotland Yard. Something which didn't seem sensible, just now. There were three of them and three of us, but in an out-and-out fight, they'd presumably come out victorious, since I couldn't really hope to match strength with any of them.

"Was it one of you," I asked, "who stopped by the Essex House Mansions last night, looking for me?"

All three of them looked nonplussed.

"Is that where you went, Hutchie?" Blanton giggled. "We wondered where you got off to. Not that we didn't appreciate the privacy, old man."

"Any time, old bean," Hutchison retorted, but without actually admitting that he was the one who had tried to get hold of me. I eyed his hair, which wasn't what I'd call fair, although I suppose in the dark, and under a hat, Evans might have made a mistake.

"I'm sorry I wasn't home when you called," I said. "I was at Sutherland House with Christopher and Lord St George."

There was a beat of silence. "We didn't see you," Hutchison said.

I smiled sweetly. "You weren't meant to. I was behind the telephone screen in the corner."

"I checked—" He cut himself off, but not quite quickly enough.

"Only the second time," I reminded him. "St George stopped you before you got that far the first time, if you'll remember."

Hutchison subsided, scowling.

"Second time?" Ogilvie echoed. "What's this, Nigel? Did you go back there after you dropped Ronnie and me off here?"

Hutchison looked like he didn't want to admit it, which I assumed he didn't. His lack of response was as good as an admission, however, and Ogilvie added, belligerently, "Why?"

"He wanted us to have the whole story," Crispin said, eyes flickering between the two of them, "now that we're all on the same side."

"What story? What did he tell you?"

"That Ronnie killed Freddie Montrose and you killed Gladys," Crispin said. "And I have to say, Ogilvie, that—"

But that was as far as he got, because now Ronnie twisted

in his chair to face Ogilvie. "You killed Gladys? *You* did? Why, Gram?"

"To protect you," Graham Ogilvie said, as if it were obvious. He glanced at Nigel Hutchison, a quick flicker of a look, before he added, persuasively, "She saw you hit Montrose, and she needed to be silenced before she could tell anyone what she'd seen."

The persuasion seemed to miss its mark, however, judging by the expression of horror on Ronnie Blanton's face. "You killed Gladys, Gram? *You* did? How could you?"

"She knew that you killed Montrose—" Ogilvie began again, but he was interrupted by a wild scream from Ronnie.

"I did not kill Montrose! I did not! I didn't kill anybody!"

"He was on the floor of the butler's pantry," Hutchison said, his voice even but with a faint tremor, "and his head was bashed in, and there was blood everywhere, and you were standing over him with the rolling pin in your hand, the marble one—"

"Was not! Was not!"

Ronnie was clearly beside himself, and as Ogilvie went to calm him down, he pushed him away and got to his feet. There were tears running down his cheeks and his face was red, but he kept Ogilvie at a distance with a stiff arm as he continued to yell at Hutchison. "You're lying! You're a liar! A liar! That's not what happened! He was on the floor, and his head was bashed in, and there was the blood, and the rolling pin, but I didn't hit him! I didn't! I didn't! I was in the lav, and when I came in..."

"You're imagining things, Ronnie," Hutchison said. "You don't remember what happened. You followed Montrose to the butler's pantry, and you picked up the rolling pin, and—"

"Did not! Did not! I went to the lav! He said he wanted the lav, so I went to the lav, and when I came out—"

There was a tug on my arm, and when I looked up, Christopher was gesturing to me. I slid out of my chair and toward him, and he slipped an arm around my waist and pulled me backwards, away from the fray. Crispin slipped quietly off his own chair and followed. He put himself half in front of me, which I didn't appreciate—for one thing, I wanted to see what was going on, and for another, I certainly didn't want or need him to protect me—but it didn't seem like the right time to get into a row about it.

"You're misremembering, Ronnie," Hutchison said, still attempting to be calm and reasonable in the face of Blanton's rising hysteria. "It happened the way I said. You followed him into the butler's pantry and—"

"Did not! Did not! You did! You're the one!"

Blanton wasn't a particularly prepossessing sight, in his bare feet and unbuttoned shirt, with his furious, tear-streaked face. But there was something both heartbreakingly real and sobering about the way he kept insisting on his innocence. There was nothing dignified or decorous about it, but he came across as desperately sincere.

The problem, of course, was that Hutchison might be right, and Blanton might not be remembering the events correctly.

Ogilvie seemed to believe him, however, because he, too, turned on Hutchison. "You said he did it! You said we needed to ensure that Gladys couldn't tell anyone what she'd seen, or Ronnie would go to prison!"

"And so he would," Hutchison said, "if you hadn't killed her."

At this, Blanton gave another shrill scream. "You killed Gladys! You killed Gladys! Why would you do such a thing, Gram?"

"He said—" Graham Ogilvie began, and Blanton turned back to Nigel Hutchison.

"You bastard, Nigel! You bastard!"

He launched himself at Hutchison, who barely got his hands up in time.

"Come on," Christopher murmured in my ear. "This is going to turn into another murder in a moment. We'd better get out of here before it's one of us."

I nodded. It certainly had that look, didn't it?

"Get Crispin," Christopher said.

That was easier said than done, especially since Crispin appeared to be thinking of joining the fray, but I reached forward and nipped his sleeve. He shot a glance over his shoulder at me. When I inched back, pulled by Christopher, Crispin followed.

By now, Ogilvie had joined the fight, and was trying to pull Blanton off Hutchison, but this only resulted in Hutchison punching Blanton when Ogilvie got him to the right distance, and then Ogilvie waded in and attacked Hutchison, too. Meanwhile, I and the two Astleys managed to scurry to the door and out into the hallway without being called back.

"Someone's knocking," Christopher said breathlessly as we emerged into the hallway. "They're so loud I couldn't—"

"Probably the neighbors complaining about the noise." Crispin headed towards the front door, his steps long and his face grim.

"Shouldn't we do something?" I asked Christopher, with a look over my shoulder into the drawing room, where they were all three now throwing punches at one another and rolling around in the middle of the floor, bumping into chair legs and tables.

He glanced at me. "If you want to get involved in that, you're a better man than me. I'd rather not risk my skin for any of them."

"But they'll kill each other."

"They might prefer that to the gallows," Christopher said, which certainly might be true.

And then it was out of my hands anyway, because Crispin had opened the door, and Tom and Finchley and Chief Inspector Pendennis boiled through, followed by a couple of constables in uniform.

EPILOGUE

 Christopher said later that day.

We were having tea at Sutherland House, and Tom had stopped by for a cucumber sandwich and to give us the lowdown on what was going on at Scotland Yard.

After he and the others had burst through the door of Ronnie Blanton's flat this morning, it hadn't taken them long to subdue the combatants. Ronnie was still shrieking accusations and declaiming his own innocence as he was hauled out the door, while Graham Ogilvie shouted obscenities at Nigel Hutchison when he wasn't pleading with Blanton. Hutchison was quiet, as he had been all along, and didn't say a word to anyone, but the look he directed our way on his way through the passage and out the door, didn't bode well. If Nigel Hutchison wasn't indicted for murder, we'd all have to take refuge in the country, I thought.

Tom nodded. "Once everyone had had their say, it was pretty obvious what had happened."

"But if Ronnie hadn't remembered going into the lavatory

because he thought Freddie Montrose was there, he might have gotten away with it," I said.

Tom glanced at me. "Hutchison gotten away with it, you mean? Yes, he was quite clever about it. He found Montrose in the butler's pantry, listening in on the conversation between Dominic Rivers and Gladys Long. And he grabbed the marble rolling pin from the counter and brought it down on Montrose's head. The butler door—it swings, you know—"

Of course it did. That was what made it a butler door.

"It swung open when Montrose fell against it, and Hutchison saw Gladys through it. He thought she had seen him, too, so he decided he had to get rid of her."

"Cold-blooded bastard," Crispin grumbled, and Tom nodded.

"Just wait. You haven't heard the half of it yet."

"Go on, then."

"Blanton stumbled into the butler's pantry, and saw Montrose dead and Hutchison holding the rolling pin. But Hutchison held it out to him, and Blanton grabbed it by the other handle while Hutchison pulled Montrose's body away from the kitchen door."

"He remembers this now? Ronnie?"

"He remembers some of it," Tom said. "Some, Hutchison admitted, and some of it Graham Ogilvie imparted. He came in at this point, and saw Ronnie Blanton holding the murder weapon and, as he assumed, Nigel Hutchison checking whether Freddie Montrose was still alive. It's pretty obvious where he got the idea that Blanton killed Montrose."

Yes, it was. "Hutchison might not even have had to say straight out that Blanton did it. But I don't suppose he did anything whatsoever to disabuse Ogilvie of the notion."

"Not at all," Tom confirmed. "They sent the three of you off with the body. Dominic Rivers high-tailed it out of there, and took Gladys Long with him, and Hutchison and Ogilvie put Ronnie Blanton to bed before they cleaned up Blanton's flat. Hutchison cleaned his own fingerprints off the rolling pin along with Blanton's."

I rolled my eyes. "Of course he did."

"Ogilvie spent what was left of the night with Blanton, and Hutchison took the Morris Oxford to drive home. We don't know exactly what happened after that—"

"Hutchison isn't talking?"

Tom shook his head, "But we know that Hutchison showed up at Blanton's flat around noon—looking like death, is how Ogilvie put it—saying that Ogilvie had to come with him. Blanton confirms."

"And the two of them took off in Blanton's Morris Oxford?" The Morris Oxford Crispin had seen parked on Eccleston Street?

"So it seems," Tom nodded. "By the time you and Kit made it to Blanton's flat, the other two were long gone."

He shook his head. "I honestly don't know how much Gladys Long saw or didn't see of what happened in the butler's pantry on Sunday morning. Hutchison seems convinced that she saw him, but if she did, she didn't mention anything to anyone about it at any point."

"So she might have been killed for no reason at all?" Crispin looked sick.

"No reason other than that Nigel Hutchison wanted to cover his tracks," Tom said. "He convinced Graham Ogilvie that Ronnie Blanton would be safer with Gladys Long dead, and after Ogilvie dropped Hutchison off at the Albert Hall Mansions, Ogilvie took the Morris Oxford to the Ellery Mews and waited for Gladys to come back. When you asked him later, Hutchison denied having been outside at all."

"And did they plan to frame Crispin," Christopher wanted

to know, with a glance at his cousin, "or was that just luck, or unluck, that he was there and went inside with Gladys?"

"I didn't get the impression that they cared much one way or the other about the extra smoke," Tom said dryly, "although it didn't seem to be a deliberate frame, at any rate. They were happy to have someone there, to bleed off some suspicion, but I didn't get the feeling that it was on purpose."

"That's one thing to be grateful for, anyway," I told Crispin, who looked at me down the length of his nose.

"Not sure I care at this point, Darling. Between them, they murdered two people I knew. The fact that they didn't deliberately frame me for either murder is minor by comparison."

And so it was. I turned back to Tom. "Did Hutchison say why he did it? Killed Montrose, I mean? In the first place?"

"I imagine it was for several reasons," Tom said, putting his teacup on the table and folding his hands. "Freddie Montrose was a journalistic hack, who had recently written a nasty exposé on Ronald Blanton—I looked it up, you know, and it was nasty—and he was in Blanton's flat, taking advantage of Blanton's hospitality, to spy on Dominic Rivers. If Montrose did anything to expose Rivers, and Rivers got arrested, Blanton would be, as they say, up a creek without his dope. I'm sure Hutchison knew exactly what that would do to Blanton, and as you said the other day—" he nodded to Crispin, "—they do seem to be close."

After a second he added, pensively, "Or they were, before all this happened and Hutchison decided to blame Blanton for a murder he himself committed."

Yes, I could see how that wouldn't be conducive to further friendship.

"But in addition to that," Tom said, "there's the matter of Clara Hutchison."

It took a second, and then— "Nigel's sister? The one who went to Newnham?"

Tom nodded. "Something happened to her the day of the vote. I'm not sure what. Nigel Hutchison wouldn't say, or perhaps he doesn't know the details. But she's disturbed in her mind, and came down from Cambridge without finishing her schools."

He hesitated. "We were in the same year, you know, although I was older. But I remember her. She was clever, and quick, and opinionated. I don't think she would have thought to stay away from the King's Parade that day. She would have thought she could handle it, whatever it was. But something happened to her, something bad enough to change her into a different person. Someone afraid, who has spent her life since then hiding in Shropshire."

I nodded. "And Frederick Montrose, in his editorials for The Granta, passed off the events of 20 October as a rag and a bit of fun, and said how it was the male undergraduates who were the real victims in the conflict. And when Nigel Hutchison was faced with him in Ronnie Blanton's butler's pantry on Saturday night, I'm sure that that was in the back of his mind, too."

There was a pause.

"So even he isn't a complete blackguard," Crispin said. The thought seemed to depress him.

"They rarely are," Tom answered. "Every murderer—or almost every murderer—is a human being first. Someone's brother or sister or best friend. You should know that better than anyone."

After a second, less than that, he seemed to realize that the comment might have been a bit too pointed, and he added, "You three."

There was another pause, longer this time.

"So what happens now?" I asked, and Tom turned to me, seemingly relieved to have something else to talk about.

"There'll be the inquests. You three will have to give evidence. Nigel Hutchison and Graham Ogilvie will go to trial. Graham Ogilvie's defense will be that he was trying to protect Ronald Blanton, so that will be a big scandal."

"Unless Blanton Senior manages to pay him to keep his mouth shut," Christopher muttered.

Tom nodded. "The jury might feel sorry for Ogilvie and let him off with a lesser sentence. Or not. That remains to be seen. Ronnie didn't actually do anything criminal—he uses dope, but he doesn't sell it or distribute it—so he'll get off with a warning."

"He helped cover up a murder," I pointed out.

"So did the three of you," Tom retorted, "and we can't charge him if we don't charge you, can we?"

"For the last time," Christopher said, "we were going to tell you—!"

Tom waved him to silence. "His family will get him to a doctor who will help him kick the dope habit. Whether it sticks will be up to him. But if he picks it up again, he'll have to find a new supplier. We haven't collected Dominic Rivers yet, but it's only a matter of time. A few days of following him around, and we should have enough evidence to arrest him for dope-dealing."

"And will he be going to Portugal," I asked, with a look at Crispin, "or Peru?"

"He'll be going to Wormwood Scrubs," Tom said. "But he's an English national, unlike Billy Chang, so we can't get rid of him entirely, I'm sorry to say."

"But he'll be off the streets," I said, "and that's something. You'll have to find someone else to supply your candy, I suppose, St George."

"I'm going to pretend I didn't hear that," Tom remarked, while Crispin scowled.

"I haven't indulged in anything illegal in months, I'll have you know, Darling."

"You've indulged in plenty of other things," I shot back, and Christopher smirked.

Tom pushed to his feet. "I should go. Plenty to do. What will the rest of you be doing?"

"I'm for Wiltshire until I'm needed," Crispin said. "Father has already sent two telegrams asking when to expect me back."

"Doesn't Uncle Harold realize that you're helping the cause of truth and justice?"

"Apparently not, Darling," Crispin said.

I huffed. "Besides, you're with us, aren't you? It's not as if you're spending your time with unsuitable women."

"No, Darling." The corner of his mouth turned up, and so did Christopher's. Tom, for some reason, coughed.

"Good luck with it," he told Crispin, and the latter grinned.

"Thanks, Gardiner."

"Can I give the two of you a lift?" Tom turned to Christopher and me.

We exchanged a glance. "I don't mind if you don't," Christopher said, and I nodded and pushed to my feet.

"Safe home, St George. We'll see you for the inquest, I suppose."

"And if not," Christopher added, "there's always Francis's big birthday bash next month."

"The big three-zero." Crispin smirked. "I'll be there."

"So will we all." I turned to Tom. "I'm sure Francis—and Aunt Roz and Uncle Herbert—would be delighted to see you, Tom. For something other than a murder investigation for a change."

Tom nodded. But—

"Careful, Darling," Crispin said, "or you'll jinx things."

I rolled my eyes and headed for the door. "Don't be silly, St George. It's a birthday celebration at Beckwith Place. What could possibly go wrong?"

"Famous last words," Crispin muttered, and bowed me out the door.

Dear Reader,

Here we are again: book 3 of the Pippa Darling mysteries. As always, the standard warning about the language: This book is written in a mixture of American and British English. I'm neither, but I spent my formative years learning British English and every year after 21 living in the US, so while one is foundational, the other comes more easily these days. The characters in these books are British—with the exception of Pippa, who's half German—so I do my best to make them sound British. There are flats and lifts and pavements instead of apartments, elevators, and sidewalks, and because this is 1926, there are motorcars and dalliances and unmentionables. People ring up instead of call and knock up instead of wake—and get someone with child instead of knock up, if it comes to that. I'm absolutely certain I have made mistakes with both British/American and 1926/2024, so if you catch any, feel free to tell me about them, but you probably won't be telling me anything I don't already know.

In the first Pippa Darling mystery, *Secrets at Sutherland Hall*, I touched on the drag balls that Christopher, as his alter ego Kitty Dupree, attends. They took place in London during this period, in various out-of-the-way venues where the arrangers hoped to avoid raids due to the fact that homosexuality was still illegal. Rectors Club was a real place—it was located at 31 Tottenham Court Road in Fitzrovia, and had been the Tabarin Club before it became Rectors—and it was forced to close its doors in 1924 for violating the liquor license. In other words, they served drinks after hours, and were ordered to shut down for 12 months. Over the next two years the owner, an American by the name of William Mitchell, lost all his businesses, and it is assumed that he went bankrupt. I decided that it made sense for him to have leased Rectors to Lady Austin for June's drag ball, in an effort to make ends meet.

Here in the real world, the location isn't heard from again until January, 1928, when it opened as the Carlton Club for a few short years, before going back to being Rectors. Eventually, it ended up as the UFO Club by the late 1960s. The UFO Club's main claim to fame was that their first house band was Pink Floyd.

The story about the nun gatekeeper is from a raid on a drag ball that took place in Hulme, in the city of Manchester, in 1880. Police arrested quite a few young men for wearing ladies petticoats and dancing with other men, after gaining access to the venue by giving the nun guarding the door the password 'sister.' The other passwords mentioned are current, in case you're curious. Yes, there are hidden bars in London these days, where you need a password to get in. They're all for fun, of course, and not all that secret, and they can be found on the web if you do a search for them.

Stephen Tennant and Cecil Beaton, mentioned by Crispin, were both members of the Society of Bright Young Persons.

Many of the photographs from London high society in the 1920s were taken by Cecil Beaton, who went on to have quite an illustrious career as a photographer.

June 1926 did start out very cold, with only 11° Celsius / 52° Fahrenheit on June 1st. Crispin's birthday, June 5th, really did fall on a Saturday that year.

There was quite a lot of drug use in England during the teens and 1920s. Up until 1916, using and selling cocaine and heroin was legal, but during the Great War, there started to be concern about cocaine use among the soldiers. Then, in 1918, promising young actress Billie Carleton died of a cocaine overdose, and in 1920, the Dangerous Drugs Act was put into place.

It didn't make much of a difference. Cocaine continued to be popular among the upper classes, as well as among the Bright Young People, who were willing to try most everything once. Hard drugs and party drugs also didn't have the stigma back then that they do now.

If you're a fan of *Peaky Blinders*, you may have come across Billy—Brilliant—Chang before. He was a real person, a Chinese national by the name of Chan Nan, and a restauranteur who ran dope in London in the early 1920s. Everything Pippa says about Billy Chang is true: He was implicated in the death of Freda Kempton in 1922, and was eventually arrested and convicted of drug dealing in 1924. He spent fourteen months in Wormwood Scrubs, followed by deportation. What happened to him after he left England is not known, but rumors abounded.

Sax Rohmer wrote quite a lot of sensational books about the London drug scene and the Chinese involvement therein, if you can stomach the inherent racism. The 1925 release *Yellow Shadows* features a villain by the name of Burma Chang, who is said to be modeled on Billy, although

Rohmer's supervillain Fu-Manchu is quite a lot better known, of course.

Everything I—and Pippa—say about the Newnham College riot is true, with the exception of anything pertaining to Clara Hutchison, who is entirely fictional. The vote took place on October 20th, 1921, in the Cambridge Senate House, to decide whether the women's colleges, Newnham and Girton, would be allowed membership in the university. There had been women students in Cambridge for more than 50 years by then—Girton was founded in 1869 and Newnham in 1871—but the students did not receive degrees and were not full members of the university. Nor did they achieve that right in 1921. In the end, at around 8:30 that night, all the votes were in and the second option was passed: no degrees for women. The Reverend Howard Percy Hart exhorted the 1,400 or so male undergraduates who were gathered in the King's Parade waiting to hear the verdict, to "go tell Newnham and Girton," and off they went. Girton was located out of town, so Newnham bore the brunt of the assault. The male undergraduates did hundreds of pounds worth of damage, including to the bronze Clough Memorial Gates, and in the aftermath, The Granta did publish editorials lamenting how the male students were unfairly judged for what was only meant to be a rag, ie. a prank. Frederick Montrose did not write any of them, however.

It was 1948 before women students were awarded degrees from Cambridge University.

ABOUT THE AUTHOR

New York Times and USA Today bestselling author Jenna Bennett (Jennie Bentley) has written more than fifty books, most of them in the genres of mystery and suspense.

For more information, please visit her website,
www.jennabennett.com

If you'd like to purchase her books, please visit
JENNA BENNETT BOOKS:
www.jennabennett.myshopify.com